T.A. WHITE

Threshold of Annihilation

The Firebird Chronicles

First edition

This book was professionally typeset on Reedsy.
Find out more at reedsy.com

Contents

ONE

"WHY DON'T YOU say that again," Raider suggested in a deceptively soft voice.

The man who had served at her side for years, through thick and thin, during a war that threatened to decimate the human race seemed calm. Serene even. Unnaturally so, given the life-altering revelation that he had a daughter he'd never known with a woman long since thought dead in said war.

It was his eyes that gave him away. They burned with suppressed emotion.

Raider was on the brink, and Kira was standing directly in the blast zone.

The waif responsible for this whole mess kicked her feet from where she was seated beside Kira, utterly unconcerned over the repercussions of her dramatic revelation.

Oh, to be young and convinced of your own invincibility again.

Years of planning wiped clean by a few careless words.

Kira had known this day was coming. If she was honest with herself, this showdown had been inevitable from the instant Kira learned of Elena's existence and chose not to track Raider down to inform him that his and Elise's love bore physical fruit.

None of this made the coming explosion any easier to take.

You didn't drop a bomb of this magnitude and expect to walk away unscathed.

There were consequences to your actions. No matter how you struggled, they always came due.

This was the calm before the storm. You could see it on the horizon, feel the gathering pressure in the air, but there was no way to outrun it. No way to hide from it. All you could do was batten down the hatches and pray that the storm would leave you battered and bruised, but otherwise alive.

Kira's uncle frowned unhappily from his spot next to the doorway. Piercing golden eyes lingered on Elena. "I'm interested in hearing this as well."

The Overlord of House Roake was built like an armored tank. Power was written in every line of his body and stamped on his features.

A stranger to Kira until recently, even she could admit the family resemblance between them was unmistakable. They looked like father and daughter rather than uncle and niece.

The line of their noses and the stubborn jut of their jaws were nearly identical. It was the hair, however, that clinched it. A distinctive deep wine color that verged on burgundy.

A vertical scar bisected Harlow's eyebrow, narrowly missing his eye before dragging down his cheek. Already physically imposing, the scar made Harlow even more intimidating. Kira was betting none who served him ever questioned his orders. One hard stare would have his warriors swallowing any protests.

Of those present, Harlow was the one most likely to understand why Kira had chosen this course. Why she'd made the decisions she had. Like her, he hadn't lived an easy life.

He'd been forced to assume leadership of a broken House when an attack from a shadowy organization left his twin brother dead and his baby niece stolen.

He knew sometimes choices had to be made that hurt the people around him, even as it kept them alive.

House Roake had not only survived but thrived under his leadership.

Already she could see him doing the calculations and arriving at answers that threatened her future wellbeing.

Elena frowned. "Auntie, you never told me the sperm donor had a hearing problem."

"Not helping," Kira told her niece in a sing-song voice.

Elena harrumphed, folding her arms over her chest.

Raider pointed at Kira. "Explain. Now."

At that, a mischievous expression crossed Elena's face. "Didn't anybody ever teach you that pointing is rude, sperm donor?"

Raider's nostrils flared as he took a deep breath, holding onto his temper by a thread. He kept his gaze locked on Kira, not acknowledging his daughter's existence.

Mistake, Raider.

Elena might have biologically come from Elise, but there was a lot of Kira and Jin in her. Evidently, nurture was as important as nature when it came to personality, and a few of Kira and Jin's less than desirable traits had rubbed off on her, including the fact that none of them reacted particularly well to being ignored.

Sensing the danger, Jin inserted himself between the two. "Let's all stay calm."

In a universe filled with odd things, Jin's existence was unique unto itself. Once a Tuann boy in the same hellish camp as Kira, Jin's soul was now housed in a military combat drone that took the shape of a sphere the size of Kira's head.

Jin was Kira's best friend, her partner in crime. He'd saved her life and sanity more times than she could count.

"Don't tell me to stay calm, Tin Can." Raider's composed mask shredded, leaving him looking vaguely homicidal. "You don't get to say that to me. Not when you knew about this."

Jin was silent in the face of Raider's accusation. Guilt and regret filtered through Kira and Jin's bond, his feelings tangling with Kira's complicated ones.

There was a kernel of hurt that Kira buried almost as soon as it registered—especially in light of all the progress they'd made at rebuilding their relationship in the past weeks.

With that hurt came resignation. She knew she deserved his recriminations. She'd made decisions on his behalf that she had no business making.

"Are you going to say anything?" Raider snapped at Kira.

Emotion clogged Kira's throat as she sought for the words to make this right. An impossible task. Where would she even start?

"She can't." Elena kicked her feet, unconcerned by the imminent explosion.

Graydon finally stirred from his place in the doorway. "What do you mean by that?"

There was something about the man known as the Emperor's Face that always made Kira feel like she was standing on the edge of a storm front, watching it roll in, breathless at the magnitude of what she was facing. The cloud formations would be ominous, even as they whispered to the adrenaline junky inside. How much fun would she have pitting herself against its fury?

He was handsome. Almost brutally so with the kind of presence that punched you in the chest. Dark hair framed features that contained a harsh edge that drew the eye.

It was a good thing he rarely ventured into human space. The paparazzi there would have been all over him otherwise. Photos of him would have spawned a renewed interest in stories about human women falling in love with powerful and dangerous aliens.

Graydon didn't need any more reason to be arrogant. His ego was already big enough.

Kira wasn't a small woman, but Graydon towered over her. He was six feet plus of pure muscle, not an ounce of fat anywhere to be seen.

Memories of how exactly Kira came by that knowledge drifted through her brain before she firmly shoved them into the box marked "things you are to never think about".

Kira looked over in time to see Elena aim a sweet smile at Graydon.

"She made a promise. Auntie always keeps her promises."

Faint amusement touched Graydon's face. "Is that right?"

"Elena," Kira warned.

Her niece was getting too close to secrets Kira didn't want getting out. Beyond the fact that it could place Elena in danger, there were others Kira protected. A few of whom would stop at nothing to bury the past. Kira wasn't certain even she could rescue Elena if they decided to move against her.

"Please continue." Graydon sauntered across the room, sprawling in the copilot's seat opposite her niece. He aimed a conspiring look at Elena.

Like a flower drawn to the sun, Elena leaned toward him.

The sight snapped Kira into the present. She stepped between the two and shook her head. "Nope. Not going to happen."

Elena frowned up at her, but Kira didn't budge. Elena could sulk all she liked, but Kira knew exactly how irresistible Graydon was when he wanted to be. No way was she going to let him charm her niece into revealing dangerous information. That way lay disaster.

Kira narrowed her eyes at Graydon as she considered him carefully. What exactly was he up to?

There was none of the anger she'd anticipated. The disgust she'd braced herself for, even as she regretted the loss of midnight strolls that lulled her into losing all semblance of reason. The drugging kisses that made her think "what if".

Yet, despite expectations, he was acting as if nothing had changed. Almost like he'd known all along.

Hope tried to bloom before she ruthlessly squashed it.

Graydon was the consummate hunter. There was every chance he was simply playing a part and masking his thoughts. Lives other than her own depended on her actions. She couldn't risk the others because she was lonely and tired and wanted someone to help her shoulder the burden. Not take it from her, but lighten the load when things got hard.

Kira shored up her defenses, rebuilding them inch by inch. Only when she felt in control again did she focus on Graydon. She stilled as she caught something in his expression. Something that seemed to say, "Gotcha. I see you now, and there's no escape."

Before Kira could react, Graydon's attention settled on her niece. "You were saying?"

Elena answered without hesitation. "The kind of promises people kill to keep."

Kira blew out a frustrated breath as she aimed her eyes at the ceiling. Perhaps this was her punishment for a youth spent purposely antagonizing Himoto and other authority figures. She loved Elena like her own, but lord, the girl could try the patience of a saint.

Suddenly, Kira had way more sympathy for the young Himoto who'd gotten stuck raising her.

"I suddenly have so many regrets about our youth," Jin grumbled.

Kira nodded in agreement.

"This isn't possible," Raider insisted suddenly. "Elise and I never had kids. I would have known."

Elena's gaze dropped, some of her bravado draining as she shrank in her seat.

Regret moved through Kira. Elena had always known about her father. Kira and Jin had each made a point of telling Elena stories about Raider and Elise. Neither of them had had parents or memories to keep them company, and they didn't want that fate for Elena. Circumstances had separated her niece from her parents, and the least Kira and Jin could do was keep their spirit alive.

Perhaps that had been a mistake. If they hadn't, Elena wouldn't have built this encounter up in her head. She wouldn't be hurting now as she learned that fantasies rarely matched up to reality.

Too late now.

Kira cast her eyes around the bridge, hoping for an answer. There were none to be had. It was time for the truth.

Kira cleared her throat, forcing her emotions into their respective boxes. "The Gregory detail."

Raider's lips pressed closed, his expression going blank.

"She was gone nearly six months, remember?"

Raider rubbed his head as he stared unseeing at the bridge of the *Wanderer*.

She could see the wheels starting to turn. He had all the pieces; he simply needed to put them together.

"She was distant for a month or two before that," Raider said slowly. "She was always busy; she barely had time for me. I thought it was because of the op tempo."

Kira nodded.

Raider wasn't the only person Elise had avoided in the months leading up to the detail. She'd pulled back from everyone. Even Kira.

"The mission was a cover story. Instead of the escort detail we thought she'd been tapped for, she headed to the planet Rosetta where she gave birth. Afterward, she returned to duty with no one the wiser."

"Why didn't she tell me?" Quiet devastation lurked in Raider's eyes.

Kira mutely shook her head. She didn't know. Even all these years later, Kira could only guess at Elise's reasoning.

Kira could understand concealing the pregnancy and giving birth in secret. Elise's identity had practically demanded such precautions. Keeping it from Raider and Kira, the two people she would have sworn Elise trusted unreservedly? Kira never expected that.

But Elise had, leaving Kira to deal with the fallout all these years later.

Raider looked at Kira like she'd betrayed him. Like she'd walked up and sunk a blade in his gut.

A part of her shriveled seeing that look on his face, the same one he'd had when he learned Elise had perished in the battle for Rothchild.

The worst part was she couldn't even defend herself.

While she hadn't known about Elena then, Kira also hadn't taken steps to correct the wrong in the years since she'd discovered Elena's existence. She'd been too hindered by fear of the Tsavitee finding out about Elena and guilt she'd survived Rothchild when her Curs hadn't.

Even now, Kira wasn't sure she would have done anything differently. Not when the result was sitting right next to her, disobedient pain in the ass though she was.

"It's because the girl is Tuann, isn't it?" Harlow folded his massive arms over his chest, leveling a hard stare on Kira. "You told me you were the only one rescued."

"Technically true. I *was* the only one rescued."

Well, with the exception of Jin, but Kira couldn't say that without revealing Jin's special circumstances.

When Himoto and his team saved Kira, they'd also brought with them the drone lying beside her, thinking it would answer some of the questions they had about the smoldering stretch of forest surrounding her.

It did, just not in the way they'd expected.

Understanding dawned in Graydon's expression. "The others escaped."

Gold star to the Emperor's Face.

Truthfully, Kira wasn't surprised he was the one to figure it out. He was entirely too perceptive for Kira's peace of mind. Also, he'd had access to a small slice of Kira's memories. It wasn't much to go on, but it was enough for a man like Graydon.

In the back of her mind, she had to ask herself what else he'd managed to glean from that brief trip down memory lane.

At that thought, Kira shot an accusing glare toward Jin, the being responsible for Graydon venturing where he had no business being.

Jin whistled to himself, rotating so the primary lens on his casing was facing away from her.

"How many survived?"

Kira's expression turned stubborn.

Harlow's eyes narrowed at her refusal. "They're our stolen children. They deserve to be protected."

Maybe so.

Only problem was they weren't little kids. They'd grown used to relying on themselves.

Kira didn't think they would react well to the Tuann's version of love, which could be considered overbearing with a side of patronizing on a good day.

"Have we treated you so shabbily that we deserve this level of distrust?" Harlow demanded.

The simple answer was no.

When she'd first been forced into House Roake, she'd been certain she'd obtain her freedom in short order. Instead, she'd found a place and people that felt astonishingly like home.

The Tuann were hardheaded and arrogant, thinking they always knew best. It was something they and Kira had in common. Despite that—or maybe because of it—they called to the lost, broken pieces of her.

But the others weren't like her. They weren't looking for a home or friends. Those who wanted those things already had them, and the rest were so broken that trying to fit them into the Tuann rules would cause them to lash out.

If she revealed who they were, the Tuann would spare no effort in reclaiming their lost progeny. She didn't have to be a fortune teller to know how that would end—with blood and mayhem and a whole lot of hurt feelings on both sides.

Better if that never happened.

Elena planted a boot on the deck and swiveled her chair side to side. "It's not her decision. The others don't want to be found right now."

Harlow's gaze dropped to her niece. "What do you mean?"

Elena sat forward eagerly. "Shall I tell you a story?"

"No." Kira sent her a warning look.

Rebellion flared in Elena's expression. "You made promises, Auntie, but I didn't."

"Don't you dare," Kira growled.

"Let her speak." Raider's gaze held Kira's, a silent dare there. "You owe me."

Kira shook her head. He didn't know what he was asking.

Elena ignored Kira, bouncing in her chair with excitement. "It all began long ago on the night Auntie and Uncle Jin were rescued."

Kira held in a groan. Why, why, why, couldn't she have raised an obedient child?

A soft rumble of amusement came from Graydon. Kira stiffened but didn't look his way.

"The others had planned their escape for weeks. That night Uncle Jin failed a test and was thrown into a punishment cell. The rest knew escaping from there would be impossible. They regretted his loss but not enough to postpone their plans. Only Auntie was willing to sacrifice herself for him."

Harlow had a frown on his face as he studied Kira and Jin, suspicion moving through his eyes.

Kira's expression smoothed out, no hint of emotion revealing what she was thinking. This right here was reason number one why she would have preferred this story remain buried.

Someone smart would be able to take what was revealed and read between the lines, arriving at a truth that only a handful of people had ever touched upon.

Because Jin hadn't always been a machine, made of metal and spare parts. Once he'd been flesh and blood, just like her.

Kira readied herself, prepared to defend Jin and Elena if Harlow or Graydon decided they were monsters to be exterminated. It'd kill something inside of her to hurt either one of them, but she'd do it.

Blissfully unaware of the danger, Elena continued, "When the others fled, Auntie and Uncle Jin made their own escape. For years, each group suspected the other had perished that night, but they had no proof. Then the war with the Tsavitee came, and out of its ashes a woman known as the Phoenix rose to acclaim. Hearing the stories, the others sent someone to investigate."

"Elise," Raider said flatly.

Elena nodded happily. "Yes, Mother."

Kira's expression was carefully blank as Raider studied her.

"They feared this unknown woman would expose their existence—or worse, that she was a trap laid by their former captors," Elena continued. "Never in their wildest dreams did they think they'd find the two they'd abandoned."

Nor were they entirely happy when they did.

By then, Kira and Jin had made a name for themselves, drawing attention from the very sort of people the others wanted to avoid.

"Mother had orders to stage the Phoenix's death and bring her into the fold where it was safe. Only, the Phoenix refused to go, and not even Mother could force her."

Raider focused on his daughter as he compared Elena to the woman he'd once known

Physically, Elena was an almost exact replica of her mother. Enough so that Kira had been tempted to think she was a cleverly designed clone when they'd first met. Jin had been the one to assure her he'd found genetic material in her DNA that could only have come from Raider.

Her ears were as pointed as Elise's and Kira's had once been before they were docked. She had the same delicate features, complete with a pert nose, lips in the shape of a cupid's bow, and a pointed chin that only made her look more mischievous.

"Mother struck a deal with the rest. No matter how bad the war got or how much she needed help, the Phoenix would never reveal their existence by word or deed. She would face her enemies alone with no help from the rest."

What Elena left out—because she didn't know—was the fact that Elise had tried to kill Kira a time or two before they came to that happy compromise.

While Elise was the sister of Kira's heart now, she hadn't always been that way.

Not that Kira blamed her or the rest. At that time, she'd been an unknown entity, and their existence was precarious.

None of them had wanted to chance being someone's science experiment again.

Kira understood.

There was no way she could assure them that humans wouldn't resurrect the project again, their aim to create a super-soldier.

Alone, Kira had been deemed a freak, her abilities mostly kept under wraps and categorized as top secret, courtesy of Himoto. Only people like Raider and the Curs knew the full extent of what she could do. Everyone else had simply thought there was a new weapon or that the Curs were exceptionally lucky.

If the others came forward, the Consortium might have considered how they could replicate their abilities, and then the whole nightmare would have started again.

Knowing how painful this subject was for her, Elena slipped her hand into Kira's and squeezed. "Mother couldn't abandon the Phoenix so she joined her. For a time, the Phoenix and Sunshine were happy. Then Mother became pregnant. Sunshine knew a child of hers would draw the attention of those who sought nothing but death and destruction. To protect her child, she hid her—even from her lover and sister. In fact, she hid the child so well that it took the Phoenix and Tin Man years to find her again."

Raider was quiet as his gaze lifted to Kira's. "Did you know back then?"

"Raider," Kira started.

"Did you?"

"No," Jin said, answering for her. "It took a long time to put the pieces together. Kira was still in her coma when I finally tracked Elena down."

Raider's eyes held a glassy sheen as he dropped his gaze to his feet.

"I knew it was too dangerous for Elena to be in our vicinity, especially with Kira out of action. I placed her with a guardian I trusted," Jin said.

"Did you never think I had the right to know?" Raider asked through gritted teeth, clinging to control by only the slimmest of margins.

"I couldn't do that without risking Elena's safety."

Raider made a harsh sound rife with disbelief.

"Think about who you were then," Jin snapped. "You were damn near crazed. You both were. You'd just lost your surrogate family. Kira threw herself into the war. She damn near killed herself a dozen times. What did you do?"

Raider started to turn away.

Jin didn't let him, invading his space and hovering menacingly over Raider. "Because I remember the words you said after it all went down. How you wished it was Kira who died. I remember the messages I sent that you ignored."

"So that justifies keeping this from me?" Raider roared.

"Of course not," Jin snarled. "But it helps explain it. The war had just ended. You and any other Cur who survived were being shielded by the military, your whereabouts considered classified so our enemies didn't try to kill you. You were all targets."

Raider's eyes flared. "Do you really expect me to believe the great Jin couldn't have hacked that information?"

Jin scoffed. "Of course I could have, but not without arousing suspicions and possibly revealing Elena's existence."

Interest crossed Graydon's face. "Why would they have cared?"

Elena perked up, the tilt of her head coy. "Because I'm the first of my kind. Tuann, human—and other."

Kira tensed as silence descended.

Graydon and Harlow were still, motionless, as if they barely dared to breathe.

Kira watched them for signs of aggression.

Several long seconds passed as they considered each other.

Kira waited.

"That explains some things," Graydon said thoughtfully.

"Maybe to you," Raider spat. He glared at Kira. "Explain."

Elena opened her mouth, only for Kira to cover it before she could speak.

"I think you've done quite enough for now," Kira told her niece.

Elena glared unhappily over Kira's hand. Kira waited for a sign of grudging agreement before letting Elena go.

"It's simple, Raider," Kira bit out, emotion making her unwise. "Elise was in the same camp as me. A camp ultimately controlled by the Tsavitee. Genetic manipulation was one of their favorite experiments. Understand now, or do you need me to continue?"

The mood in the air went electric, the tension threatening to turn explosive.

Raider bared his teeth at Kira, looking an inch from going for her throat. In retrospect, sarcasm probably wasn't the best tactic to take.

He pointed at her and shook his head, aggression pouring off him. Even then, he didn't trust himself to speak, slamming off the bridge without another word.

Kira scrubbed one hand over her face, regret at her hasty words giving rise to the sick feeling in her stomach. "That could have gone better."

Jin snorted. "Really? I thought it went great. He didn't try to kill either of us. I count that as a win."

This was true. Raider wasn't a turn-the-other-cheek kind of guy. He was notorious for seeking retribution for any and all insults.

And Kira had wronged him way worse than any before.

The situation could have easily ended with blood shed. It hadn't. His restraint had been admirable—and unexpected.

He'd retired from the battlefield with barely a shot fired.

Kira didn't know whether to be relieved or worried.

A hurt, lost sound distracted Kira from her thoughts. Her niece's lips quivered, cutting Kira to the quick.

She closed her eyes, wishing for a split second she could kick her own ass. Great job, genius. Look what you've done.

Kira knelt by Elena's side, setting a gentle hand on her shoulder. "I'm sorry. You should know his reaction has nothing to do with you. It's entirely my fault."

Elena's nod was small, reminding Kira that her niece was still very much a child. Elena might act with a bravado and cockiness only present in the very young, but she had the same need to be loved as all children. The desire to be part of a family.

Kira's hand closed into a fist and knocked Elena softly on the head. "Cheer up, buttercup. He'll come around in the end."

Even if Kira had to spend a little time beating sense into that thick head of his.

TWO

ELENA FINALLY SMILED. "I suppose this means I should have listened. Maybe the big reunion would have gone better that way."

"Reality rarely lives up to our expectations," Jin said. "It's not wrong to want what you don't have. Kira's right; he'll come around eventually."

Elena perked up. "Does this mean I have permission to disregard your orders next time?"

"No," Kira and Jin both said at the same time.

Elena sat back in her chair, crossing her arms over her chest as she pouted. "Mean."

Elena's upset didn't last long. After only a moment, she sobered and looked at Harlow and Graydon. "I'm not only here to find Auntie. The others wanted me to pass a message to you."

Kira felt a sense of dread as her niece conspicuously avoided her gaze.

"Elena," Kira started.

Knowing Kira would try to stop her, Elena's shoulders straightened as the words poured out of her. "The others wanted you to know they're watching and waiting. What you do next and how you treat the youngest will determine the direction they take."

Kira bit back some choice words that wanted to escape. She was going to kill whoever had sent her niece here with that kind of message.

Bad enough they had a habit of sticking their noses into Kira's business, but now they were using her niece for the same purpose.

Seeing her growing anger, Harlow finally spoke. "I think we could all use some time to come to terms with this situation. Come. We'll discuss the rest at home."

His reasons for getting them off the ship were obvious. He didn't trust either of them remaining behind while he wasn't also on it.

Kira was afraid this was coming.

Elena had practically handed House Roake what they wanted most in this world—to recover the children lost in the Sorrowing. Nearly a century had passed, but for the Tuann it was barely a breath. No way was Harlow or Graydon going to let them walk away that easily.

Leaving her anger behind for the moment, Kira prodded Elena in the shoulder when her niece didn't move. "He means you too."

Elena straightened and blinked at Kira. "I can return to the ship, right? After we've had this 'conversation.'"

Jin guffawed. "That's not how the Tuann work."

Especially not House Roake, who was overprotective in the extreme.

The only bright side of this was that Kira now knew Harlow didn't care that Elena's DNA had a little bit extra in it. Neither Harlow nor Graydon were the sort to pretend an acceptance they didn't feel.

If they saw Elena as a threat, they would eliminate her here and now.

That wasn't to say the rest of Roake or the Tuann in general wouldn't have an opinion about that if they ever learned of it.

At least Harlow and House Roake had a chance of keeping her niece on lockdown rather than let her gallivant halfway across the galaxy on a whim.

Elena sent a furtive glance at Graydon and Harlow. "Didn't that person talk to you about Mom? We have a location. We can go there now."

"First—what is this 'we'? There is no 'we' in this plan. If by some miracle we've found your mom, you will not be anywhere in the vicinity when we go after her."

A mulish expression crossed Elena's face.

"Second—even if the intel is right, there is no guarantee your mom will be there when we finally arrive. This has always been a stab in the dark."

The chances of success were small. Minuscule. Despite that, Kira couldn't make herself give up. The girl in front of her was a small piece of that.

"Finally, do you think either of those two will let us go anywhere?" Kira tilted her head at the two in question.

The Overlord of Roake stared at them, his expression reserved and uncompromising. They were getting off this ship even if he had to drag them.

By contrast, Graydon's enigmatic gaze did nothing to conceal how entertaining he found this predicament of Kira's.

Elena waved her hand at them. "Can't you do your thing and take care of them?"

"My thing?"

Exactly what did her niece think Kira could do against two highly trained Tuann warriors?

At her peak, Kira might have been able to take one of them. If she was lucky and they erred along the way. But both? Not unless she had many, many more years of training—or reverted to her primus form. Even then, Kira judged her chances of success as iffy.

She'd never seen Harlow fight, but she had seen Graydon—and Harlow was the one who trained him. He'd be every bit as good as the Emperor's Face, if not better.

Elena crooked her fingers in what Kira was pretty sure were claws and made a "rawr" sound before swishing her hands through the air like a bomb exploded.

"Yeah. Your thing."

"I learn so many interesting things with your niece around," Graydon observed as Jin broke down in hysterical giggles. "I'm not entirely sure what the second was, but the first was pretty clear."

Kira ignored the mountain-sized pain in her ass in favor of bending toward her niece and fixing her with a hard look.

Elena blinked innocently up at her. "What? I didn't say anything."

Kira flicked Elena in the forehead with a finger. "Charades and hand gestures count too."

Harlow and Graydon weren't stupid. With enough hints they'd put things together.

Even if Kira wanted to go against the two, it wasn't possible. The inhibitor she still wore suppressed a large portion of her powers—though not as much as when she'd first donned it. Part of the reason she ended up in House Roake was to see if they could fix her.

Until now, her *ki* was killing her slowly. Harnessing it and building up her inner *ki* channels was a necessary component for her long-term survival.

Until the healers of Roake determined she was strong enough, the inhibitor wasn't going anywhere which meant there would be no flashy saves.

"Up." Kira's tone left no room for argument.

Grumbling softly to herself, Elena climbed from her seat. "How long am I supposed to stay on this rock?"

"Until I decide otherwise." Harlow headed for the exit ramp without giving Elena time to argue.

"Chances are it'll be a while, kid," Jin told Elena. "They don't even think Kira can take adequate care of herself."

Elena's eyes widened in protest. "Auntie!"

"Don't look at me. I'm not the one who got caught."

Elena sulked.

"I'm beginning to see the resemblance," Graydon murmured in Kira's ear.

Kira ignored him, following behind as her niece dragged her feet on the way to the door.

"Will she be safe here?" Kira asked, unable to resist.

Graydon's expression thawed. "He will protect her as his own, and if by some chance he doesn't, I can make alternate arrangements."

Kira closed her eyes in relief. Graydon didn't make promises he couldn't keep. If he said her niece would be protected, Kira trusted he meant it.

"Thank you."

Their little group was somber and silent as they made their way to the belly of the ship and the landing ramp.

Elena slowed as they approached, finally coming to a stop at the top of the ramp. Her gaze dropped to her feet, appearing deep in thought.

Kira was the first to notice, stopping a foot past her niece. Graydon continued a few steps down the ramp before looking back with a questioning expression. In the lead, Harlow had already reached the bottom of the ramp.

"Elena?"

Elena nodded to herself as if listening to some silent voice.

Oh no. Kira knew that particular combination of determination, stubbornness, and guilt. Usually, such an expression boded ill for Kira.

"Sorry, Auntie. I've decided I don't want to stay here. I've come up with a new plan. A better plan." Elena licked her lips, her gaze darting to Harlow and Graydon. She reached for the smart watch on her wrist, pressing the side.

"Wait!" Kira shouted.

Too late as the ship came alive around them.

"Intruders detected. Defensive actions will be taken. You have t-minus zero seconds before you're singing with the fishes," a recording of Jin's cheery voice came over the speakers.

"Fuck," Kira cursed, grabbing a handhold and gripping it tightly.

The deck heaved violently as the ship's thrusters roared. The nose of the ship shot into the air. The deck bucked, much like a horse who suddenly found itself with an unwanted rider.

Only these riders didn't have a saddle.

The violent movement spilled Harlow to the ground where he landed in a crouch.

Graydon leapt toward Kira, concentration and determination twisting his expression. His fingertips missed her by mere inches. The ship bucked again, expelling him.

The landing ramp began to raise.

Jin squawked. "Don't you dare leave me here."

He powered toward the opening of the ship. The ramp slammed closed seconds before he reached it.

"Captain's override!" Kira shouted

"So sorry, but not sorry. That command isn't recognized."

Kira cursed.

"Kira! Open the ramp! I'm still outside," Jin shouted through their comms.

"I'd love to, but I'm currently locked out of the ship."

"I thought you reset the command codes."

"I did."

"Apparently not, or this wouldn't be happening!"

Kira gritted her teeth as she reached for a second handhold, muscling her way further along the wall. "I suggest you figure out a way inside so you can fix it then."

"How am I supposed to do that?" Jin wailed. "I designed the *Wanderer's* defenses. It's not like I left any holes for nefarious sorts to slip through."

Not Kira's problem. Right now, she had her hands full avoiding being flung around the ship like an oversized rag doll.

"You're smart; I'm sure you'll figure it out," Kira snapped, watching as Elena moved step by slow step toward the bridge, the distinctive clink of her boots locking and unlocking as the ship shimmied and shook under her.

Mag boots. Of course. Why didn't Kira think of that?

Oh yes, because she didn't have any inkling her ship would do an impression of a demonic possession.

So good to know her niece had this all planned out ahead of time. Kira would be impressed if she wasn't so furious.

"Glad to see you managed to stay on board," Elena said cheerfully. She swayed and took two steps sideways as the ship flipped onto its side.

Kira took advantage of the brief respite, using brute force and luck to make her way to the next handhold, one closer to the hallway—and the bridge.

Elena steadied herself before resuming her slow, steady progress.

"It'd be nice if you turned the defenses off," Kira snarled.

"Sorry, Auntie. No can do. At least not right now." Elena reached the first T in the hallway. "You're welcome to join me on the bridge—or you can find your way off. Up to you."

Kira's response was stolen as the ship abruptly flopped onto its back, tearing the hand hold out of Kira's grip. She careened toward the ship's ceiling, flipping so her feet landed first.

The ship's thrusters fired as it prepared for its next maneuver. Jin had always called this series "a flea on a dog's back". Kira was beginning to see why.

Anticipating its next move, Kira leapt sideways, landing on the ship's starboard wall and running along it before leaping again when the ship started its next maneuver. Lucky for her, she guessed right.

"Jin, I don't care what you have to do but get me control of this ship," Kira ordered.

Silenced answered Kira.

She'd worry if she couldn't still sense him through their link. A barely audible grumbling was coming from his side. She got a feeling he was concentrating. For now, she'd leave him to his task and hope he figured out quickly how to access the ship's brain before they all ended up as a burning tangle of wreckage.

Dumping Graydon and Harlow out of the ship like they were discarded trash was bad enough—and would definitely have consequences down the line—but what she really worried about was what the planetary defense systems had in store for them. There was a reason Elena and Odin hadn't tried to leave before now. Ta Sa'Riel was home to the emperor and the overlords of several Houses. There was no telling what sort of nasty surprises the Tuann had in store for unwelcome visitors.

Kira very much feared if she didn't take control of the ship soon that they wouldn't have the time to regret the poor decisions that had led to their demise.

Kira pushed harder, an invisible clock in her head counting down the precious seconds.

Two more leaps allowed her to clear the cargo hold. It was easier once Kira reached the hall. She raced along the side of its walls, shifting her balance every time the ship tried to surprise her.

By the time she reached the bridge, the ride had mostly smoothed out. Elena was already strapped into the copilot's seat, her hands on the ship's manual flight controls.

"Good, you're here." Elena didn't look away from what she was doing. "Just in time too. We're being targeted by an unknown weapons system. Would you care to take over?"

Red flashed over the data screens and a recording of Jin's voice came through the speakers. "Uh oh. Looks like you've pissed someone off again. You should probably do something about that."

Kira plopped herself into the captain's seat, barely taking time to strap in before she assumed command of the controls. "This right here is why I would have preferred you didn't hijack my ship."

"Yell at me later. Save me now."

Kira bared her teeth as she jerked hard on the controls, sending the ship into a sharp barrel roll. The horizon outside the windows spun before Kira righted them again. Seconds later, she pulled hard on the control stick to send them into a hard right.

Whatever had locked onto them wasn't budging.

"Persistent little thing," Kira observed.

Elena clutched the armrests as Kira rolled the ship again. "Perhaps you could save your admiration for when we're not fighting for our lives."

Kira didn't answer, too busy trying to keep them alive.

If they couldn't outmaneuver their shadow, maybe they could outrun it. Kira hit the thrust. A great force punched her deeper into her chair.

"Warning. You're in danger of imminent death. Do something now."

"We are going to have a very long talk when this is over." Kira didn't look away from her monitors.

"Only if we survive,"

Here's hoping they lived long enough.

***

Graydon landed in a light crouch beside Harlow, already tensed to spring toward the ship again. Feared across half the galaxy yet outsmarted by a girl only a few years out of her first decade.

The emperor would laugh himself silly when he heard about this.

Above him, Graydon caught the squawk of protest as Jin's round form darted toward the exit Graydon had just been launched from.

All plans to return to the ship were abruptly abandoned as Graydon raised his *ki* shield an instant before heat from the ship's thrusters washed over them. A second's delay in his reaction would have seen him and Harlow distilled to ash and bone.

For now, they were safe enough behind the shield, but eventually the extreme heat would penetrate even Graydon's *ki.*

Behind him, Graydon sensed the flow and movement of *ki.* Years of working at the Overlord's side told Graydon what the Overlord planned.

As if they planned it, Graydon dropped the shield the second it was safe. A dark blur shot past him. Harlow reached for the ship, even managing to get one hand on it.

As if sensing his presence, it veered at the last second, bucking and rolling like a wild ooros intent on keeping its freedom. Even a Tuann as strong and versed in *ki* as Harlow had no chance to punch his way through.

He flew off the ship, hitting a tree and breaking it in half before sliding to a stop.

Harlow climbed to his feet, looking no worse for wear, his synth armor along with his *ki* protection enough.

Frustrated, Harlow looked up at the rapidly ascending ship which was being desperately pursued by Jin.

"This is an unwelcome turn of events," Harlow said.

Graydon grunted in agreement, watching the ship's dark shape disappear into the night sky.

They could have brought it down with a well-placed *ki* blast, but it would have been risky. Kira hadn't been strapped in and she'd barely been holding on the last time Graydon saw her. A crash landing could have proved fatal for one or both of the women.

That was something Graydon refused to chance. Even without asking, he knew Harlow felt the same.

"The emperor is going to have a lot to say about this," Graydon said.

A stream of yellow streaked across the sky, lighting it up for a brief second and highlighting Kira's ship.

It rolled, barely evading before the yellow streak swung around for another attempt at bringing it down.

"The planet's defenses just went active," Harlow snarled.

Graydon cursed.

"I'll buy you as much time as I can," Harlow said.

Graydon pressed a finger to his left forearm. "Open channel, priority. Access code, Stormfront."

Next to him, Harlow brought his hands together with a harsh clap that sent the tops of the tree swaying away from him. His eyes closed as beads of sweat formed on his face. He ripped his hands apart in a quick movement, his left hand sweeping up, around, then away from his face. His right hand mirrored the move, sweeping down, around, and away, dark light following in each hand's path.

Ki built before bursting from the center of the pattern, shooting across the sky like a black spear. It crashed into the streak of yellow, its darkness eating away at its light as the ship dove in the opposite direction.

"This is a surprise," a warm voice came over the line.

"Shut down the defenses."

There was a startled silence.

"I expect you to have a reason for this."

Graydon heaved a sigh of relief. He was going to do it.

In the distance, countless streaks of yellow rose into the air. For a brief moment, they resembled a blossoming flower before they broke apart to arrow at the little ship.

Graydon could only hope and pray his interference was in time.

Harlow was already moving to intercept the rest of the streaks. Two, sensing the output of *ki,* veered off course heading in their direction.

A great bark of sound came as Graydon sank every bit of his reserves into a triple *ki* shield. The outer layer shattered as soon as the streak collided with it. The second went moments after the first. The third caught and held the streak as it pushed against it.

Graydon gritted his teeth as he strained to keep the shield from collapsing. Pain spiked deep in his brain. He breathed through it, roaring a challenge seconds later.

Abruptly, the streak dissipated, specks of gold light floating up in the air.

Above, the same thing was happening to its companions.

"I expect you in my chambers immediately to explain the reasoning for this, Little Storm," a voice said in Graydon's ear.

"I'll report as soon as I'm done here."

"Don't keep me waiting."

The presence that accompanied the voice dissipated.

Graydon and Harlow shared a long look, understanding of the implications reflecting on their faces. The loss of Kira and Elena was bad enough, but the knowledge that many of the children lost in Sorrowing had survived would have far-reaching repercussions. If true, Graydon feared keeping it from the rest of the Houses would only work in the short term.

Already, the other Houses were clamoring for news of Kira and demanding to know how she survived in hopes that their own children had as well. The children were the future of their Houses. If there were even the smallest hope, the other major Houses would be ruthless in reclaiming what they considered theirs. If they found out about Kira's disappearance, they would search for her. Roake wasn't likely to allow outsiders interfere with one of their own.

Harlow turned to make his way to the Fortress of the Vigilant. "I'll leave you to deal with the emperor. I'll make the necessary arrangements on my end."

Graydon let the Overlord go, tilting his head back to take in the night sky, the stars glittering above. Kira's ship was long since gone.

You left me with quite the mess, coli.

His lips curved up as he started toward the city and the fortress at its heart. Good thing he excelled at messes.

* * *

Graydon stalked through the halls of the Shining Palace. Despite its delicate name, the palace was every bit as heavily fortified as Roake's Fortress of the Vigilant.

Normally, if one wished entry into the Shining Palace, they were required to approach from one of the five avenues extending out from the palace like the spoke of a wheel, their ends connecting to the five major Houses.

It was tradition among the Tuann that to approach the emperor, you first needed permission from a House. It was an old custom, the origin stemming from a time when the Houses would shed every drop of their own blood in defense of the emperor, choosing death rather than letting an enemy march through unobstructed.

The measure had never been put to the test, but the Houses still kept to the old ways.

If Graydon had been anyone else, he would have been turned back the moment he landed at the entrance Roake defended.

Instead, he passed unchallenged.

Where Roake's fortress resembled a stalwart sentry, imposing and vigilant, the Shining Palace was a crowning gem. Her face delicate and refined but her spine pure titanium.

At the palace's heart was a single tower. Its top was the highest point in the city, allowing it to be seen for miles in every direction.

It was there Graydon would find the man who'd demanded his attendance.

It didn't take long for Graydon to reach a pair of large doors with ornate designs carved into them. His steps didn't falter as a tingling sensation brushed along every inch of his skin. Though currently gentle, Graydon knew the sensation could turn painful in a second if the defenses decided he was an enemy.

Whether that pain would reach lethal levels would depend on the level of threat he posed.

The precaution was designed to safeguard the man inside against the incredibly small possibility of an assassin or enemy force penetrating this far into the palace.

Sensing his approach, the doors opened silently as if by invisible hands.

Graydon swept into the room beyond, not pausing to admire the beauty within as he headed to the set of staircases leading to the floors above.

Only the most trusted ever gained access. Of those, even fewer saw the views from the top floor.

Graydon didn't even pause as he bypassed the first landing. At the top of the stairs, he raised his hand and sent a pulse of *ki* into the air in front of him.

His *ki* vibrated as he manipulated it to a frequency known only to four.

To the naked eye, nothing would seem to be amiss. Only someone with an exceptional mastery of *ki* would feel the field millimeters in front of Graydon's hand. If he were to step forward before he finished calibrating his *ki,* he would die a gruesome death.

Not even his *ki* or synth armor would be able to save him.

Seconds later, the field dropped and Graydon stepped into a room. A bank of windows on one wall offered a view of the city and ocean beyond. A large bed sat against the opposite wall with several sitting areas set up throughout the space.

Gold seemed to be the dominating color, fabric spilling from the bed's posts.

Despite the luxury, the room was welcoming, the air carrying the faint smell of a forest.

The space was empty except for the man in a chair by the windows.

Despite Graydon's presence, he didn't look up, engrossed with the object in his hands, a small puzzle box. Only instead of manipulating it physically, the tiny metal pieces were shifting on their own.

As a demonstration of the finer theories of *ki* manipulation, it was impressive—and rare. Graydon didn't think he knew anyone with such pinpoint control.

"You've come." The small snick of the puzzle pieces filled the room.

Unlike Graydon, the man wasn't dressed for war. He was clad in simple pants and wearing a black robe that glittered when he moved, like someone had trapped a galaxy in its depths.

"As you ordered," Graydon said.

The man's head lifted, a pair of eyes the color of gold staring coldly at Graydon from a face that was unlined with age despite the many centuries the man had lived. "Care to explain why you allowed an unauthorized ship to leave this planet."

"Roake's heir was on that ship."

Shooting it down would have effectively severed Roake's ties with them.

Roake would make for a difficult enemy. They were ruthless in their pursuit of justice. A blood feud with them would have resulted in consequences for the entire empire. Their House was small, but they were fierce.

The man went still, only the snick, snick of the puzzle box continuing. "How did that happen?"

"Through a series of unexpected events."

"Oh?"

Graydon hesitated, trying to find the best explanation. "Our suspicions were correct. Kira isn't the only survivor."

The movement of the puzzle box stopped. "Another survivor was on the ship."

"Not exactly." Seeing the question on the other man's face, Graydon said softly, "A daughter borne of one who was lost."

The man set the puzzle box in his lap and stared unseeing out the window.

Finally, he let out a heavy breath. "We knew we were biologically compatible with humans. Do we know which House the child belongs to?"

Graydon paused. "Likely Roake's."

The man lifted his eyebrows.

"There was some resemblance," Graydon admitted.

A frown crossed the man's face. "As glad as I am for them, it would have been easier on us if this child belonged to one of the other Houses."

Graydon understood the man's concerns. The other Houses were jealous of Roake's good fortune and wanted their own children returned. If Elena belonged to any of those Houses, it would have relieved some of the pressure.

The man slanted a look at Graydon. "Though considering we now no longer possess either child, perhaps it's for the best they belong to Roake."

The man propped his head on his fist and crossed his ankle over his knee. "How exactly did they slip through your fingers?"

Graydon avoided the man's gaze.

The man lifted his head off his fist. "They outsmarted you."

He threw his head back, a warm chuckle rolling through the room.

"A ship is being prepared as we speak. I can set off after them as soon as it's ready," Graydon said, hoping to steer the conversation back on target.

The man hummed thoughtfully and shook his head. "Your agenda will have to wait until after the quorum."

Graydon fought his sense of impatience. "Assign another Face."

"I plan to, but everyone already knows you're slated to attend. Sending another at this late stage will cause questions we can't afford."

Much as Graydon wanted to, he couldn't argue with that logic. If word got out about Kira leaving, and the manner in which she did so, it would create trouble for Roake. To say nothing of the danger Kira would be in when Roake's enemies discovered her.

For now, they could only keep the matter to themselves for as long as possible and hope they could recover Kira before anyone noticed.

The man's gaze turned inward. "Besides, I have a feeling your presence will be needed there."

Graydon went on alert. "You've sensed something."

"I'm not sure, but something feels off."

There was no choice then. Graydon had to attend. The man's premonitions were never wrong.

"Don't worry; you can still search for her and the rest while you're there."

Graydon's expression turned wry. "That might be difficult. You know as well as I do how much is involved in the quorum."

Graydon would be lucky to eat and sleep during the ten days and nights.

For the first time, the man smiled, his expression playful. "You won't be alone. I'm sending another Face with you."

That would free up Graydon from the countless demands people would make on his time. Depending on the Face, Graydon's presence could be reduced to a formality.

Graydon looked up to find the man watching him carefully.

"Why do I have the feeling you're keeping something important from me?" the man asked.

Graydon debated the merits of revealing what he'd learned.

Something stopped him.

One of the hardest things any Face learned was the precarious balancing act that came with the position. Some secrets needed to be kept. The last thing any Face should do was force the emperor into a corner where he'd have to act.

Sometimes discretion was the better part of valor.

From what Graydon saw in Kira's memories, Jin's existence was a thorny problem. If his suspicions were correct, Jin was the first soul bound since the Tuann seized freedom from their masters.

According to their stories, Jin should be nothing but a mad creature, thirsting for blood. A danger to all Tuann that needed to be eliminated at all costs.

Yet, from what Graydon had seen, Jin was none of those things.

Until he knew more or at least why Jin was different, Graydon's best course of action was to stay silent.

He shoved aside the voice inside saying the real reason for his inaction was the fear he'd lose Kira forever if he brought danger to Jin.

"There are many things," Graydon allowed. "I will share when the time is right."

Graydon was a man defined by duty. He'd do what was right even at the cost of his own self-interest—but only if it became absolutely necessary.

They hadn't reached that stage yet.

The man studied Graydon with eyes that seemed to see through him. "I'll trust in that promise."

Graydon started to leave, then hesitated. "There is one thing I forgot to mention."

The man waited patiently.

"The girl, Elena. She had a warning for us. She said the others are waiting to see how we treat the youngest before they make their decision whether to trust us or not."

"That is an interesting choice of words."

They shared a look, each thinking the same thing.

Kira wasn't the youngest child taken. That was the emperor's eldest son, born three hours after Kira.

THREE

THE HOSTILES CLOSING in on the *Wanderer* dispersed in specs of golden light.

"We made it," Elena whispered in relief.

"Yes, we did." The question was how?

Elena punched her fist in the air. "I knew you could do it."

Kira shook her head grimly. "That wasn't me."

No matter what tricks she had tried or how hard she had pushed the *Wanderer* to its limits, she couldn't lose the target lock. For a minute there, she'd debated the merits of ejecting in a last-ditch effort at survival.

Graydon or Harlow had to have called the beams off. It was the only explanation.

Kira didn't waste time questioning their luck further. Those anti-aircraft defenses could come online at any moment. She needed to be as far as possible from her current position before that happened.

After only a second of hesitation, Kira pointed the nose of the *Wanderer* toward the sky and punched the ignition. The ship jolted before it leapt forward, heading for the upper reaches of the atmosphere.

The hull shimmied around them as Elena whooped with excitement in her seat. That same excitement caught hold of Kira, and she smiled before shaking her head in resignation.

The pull of the planet lessened as the *Wanderer* broke from its gravity. There was a sucking sensation on Kira, as if the planet's soul was reluctant to let her leave. The warmth and energy from the Mea'Ave she'd gotten used to over the last weeks drained away, only a small thimble full remaining.

Kira exhaled as her body adjusted to the sudden loss.

"I guess I know now why the Tuann rarely choose to leave their planets."

If this was what they felt every time, it was a small wonder they left at all. While not painful, Kira couldn't say the sensation was comfortable either. It was like an entire set of senses had been stolen from her. The vibrancy of the world around her dialed down a few notches.

It was possible this was another symptom of her *ki* poisoning. Quillon, the Tuann healer overseeing her treatment, had warned her she'd need to stick close to planets with a Mea'Ave until she was further along in her healing.

Now she saw why.

The Mea'Ave's loss was akin to going from an oxygen-rich environment to a depleted one. Kira could still sense the invisible force she associated with the Mea'Ave, but it was considerably scarcer.

Elena shook herself all over. "It's definitely weird."

"What does it feel like to you?"

Elena pursed her mouth as she considered. "Like fizzy bubbles in my middle. Nice, but it gets itchy after a while."

That was different than Kira's feeling. It could be because of Elena's non-traditional heritage. She wasn't full Tuann, whereas Kira was.

Kira shrugged off the questions, putting them aside for later. Even if she wanted to, she wasn't likely to get answers now. Only a Tuann who understood the Mea'Ave far better than Kira would have an answer.

From above, the sound of knocking came. Almost like something was hitting the sides of the air vents.

Kira and Elena looked up.

Cautiously, Kira unlocked her safety harness, wanting to be free to move in the event of danger.

Before she could do more than touch the release button, a grate popped open, and a ball rolled out.

Elena caught it before the object could hit the deck, peering at it in puzzlement.

"Uncle Jin, where did you come from?"

Jin re-oriented himself, his antigravs whirring as he lifted himself out of Elena's palm. "A place no one should have the misfortune of venturing."

A foul stench invaded the air. Upon closer examination, Kira could see small specks of matter stuck to his shell.

With a grimace, Kira covered her nose. She had a feeling she knew what avenue he'd taken to get here.

"Darling child of my sister, do you know what hells I had to travel? What horrors I've seen?" Jin asked with a false sense of calm that did nothing to hide the brewing storm.

Elena looked like she was about to throw up as she held the hands that had touched Jin as far away from her body as she could. "I think I have some idea."

A sense of menace came from Jin as he crept toward Elena. "No, my dear, who is in the most trouble she's ever been in during her short life, you don't, but you will."

At that, Jin swooped toward Elena, evading her hands as she tried to bat him away. He rubbed his sides along her face and torso, ignoring the wails of dismay and the flailing. He was merciless as he smeared the matter on his shell all over Elena.

"Auntie! Help!"

Kira shook her head. Not a chance in hell. Kira knew better than to get in the way of Jin's revenge. Not unless she wanted to fend off the same attacks.

"Oh no, you're on your own for this one."

"Auntie!" Elena screeched in protest.

"Let this be a lesson, my dear." Jin finally backed away from Elena. "If you're going to steal the ship, at least give your Uncle Jin a heads up so he can be on it when you do."

"Or she could not steal the ship at all. That'd solve all our problems."

Elena bolted out of her seat, making a beeline in the direction of the ship's pitifully small passenger level—and the enzyme shower that waited there.

In her absence, Jin threw himself at Kira, only for her to dodge away. After guessing how he got into the ship, Kira wasn't going to let him touch her. No way; no how.

"Kira," Jin started.

"You stay away from me." Kira pointed at him. "While you're at it, go get cleaned up."

"You forget there's only one enzyme shower on this ship, and the brat is currently in it."

Kira grimaced. Maybe she had been a little hasty denying her niece aid earlier.

"This is a cluster fuck of epic proportions." Kira could feel a headache coming on, its origins residing in her niece and this entire situation.

"We've become a cliché; we're runaways from home," Jin whimpered.

"Technically, the *Wanderer* is our home."

It was hard to be considered a runaway when you were standing on the bridge of said home.

"You know what I mean."

Sadly, Kira did.

Current events were so far outside her plans that it was a little concerning. What was supposed to be a quick jaunt—out and back before anyone knew she was gone—had turned into a situation spiraling out of Kira's control.

Nowhere in her plans had there been an impromptu trip off-planet.

Now, not only did Harlow and Graydon know about Elena, they knew about the existence of the forty-three as well.

On top of that, Kira's hope to use the quorum as a chance to search for Elise in Haldeel space was gone.

They could try to return, but Kira was pretty sure the planet's defenses would shred them before they even got through the upper atmosphere.

Even if she could land, what would she say to Harlow?

Sorry. I'm back, please forget my temporary escape?

Elena and Kira would be lucky if they weren't locked up after this stunt. Forget any chance of attending the quorum.

"As much as this has really thrown a wrench in everything, I kind of understand where she's coming from." At Kira's look, Jin got defensive. "Don't tell me if Himoto or Jace came up with a plan to rescue Elise that you wouldn't insert yourself into the mission."

"That's different."

"Oh? Because you're you?"

Kira scowled. "She's a kid."

"Physically she's older than we were when we staged our escape from the camp," Jin pointed out. "Developmentally, you were only a few years older than her when you started fighting in the war."

Because of Raider's contribution to her genetics, Elena matured at a faster rate than either Kira or Jin. She looked like the thirteen-year-old she biologically was. By contrast, Kira was ninety-two and still looked to be, at most, in her mid-twenties. As near as Kira and Jin could figure it out, once a Tuann reached physical adulthood, their aging stagnated.

One example of this was Harlow who despite being nearly two thousand years old, didn't look any older than his mid to late thirties.

Kira and Jin would have been Elena's equivalent age when they were forty or fifty—right around the time they rebelled against the camp's masters.

It was anyone's guess whether Elena would have a lifespan closer to a human's or a Tuann's. As the first of her kind that Kira knew of, Elena's existence raised a lot of questions but not a lot of answers.

They couldn't risk a scientist becoming aware of her and using the information for their own experiments.

Their best source of information was on the planet shrinking in their rear view.

"Elise didn't entrust us with her daughter so we could put her in danger," Kira argued.

"I would say Elise didn't do a very good job of entrusting us with anything."

There was a bitterness in Jin's words that Kira understood.

After Rothchild, it had taken far too long to find Elena. Nearly four years passed before Jin caught whispers about her existence.

Kira only knew the barest of details of that time. Enough to know their niece's earliest years hadn't been sweet and easy. The person Elise left her daughter to was long since gone, either dead in the war or for having abandoned Elena.

Jin bore the brunt of finding her a new home, knowing it was far too dangerous to have her with them while Kira was in her coma. Even after Kira recovered, they had only been able to manage short, periodic visits.

It was no wonder Elena wanted a family. In a way, she was much more restrained than either Kira or Jin at that age.

"I don't want Elena to go through what we did," Kira said. "She deserves to have the adults in her life protect her."

It was why they had placed her with that guardian—so Elena would have a place to grow up where she'd be safe and loved. Where she didn't have to fight every second for survival or have her personality twisted by forces outside her control.

The stakes of the game Kira and Jin were playing were harsh. Here, death would be far preferable to capture. To the Tsavitee, Elena would be a priceless treasure—the culmination of years of experimentation, fallen into their lap by chance.

"Elena is far too much like us and her parents to sit idly on the sidelines for long. You need to figure out how to handle that aspect of her or you risk having more events like today in your future," Jin said seriously.

Much as Kira wanted to deny it, Jin had a point.

Her expression turned mournful. "When did we start raising a rebellious teenager?"

Jin bobbed in front of her. "I blame you for this. Being raised by the Phoenix—of course she'd be a little hardheaded and rash."

"Me? You're the one who told her bedtime stories about the Curs and their exploits," Kira accused as she turned to the console, her hands flying as she initiated a system check.

The ride through the atmosphere had been bumpier than normal. Probably courtesy of the golden lights getting too close for comfort.

It was best to know the extent of the damage here, where they could still signal for help, then out there where there could be millions of miles between them and the nearest source of assistance.

Kira frowned at what she saw.

The ship itself looked unharmed for the most part. A few scratches on the hull, but nothing that would affect its integrity. The power readings also looked good. No overloads anywhere she could see, nor any sign of damage to the engine.

For having escaped a planet protected by the pinnacle of Tuann technology, they were remarkably intact. Unnaturally so.

"I'm getting some weird readings around the cargo bay. You wouldn't have anything to do with that, would you?" Kira didn't look away from the console as she tried to understand how they'd come out unscathed.

At least two of those golden lights had struck the ship. There should be more damage than this.

Jin hovered over Kira's shoulder. "I came through the pipes we use to offload our waste. I was nowhere near that area."

Kira extended the parameters of her search, pausing when she noticed two major spikes in that area coinciding with the timing of the lights hitting them.

Kira tapped her finger, thoughtfully.

She stood abruptly. "Come with me."

Jin bobbed along behind her as she strode off the bridge. "What about my shower? I need to get this stench off me."

"You don't have a nose, which means you have no sense of smell. If I'm willing to put up with it, you certainly can."

Jin moaned but didn't argue further. "Where are we going?"

"To see if we have a stowaway."

Jin abruptly stopped. In the next second, he darted in front, spinning so his 'eye' faced her. "Impossible. My scanners would have picked them up."

Kira didn't stop walking, forcing Jin to drift backward.

They rounded a corner only to find their passage blocked. A tall Tuann stood in the middle of the corridor, his hand wrapped around the neck of a much smaller figure. The Tuann held the person up in front of him, his victim's toes barely brushing the floor.

Kira shot Jin a look that said *see*. "Those same scanners that continually fail to detect Graydon or any oshota?"

Jin lowered several inches, his tone sulky. "I suppose you're never going to let me forget this."

Kira glanced at the two figures in front of her. "You suppose right."

The figure in Finn's grasp lifted a hand in a halfhearted wave. "I'm guessing you have a lot to say right about now."

"You've got that right," Kira said grimly

"Have the oaf put me down, and we can discuss."

Kira glanced at Finn to see one very unhappy oshota. Something told her he wasn't in the listening mood. Considering recent events, she didn't blame him.

As her accepted oshota, it was his duty to protect her from all dangers. Something that became exceedingly difficult when Kira went off on her own.

Unsurprisingly, Finn didn't loosen his grip, Odin dangling like a scolded cat.

An eye patch covered one of Odin's eyes, the other a green so brilliant that it looked like an emerald. No glint of an earring could be seen, signifying Odin was in his masculine persona. His features a little less feminine than the last time she'd seen him.

The change was subtle. The line of his jaw a little sharper, his nose and cheekbones a little blunter. Even with these changes, his face had a certain androgyny to it. Not female but not male either, rather a perfect blend of both.

Odin came from a rare race that had minor shape-shifting capabilities. They didn't experience gender in the same way humans did. For them, there were three possible genders: masculine, feminine, and the *sye*—which as near as Kira understood meant all and none. It was a sort of nongender that refused definition.

For as long as Kira had known him, Odin had flipped through the three forms according to whim. She'd once asked him how he decided between the three. He'd told her that the spirit knew and the body followed.

When Finn's expression didn't relent, Kira focused on Odin. "Something tells me you're on your own."

Odin shot her a sour look but didn't struggle.

"I suppose I don't need to ask how you got on the ship," Kira said, glancing at Finn.

As they'd seen more than once over the last month or so, Jin's scanners weren't fool proof when it came to the oshota. Their synth armor combined with a very interesting manipulation of *ki* shielded them from detection. Her time on Ta Sa'Riel had opened her eyes to the wide world of *ki*'s application. Everything she'd thought she'd known before only touched the barest surface.

Nor was she surprised Odin had managed to circumvent the scanners. Like Finn, the hacker had probably been on board the entire time, only being discovered by Finn once the excitement faded.

Odin was always quite good at finding his way into places he didn't belong. Kira simply hadn't expected for her ship to be one of them.

For the moment, Kira ignored Odin, focusing on Finn. "How much did you hear?"

"Enough."

Kira took that to mean he knew who Elena was—and probably everything else that had been discussed.

"Pretty smart to stay hidden."

"I thought so."

"Right about now, I bet you wish you hadn't agreed to Graydon's request to be my oshota," Kira ventured.

"It had occurred to me."

Kira supposed she deserved that. Sneaking out of the Fortress without notifying him, getting stuck on a ship heading off-planet, not to mention the major secrets she'd been keeping—yeah, he had a reason to be touchy.

Elena appeared at the end of the corridor, her hair slightly damp and she was wearing a fresh change of clothes. She stopped short, a towel hanging forgotten in her hand.

Her gaze flicked cautiously between Kira and the other two.

The lack of surprise in her expression told Kira her niece had known about Odin's presence the entire time.

Her niece hadn't been the one to launch Jin's defense sequence. Odin had. Elena had just gone along for the ride.

A murderous aura seeped from Kira even as a gentle smile formed. "That reminds me—I have a score to settle with you, Odin."

Wariness registered in Odin's eye.

Not enough. Not nearly enough to satisfy Kira.

That was okay. She could fix that.

Sensing the shift in Kira, Finn slowly set Odin down.

"Let's not be hasty." Odin backed away holding up his hands.

"Jin."

"My pleasure." A maniacal cackle came from Jin as he advanced.

Odin retreated. "Don't do it. You know what happened the last time you went against me."

"This time's going to be different," Jin snarled.

Electricity crackled along his shell, striking the walls with arcs of lightning. Odin jumped as a bolt impacted the floor right in front of him.

Jin chuckled, the sound echoing in the ship's speakers. "You've never fought me on my home ground before."

Odin smirked. "We'll see."

Blue arcs shot from his fingertips to the closest set of wiring embedded behind the ship's walls.

Jin cursed and flew toward him. "It's not going to be that easy."

"Auntie, shouldn't you stop them?"

"Don't worry. Jin won't kill Odin. The Allfather is far too useful for that."

But if Jin wanted to extract a pound of flesh for the many grievances he had against Odin, who was Kira to stop him?

"Have you decided on a course?" Elena asked.

"We're taking you home. I'll decide what's next after that." Kira tilted her head at the bridge. "Why don't you input the coordinates?"

Pleasure flashed across Elena's face, and there was a bounce in her step as she did Kira's bidding.

Beside Kira, Finn didn't bother concealing his disapproval.

Kira pinched the bridge of her nose. "I need a drink for this conversation."

Kira strode away, leaving Finn to follow—or not. His choice.

It took only seconds to reach the galley. The *Wanderer* wasn't a large ship by any means. You could get anywhere on it within a matter of minutes.

The galley was small, really no more than a nook filled with only the barest of essentials—a food synthesizer, a cupboard of ready to eat blocks, and a table with two sad-looking chairs pulled up next to it.

It hadn't always been this way.

The original galley was much bigger, located in a room twice the size of this one. Since Kira was the only person who required sustenance, she'd decided it was much better to repurpose the old galley as a weapons room. The new one was relocated to an old closet.

What could Kira say—she had a lot of weapons.

Finn eyed the small space with distrust as Kira fixed two cups of chai. With his much larger body, the galley seemed even more cramped than usual.

Kira set the two cups on the table and took a seat before nodding at the chair across from her. Kira took a sip of her chai, waiting as Finn eased into it. His uncomfortable expression made it clear he didn't entirely trust it to hold his weight.

Finn picked up his mug and sniffed. "What is this?"

"Chai. I've had better, but it fills the craving."

Finn took a cautious sip, surprise flashing across his face.

"You disagree with my choice not to return to Ta Sa'Riel," Kira said, getting down to business.

Sometimes it was best to rip the band-aid off. Beating around the bush would only delay the inevitable. She didn't want that.

With a guarded expression, Finn set his chai on the table.

Kira stared into her mug as if it had all the answers. "Could I land safely on Ta Sa'Riel in the current circumstances?"

Finn was quiet.

Good. He was giving her question consideration.

He tapped the table with a finger. "Not unless we call and gain clearance first."

That fit with Kira's reading of the situation as well.

"And is there a way to establish a direct link to Roake?"

Finn opened his mouth, then closed it again. "If you had one of their communication stones."

"I don't. Do you?"

All expression disappeared from Finn's face as he realized where she was going with this.

Kira propped her chin on her hand. "If I wanted to contact Roake, I'd have to broadcast on wide band."

Which would alert any potential enemies to their position.

Since Kira didn't have the codes for the Tuann comms nor was her ship compatible with their method of communication, she was stuck screaming into the void in the most unsecure way possible.

If Elena wasn't on the ship, she could take the risk.

But Elena was on the ship, leaving only one path before Kira. Find Elena a safe port, then reassess.

"By now, I think you have a sense of what's at stake." Kira met Finn's gaze. "Can you promise me beyond any shadow of a doubt Elena will be safe on Ta Sa'Riel with Roake?"

"There are none in your father's House who would hurt her."

Kira raised an eyebrow. "What about Loudon?"

The traitor was now dead, but the fact he'd existed at all proved Kira's case.

Loudon was a trusted member in the highest ranks of the House. His betrayal and involvement in the events that had led to the deaths of Kira's parents and her subsequent capture by the Tuann's enemies proved that. He was dead now, but that didn't change history.

Where there was one, there could be more.

"Can you swear that no others like him exist? If you can, I'll roll the dice and make contact with Roake."

Kira would far prefer her niece to be ensconced in a House with hundreds of oshota willing to give their lives to protect her.

Finn stared at his cup of chai and closed his eyes. "I can't."

That was her answer then.

"Then our course is set."

Kira was surprised at the level of disappointment that answer brought.

"It would be a mistake to cut ties with Roake," Finn warned.

"I happen to agree with you."

Even if she hadn't regretted the manner of her leaving, there was the little problem of her health.

While she'd made great strides in her treatment for *ki* poisoning, Quillon hadn't pronounced her healed.

If she was going to go against the Tsavitee and the masters controlling them from the shadows, it would be better to do so in peak form.

"I'll drop Elena off with her other aunt, and then rendezvous with Roake at the quorum."

It'd be the easiest place to reinsert herself into their number. Not to mention, doing so would put her in the vicinity of where Elise had last been seen.

"That could be a problem," Odin said from the threshold.

A piece of metal glinted. Kira caught the object Odin tossed.

"What's this?" Kira lowered her hand, seeing Odin's scroll. The latest model from the looks of things.

Kira pressed the tip of a finger into one of the groves. A small light flashed. She tapped the end to the table. A small screen spread across the table's surface, its smart feature displaying the information Odin had pulled up for her.

The crease in Kira's forehead deepened the longer she read. "Why are the Haldeel having the quorum on Jettie?"

True, the planet was in Haldeel space, but just barely.

It had a large population of human refugees—those who'd been displaced by the war and chosen to shelter under the shade of the Haldeel empire rather than relocate to a human planet.

Also, coincidentally, it was where Jin had chosen to hide Elena.

"It's an interesting choice on the Haldeel's part, but not out of character. The Haldeel move the site of the quorum every time so as not to put undue burden for hosting on any one planet," Finn said.

The answer didn't make Kira any happier. She didn't like coincidences, even when they were in her favor.

"Read further." Odin crossed to the small kitchen counter and hopped up, sitting cross-legged on it.

Jin moved out of the corridor, scorch marks decorating his sphere. Every so often, he would shudder in place as if he were having issues with his antigravs.

Odin wasn't unscathed. There was a bruise on one cheekbone and his cloak had been shredded, revealing the bodysuit beneath

Kira ignored him, scrolling down the lines. She stopped as she reached a particular paragraph. "This could present a problem."

"What sort of problem?" Jin nearly clipped Kira in the head as he moved to get a glimpse of what she was reading. It only took him moments to spot the same thing Kira had. "Oh."

Yes. Oh.

"Jettie is only allowing those who are already registered citizens or participating in the quorum to the planet," Odin explained to Finn.

For Elena, it wouldn't be a problem. She'd had status as a citizen since her fifth birthday. The rest of them were a different story, however.

"Chances of sneaking down unnoticed?" Jin asked.

Odin fixed a look on Jin. "What do you think?"

Getting down to the planet was possible. Doing so without drawing attention to themselves—unlikely.

Even if they slipped through the Haldeel's net, it was bound to raise some red flags—exactly the kind of thing Tsavitee spies would be on the lookout for.

Finding himself the center of attention, Jin said defensively, "It was just a question."

"A stupid one," Odin retorted.

"Well, this stupid one fried all your nasty little friends, so who's really the idiot now?" Jin returned.

Odin regarded him with a flat stare. "Still you."

Jin sputtered.

A crafty look overtook Odin's face as he smiled suddenly. "How's it going finding the surprise I dropped into your positioning system?"

"Fine," Jin said stiffly.

Kira ignored them, still engrossed in the dossier that Odin had put together for her. He must have known the quorum was coming because he had gathered quite a lot of information. All of it useful.

"I think I know how we can get onto the planet," Kira said before the argument could escalate.

Jin and Odin fell quiet.

"I thought you'd be interested in that route," Odin said.

Not one to let others know something he didn't, Jin scanned the document over Kira's shoulder.

"You're going to enter one of the hoverboard races," he guessed.

Kira ducked her chin in a nod.

Odin drummed his fingers against his knee. "It would take care of the most pressing of your problems."

"Not your; our." To Odin's argumentative expression, Kira added, "You're the reason we're in this mess."

Kira wasn't entirely sure he hadn't orchestrated this whole scenario. She wouldn't put it past the manipulative bastard. The question was how complicit was Elena in his schemes.

Knowing she wasn't likely to get an answer that would satisfy her, she left the matter alone.

"You're awful quiet." Kira glanced Finn's way. "Have anything to share? Of all of us, you're probably the most knowledgeable about the quorum."

The quorum was still a relatively new concept for humans. To them it would seem like a particularly extreme version of the Olympics—simply more deadly for contestants and with a lot more political moving and shaking.

The Tuann, on the other hand, had participated for centuries. Of them all, Finn would understand the undercurrents best.

Finn took a thoughtful sip of his chai. "There are no restrictions on who may participate. Whether you're sponsored by one of the three powers doesn't matter. Any may showcase their abilities and rise or fall under their own merit."

How egalitarian of them.

Of course, the truth of the matter was a little less transparent. Although any could compete, the odds were tilted very much in favor of those who had a powerful backer. Housing, food, equipment—even the credits needed for registration—all of those had to be taken into consideration.

For most, the price of competing would simply be out of the realm of possibility, no matter how talented.

That didn't even touch on the specialized training you'd need to be competitive in your chosen field.

From the dossier Odin had put together, the hoverboard races were relatively new as events went. It was why Kira had picked them as her point of entry. The field would be much more even with humans holding a slight advantage. The rest of the galaxy wouldn't be as familiar with the rules, whereas hoverboard racing was one of the most popular sports in human space.

Add in Kira's history with the sport and the fact she already held a waveboard license, and it was the easiest avenue to take to accomplish her goals.

"If you don't qualify, you'll be kicked off the planet," Finn warned. "Only the support staff of a contestant or those who have won an event in the past are exempted from the requirement."

Kira could see why the quorum was such a big deal. Its structure was flawless, feeding into the psychology of all three races.

They'd limited attendance to make those with a coveted slot perceive it as a rare honor. Throw in the chance to brush elbows with the most powerful individuals in the galaxy while fostering an environment where issues of state could be discussed unimpeded, and you had an irresistible recipe for success.

With one move the Haldeel earned their spot as one of the most influential and powerful in the galaxy—and they'd done it without having to fire a shot.

"It's decided then. I'll resurrect my old alias so as not to draw attention," Kira said.

It was her only choice.

Graydon and Roake were almost guaranteed to be there. While they wouldn't necessarily assume she was also in attendance, it paid to be cautious.

She didn't plan to evade them forever, just until she got Elena's situation sorted.

Even Finn couldn't argue with her logic.

"If that's settled, I'll be in my berth." Odin jumped off the counter, only pausing to send a sly look Jin's way. "You're always welcome to join me if you'd like. Maybe I can fix that little problem you're having."

"I can fix my own problems," Jin snarled.

"Have it your way."

Odin strolled out of the galley.

To Finn, Kira said, "It might be a bit cramped over the next month. I'm afraid all the berths are taken. Find a spot anywhere and it's yours."

Finn nodded and stood, disappearing silently into the hall.

"Kira, you don't think—"

"It's not going to be a problem, Jin." Kira drained the rest of her chai. "We'll be fine. All that happened years ago. I bet no one even remembers it anymore."

And even if they did, chances were they wouldn't recognize Kira and Jin. Kira had been a lot different back then.

"If you say so," Jin said doubtfully.

FOUR

A DEEP SILENCE fell over the ship as one by one its occupants sought the release of dreamland, leaving only Kira awake.

Slouched in the pilot's seat, she held a cup of chai. It'd been a long time since she'd sat like this, watching the stars go by, the ship as silent as a tomb around her.

To think, she thought she'd missed this.

It was a long time later when Kira finally stirred, setting aside her mug and reaching over to press the record button.

"Raider, you're furious with me; I don't blame you."

A fleeting smile, lacking any semblance of warmth or happiness, chased across her face, there and gone as if it'd never been.

"To tell you the truth, I never really thought you were the mole. There are a lot of excuses I could give you for the decisions we made, but that's all they'd be—excuses. I won't insult you by listing them here. At the time they seemed relevant, but looking back, I have to wonder."

Kira's gaze turned distant. "I should have told you about Elena the moment I knew about her. I'm not even sure why I didn't."

Kira rubbed her forehead. "Honestly, I don't even know why I'm bothering to record this. You'll never see it. I've never sent any of the messages I've recorded to you."

Exhaustion pulled at Kira. The type that made her wonder if it was all worth it.

At this point, she didn't even know anymore.

In the moment, she could ignore the look of betrayal. Pretend not to feel the hot splash of pain that came with knowing she caused that grief.

Until Raider and the rest came back into her life, she'd never really questioned whether she was doing the right thing.

Now, she was left wondering if there had been a better way of doing things and she simply hadn't taken the time to find it.

"I'm tired, Raider. So bloody tired." Kira felt the truth of that statement all the way to her bones. "The worst part is I don't even know if I'd do it differently if given the chance. Elena is alive. Safe. A know-it-all pain in the ass in the way only someone that age can be, but she's happy."

Kira shoved aside her feelings of regret and sorrow. "By now, you know or have at least guessed that Elise is alive. It's not the rosy scenario you think. I promised Elena I'd bring her mother home, and I intend to do that. There are some things you need to know that I couldn't have revealed in front of the rest. Next time I see you, I promise I'll tell you everything I can. It's not much in the way of recompense, but it'll have to do."

Kira reached out and stopped the recording.

On the screen, a message popped up.

[Do you wish to send?]

Her finger hovered over the Yes button, knowing it'd be days before the *Wanderer* got close to a station where all the messages in the queue could be uploaded and sent.

In the end, she pressed the save for later button.

Finished, she leaned back in her chair, content to watch the stars for a while longer.

* * *

"Have you ever seen anything like this?" Elena asked as the *Wanderer* approached Almaluk, the station currently floating over Jettie like a second, much smaller, oblong moon.

Hundreds, possibly thousands, of ships dotted the expanse of space around the planet—the bulky shapes of human ships intermingling with the more svelte and streamlined Tuann vessels. Kira even caught a few designs she wasn't familiar with—possibly of alien origin.

Kira shook her head.

At least not in peacetime. During the war, seeing a gathering of ships this large was rare but not unheard of. Of course, back then, most of these ships would have ended up as silent graveyards if they'd actually seen battle.

Kira had known the quorum was important, but until right this moment she couldn't have guessed the sheer magnitude of the event.

Even Kira had heard of Almaluk, the floating palace of the Haldeel, crowning gem of their empire. Unlike most stations that tended to be stationary, or at least fixed to a certain quadrant, Almaluk wandered the void. To find it, you either had to have the key to its ever-changing frequency or happen upon it by chance.

The station was a relatively recent addition to Jettie's skies. The last time she'd visited, it hadn't been a consideration. Guess Kira knew how the Haldeel intended to enforce their restrictions.

"That is a lot of ships," Jin said.

"Any idea the exact numbers?" Kira asked.

Jin was silent a moment as he calculated.

Odin was quicker. "One thousand eight hundred ninety-five, with an additional two hundred outside the system."

"I was getting to it," Jin grumbled.

"Not fast enough."

Kira ignored the two, used to the sniping by now. The weeks of living practically on top of each other had required a delicate balance.

Finn had kept mostly to himself while Odin and Jin spent hours tinkering with the ship and any gadget they could get their hands on.

She was pretty sure the two had invented more than one thing that would revolutionize the market if they ever decided to offer it for sale.

Elena had kept pretty close to Kira, soaking up the rare opportunity to spend quality time together.

Overall, the trip had been uneventful.

Kira glanced outside at what basically amounted to an armada. All with one central goal—Almaluk and the planet below.

The station was the most beautiful Kira had ever seen. It lived up to its name, the metal framework curving in on itself like thousands of infinity symbols. The craftmanship showed the Haldeel's delicate hand in working metal as it created an illusion of movement, until the station seemed like a flower constantly on the cusp of blooming.

"Are we all set?" Kira asked.

"Everything has been arranged. I've already received a temporary pass to the planet," Jin said. "Once we dock, we should be good to go."

In other words, if you wanted to participate, you had to go through the Haldeel.

Only those they deemed trustworthy would be allowed to set foot on Jettie. It also meant that anyone entering would have to go through a Haldeel security check. As safety measures went, you couldn't get much better.

"Are you sure I can't go with you?" Elena asked.

"There are too many eyes. If we're recognized, I don't want you associated with us."

Kira wasn't exactly happy allowing Elena to go down separately, but it was better than the alternative. If a Tsavitee agent was present, it would be best if they never saw Elena—especially in relation to Kira.

It was hard to hunt for something you didn't know existed.

For that reason, Kira, Jin, and Finn would go first with Odin and Elena leaving long after them.

It wasn't Kira's favorite plan, but given the circumstances, it was the best she could do.

"Don't screw this up," Kira told Odin. "If you do, you'd better run very, very far and hide really, really well."

If something happened to her niece, she would actually kill him this time.

"And you," Kira said to Elena. "Don't stray off book."

"Geez, it's like you don't trust me."

"I wonder why." Could it have anything to do with their current predicament? Let Kira think. Why yes, yes it could.

Elena's grimace was sheepish. "I promise to be careful."

That didn't really make Kira feel much better. A preteen's idea of careful and hers differed greatly.

Elena was more trained than most her age and more cautious as a result, but her decision-making priorities sometimes left Kira with a headache.

"I don't suppose you'd let me watch the quals?" Elena asked, trying her luck.

Yup. That headache definitely had Elena's name all over it.

"Which part of 'be cautious' didn't you understand?" Kira asked.

"I can stay out of sight. Besides, you'll need Odin's help for the race," Elena said, not allowing herself to be dissuaded.

"Kid has a point. You're going to need some talented seconds to help you with pre-race calibrations and during the race itself," Odin pointed out.

"Excuse you," Jin objected. "Kira has me for that."

Odin held up one slender finger proportionally longer than any human or Tuann's. "Race rules—all racers must have at least one controller, and it can't be a machine. As handsome as tall and dangerous over there is, he doesn't have the right skills for the job."

Finn didn't react to either the compliment or the insult beyond a faint tightening of the skin around the corner of his eyes.

"That leaves yours truly." Odin pointed at himself.

Kira had already considered all of that. No waveboard pilot could see everything at one time and also keep an eye on the ever-changing conditions.

While it was possible to race without a controller, it was a lot more dangerous. Only the crazy or the extremely talented ever tried, let alone succeeded. Kira could do it and had even considered that route before discarding it.

Such an action was bound to draw attention.

Since she planned to hide her identity for a time—at least until Elena's situation had been taken care of—Kira planned to have Finn stand in with Jin coaching him in the background.

Odin's way was a lot simpler, and if it hadn't been for Elena, Kira would say yes.

"I can stay in the stands. No one's going to pay attention to a kid. I'll keep my cloak up and my head down," Elena promised.

Kira hesitated.

"We're going to have time to kill anyway," Odin said. "Your contact hasn't responded yet, and we don't want to fall afoul of the Haldeel rules. You know how sensitive they can be."

Yes, Kira did.

The Haldeel prided themselves on their adherence to the laws and rules set in place. They wouldn't break them, even if doing otherwise resulted in death.

They expected those competing to do the same. If you were known to break a vow or rule, they would blacklist you.

The Consortium had come remarkably close to trespassing against this cultural ideology in the beginning of their relationship. It was only because of the battle of Rothchild and the sacrifices made there that the Haldeel gave them a second chance.

By that point, humans had been desperate to curry favor with their powerful ally. As a result, several key military and political leadership roles were reassigned to people who would be a little more honorable in their dealings.

What few seemed to realize was that although the Haldeel were rigid in their views, they also loved loopholes. It was considered something of a coup to be able to use one.

In that, Kira and the Haldeel were of one mind.

"Let's hope the contact is prompt then," Kira finally said.

"And if not?" Elena asked, her eyes brightening.

When Kira didn't answer, Jin interceded. "I have something that might set your mind at ease."

There was the small click of metal against metal as a silver turtle crawled across the floor of the bridge.

It reached Elena's feet and stopped, its little head craning as it blinked metal eyelids over the impression of metal eyes.

"Jin, what is that?" Kira said in a carefully controlled voice.

It bared a striking resemblance to the lizard Jin had called Min, the small avatar he'd given Kira so he could still interact with her on Ta Sa'Riel when he was supposed to be keeping a low profile.

The lizard hadn't survived their showdown in the Trial of the Broken and had had the core of its essence extracted so Kira could save Wren.

No bigger than Elena's palm, the turtle was as cute as that lizard had been.

"Meet Min Junior," Jin said. "Or Min 2.0. I haven't decided."

"I thought the days of making a mini you were over."

The turtle opened its mouth, a small croak coming from it as it begged to be picked up.

Elena obliged, bending and setting her hand in front of it. The turtle considered it before padding forward. Elena picked the small avatar up, petting it with one careful finger.

"So cute!" she said, engrossed in her new friend.

Kira glared at Jin.

"This one is better than the last one," Jin promised. "MinMin, attack."

The little turtle scuttled around on Elena's palm until his head was facing away from her. Its mouth opened and a pinprick of light roared from it. No smaller than a laser, it still had a big impact as it melted a perfectly round hole in the wall.

"Are you kidding me?" Kira asked as Finn erected a shield, containing the rest of the blast. "You fit him with a modified *zuipi*? Are you trying to kill us?"

"Cool, right? I took Blue's designs and modified them. The power output is a lot more efficient now." Jin blathered on, unaware of the way Finn's expression darkened. "I don't know why they didn't do it that way from the beginning."

For once, Kira was speechless.

"What?" Jin asked, realizing how silent it was. "You wanted her protected. Now she's protected. My spawn will keep her safe."

"You can't call it a spawn when it's basically you in a smaller body," Kira shouted.

"I told you—I made improvements. This one has its own base personality. Introduce yourself," Jin invited.

"Hello, my name is Min Junior. You can call me MinMin as directed by the one who spawned me," the turtle said in a cute, squeaky voice.

"I'll admit his personality is a bit basic at the moment, but he'll get the job done. Even better, as long as he's on Elena, I will always be able to find her."

Elena's glance at Kira was hopeful.

Kira's shoulders sagged. She wasn't going to win this battle. "Fine, if our contact is late, you can come. Remember your promise, stay in the background and don't draw attention."

Elena hopped up and down. "Yes, I'm finally going to get to see you race!"

The turtle yawned, padding up Elena's arm and into her hair where he sank down, for all the world appearing as if he was an ornate hair clip.

Kira shook her head, wondering how she had lost control on her own ship. She could only hope their contact would be prompt. Last thing she needed was for Elena to decide on a career as a waveboard racer.

* * *

Hours later, Kira wove through the crowd, Finn a grumpy sentinel at her side.

After some skillful arguing on her part, she'd managed to convince him to cover his synth armor with a cloak. As disguises went, it wasn't foolproof, his size alone guaranteeing anyone who noticed him would assume he was some kind of a warrior.

At least with the covering, any prying eyes wouldn't be able to pick him—and by extension Kira—out of a crowd at a glance.

Kira was a little more inconspicuous, playing the part of a fashion-challenged teen. She'd reunited with one of her many hoodies. Currently, she had her hands stuffed in its pockets, the hood drawn to hide her distinctive hair color.

For once, Jin was playing it safe, hiding out inside her hood, using it and her hair to go unnoticed.

He'd had to condense his sphere, something he only did when he needed to fit into small spaces. Right now, he was closer to the size of a softball. Even then, he barely fit.

Kira knew the hood looked a little misshapen. The ruse would never fool the Haldeel scanners located at nearly every hall intersection, but it didn't need to.

The Haldeel weren't the ones she was trying to deceive.

"Any issues?" Kira asked, her lips barely moving.

To her surprise, there were a lot more Tuann present than she'd anticipated. It had left her feeling a bit twitchy and paranoid, like she had a target painted on her.

"Not yet."

"Any sign of Graydon?" Kira asked.

Jin hummed in thought. "No, I don't think he or anyone from House Roake have docked yet."

Or maybe they had and Jin was simply more confident in his skills than he had a right to be.

It wouldn't be the first time one of the Tuann had come out of their blind spot.

"Either way, stay on guard. If we're caught here, they're going to go after Elena."

Kira didn't have to explain how bad it would be if Elena was spotted so close to her other protectors.

Certain people would find that information interesting. They could even decide to investigate further. The results of such a fact-finding mission would endanger a whole lot more than the safety of her niece.

"I know."

They moved out of the corridor that connected the shipyard docks to the station.

Kira flicked her eyes up and to the right, accessing the map Odin had uploaded into her optics.

Tiny glowing lines formed in the upper right of her vision, a representation of the station and its features.

Their destination was the docks where drop shuttles would ferry visitors planet side.

Seeing they were still heading in the right direction; Kira dismissed the map.

"You'll find this interesting," Jin chirped. "Luatha is here."

Kira dodged around a slow-moving clump of humans, noting the insignia embroidered on their uniforms. Two crossed swords framed by a sunburst on either side.

Zepher.

Kira's lip curled. She could have done without seeing them ever again.

"What's my cousin's House doing here?"

"Probably the same thing everyone else is."

Kira couldn't catch a break. One more group capable of recognizing her and Jin at a glance.

She'd known the chokepoint of the station would pose a problem, but she hadn't thought she'd be so thoroughly surrounded on all sides.

Kira forced her pace not to quicken.

This little deception hinged on going unremarked. She was one of thousands of hopefuls looking to earn recognition and praise through her own skills and talent.

For that reason, she needed to act the part of tourist as she admired the interior of the station.

It mimicked a city. Tall buildings were framed by the same swooping metal arches she'd seen on the exterior. Here, she could better appreciate them. The loops weren't simply flat metal. Instead, they twisted and turned in a relaxed spiral.

It made it easy to show fascination as she walked.

Although technologically advanced, the Haldeel had an appreciation for beauty, entwining form with functionality.

It was apparent in this brief visit how ingrained that mentality was in the Haldeel mindset.

It wasn't enough to build something. It had to be effortlessly beautiful as well. Extra points if it was also insanely complicated.

Too soon, Kira and her companions reached their destination, a massive room filled with small ships arranged in neat little rows.

On one side of the room was the black of space, the planet taking up a large chunk of the view. A small membrane ensured those who entered weren't immediately sucked into the vacuum of space.

A disturbance mere feet away drew Kira's attention from the breathtaking view.

A group of humans faced off against a Haldeel.

The person in charge was a short man with a barrel chest. He, like his companions, was dressed sharply in a uniform of tailored pants and a tight-fitting jacket.

Like the humans Kira had passed earlier, the emblem of Zepher was displayed prominently over the left side of their chest.

"There are plenty of other vessels. There's no need for you to allow these aliens to board ours," the man was saying.

Kira glanced at the people he indicated, feeling her heart lurch at the sight of five people clad in the forest green of Luathan synth armor.

Speak of the devil and he shall arrive.

Liara's gaze was cool as she watched the drama with an impassive expression. Unlike the first time Kira had met her, Liara's armor was more subdued. She'd left off the long cape in favor of blending in with her oshota.

Next to her, Roderick's face displayed his displeasure at the humans' behavior.

"We, too, would prefer not to share space with ones such as these."

Disdain dripped from Liara's words.

The Haldeel in front of them inclined his upper body in a small bow. "I apologize, esteemed guests. Our ships must be filled to capacity before they are released to the planet. You can wait for others in your party if you would prefer."

The humans from Zepher didn't look happy at that response.

"Our party is taking part in the quals. We don't have time to wait for the necessary numbers," a woman standing beside the man said.

"Then your path is clear," the Haldeel said, unfazed by their argument.

Luatha looked on dispassionately.

"We will wait for another ship," Liara said.

The Haldeel inclined his head. "That is also an option."

Luatha and the Haldeel moved away, leaving the humans standing in front of the transport ship.

"Fucking wizards and squids," one grumbled.

"Hush," the man in charge said. "I don't want to hear you talking like that while we're here. You never know who is listening."

The man grimaced but didn't argue further.

"They might be squids, but they have their uses," the woman said, looking around her. "We can't afford to offend them."

The humans from Zepher shot a glance in Kira's direction as she moved past them.

Finn picked up on Kira's dislike. "Those humans—they're not like your Curs."

Kira's pace was steady as she made her way to a dropship on the other side of the hanger, choosing one at random.

The quals weren't for another couple hours. Judging by how quickly people were pouring in and ships were taking off, even if Kira wasn't at the front of the line, she should still make it in time.

"You could say that again," Jin said from inside her hood.

"I didn't recognize their affiliation," Finn ventured after a small pause.

"You wouldn't. Zepher didn't contribute a lot to the war." Kira kept her gaze focused on the ship, looking neither left nor right.

Finn paused. "How is that possible?"

Jin answered when it seemed Kira wouldn't. "The planet Zepher enjoys a unique natural defense. It's located in the middle of a perpetual solar storm. Only those who have a map can reach the planet. Anyone else risks their ship being ripped apart from the fluctuating gravitational fields and ion winds."

Those attributes allowed them to ride out the safety of the war from the comforts of their own planet. While the rest of the Consortium was in a fight for their lives, Zepher sat back and watched.

They contributed the bare minimum to the war effort.

That hadn't stopped them from a shameless power grab afterward. Since they'd suffered little in the way of losses, it had allowed them to attain a position of power in the Consortium, bought in large part by the sacrifices of others.

Kira could have forgiven them for that. After all, who wanted to send their sons and daughters to war?

However, Zepher was also highly xenophobic. Anything that smacked of aliens was abhorred and treated with extreme prejudice.

"I'd be on your guard with them," Jin advised. "They're tricky little bastards."

There was no love lost between Zepher and them. If Kira had her way, she'd stay far from anyone associated with that planet.

Kira ignored how Finn studied her, knowing he'd realized there was more to this story.

Unfortunately for him, Kira didn't intend to let any of her secrets slip on this trip.

"Much as I hate to agree with someone from Zepher on anything, they did have a point. There's not a lot of time before we have to be at the quals," Jin said as Kira targeted a ship in the corner, hoping its location far from the dock's entrance would mean they wouldn't run into anyone they knew. "You sure you want to pick this one?"

"Really, old friend, I would think you'd know by now not to question me," Kira said, marching toward the ship she'd picked.

A much richer and luxurious cousin to the dropships they'd used in the military, the ship didn't have anyone lingering near its boarding ramp.

"Oh no, you haven't gotten arrogant at all," Jin griped.

Kira allowed herself a small smile. "I don't want to hear that from you, Mr. I'm-going-to-invade-someone's-nexus-and-get-caught."

There was silence and then a sulky, "I didn't get caught. I just tripped the sensors, set off the alarm, and got knocked out for a few hours."

"If you think my uncle hasn't put together that incursion with your presence, you're even more dimwitted than you sometimes act," Kira said lightly as she approached the Haldeel steward waiting outside the ship, his eyes bored.

"Hello, I'd like to inquire about passage," Kira said in accented Haldeel.

Meanwhile, she gave him a simplified greeting, her wrists lifting in a gentle hello, her fingers fanning out in a gesture meant to convey good fortune and favorable tides.

The Haldeel language was filled with a surprising amount of nuance. It contained two parts, placing as much significance on your nonverbal physical cues as it did on what you said.

Vaguely resembling a simplistic form of sign language, there were countless variations that changed based on the tilt of the head, the flick of a finger, or the twist of a wrist. Get even one wrong and you significantly changed the meaning.

An appreciative smile appeared on the Haldeel's face. "You're familiar with our language."

"A novice still." Kira changed her posture to denote gratefulness for the compliment.

"Welcome, *za*." The Haldeel's limbs flowed into a much more elegant version of the common greeting Kira had given him. "This humble one would be delighted with your company."

Kira smiled at the Haldeel, allowing herself to feel the pleasure the exchange had brought her.

There was an aspect of communication with the Haldeel that most never considered—the empathic nature of the race.

It wasn't enough simply to express what you were feeling. To truly communicate on a level the Haldeel respected, you had to feel what you were trying to get across.

Surprised pleasure suffused the Haldeel's expression. Often called squids by humans, the Haldeel had many traits in common with a cephalopod.

From the waist up, the Haldeel resembled humans.

The first difference most noticed was the two-toned pigmentation unique to their species. The Haldeel in front of her possessed a creamy coloring that was overlaid with a tracery of dull green markings. The green marched along his limbs, up the sides of his neck, to end in tattoo-like patterns along the edges of his face.

Not many out there realized how their unique pigmentation allowed them a biologically based camouflage. Kira still had nightmares about how she'd learned that little factoid.

Like most of the Haldeel Kira had come across, the man before her favored the long flowing robes that were popular in Haldeel fashion.

The robes hid their lower half, which was where things got interesting.

Like the cephalopod they got their name from, the Haldeel had eight flexible, prehensile appendages which made them an absolute nightmare to fight.

"May I ask what event the *za* will be competing in during the quorum?"

"The Pinnacle." Kira supplied the common name for the waverunner races.

The Haldeel clasped his hands before his chest, interlocking his fingers and dipping his chin in a gesture meant to denote accepting a task and promising its completion.

"Then we will endeavor to allow you to arrive on time."

Kira let gratitude flush through her as she changed her stance to one of gratefulness. "I would be in your debt."

The Haldeel moved aside in a gliding movement no human or Tuann could hope to replicate and gestured for Kira to enter.

"Where did you learn to speak Haldeel?" Finn asked in a low voice only meant for Kira's ears.

"Here and there."

She didn't want to get into the short span of time she'd spent on the edge of Haldeel space, or the little girl and her bodyguard she'd met there.

The two were the lone bright spots in a very dark period of Kira's life. Being here, interacting with the Haldeel again, even on a superficial level, Kira couldn't help but wonder how the other two were doing these days.

Sensing Kira had said as much on the topic as she planned, Finn fell silent, his gaze speculative.

That was okay. As long as he kept his questions to himself and let her do what she needed.

"You sly woman, how did you know they'd be willing to take off even if they weren't at capacity?" Jin asked.

Kira allowed herself a small smile. "One word—loophole."

Jin snorted. "Of course, the thing Haldeel like best."

Kira had bet on the fact the Haldeel would leave their options open. Although the rule the Haldeel at the entrance had quoted was likely real, Kira had known the Haldeel would likely include a clause that if waiting jeopardized a passenger's ability to participate in an event, the vessel could take off sooner if the captain wished it.

The quorum was a showcase of the best and brightest after all.

Of course, it also helped that Kira knew the Haldeel were more likely to respond well when they were treated with respect and kindness. If she'd been rude or presumptuous, Kira doubted they'd be so willing to take off.

It was a test. A cleverly designed one she was quite sure most didn't pass.

That was the Haldeel for you. Simple at first glance. Only the observant realized the nuances behind every action they took.

Kira paused on the threshold of the dropship, noting the empty seats and the handful of bodies currently occupying the ship.

Good.

Just the way she liked it.

Kira started down the aisle when a piping voice reached her.

"You haven't told me where my *seon'yer* is," a little girl said from directly behind her.

Jin choked in surprise, Kira not faring much better.

A shot of adrenaline ran through Kira, and only years of training kept her from whirling and destroying her cover.

Because she knew that voice. And the other three with her.

It belonged to Ziva, one of two children Kira had rescued from a hovercraft that was in the process of crashing. The act had precipitated her discovery by the Tuann and the subsequent realization that she wasn't human at all.

Next to her was Joule, the other child Kira had rescued.

They weren't alone. Devon, someone she suspected was the son of the Tuann Emperor and another she'd saved at one time or another, accompanied them.

Lastly was Rheya, who with Joule and Devon, had participated in the *uhva na*, the Trial of the Broken, with Kira shortly before she left Ta Sa'Riel.

"Ziva, I'm not sure Kira would appreciate you calling her that," Joule chided.

Ziva harrumphed. "What would you know? My *seon'yer* is not like all these others."

This time it was Kira's turn to choke.

"Is that so? Tell us what your *seon'yer* is like, little sister," Rheya teased.

Ziva rose to the challenge. "She's wise and fierce. No one is as devious or good at fighting as she is."

Jin shook in silent laughter against Kira's neck.

She slapped one hand over his body, hoping no one had noticed the movement.

"That description is rather accurate," Devon observed.

Kira stiffened. "I'm not devious."

"That's the part you take umbrage with?"

"I'm not," she muttered.

"Uh-huh."

Finn had turned into a statue at her side, staring rigidly into empty space.

Kira grabbed his arm, shuffling him forward. Picking a seat at random, one thankfully in the far corner of the craft and as far from the door as possible, Kira shoved Finn into it before taking the one right beside him.

Only once seated did she force herself to relax, stretching her feet out as she pulled her hood forward to shield her face. She fiddled with it. Only when she felt it was secure enough did she chance a furtive look at the others.

With the exception of Ziva, they were all apprentices in service to their own *seon'yers*.

Devon was the tallest of the four, his height approaching Graydon's. Dressed in a matte black armor, he was a smaller, less muscular version of the Emperor's Face.

Though much younger than Graydon, Kira had a feeling it was only a matter of time before Devon bulked up, rivaling the other man in terms of size.

With yellow eyes that always reminded Kira of daisies, Devon observed Ziva with an amusement that had been lacking the last time she'd met him.

Kira remembered another set of eyes that looked exactly like those, the former owner of which was currently hiding in her hair, completely oblivious to the resemblance.

Beside Devon, Rheya had one hand propped on her hip as she teased the small girl in front of her.

The youngest of the four, Ziva could be mistaken for an eight-year-old child—though her true age was likely around thirty years.

Because of her white-blond hair and deep blue eyes, people tended to underestimate her, never realizing the fierce heart that lay within.

Though young, Kira had a feeling Ziva would be a force to be reckoned with in a decade or two.

She was a scrapper, disregarding her limits, more than willing to come out swinging no matter the opponent.

Kira couldn't help but admire someone who possessed that sort of stubbornness. They were the ones who held the power to change the universe because they didn't pay attention to what was but rather devoted their attention to what should be.

The final person in the party was also the one who'd spent the most time at Kira's side.

Joule's face had thinned out since she last saw him, nearly a month ago, losing some of the softness it had had when they'd first met.

It looked like his training was beginning to have an effect, packing his small frame with muscles.

There was a world-weary look in his eyes that was new. Something that said he'd seen the dark side of life and knew things weren't always going to turn out the way he wanted.

Kira couldn't help feeling like she shared some of the blame for that look. People around her tended to lose their innocence far sooner than they had a right to.

The loss of his parents might have started the process, but Kira had finished the job.

Despite that, he still had an earnestness to him. A goodness that Kira hoped he preserved.

All this wouldn't be so bad if not for the oshota keeping watch on the group from several feet away.

"Your luck continues to trend toward the shittier side," Jin observed.

Of all the ships on the docks, they had to choose this one to board.

Kira supposed it could be worse. Graydon could be with them.

FIVE

FROM THE SAFETY of her hood, Kira allowed herself to study the four as they moved further into the craft. They had the same idea as Kira, selecting seats far from the other passengers where they could place their backs against a wall and see anyone who entered.

Curious looks were aimed Kira's way, but none of the others recognized her or Finn with their hoods concealing their faces.

A relief really.

"What do you think they're doing here?" Jin asked.

Kira's head shake was slight.

That was a good question.

She also wanted to know how Ziva came to be here. Liara and House Luatha were supposed to be taking care of the girl.

Kira would be curious to know how Luatha finagled this—especially in light of the visitor restrictions.

"I'm going to see if I can get closer and hear what they're saying," Jin said.

"Don't you dare."

"But—"

"No buts. Sit still and don't draw attention," she ordered.

"Boring," Jin pouted.

And Kira wondered where Elena got her sass from.

Seconds later, Jin nudged forward inside the hood.

Kira slapped a hand over him. "What are you doing?"

"Looking for the seatbelt. I don't see it."

"Don't even start with that again," Kira said through gritted teeth. "The objective is to appear normal. Not like we have a few screws loose."

Even if their screws had long since come undone and been lost to the void.

Before Jin could respond, a figure wearing dark clothes and a hat pulled low over his face dropped into the seat across from her. "Fancy meeting you here."

"Jace." Kira blinked dumbly at him, caught off-balance.

She glanced around.

"I'm alone," he assured her.

"How did you find me?" Kira asked, thankful Joule and the rest had chosen seats out of hearing range

Jace made himself comfortable in his chair, stretching out his legs until his feet edged close to the aisle. "I'd like to say this is on purpose, but it's quite by chance."

Kira didn't believe that.

One coincidence maybe. Two? Unlikely.

She could have overlooked Joule and the presence of the others. For Jace to pop up as well, that strained the threads of credibility.

Jace's lips quirked as he sensed her doubt. "You're starting to rub off on us. I simply needed to ask myself what ship Kira would take and then wait. The hoods are a nice touch and the big guy threw me off for a moment."

Finn shifted at the comment, his expression not entirely friendly.

"Don't worry, I doubt anyone besides those who've had close contact with you would think this way," Jace assured her.

Finn grunted. Whether in amusement or grumpiness, Kira couldn't say.

"Also, Himoto stationed a few of his most trusted around the dock with orders to report any unusual behavior." Jace grinned. "Speaking Haldeel—that's a bit attention-grabbing."

There it was. The truth.

In her defense, she hadn't expected the ability to be considered unusual.

To her, it was a no brainer to have at least a basic understanding of your host's language, even if the extent of that knowledge was only a common greeting.

Kira let herself relax a tiny bit, satisfied the risk was still at acceptable levels.

"How was your trip?" Kira prodded.

Jace couldn't hide his scowl.

Kira snickered. "That bad, huh?"

Not surprising, really.

The Tuann were like a group of bristly porcupines, intent on not letting outsiders get too close. Traveling on a ship filled with them would have been hell—especially when most didn't have a favorable view of humans.

Jace and the Curs had won some goodwill with their actions on Luatha, but still, Kira didn't imagine it was an easy voyage.

What she wouldn't have given to be a fly on the wall.

"Thanks for that," Jace said, sounding anything but thankful.

"Himoto asked, and I delivered. Not my fault you're his lapdog."

"Still angry at him, I see," Jace observed.

Kira lifted a careless shoulder. "Not really."

"Liar."

He was right, but Kira had no intention of letting him know that.

She preferred to strike from the shadows when a person's guard was lowered. Made everything so much easier.

"Think those ships will make a difference?" Kira asked.

"Only time will tell," Jace said. "The scientists have already started digging into the technology. I don't think I've ever seen grown men and women so giddy."

Best case scenario was the scientists cracked the Tuann technology and replicated it throughout the fleet.

The problem was that would take time. Even if they could figure out a substitute energy for *ki,* they'd have to build new ships using that technology. Something like that didn't happen fast. It'd likely take a decade or more to disseminate on a large enough level to make a difference.

With the Tsavitee on the move again, the changes wouldn't come soon enough.

"I've been looking into that matter you told me about before," Jace said with a meaningful expression on his face.

Kira's gaze cooled, highly conscious of Finn's presence next to her as he listened to every word they said.

"I didn't tell you about that for you to go digging where you don't belong," she said through stiff lips.

His gaze was chiding. "What did you say before? We all face death every time we put on that suit?"

Kira flinched at having her own words thrown back at her.

"This is me facing death in place of you," he said with a resoluteness that caused Kira's eyes to drop to her lap.

Jace reached out, tapping her on the side of the knee. "You've carried this burden for so long. Let me help. It's what a battle buddy is there for."

"What matter?" Finn asked, his drawn hood moving as he glanced between them.

A question flickered across Jace's face.

Kira kept her expression blank, leaving it up to him to decide to tell or not.

"A traitor within our military is responsible for the losses at Rothchild and in several other battles," Jace said.

A somber quiet filled the air.

"This is why you find it so hard to trust Roake even though I know you want to," Finn said, his voice soft with discovery.

It took willpower to duck her chin in the smallest of nods.

Finn didn't say anything more, lapsing into silence.

Kira's hands clenched.

Much as she wanted to reject Jace putting himself in danger, she couldn't. She'd be a hypocrite if she did.

She'd hit a wall in her own investigation. Being as high up in the ranks as he was, Jace was in a better position to learn more.

The Haldeel bustled around the cabin, closing the hatch doors as they prepared to launch.

There was none of the insistence on seat belts or safety harnesses that you'd encounter on a human vessel.

Unless there was an issue during re-entry, such things would be unnecessary. At that point, it likely wouldn't matter what kind of restraints they wore.

The ship lifted off the platform with the faintest of jolts. There was a sense of movement as they slipped out the membrane separating the dock from the void of space.

The gravity switched seamlessly from the station's to the ship's, the faint sensation of weightlessness there and gone in an instant.

"What did you find?" Kira asked as they started their descent.

"You were right about a mole. They're good too."

They'd have to be to go this long without discovery.

"If I hadn't known they existed, I don't think I'd have caught their trail so easily," Jace admitted.

Outside the viewing window, the small orb that was the planet grew until it filled the screen.

"They're pretty high up in the ranks," Jace said. "I'd say an admiral or rear admiral. It could also be someone who had regular contact with the Curs."

Kira shook her head. "I thought of that. Most of them are dead."

"It could be a survivor from one of the ships present at Rothchild," Jace pointed out.

"If that was the case, they would have been on the CSS *Vega*. They couldn't have guaranteed their survival."

The handful out of thousands who'd survived had done so by chance. Kira didn't see a Tsavitee double agent taking that sort of risk.

"That leaves someone who had knowledge of troop movements and highly classified information," Jace said.

Of which there was only a small number.

"Tell me one thing," Kira said. "Do you suspect Himoto?"

The muscles in Jace's face jumped as he quelled his instinctive denial.

Kira's stomach twisted as she waited for his answer. It wasn't easy contemplating whether Himoto was a traitor. He'd raised her after the camps.

At one time, he'd been her hero.

"At first glance, he would seem to be a prime candidate," Jace allowed before shaking his head. "I simply don't see it. Himoto would do many things to safeguard the Consortium, but I can't see him being capable of that. He'd have to be a much better actor to pull something like this off."

That fit with her assessment as well, but she'd also known she was too close to the matter to be objective.

"There are multiple people who were at Rothchild and at other battles now in positions of high authority," Jace said, sliding a microscopic data unit her way. "I've included dossiers on all of them. I think you'll find one of particular interest."

Kira took the device and held it up to Jin. He scanned, pulling the data off it, and frying its circuits when he was done.

"Kent," Jin said.

Jace inclined his chin. "The thing I find most interesting about him are his ties to a certain faction that has its roots in Zepher."

Kira's lips curled. "Why doesn't that surprise me?"

"That brings me the second piece of information I have for you—one Himoto wanted you to have. Factions are forming in the Consortium."

Kira sent him a quizzical look. That was nothing new. There had always been factions in the Consortium.

"They're the kind that could tear it apart and jeopardize our alliances." Jace's face was grim. "Himoto and I have come across some disturbing communications. Nothing concrete enough to allow us to act."

Everything in Kira stilled. "What does that mean?"

Jace didn't look away from her as he confessed, "Someone wants to restart the project."

Emotions fractured the bond between Kira and Jin. Anger and frustration assaulting her senses as a gnawing feeling of helplessness grew.

Kira took a breath, steadying herself as she reached for composure. She was Kira Forrest. The Phoenix. Scourge of the Tsavitee. War hero and villain at the same time.

Neither she nor Jin were helpless anymore; they hadn't been for a long time.

If the project was being relaunched, she'd deal with it as she had whenever people thought they could trespass into realms they had no business visiting—by destroying anyone and anything that had a hand in it.

"Himoto gave me a message for you," Jace said carefully. "We'll handle this. There's no need for Kira-chan to get involved at this stage."

For Jace to repeat the message verbatim said how aware Himoto was of her activities both before and after the war.

This wasn't the first time someone had gotten the idea to revisit the objective of the camps. Jin and Odin had protocols in place designed to find and root out those interested in using bioengineering with the goal of creating the perfect soldier.

What happened to her and the rest would not happen again.

"Himoto has gotten bold in his old age." Kira's expression wasn't exactly friendly as she said that.

"Perhaps that's why he's chosen to train me as his successor."

Kira frowned. There were dozens of talented officers in the Consortium. Why pick Jace?

Her hands clenched. "If that's what you want."

"It's what's needed."

She made a scoffing sound. "Now you sound like him."

Jace's expression lightened as he teased, "Such compliments will make me blush."

Kira rolled her eyes. Her expression sobered as she considered all that he'd revealed.

"Do we know if this faction has any ties to Zepher?" Kira asked.

A glint entered Jace's eyes and he pointed at her as if to say bingo.

If they had a hand in the most recent incarnation of the project raising its nasty little head, they were likely looking for new genetic material.

It explained why Tsavitee agents had tried to abduct Devon.

Kira didn't fool herself into thinking the Tsavitee and their masters ever had only one agenda, but she didn't think it was a coincidence that they went after Devon.

He had links to the emperor, ostensibly the most powerful Tuann alive. Genetically, he was a prime specimen that could advance their research by decades.

Most importantly, he was related to Jin. Brothers, if Kira's suspicions were right.

It was no wonder they'd made such a bold move.

The question became did they target Jin's line because of his former status as one of their toys or were they beginning to suspect the truth behind Jin's current existence?

Only two people knew the truth of that night—Kira and Jin.

It wasn't outside the realm of possibility that the Tsavitee were trying to replicate what they did.

"And I thought my mission was already hard enough," Kira grumbled.

Now in addition to tracking down and saving Elise, she had to be on the lookout for that project resurrecting itself from the ashes. Oh, and she had to make sure the Tsavitee didn't get their hands on any more Tuann children.

An already impossible task just had a whole bunch of awful dumped on top of it.

This was why Jin was always telling her she could never do things the easy way.

Sympathy settled on Jace's face. "I'll keep digging and inform you of what I find."

"Very well. Do what you want, but make sure you're not caught," Kira said, relenting. "I have no intention of attending your funeral."

Before he could respond, a strange sound issued from within Kira's hood, nearly blowing out her eardrum. A combination of a shriek and a roar, it caused those in the cabin to come to their feet.

Kira's heart dropped as a force yanked her sideways out of her seat, nearly sending her ass first to the ground.

She recovered in time, lurching forward, and grabbing Finn's arm as he reached for his synth blade.

If he drew his weapon, they'd be exposed. Devon and the rest would know they were Tuann and become suspicious.

"Spider, spider, spider." Jin whimpered right next to Kira's ear.

Finn's arm remained tense under Kira's hand. Only when she was sure he wouldn't do anything did she remove her hand.

Jace stared at her like he thought she had lost her mind, one hand hovering over the place where she knew he liked to keep a hidden blade.

He wasn't the only one.

The smell of burned ozone permeated the air. Someone had used *ki.*

It wasn't hard to see who.

In the aisle across from theirs, Joule had his hands up in a gesture she recognized, a nearly transparent shield extending inches from the tips of his fingers. It covered the small section of the ship where he and his companions had set up shop.

Behind the shield, Devon and Rheya had adopted a defensive posture, their blades drawn.

A flicker of fire shimmered on the surface of Devon's blade, whereas black lines slowly snaked across Rheya's face, a result of her drawing heavily on her *ki.*

The oshota guarding them stared suspiciously at Kira and Finn.

The Haldeel from before regarded Kira and Finn carefully. Any goodwill she'd earned was likely gone.

Seeing the situation, Jace laughed, moving his hand away from his hidden blade. He stepped forward, one hand dropping onto Kira's shoulder.

"I apologize everyone. My friend had a fright." Jace's smile was meant to be reassuring and conciliatory.

He bent to say into her ear. "What the hell was that?"

"Spider." Kira pointed at the cause of this whole mess.

A creature roughly the size of a cat uncurled, scuttling down the wall and onto Kira's former seat.

A gibbering came from Jin, and he slid further into her hood.

Jace fought laughter as he heard the word, finally realizing what had happened—and who was responsible for the fuss.

The creature that had so terrified Jin lifted its body, its head canting curiously.

Kira hadn't ever thought she'd meet an *ilsa* in person. Although it resembled an arachnid with its eight legs and many eyes, that was where the similarity ended.

Covered in a light creamy colored fuzz, the *ilsa* had pink rosettes on its torso and legs. It also had a snout no spider would ever have. Wearing a tiny top hat and jeweled collar, it looked rather adorable.

"Kill it. Kill it now," Jin whined.

"I'm not going to kill it," Kira argued in an undertone.

"It's a spider. Destroy it in a way where even its ancestors will feel it's pain."

"It's not a spider. It's an *ilsa*. Totally different."

"It has eight legs and eight eyes. Close enough."

"Excuse me," a soft voice said as a slight figure moved forward.

She was Haldeel and had dark purple markings edged with black. She looked young, not much older than Elena and Devon.

"I apologize if Jaks scared you."

Jaks scuttled down the chair, hopping onto the floor, and then scurrying over to his owner. She bent and picked him up, cradling him in her arms as she faced Kira and Jace.

"The apologies are ours," Jace said in a polite tone. "My friend is a little irrational at times."

"Heh." Jin snickered.

"He means you, dumbass," Kira said out the side of her mouth.

Jin made an insulted sound and would likely have done more if Kira hadn't slapped one hand over his body under the hood.

Jin grumbled to himself but didn't fight her further.

To the teen in front of her, Kira made a slight bow, but didn't speak.

Devon and the rest were on their guard now, paying attention where they hadn't been earlier. If she said anything now, they'd likely recognize her voice.

"Are you heading to the planet for the quorum?" Jace asked, picking up on Kira's predicament.

The girl inclined her head.

"What event will you be joining?" Jace asked.

"The waveboard races."

That was an interesting answer.

While the races were popular among humans, the same couldn't be said for the Tuann and Haldeel. They were only now beginning to find traction among the other species.

For this girl to choose it as her event was unexpected. Kira had assumed it would take much longer before the Haldeel embraced it.

Then again, there were those among the Tuann who shared the same obsession with the races, Kira thought just as Ziva bounced forward.

"He is too." Ziva gestured at Devon.

"It seems this ship has several contenders for that race." Jace patted Kira on the shoulder. "This one is also competing."

Kira stiffened under his hand. "What do you think you're doing?"

Jace leaned closer to her. "Remember on Duo when you and Raider antagonized that gang and then left me to deal with the consequences? Consider this my long-overdue revenge."

Kira choked down her response. "You've gotten a lot braver over the years."

Jace patted her on the shoulder again. "I learned from the best." To the rest, he said, "I hope you can show my friend some interesting things."

Devon regarded Kira with suspicion. "You're a racer?"

Kira shrugged.

Devon looked about to say something when the Haldeel steward approached. "We'll be landing soon. Please take your seats."

The Haldeel girl sketched a small bow before making her way to her seat.

Devon and the others followed suit, leaving Kira and Jace alone.

"That's one thing I've never envied about you—having to deal with Jin," Jace mused.

Finn's shoulders jerked next to her.

"Rude, meat sack," Jin grumbled from Kira's shoulder.

From his own position, Devon eyed their trio with a contemplative look. "Both of you be quiet. We've already drawn enough attention."

Jace glanced in the direction of the Haldeel teen. "I do find it interesting that an *ilsa* appeared here and now."

Kira didn't have to ask what he meant.

The *ilsa* was a rare breed that not many had the opportunity to befriend. Although it looked like an adorable pet it was much more. Some knew the *ilsa* by its less common name—the *alja*. Or spy.

Jin's actions on the surface may have seemed like that of an idiot, but there had been purpose behind them.

If he hadn't acted in such a way, there was no telling how long the *ilsa* would have sat there and listened.

Kira could only hope Jin had noticed him before they revealed too much.

* * *

Graydon contemplated the Tuann in front of him, trying to decide if he cared about the repercussions that would come if he ripped the man's limbs from his torso.

He could already envision how that conversation with the emperor would play out.

"And why did you feel it necessary to maim one of my most loyal subjects?"

The emperor wasn't likely to be satisfied with the excuse "Because his face offended me".

Pity. Such an action was sure to satisfy and work out some of this tension.

It had been weeks, and there was still no word on Kira.

His resulting bad mood had ensured those with an ounce of self-preservation steered clear of him.

A quality that didn't seem to extend to the Chancellor of House Kashori. The man was dogged in his determination to win concessions for his

House.

"There are hundreds of Tuann who plan to go down to the planet. It is unreasonable to expect all of our people to use the Haldeel dropships to come and go," Torin said.

Graydon bared his teeth at the man, his expression not particularly nice. "These are the terms of the quorum, as set by the Haldeel."

Did House Kashori think they were special in some way?

"They've never had those requirements before," Torin argued, unwilling to let the matter drop.

True enough. The restrictions on who could visit and how they would get there were new but well within the rights of the host to set.

"They don't need to explain themselves to us," Graydon ground out. "Just as we have no need to explain ourselves to them. These are the conditions for us to attend. They will be followed to the letter."

Even if Graydon had to break a few bones to ensure the cooperation of the various Houses.

Part of the reasoning behind the Haldeel's request was easy to see—at least on first glance. They likely hoped to foster an air of cooperation and camaraderie among the Tuann and the humans whose relationship could be classified as uneasy at best.

Only a very select few attributed the truth of the new requirements to the Tsavitee.

A short distance away, two Tuann of different Houses bumped into each other. Instead of apologizing and moving on, they bristled, violence and antagonism threatening to spill into bloodshed.

Graydon strangled his urge to flatten the idiots. He signaled for one of his oshota to take care of it.

Diplomacy required a delicate touch, and Graydon simply didn't have the control for it today.

He was too volatile, impatience lurking under his skin like a constant itch.

Noor bowed before heading toward where the two idiots were now shoving each other. The smaller one stumbled, bumping into Noor's chest.

He whirled; an arm already cocked.

Catching sight of the matte black of Noor's synth armor, the Tuann's eyes widened in horror.

Noor simply looked at him.

The man who'd shoved the Tuann finally displayed a hint of common sense. He spun on his heel, striding away at a pace that wasn't quite a run.

The man who had collided with Noor dropped his fist. He muttered an apology before disappearing into the crowd in the same direction as the first.

Noor caught Graydon's eye, a small quirk to his lips.

Solal moved up to his side. "I've received a message from Baran."

Graydon didn't react outwardly. To Torin, he said, "You're dismissed. House Kashori will abide by the Haldeel's rules, along with everyone else."

Graydon didn't have to include a threat in that statement. Noor's actions were a perfect example of what would happen if Graydon wasn't obeyed.

Graydon strode away, leaving Torin gaping at him like an out of water fish.

"Where is he?" Graydon asked Solal.

"Waiting in your quarters."

Graydon picked up his pace, feeling a sense of rising anticipation that burned away the frustration and boredom of the past couple of weeks.

Just wait, Kira. This was only the start.

* * *

Baran wasn't the only one Graydon found waiting for him when he reached his quarters. His oshota stood at attention on one side of the room, watching Graydon's other guests.

A man stood guard over a seated woman as she sipped from one of his teacups.

She didn't look up as he entered, seemingly engrossed in the contents of her cup.

Despite the long flowing robes she wore, the woman was Tuann. Her face had a kind of perfection that was rare. A cold beauty a man could get lost in. She looked like a goddess descended onto the mortal realm.

Black hair fell in a thick sheet down her back, her eyes large and her lips painted red as they curved into a chilly smile.

"Little storm, you've finally seen fit to join us."

Graydon raised one eyebrow. "I wasn't aware I was expected, Yukina."

Graydon gave a nod of respect to the imposing man at Yukina's side. Tall, with a build similar to Graydon's, he had brown skin and gold eyes that seemed to see everything.

He'd positioned himself in the role of an observer.

"What are you doing in my quarters?" Graydon asked.

Yukina took another sip. "You seemed so interested, how could I not be curious?"

Graydon didn't ask how she'd found out about Baran's presence or why she felt the need to pry.

As an Emperor's Face herself, Yukina had her own way of doing things.

He should have known the woman would find her way into this matter.

Graydon prowled into the room, taking a seat opposite the woman and her oshota.

He triggered the room's privacy mode, a bubble of electricity and *ki* forming around the occupants. The field acted as an additional safeguard to guarantee the content of this conversation wouldn't be heard.

No sound could enter the bubble, but more important, no sound could leave. Any bugs would be rendered obsolete.

As soon as it went live, Yukina set her cup down with a clink, the lazy grace she'd had earlier disappearing to be replaced by a penetrating intellect.

"I assume this is the oshota you sent to investigate the little heir's background."

Graydon inclined his head.

"What did you learn?" Yukina asked Baran.

Graydon's oshota sent a questioning direction in Graydon's direction. Graydon waved a lazy hand in answer.

Anything Baran shared was bound to reach Yukina and the emperor's ears anyway. They had their own methods of investigating if they so wished. Might as well expedite the process.

"Something that I still can't quite believe," Baran said.

With an excitement rare in Baran, he pressed three buttons on the inside forearm of his synth armor. A small sheet of metal popped out. Baran set it on the ground in front of them.

An image appeared.

Graydon leaned forward with interest as a planet's sky took shape, one under attack.

The camera was pointed up, catching a worm's eye view of the aerial battle. Screams sounded in the distance as a Tsavitee raptor hit a tall, spiral shaped building.

"This is what you wanted to show us?" Yukina asked.

"Keep watching."

The view jostled and moved, difficult to follow as the person filming ran for their life.

Graydon sat forward as he caught a glimpse of a solo waverunner.

"What's this?" he murmured.

An arc of purple light trailed behind the person, glowing brighter and brighter until it swallowed the person inside.

"The reason I'm so late in returning," Baran answered.

The light condensed into a single point, the world turning dark and gray as if it had sucked in all the color.

The purple light exploded, spreading out from the rider in an ever-widening sheet until it encompassed the entirety of the sky.

Anything it touched disappeared.

"The Heaven's Wrath," Yukina whispered.

People out of sight prayed to gods Graydon had never heard of as their savior dropped from the sky as the purple light reached the hull of the ship currently bombarding the planet.

The vessel was destroyed in seconds.

The images disappeared, leaving silence.

"I guess we know now how the humans managed to win their war," Solal said in a soft voice.

And how Kira came to have *ki* poisoning.

"It's a rudimentary form, but it's definitely the Wrath," the man behind Yukina said. "I'm interested to know how she stumbled onto that ability."

In all of the Tuann's history, only four had been capable of that technique. It was considered one of the most valuable defenses to the Tuann and had been a deterrent against their old enemy since the Tuann's break from them millennia ago.

"This isn't the only instance I've found of its use." Baran waved his hand, and the view changed.

They watched in silence as a similar situation played out. First on a planet, then in space, then another planet. The only thing all of the videos had in common was the waverunner, sometimes alone, more often accompanied by a small contingent.

The waverunner's armor was entirely black except for the bird born of fire emblazoned on her back. The board she rode was a flaming red—almost as if her intention were to draw the enemy's focus and keep it entirely on herself.

"Repeated use on a scale such as this would cause massive damage to the wielder if they did not replenish their *ki* by interacting with the Mea'Ave," the man said in an emotionless voice. "She would have been in near-constant pain as a result."

It would take a considerable strength of will and determination to accomplish.

Such a person would be a credit to their House and the Tuann as a whole.

"Her line has not demonstrated this ability," the man added.

"The Mea'Ave has been known to bestow gifts on a line when it deems it appropriate," Yukina said.

What she left out was how rare such an occasion was. They only had record of it happening twice. Both times when they'd faced annihilation.

"Perhaps," the man conceded.

"I'm surprised you found this," Yukina said to Baran. "The humans don't strike me as being so careless."

Baran shook his head. "They aren't. The military and Consortium weren't obvious with their efforts, but they did their best to steer me away from any information dealing with Kira and her former team."

Yukina raised an eyebrow. "And yet somehow you managed."

Baran sketched a mocking bow. "I have never been one to consider myself ordinary. The task took some doing, but the results speak for themselves."

Yukina suppressed her smile, unwilling to stroke the man's ego any further.

"You've found quite the monster, little storm." Yukina rose from her chair. "I hope she doesn't swallow you whole."

With those words as a farewell, Yukina strode through the field, the door opening without a touch from her.

The man beside her nodded farewell to Graydon. A hood rose from his synth armor, a small disturbance field shielding his features as he followed the Emperor's Face.

"What now?" Solal asked.

"We find Kira," Graydon said.

"That's not going to be easy. She could be anywhere in the universe."

Graydon's lips spread in a wicked smile. "Nothing fun ever is."

SIX

LANDING ON THE planet went smoothly.

It didn't take long for the passengers to disembark, Kira and Finn purposely lagging behind.

Jace paused to touch his fingers to the brim of his hat in a brief salute. He stuffed his hands in his pockets and rounded his shoulders, his stride quick as the crowd swallowed him in seconds.

"Status update," Kira said, joining the slow-moving pedestrians as they made their way off the landing pad and into the city proper.

This wasn't Kira and Jin's first visit to Zara, the capital city of Jettie. They were prepared as they stepped out of the space port, diverting around the clumps of first-timers overcome by the view.

"Elena and Odin have left the *Wanderer*. If they kept to the timeline, they'll just be reaching the dropship," Jin whispered.

"Any problems?"

"Not yet."

One could only hope it stayed that way.

Kira took in the roofless colonnade, its columns supporting arches every third opening. Beyond those arches, visitors could glimpse the more modern architecture of the city proper.

That was breathtaking enough, but it wasn't what caused visitors to stop and stare. That was the avenue the colonnade framed.

A flat road of water stretched into the distance, its color changing depending on the season and weather.

Today, the sky was bright and clear, small fluffy white clouds high in the atmosphere.

The water acted as a mirror, creating the illusion of a never-ending sky, the columns appearing to float upon clouds.

"Looks like the Haldeel spared no effort in welcoming their guests," Jin observed as Kira stepped onto the avenue.

Instead of her foot sinking into the deep water beneath her, she walked across it as if it were solid land.

Beneath her, countless flowers in every shade of red and pink floated in the still water. Brightly colored fish darted among the flowers.

The columns of the colonnade were also decorated in the same shades, ribbons and banners wound around them, threaded through with more flowers.

Water was a sacred concept to the Haldeel, whose home planet primarily consisted of oceans. They'd evolved in its depths, and they held that memory close even as they journeyed into the stars.

Zara's avenue wasn't unique. Nearly all planets in the Haldeel empire had something similar.

That didn't make it any less impressive.

Kira's pace didn't pause as she bypassed those who'd stopped to take in the beauty of their surroundings, Finn a silent shadow behind her.

She tailed Devon and the rest as they continued along the avenue, traveling deeper into the city. When they turned off the avenue, stepping through one of the arches and into the city, Kira did too.

Growing more modern the further they traveled from the avenue, the city sprawled around them. Water gardens and parks were abundant, smaller shops and homes crouching in their shadow.

The juxtaposition of nature versus man-made, new versus old, was an interesting one. Kira could have spent hours wandering the streets and not getting her fill of the unique surroundings.

Sadly for her, she was on a deadline.

She turned her feet toward the registration building, leaving the more interesting residential districts behind.

The gardens and water ponds became scarcer as the crowd thickened around her.

"So many people," Jin complained.

"The quorum is quite popular. Every major power attends, to say nothing of the smaller powers hoping for their piece of the action." Finn was never still, continuously studying their surroundings as if anticipating the possibility of an attack.

A tall, expansive building loomed in front of them, its grounds inundated with a crowd.

Kira hesitated on its edge, allowing Devon and the rest to disappear into its depths.

Finn shot her a sharp glance. "You're not going to follow them?"

Kira shook her head. "It's best if we don't meet for now."

If the quals were arranged anything like they had been in previous races, those who registered around the same time would be dumped into a group.

"Aw, aren't you the sweetest, not wanting to knock him out of the competition on his first race," Jin crooned.

Kira ignored his teasing in favor of studying the crowd. Humans made up the majority of those signing up. Most of those present were newcomers to the races, not having earned a reputation or ranking yet.

Racers who'd won on the circuit and made a name for themselves could skip this part of the process and simply submit their name to qualify.

Kira could have done that as well, but this way seemed more inconspicuous.

"I took a look at the brackets. Devon's has already been filled. You should be okay to sign up now," Jin said.

Kira started forward, threading her way through the clumps of people before joining the queue for sign up.

Dozens of kiosks with Haldeel attendants positioned next to them guaranteed the process went smoothly.

Finally, Kira stepped into the space where the sign up was taking place. She picked the kiosk with the least number of people in front of it.

She'd have chosen differently if she'd known what awaited her there.

A group of humans clumped around the much smaller form of a

Haldeel—one familiar to Kira.

It was the teen from the dropship. Her face remained expressionless as she inputted her information in the kiosk, handing her identification and pilot's license to the Haldeel attendant.

"A squid using a waveboard—that's something you don't see every day," a young man jeered.

"How would a squid even ride it?" the woman next to him asked.

"Maybe by wrapping its tentacles around it?" another person answered.

The Haldeel race representative frowned, asking if the teen needed assistance with one subtle hand gesture.

The teen responded with a negative. The entire silent conversation went unnoticed by the group.

"Zepher again," Jin muttered. "Could they please refrain from perpetrating certain human stereotypes."

Kira stepped forward amid the taunts. "I'd like to register now."

"We were next," the young man from Zepher argued.

Kira didn't face them. "Oh? I could have sworn you were too busy hearing yourselves talk to bother."

Heated glares burned into Kira's back as she approached the two Haldeel, one taller than the other.

The attendant didn't react to Kira's cutting the line, showing just how dissatisfied she was with the Zepher representatives behind her.

"Who the hell do you think you are?" someone demanded.

Kira didn't answer, handing her credentials to the Haldeel woman instead.

The teen's neutral expression shifted as the kiosk exposed Kira's details.

Call sign: Sparrow.

Status: Expert.

Titles: Champion of the Dragon Circuit, Champion of the Fanged Winds, Champion of the Broken Levels

There were other titles, but those were the ones that stood out.

Seeing the information, the attendant bowed. "This is a rare honor. You did not need to sign up in person."

Kira shrugged. "I had the time, and the view was well worth the trouble."

Hushed whispers came from those behind her.

Kira hid her smile. She thought that would be enough to shut them up.

It was one thing to tease a kid, another matter entirely when faced with someone who had already reached the pinnacle of the mountain you were trying to climb.

The Dragon Circuit alone enjoyed a bit of a reputation among racers. The race was considered highly dangerous with only exceptional pilots ever attempting it.

Winning the crown could launch you into fame and fortune. It was one of those rare titles that most could only dream of attaining.

Yet here Kira stood.

"I suggest you let your talents speak for yourself," Kira warned, not looking back. "Otherwise, you may find yourself eating those words."

Kira focused on the Haldeel teen. "I am looking forward to seeing you race."

A small glint shone in the teen's gaze.

"I'm Skye."

"I'll remember it," Kira said, smothering her smile at the girl's serious expression.

Still cradling Jaks, Skye glided away, disappearing through the doors as she headed for the race's preparation area.

Kira ignored the hushed whispers behind her as she completed her registration.

The attendant glanced at Finn. "Will this be the entirety of your team?"

"There is one other who should be joining us shortly. I've included his name and details in the data packet."

The Haldeel checked over the information, nodding her approval. "Do you have a compatible device for the race packet?"

Kira nodded, holding up the thin Scroll Odin had given her.

The Haldeel's movements were quick as she transmitted the information, keeping up a running commentary. "You've been placed in bracket two oh four. The first qual of that bracket is in an hour. Each bracket will allow those with the top three times to advance to the next bracket. I've assigned you bay two hundred. Your items should be there by the time you reach it."

Her spiel finished, the Haldeel smiled at Kira. "May the tides favor you."

Kira bowed. "And you as well."

Kira set out at a brisk pace, Finn trailing behind her, keeping one eye on the humans.

Kira wasn't as concerned. Zepher wasn't stupid nor were they particularly brave.

If they planned on getting back at Kira for the small slap in the face she'd given them, they'd do so when they thought they could get away with it. Until then, she was safe.

Stepping through the doors was like stepping into another world. Those on the other side bustled back and forth, the bays a frenetic swarm of energy as they raced to finish last-minute adjustments.

The smell of oil and sweat filled the space. It was as familiar as it was comforting.

"This brings back memories," she said softly, the high-pitched hum of tools mixing with the shouts of the individual bays' occupants.

"It was a lot smaller then," Jin agreed.

Kira's lips quirked as she set off to search for their bay.

"Who would have ever thought our little hobby would grow to be such an event?"

Not Kira. That was for sure.

"You've competed before?" Finn asked.

Kira hummed in ascent. "You could say that."

"The Curs started the races," Jin volunteered.

It all started with a bet to see who was the best. From there, it had grown. Of course, by then, most of the original founders were already dead.

Kira competed every once in a while to keep her skills fresh, but it had been a few years since then. She doubted anyone would remember her. It was why she had taken a chance and used her alias from during the war and after it.

Sadness pulled at her. There was more than one reason she stopped racing.

"You going to be all right?" Jin asked.

Kira walked with renewed purpose. "Why wouldn't I be?"

Jin made a sound that said he wasn't convinced, but he didn't pry.

"This is our bay," Jin said.

From the stands outside, they could hear the roar of the crowd over the rumble of the waveboards.

Their bay stood empty except for two pallets in the center of the room. Kira caught sight of basic mechanic tools and a workbench along the wall.

Most of the surrounding bays had their privacy screens up. The thin, electric field rendered anything on the other side invisible.

Jin barely waited for Kira and Finn to step inside before activating their own shield.

He zipped out from under her hood without waiting for permission.

"Someone's happy," Kira commented, watching him zoom around the room.

"Wouldn't you be if you were cooped up inside a tiny space for hours?" he asked.

Spotting the pallets, he zoomed toward them, hovering over the nearest one. "Let's see what goodies Odin got for us."

A small laser cut through the packaging, exposing the contents inside.

Jin made approving noises as he went through the items, lifting them out with his antigravs one by one.

"How are we looking?" Kira asked.

"Not bad. I don't see anything missing," Jin said.

Most of the items, including her board and the tools needed to maintain its functions, came from the *Wanderer*.

Odin had been responsible for ordering the odds and ends they needed while Kira and Jin were in transport.

A small mask flew through the air.

Kira caught it before it hit her face.

"What do you think?" Jin asked.

She held it up, examining it carefully. Its surface was white with two broken red lines carved vertically on the right third.

Kira held it up to her face, satisfied when it sealed to her skin. A holo screen appeared in front of her eyes.

[Connect]

Kira blinked once in *yes*. A bright pinpoint of light pierced her right eye as the lens there communicated with the system of the mask.

The transition was smooth.

Information such as temperature, air pressure, and humidity levels scrolled across the display.

Kira took a look around the room, getting used to the headset. Small screens with additional information popped up. Heat signatures flared and then waned as she dismissed the functions one by one.

She shook her head back and forth, up and down. The mask didn't budge.

Good. Exactly what she was hoping for.

She touched the sides, and the seal released, allowing her to pull it away from her face.

"Pretty nice," she said.

Jin snickered. "That's a best-in-class, ocular interface. We're talking a top-grade warning system, complete with some of the most advanced radar there is. Only the military or maybe assassins would have anything better. If someone farts a mile away, this thing will warn you."

Kira lowered the mask. "And to think, all I wanted was something to keep my identity a secret."

Jin snorted. "Why would we limit ourselves to obscurity when we could reach for greatness? I have to say, I'm a little impressed Odin could dig that up."

So was Kira. Items like this weren't exactly common.

It made Kira wonder where her hacker friend had found it.

Finished with the first pallet, Jin moved to the second. He sifted through the material exposing a board the color of onyx. It was an older model, one not often seen in races like this. A remnant of a past she rarely dwelt on.

Her preference would have been to leave the board gathering dust in the *Wanderer*, but time constraints had left it as their only option.

Jin lifted the board out of its packaging and gently set it on the workbench. "Hello, old friend."

Most novice racers wouldn't consider using a board as old as this. They preferred the newer, flashier models with the latest technology. Many of them would switch out their boards numerous times over the years.

That had always been a mistake, Kira felt.

The technology for waveboards didn't really change all that much from model to model. Sure, the bells and whistles would get fancier, but the core of the board remained the same.

Most inexperienced riders never realized it was the drive chain in the board that was the true decider.

A rider could spend years of trial and error adapting and developing a base model drive chain to optimize its strengths.

The more poetic racers likened the drive chain to the board's soul. Without it, the board was a hunk of metal with a few tricks up its sleeve.

Kira's had been with her for nearly two decades—almost since the moment she first stepped onto a board. She didn't have the patience or time to train and tinker with a new drive chain.

"We're going to have to make adjustments based on your new stats," Jin said, already lifting off the under panel to get at the board's innards. "Do you want to make the adjustments or shall I?"

Kira palmed the handheld that would allow her to access the heart of the drive chain. "I'll do it."

Jin made way for her, allowing Kira to take his place.

She removed the layers between her and the drive chain one by one, finally stopping when she reached the glowing ball of golden light. Inside danced countless strands that almost looked like the twisted double helix of DNA.

Kira hummed as she took a look, pressing on one strand before moving to the next.

The entire time Jin hovered over her shoulder. "You're doing it wrong."

"I'm not doing it wrong." Kira made another adjustment.

"I'm pretty sure you are."

Kira closed her eyes, counting to ten.

This was what she got for having a best friend who was also a drone. He was even more of a know-it-all than her.

"Would you like to do it?"

"I thought you'd never asked." Jin shoved his smaller body into the spot she'd been occupying, forcing her away.

The tools she held levitated out of her hand as Jin took over.

"Don't forget to account for the fluctuations in atmospheric pressure," she instructed.

"Yeah, yeah. I got it. Why don't you go review the stats of your opponents?" Jin grumbled.

Kira lingered long enough to thoroughly irritate Jin before making her way toward one of the tables.

Much as she hated to admit it, Jin was probably better at reconfiguring the drive chain.

"Nervous?" Finn asked as she hopped onto the table behind him.

Kira lay down, stretching out and closing her eyes. "Why would I be nervous?"

Finn didn't look up as he continued to check over his weapons. He was methodical, examining every inch of them before moving on to the next.

"The stakes are high and from the sound of things, it's been awhile since you've raced. Such things would be considered normal."

Kira let out a small scoff. "There's not a whole lot that is normal about me."

Finn hummed softly, finishing with the en-dagger he held, storing it in his synth armor, before picking up another.

"That Dragon Circuit—those humans and Haldeel seemed to find it impressive."

Kira gazed unseeing at the bare bones of the ceiling above her. The bays were temporary constructs for the quorum. There was little need for frills, and the architects had left the structure of the building exposed.

"That race is little more than suicide to those who decide to compete," she finally said after several moments.

Finn paused in his actions.

Kira waited, but no questions came.

Finn resumed polishing his dagger as if she hadn't said anything.

Her lips quirked. Smart. If he'd pressed, she'd likely have clammed up. Since he didn't, he left it up to her whether to continue or not.

Her first instinct was to suppress the memories, but something stopped her. Perhaps it was being here again in an unfamiliar place that still managed to feel familiar.

"The Curs were the first to pair waveboards and racing." Kira made herself more comfortable on the table. "That's not to say someone somewhere wouldn't have eventually come up with the idea."

It was a given that any new mode of transport would eventually give way to the act of then racing it. The mentality was as natural to humans as breathing.

The Curs couldn't help but pit themselves against each other to see who was the best.

"They always were competitive little shits," Kira murmured.

Eventually, the races became a morale booster for the rest of the military and the populations of the planets they raced on. It helped that it also provided a way to give the Curs a mental break from the rigors of war while also further sharpening their skills.

Quiet fell again as Kira closed her eyes.

"The Dragon Circuit isn't a race you undertake lightly. It has a mortality rate of sixty percent."

Some of that was the difficulty of the race itself. The rest was the competitive nature of the sport. It wasn't unheard of for teams to sabotage each other. Even during the race, it was considered acceptable to dethrone a rider—which was a fancy way of saying you knocked them off their board.

Only in that race the surroundings were highly dangerous, making it difficult for the safeties to react in time. Lose your board and chances were you wouldn't survive.

"I was a different person then." One who didn't care if she lived or died. "The me of today wouldn't be so reckless."

As promises went, it was weak.

Kira didn't like to think of those days. Revealing some of it to Finn was an apology of sorts for the current situation.

She knew he didn't exactly approve. Still, he didn't try to strongarm her or talk her out of her plan. It showed a flexibility she hadn't thought possible in the Tuann.

It was something to consider for the future.

* * *

"Let's go over the plan again." Jin floated in front of Kira as the three of them made their way to the race's starting point. There were a half-dozen other racers in the tunnel, but none were paying attention to her party. "What position are you going to come in?"

"Second or third," she answered, barely resisting the urge to roll her eyes.

Jin bobbed in a nod. "Very good. I want you to remember that. Second or third. Not fourth or fifth and definitely not first."

Kira listened to Jin's spiel with a bored expression. This wasn't the first time he'd said this, nor was it the second.

He was beginning to sound like a broken record.

"Now, what did I say?" he asked.

"Not any position but second or third," she repeated by rote.

"Good. You've got it. Don't even think about coming in first."

"Don't you think it could be fun," Kira said suddenly.

Jin choked. "No. No, I don't think it would be fun."

Kira looked in Finn's direction. "How about you?"

The upraised hood made him seem even more mysterious than normal, hiding his expression and making him impossible to read. "It would be an interesting sight to be sure."

"See, Jin. Finn doesn't mind first place."

"I don't care what he thinks or how bored you are. We have a plan; stick to it."

The "or else" went unsaid.

Kira eyed the drone. "Sometimes I really wonder how you see me."

Did he really expect she'd do anything to jeopardize the mission?

"Without tinted glasses of any sort," Jin retorted in a flat voice.

Kira snickered. She really couldn't argue with that.

"I'm warning you, Kira."

She flapped a hand at him. "Yes, yes, master. I hear and understand."

"Good," Jin grunted as they approached the end of the tunnel.

Kira grabbed Jin before he could exit.

"What are you doing?" he cried.

Kira didn't answer, instead facing Finn. He let her grab his shoulder to force him to bend. She reached up and stuffed Jin in his hood.

Finished, she patted Jin on his casing. "You have to stay hidden. Remember?"

Jin sputtered. "You can't—This is—Kira, I object to this treatment!"

Wails issued from the depths of Finn's hood as Kira continued walking, stepping out of the tunnel, and squinting at the bright light that greeted her.

A small expanse of dirt stretched in front of her, ending at the feet of the audience stands.

At one end was the starting line, racers congregating as they waited for the officials. Their postures were relaxed as they threw taunts back and forth.

That wasn't what caused Kira's abrupt halt. "Why are they here?"

A sea of synth armor took up the stands. Roake's midnight blue intermixed with Luatha's forest greens. Their colors dominated the stands.

Even more concerning was the small clump of people located in the front center wearing synth armor so deep a black it seemed to eat the light.

Worst of all was the man sitting in their midst, an arrogant expression on his face as he surveyed the proceedings.

Graydon.

And right beside him was Raider.

Shit. Shit. Shit.

They weren't supposed to be here. She'd thought if anything they'd attend one of the more popular events. The ones that involved swords or fighting.

They couldn't know about her, right? She'd been so careful.

Then again, Jace had found her. Who was to say Graydon hadn't also?

Coincidences made her itchy inside. None more so than when a certain Emperor's Face turned up somewhere he wasn't supposed to be.

Thank every god that ever existed she'd had the foresight to procure a mask. If he didn't already know she was here, then the mask might allow her to slip away unnoticed.

Jin cackled, the sound strange as it issued from the depths of Finn's hood, not fitting his mysterious aura at all.

"It's like fate is drawing you two together," Jin teased.

Kira's fingers tingled with the urge to take a swipe at him. If not for their audience, she would have done exactly that.

"They can't know about us yet, right?" she asked Finn.

Finn's head lifted as he considered those in the stands. "It's hard to say what the Emperor's Face is capable of."

Kira debated the likelihood that Graydon had tailed her from the station. Jace had managed to find her. It wasn't outside the realm of possibility that Graydon had done the same.

Granted, Jace and Himoto had years of familiarity with Kira's habits, but she wasn't about to put anything past Graydon. The man had managed to surprise her in the past.

Even if Graydon hadn't known where to look for her, Raider would, and he was likely angry enough at Kira to help the Tuann beside him.

"It's possible he's here for Devon," Finn said after some thought.

"And Luatha?"

Finn shook his head. "Your guess is as good as mine."

The temptation to withdraw from the competition was strong. Too bad doing so would ruin her plans.

Kira frowned as she caught sight of Joule, Ziva, and Rheya seated beside Raider as they watched the race preparations with interested faces. They looked up as Devon joined them seconds later.

"Raider is competing," Jin said abruptly. "His status as a Cur and previous wins allow him to skip the quals and appear in the final races."

That explained his presence at least. Raider was the careful sort. She could see him gathering information on his potential opponents before the main event.

It wasn't outside the realm of possibility that Roake and Graydon's oshota had attended to see Raider and Devon race.

If that was the case, they weren't here because they knew of her presence.

It was all a massive coincidence—or so she tried to tell herself.

"Stick to the plan, and we should be fine—probably."

It was that probably that gave Kira concern.

A hand waving from the pit drew their attention. Odin aimed a roguish smile at them. "There are things to do and races to win. This is no time to stand around with your mouths hanging open."

The side of Finn's hood bulged in a suspicious manner.

Kira slapped at the bump. "Now, now, let's not go being stupid."

If Jin jeopardized their cover because of his problem with Odin, she would eviscerate him. She'd like to see how he managed if she disabled his optics and antigravs.

Jin grumbled but didn't do anything further as she led Finn over to Odin.

"I don't think this is where you're supposed to be," Kira said.

"There was an issue making contact," Odin explained, untroubled by the threat underlying Kira's words.

"What kind of issue?"

"The kind that will need your involvement to settle. In the meantime, I took the liberty of setting up our station." Odin gestured to the array of equipment in front of her. She pulled out a comm set complete with mic and handed it to Finn. "You're going to need this if you want to keep up appearances."

His distaste was obvious as he took it.

Kira couldn't blame him for his reluctance. As a Tuann, he was used to much more advanced technology. For him, the headset would be akin to a human using a tool from the stone age.

"Where's the package?" Kira asked.

Odin jerked his chin at the stands. "It's close by."

Kira glanced up at the stands, her interface already scanning for her niece's familiar face. Her shoulders relaxed as several seconds passed where she couldn't find a single sign of Elena.

Good. It looked like her niece was taking this seriously.

If even Kira, someone very familiar with her, couldn't find her, others wouldn't either.

Coupled with Graydon's and Roake's presence in the stands, Elena couldn't be much safer. If anything happened, she could approach either group and receive protection.

From the starting line, a sharp buzz announced the next group.

From the pits around her, those racers who weren't already at the starting line headed toward the rest.

"You're up," Odin said. "Go be reckless."

"That's exactly the thing we don't want her to be," Jin yelled from the depths of Finn's hood.

Kira ignored the two, stepping onto the waveboard that was already waiting for her, having been cleared by the team officials.

Its engines softly hummed as its weight left the ground. Kira pointed its nose toward the starting line.

Kira was the last to arrive. Those already assembled ignored her after taking one look at her older model board and the modest hoodie she still wore. It was clear they classified her as a non-threat.

Kira was okay with that. She'd rather be overlooked and underestimated than be guarded against.

Waverunners had a habit of going after those they saw as a threat. She'd prefer to avoid any attempts at dethroning her on the starting line.

While they were occupied with each other, she also took note of them.

The Haldeel teen from before was there, her hoverboard a little different than her competitors.

There was evidence it had been modified for her species, eight protrusions where her prehensile appendages could wrap around to hold her.

It was a pretty smart design, allowing the Haldeel to lower her center of gravity and reduce the wind resistance.

Besides the Haldeel, there was only one other non-human competing in this bracket. A Tuann wearing an unfamiliar style of armor.

The man glanced at her before dismissing her in the next moment in favor of keeping an eye on the rest of the competitors.

All of whom were human and sporting various types of exoskeletal armor.

Jin whistled in her ear. "Aren't they spiffy? Look how their armor shines."

Kira snorted to herself. That armor might look pretty, but it would be dead weight when they got started.

"I wonder if they know that grade armor is useless in this environment," Kira said.

"Doubt it," Jin responded. "No one in this group is experienced."

If they were, they'd know you needed a much higher-class armor to survive a crash.

"Seems the quality of competitors has fallen," she said softly.

A pity.

Waverunner races weren't a place to venture recklessly. If you didn't have the talent, you could very well end up a bloody smear on the pavement.

"You concentrate on doing what's needed. Leave any would be idiots to their own devices," Odin instructed.

"Enough chatting. The race is starting," Jin said.

"Roger that."

In front of Kira, a human strode onto the course, a flare gun held at his side.

Engines rumbled to life.

The official pointed his gun into the air. Silence fell.

A boom sounded, and a flare of light shot into the sky.

Kira stomped the heel of her foot on the throttle. Her board heaved before coughing and shuddering. She landed hard; her board lifeless as the rest of the waverunners rocketed forward.

SEVEN

"WHAT JUST HAPPENED?" Kira asked in disbelief as the racers left her in a cloud of dust.

Literally.

They'd already formed a pack.

She was supposed to be in that pack, smack dab in the middle until she made her move. Not still standing on the starting line with a dead board.

"Doing a system check now." There was strain in Odin's voice.

"Jin, what did you do to my board?"

"Nothing out of the normal," Jin defended. "I made a few last-minute adjustments based on your most recent training results."

Odin's head jerked up. "You didn't touch the power distribution, did you?"

Silence echoed over the comms.

"That may have been one of my fixes," Jin allowed.

A growl came from Odin. "You idiot. I adjusted the antigravs to compensate for the differences in the planet's gravity."

Kira closed her eyes and tipped her head back as she put together what had happened. The two changes must have canceled each other out. The board's safety protocol would have shut the engine down to prevent engine failure when she floored the throttle.

"Oh." Jin arrived at the same realization seconds later. "That could be a problem."

A stream of curses came from Kira as she hopped off the board. She yanked out the repair tools she stored on her person. The habit she'd picked up as a Cur would stand her in good stead now.

Squatting beside her board, she stripped off the emergency panel and stared inside, thanking every piece of luck she had that she knew how to do emergency repairs. Otherwise, it was very likely she'd be heading to her ship with her tail between her legs at the end of this race

"What are you doing?" Odin asked.

"Fixing both of your mistakes." To Jin, she instructed, "Keep an eye on the pack. I want to know the second they've begun their approach to the tower."

"You're not thinking—" Jin trailed off.

"You got a better idea?" Kira's movements were precise as she made the adjustments. "If so, I'm all ears."

"So much for flying under the radar," Jin said mournfully.

* * *

Titters and laughter filled the air as the grounded racer's plight became clear.

"Someone's having a bad day," Solal observed as the racer fiddled with their board.

Ignoring the comment, Raider sat forward, his gaze locked on the small figure.

It was the first time Raider had shown a spark of interest in anything in weeks. The typically arrogant human had become even more cold and combative since Kira and Elena's disappearance.

Where Graydon's oshota had earned the Tuann's respect during the journey to Jettie, Raider could be said to have earned the Tuann's fear. He was the opponent no one wanted to deal with. Some of that came from his vicious way of fighting, the rest on the fact he could take an extreme amount of damage and keep going.

To everyone's surprise, he fit rather well among Graydon and Wren's oshota.

"What is it?" Graydon asked, picking up on his preoccupation.

Raider nodded at where the racer was attempting to make repairs to their board. "They're rather good."

"Why do you say that?" Wren asked, looking over to see what held Raider's attention.

Raider didn't answer immediately, instead studying the racer more closely. His eyes narrowed. "Not many of today's waverunners know the technical side of their boards. They only care about going fast and performing cool stunts."

Wren frowned. "How short-sighted of them."

Raider made an expression like he agreed. "It's rare to see someone who can attempt repairs on the fly like this."

Even more so considering the pressure the individual had to be under.

"Could you do it?" Graydon asked.

A confidence that bordered on cocky chased across Raider's face before he shrugged. "Of course. All the Curs can. It's a training requirement."

"Could Kira?" Wren asked.

Raider paused. His gaze returned to the racer, a coldness to it.

Graydon guessed they had their answer.

Wren leaned forward, studying the racer with a renewed interest. If that really was Kira down there, she had a lot to answer for.

Wren hadn't been happy when he was informed of her departure. The only reason he hadn't gone after her immediately was an order from the Overlord. Otherwise, he'd have hunted her down.

Graydon considered the racer. The chances of it being Kira were astronomically small, but the woman had surprised him in the past.

"They're wearing a mask," Solal noted.

Raider shook his head. "That's not conclusive evidence. Many of the racers wear helmets."

Except those racers also wore armor, whereas the racer below was clad in a flimsy long-sleeved garment with the hood pulled up. Why would they go to the trouble of covering their face with a mask that would do nothing to protect their head in the event of a crash?

Graydon could think of one reason—to conceal their identity.

"Should we go and retrieve this racer?" Baran asked.

Graydon's oshota all perked up at the question.

Graydon hesitated, sharing in his oshota's desire to do exactly that. He shook his head. "We don't have enough evidence. If we're wrong and Kira is anywhere on this planet and hears wind of it, she'll go to ground."

The woman was nothing if not stubborn in the pursuit of her goals.

Disappointment crossed Amila's face. Even Solal seemed put out at the suggestion.

"Isn't that interesting?" Raider said with a low whistle.

"What is?" Amila asked, cocking her head.

"That person removed the limiter. Bold move," Raider explained. "With waverunners, people don't understand it's not how fast the board can go, it's how much your body can withstand. The limiter creates a biofeedback with the pilot. It regulates the power output based on that person's condition. Not many waveboard runners are adept at making those second by second judgment calls. Without the limiter, you remove your upward limits, but you also have a lot more difficulty with control."

"Why do it then?" Solal asked.

"It's likely there was a conflict in the sequence of commands in the drive chain. This is the fastest way to fix that." Raider thought about it for a second. "And the most dangerous."

"More and more this person resembles Kira," Graydon said grimly.

Raider grunted. "It does smack of something she would do. It's certainly reckless enough."

The question remained whether it would be enough. Already the clump of racers had separated into two packs, one that lagged behind the first as the leaders started to draw away from the main body. They were almost through the first third of the course.

After this would be the tower, a nearly vertical climb up to an air buoy nearly two thousand feet above the ground. From there would be a breakneck descent heading into the gauntlet, a series of obstacles designed to thin the herd and test the racers' speed, maneuverability, and luck.

"Once the race is over, I want that person intercepted and brought to me," Graydon ordered.

His oshota acknowledged the order with determined expressions, anticipation in their bearing.

Graydon looked at the racer. Soon, he promised himself.

"This should be a good show," Raider said softly. He leaned back, peering over his shoulder to the row where Devon and his friends waited. "Yo, kid, if I were you, I'd watch that racer."

Devon's expression was serious as he nodded.

Ziva straightened. "Why? Is that person important?" Her expression brightened. "Is that Kira?"

The Luatha surrounding the children all looked down at the racer with renewed interest, where before they'd seemed bored with events. Their Overlord may have rescinded Luatha's claim on Kira, but that didn't overshadow Kira's appearance in their hearts. A good number of them still felt gratitude and appreciation for her actions on Ta Da'an.

Raider smirked. "Just watch."

Graydon leaned forward. "Thanks for that."

The human knew very well they were trying to keep Kira's absence quiet.

Raider's reaction was to send him another grin.

"Do you know something we don't?" Amila asked, studying the human closely.

Raider jutted his chin at the pits beneath the stands where the race teams were. "He seem familiar to anyone?"

The man he'd indicated had his back to them.

"Finn," Wren said.

To the casual observer it wouldn't be obvious, but Roake recognized their own. It was in the way the man moved, his size and bulk, his awareness of what was going on around him. There was no doubt; he was oshota, through and through.

"I can't think of a single reason why a controller would shield their identity," Raider said in an idle voice. "Can you?"

“It does seem unnecessary,” Wren observed.

Raider smirked and nodded at the race. “There are two ways to win a race with a set up like this. You’re first over the tower—or you’re last. The thing most don’t understand is how treacherous the wind currents are up there. The slightest turbulence can send you into a free fall. Stuck in the middle of the pack, it’s hard to draw out your greatest speed. Most won’t even try for fear of crashing. But fall too far behind and you’ll never catch up to the lead by the end.”

“You’re saying that person is hoping to be last over the tower,” Amila guessed.

Raider’s expression was devious “Do you know why we’re called the Curs?”

Amila frowned. “I believe it is a term for a dog.”

“That’s correct, but you’re missing the nuance behind that term.” Raider watched the rider work. “In our language, that name has negative connotations. Simply put, it’s considered an insult. It’s another word for mongrel or mutt. Often called a mixed breed or someone who is unfriendly and aggressive.”

Wren considered him. “Why would an elite force take such a name?”

“It’s a reminder.”

“Of what?” Amila asked.

“Kira built a family out of people others considered the dregs of society. When she gave us that name, it was so we would remember that no matter how others saw us, what was important was how we saw ourselves. She took something that should have been bad and made it a name to be respected. Curs are fighters. We’re the junkyard dogs of the Consortium. Vicious and loyal only to our own. We decide how we win or lose. No one else.”

From what Graydon knew of Kira and Raider, the description fit.

“Apt,” Wren said.

“You think so?” Raider tilted his head at the racer. “I always thought that name suited Kira best.”

* * *

Finished with the repairs, Kira slapped the panel into place and straightened.

"You're running out of time. The leaders of the pack will clear the first third of the race in less than two minutes."

"What are you talking about? That's plenty of time." Kira hopped onto her board, grinning at its throaty purr when she activated the engines. Its rumble felt a lot like home after a long absence.

"Much better," she said to herself.

She lifted her head. "Locate targets."

On her ocular interface, small squares appeared, little arrows above them. The squares were spread throughout almost a mile of the course, the leaders tightly clumped together with the pursuing pack a little less uniform. The racers framed by the squares were little more than fast-moving specs at this distance.

"Let's get started then." Kira tucked her hands into her pockets as she zoomed forward. Her stance was easy and relaxed as the board slowly picked up speed. It was only when she approached the first obstacle that she got serious.

Commonly referred to as the rhythm section, it was a group of continuous jumps. Many waveboard runners used it as an opportunity to show off, executing flips and twists that did little more than add time to their run.

Kira hit the first jump and held her stance, soaring over the second and third to save time. She hit the final jump and kept it short, heading into the berm without a hitch in speed or positioning.

"Good. There are three more berms coming up, each shorter than the last. Stay low and to the outside," Jin advised.

Kira adjusted her balance, swaying left then right then left again as she followed the twists and turns.

She came out of the final turn fast, the next jump appearing before her in a blink.

"Incoming fire."

Kira flipped, rotating her body to move the board from its original position. Heat flashed past her, narrowly avoiding her.

Jin whistled. "Close, close, close."

Kira came out of the flip as the lasers lit the air up beside her.

"You're still operating in the green," Odin informed her.

A good thing. Had any of the lasers scored a direct hit, she would have taken damage and a reduction in the number of points she could get for the event.

The lasers were designed to simulate battle conditions. Because what was more fun than a race? A race where you could get knocked out of it at any moment, of course.

"The Haldeel sure like their fireworks," Odin said.

"The Haldeel didn't create this course." Kira entered a tunnel. Her ocular implant switched one eye to night vision.

Sadly, for her, there was no light beyond what her hoverboard provided. It made navigating the tunnel a tad more difficult than most riders would be comfortable with. It'd force them to slow down for fear of running headfirst into the tunnel walls.

Kira didn't have that option, relying instead on instinct and skill to find her way through.

She broke out of the tunnel in the next second.

None of her movements were particularly flashy, but an onlooker would be able to tell she knew what she was doing. There was no gesture wasted as she zipped through the various ramps and the harsh twists and turns, picking up speed rather than shedding it.

"The front of the pack has begun their ascent of the tower," Jin warned.

Kira crouched lower as she fought for every bit of speed. The last half of the course before the tower passed in a blur.

"Starting my ascent," Kira informed them as she reached the base of the vertical obstacle not-so-fondly called the tower.

The obstacle didn't look like much, but it was more challenging than it appeared at first glance. Considered one of the most dangerous pieces of the course, it required a pilot to be absolutely perfect in every aspect. From the angle of ascent, to the speed of approach, to the positioning of your body.

Get any of it wrong and you courted death.

Most racers would tell you the tower was the obstacle they feared the most as it had claimed more than one victim over the years. Not Kira. It had always been her favorite. It was like a roller coaster ride. Slowly approaching the ascent, only to race breakneck for the ground once more.

"Remember that all the other racers need to be finished with their descent before you start yours," Jin advised.

"From the way you're nagging me, you'd think this was my first time," Kira said as she picked up speed.

She fixed her eyes on the red dot high above, the buoy that signaled the turnaround point.

That was her goal. Nothing was going to keep it from her. Not even gravity.

"Perhaps that's because you have a tendency to discard perfectly good plans at a whim."

"Hello, pot; meet kettle," Odin said dryly.

Kira grinned as gravity started to push on her chest.

"Who asked you? If not for your meddling, we wouldn't need to go to these lengths," Jin grumbled.

The sky spread in a wide expanse, its fluffy white clouds seeming to beckon her until it was all she could see. Kira kept her gaze trained forward. Racers, even experienced ones, occasionally experienced vertigo on this type of ascent. It was easy to get disorientated, the ground so far below and only a thin scrap of metal equipped with what amounted to little more than an antigrav engine between you and it.

Honestly, Kira considered people who did this a little crazy. That went for herself as well.

"How was I supposed to know you wouldn't check the board's maintenance log before you started tinkering?" Odin shot back.

"Of course, I didn't. I'm the only one with permission to touch that board. Even Kira knows better," Jin cried.

Kira ignored the two as she flew ever higher. She felt like Icarus as he flew too close to the sun—only her wings weren't the type to melt so easily.

"Heart rate and blood pressure still look good," Jin announced.

"I'm not reading any issues in the board's feedback either," Odin added.

The sensation of pressure on Kira grew, until it felt like external forces would try to rip her from the board.

Kira ignored the discomfort as the red of the buoy grew until it seemed to eclipse the sky. The buoy that had seemed so small when seen from the ground was suddenly as big as her ship.

"The last of the racers cleared the bottom. You're good to go whenever you're ready," Jin announced.

"You always know the way to my heart," Kira teased.

The sound of retching came. "Please. I've held ownership of that decayed muscle since the day we first met."

Kira grinned as her engines shut off to conserve power as she bypassed the blimp, climbing up and up until gradually her pace slowed, and she felt gravity calling her back to land.

"You ready for this?" Jin asked.

"When have I not been?"

Jin chortled. "All right, prepare for ignition."

Kira let gravity drag her down, twisting to point the nose of her board toward the ground far below. She crouched, reaching for the handle affectionately called the "oh shit bar" by waverunners.

"Three. Two. One. Systems are go and waiting on you. Fly fast; fly far, Firebird."

"Roger that. Prepare the home fires."

Wind whipped past Kira as she let go of the handle and straightened her legs. She fell, her stomach climbing into her throat. Right about now should do it.

Head pointed toward the planet and her feet at the sky above, Kira punched it, opening the engine and accessing eighty percent of the board's power.

"Here. We. Go." Jin chanted.

"Commencing burn."

For a split second nothing happened. The world froze. Time had no meaning.

A dull trembling started in the board, shaking her bones. Anticipation filled her. This was going to be so much fun.

Dangerous fun—but that was the best kind.

There was a dull thump that Kira felt in her chest. Her board jolted forward, catapulting her toward the ground in a move that would have been suicide for anyone without Kira's experience.

"Trajectory and speed look good. A little feedback from removing the limiter but nothing outside our projections," Jin said with calm detachment.

In her interface, a blue dotted line appeared outlining the optimal flight path. All she needed to do was follow it.

Below her, the ground grew at an alarming rate. The journey up that had seemed to last forever went by in a blink of an eye on the return trip.

"All right Kira, we're good. You should pull up now," Jin advised.

Not yet.

The wind whipped past her as she crouched a little lower, reaching for more speed.

Just a little bit more.

Almost there.

"Kira, if you break the sound barrier, they're going to know it's us," Jin warned.

There.

Kira relaxed her stance, pulling out of the dive in the next second.

"Good, I'm glad we agree on how stupid that would be," Jin grumbled.

"Personally, I think it would be fun," Odin added.

"Don't encourage her."

Kira ignored the bickering as she shot past the first three obstacles with ease, not losing any of the speed she'd picked up during her dive.

She overtook the rear of the pack, bypassing them in a blink.

"Warning messages are starting to pop up," Odin said, sounding distracted.

"We knew that was likely to happen." Kira arrowed through the course, closing the distance between her and the leaders. She was too fast for the laser fire to present a challenge. By the time the drones registered her presence, she was already long gone.

"Which systems are we having problems with?" Kira asked as her board rotated in a smooth spiral.

"It'd be easier to tell you which systems didn't have error messages."

"You'd better make it worth it," Jin threatened.

"When have I ever let you down?"

"Do you want this week's list or the running tally?"

"Don't be ridiculous. The running tally would take much too long to relate. I'll be long done by the time you finish."

As if to demonstrate that fact, Kira flew past another clump of competitors.

Kira grinned. For all his sarcasm, she knew there was no one more worried about her current predicament than him. He was used to riding with her, ready to troubleshoot any issues she might have.

Unfortunately, the rules didn't allow for AI companions.

It left Jin with the new experience of being sidelined and forced to watch as someone else did all the work.

"How's my fuel looking?" Kira asked.

Jin grunted. "Not good. You're going to be close."

"Let's hope luck is in my favor today."

Kira pointed her board toward a series of obstacles nicknamed the gauntlet. A shorter version of the tunnel from before, this one was ten feet long and had fixed-point drone fire on each side.

Where the tower was an exercise in stamina and precision, the gauntlet was designed to test your maneuverability and luck. It was responsible for knocking out about a third of the riders who made it to this point.

Only four people stood between her and the finish line.

"Approaching the gauntlet now," Kira said.

"Operation Thread the Needle commences in three, two, one. Punch it."

Kira hit the boost on her board, her stance almost lazy as she approached the last stretch that stood between her and a win. Already, the lasers had started firing, creating an almost impossible to navigate screen.

There was really only one way to face the obstacle—to get through it as fast as possible and pray your luck held.

Kira's speed remained unchecked as she dove into the middle. The lasers were an overwhelming din all around her. Kira used the underside of the board to catch the stray lasers she couldn't quite shake.

She came out of the tunnel arrowing for the finish line.

"Yas! Nicely done, Nixxy," Jin crowed. "That's how we do it."

"Don't celebrate yet," Odin cautioned. "The energy drain from the laser fire is causing a chain reaction."

"How long do I have?"

"Three, maybe four minutes."

"Good enough."

Kira rounded the final corner. The racers in the first three positions came into view as Kira barreled down on them.

"Critical failure imminent," Odin warned. "If I were you, I'd consider taking drastic measures. The board is literally about to shake itself apart under you."

As if he'd jinxed her, there was an ominous clanking from her board seconds before a tail piece snapped off.

"Hm. I see what you mean."

"Good. Then do something about it," Jin cried.

Kira snorted. He said that like it would be easy. Did he imagine she could wave her hands and magically fix the problem?

The Tuann from the starting line was in the lead, the Haldeel right behind him, the racer from Zepher bringing up the rear. Only a length of a board separated them, the Haldeel and human almost neck and neck.

Kira swung her board wide, hoping to slip around them.

The human moved to block her.

So that's how he wanted to play it. Very well. The idiot was a few decades too young to truly be a nuisance.

"You're not going to make it. Your fuel just dipped below the red," Jin warned.

"I will."

"You won't. Even you can't argue with physics."

"I have a plan."

Silence crackled over the comms.

"Wait. Please don't tell me you mean what I think you mean."

"Yup." Kira sounded chipper. "I absolutely mean that."

Kira surged forward as Jin wailed, straining for the finish line as it came into view. Her focus narrowed to that line and the victory it promised.

"That's such a bad idea! You know they'll never consider that a win."

Kira smiled. "We'll see."

"Critical failure imminent," Odin announced.

The board sputtered.

Eight meters left.

Six.

She edged up beside the Tuann, fighting him for first place.

This time when the board coughed, there were no further sounds. It went silent and still, coasting along at its current speed.

The front of the board started to dip.

"Now, Jin!"

"Why do you always drag me into your crazy schemes?" he snarled as he overrode the safety protocols, causing a chain reaction in the drive chain.

For one endless moment, Kira thought they'd missed their window. Too early and she'd never make the jump. Too soon and she'd face plant directly into the ground, likely breaking her neck and killing her instantly.

There was a whoosh and then a thump as the board exploded. Kira wrapped a *ki* shield around her feet, using the force to spring forward with one powerful leap.

She barreled headfirst over the finish line, milliseconds before the Tuann.

Kira barely had time to feel victorious before gravity reclaimed her. She plummeted. She had just enough time to think this was going to hurt before she hit, her right shoulder first.

She was right. It did.

Kira rolled and then kept rolling for several seconds before coming to a stop. She lay there, taking stock of her injuries.

If one discounted the ache in ninety percent of her body, she was in surprisingly good shape. No broken bones. No internal injuries.

Score one victory to the Tuann.

"This stuff is even better than we thought." Kira slid up the sleeve of her hoodie, exposing the undershirt she'd worn. The dark gleam of Tuann fabric greeted her. It was a present House Roake had given her when she'd completed her *uhva na*. It was the only thing she'd managed to bring. She'd been wearing it when Odin and Elena commandeered her ship.

Kira had to admit. She was more than a little impressed with the shirt.

If she'd had this during the war, her life would have been so much more comfortable. Human armor couldn't compete. To replicate the same effects, she'd have needed a full battle suit. It would have been the only thing strong enough to protect her from a crash like this.

"Very nice," Jin quipped. "But I suggest you get moving. That little stunt hasn't gone unnoticed. The mountain and his smaller mountain friends have guessed it's you and are now on their way. It's time to pop smoke and make yourself scarce."

Kira glanced into the stands.

Graydon caught and held her gaze, a slow smile spreading on his face.

"That's not good," she observed.

As if hearing her, his smile widened.

"No, it's not, and oh look, that's not all. The race officials are also on their way. Probably to disqualify you. Congratulations, the prize for most attention-grabbing landing goes to you."

Kira stood and swept a cocky bow in Jin's direction. "Thank you. I'd like to thank my partner in crime, Jin, for this honor. Without him, none of this would be possible."

Kira could almost feel Jin rolling his metaphorical eyes.

"You deal with the officials," he instructed. "Odin and I will work on delaying your mountain."

"How? And he's not my mountain."

"Pretty sure he wants to be," Jin shot back. "And we'll think of something."

Kira ignored the quagmire in Jin's first statement. The draw between her and Graydon was something she tried very hard not to think about. He was a black hole of magnetism that she could very easily get lost in.

Instead, she faced the sidelines where the rest of the top four racers had already congregated.

Her gaze lifted to the board where the winners were typically announced, only to find it blank.

Jin was right. Kira needed to fix this.

She knocked the dirt off her clothes as she considered her options. Graydon and company would need at least three minutes to free themselves from the chaotic mess the stands had turned into upon Kira's win.

She had the time but barely.

Kira sauntered in the direction of the race officials, ignoring the small stabs of pain as her body protested.

"That racer should be disqualified for reckless endangerment," the man from Zepher was saying as Kira walked up.

"That seems a little extreme," Kira responded.

His expression turned nasty. "You could have killed yourself or us."

"But I didn't."

Nor was anyone except Kira in any real danger.

Ignoring her, he faced the officials again. "This sets a bad precedent for the future. What kind of stunts do you think other racers will try if you let her get away with this?"

"The same kind of stunts they always do?" Kira guessed.

"You can't allow someone to break the rules in this way," he said in a carefully controlled voice that didn't quite hide the fact Kira was getting to him.

His hands had curled into fists and she sensed he was about one snarky retort away from attacking her.

Kira checked on Graydon's progress, noting how he and the others were almost out of the swarm of people. If she'd had time, she might have humored the man. As it was, she needed this done—and fast.

If she left without her win having been declared, chances were she'd be disqualified—if only because there was no one to argue her case.

She didn't do all that to lose in the final hour.

"Technically, she broke no rules," Skye observed.

"Of course you would think that, squid," the man said snidely.

Skye's eyes flickered but otherwise she didn't react. Beside her, the Tuann's expression went cold.

"She broke the rules; she's disqualified," the Zepher representative said again.

"Check again," Kira invited. "There's nothing that says the racer needs to be touching their board when they pass the finish line."

Kira would know. She and Jin had helped Bayside and Courtland draft the original set of rules, and they hadn't changed much over the years. She'd read them over before they reached the planet just in case.

While her interpretation allowed her to win on a technicality, it still very much counted—especially on Jettie, a Haldeel world where they were sticklers for the letter of the law, and there was nothing they enjoyed more than seeing someone wiggle through a loophole.

A small glimpse of amusement appeared on Skye's face. The Tuann looked at Kira with something resembling respect.

"I'm not sure," the male official told his companion.

The woman looked calculating as she considered.

Kira tensed, sensing she was about to lose control of the situation. It was her win. She could force the issue, but it would take time. There was no way Graydon wouldn't stake out the race headquarters. He'd lock that place down until not even an ant could go in or out without being noticed.

A Haldeel with black markings approached with a neutral expression. The wide robes he wore fluttered around his quick-moving appendages. "What is the problem? Why haven't the winners been announced?"

"Apologies, *Za*. We were debating the merits of the lady's win," the woman said with a small nod.

The Haldeel's head tilted as a dissatisfied expression appeared on his face. "Why would debate be needed?"

"This man argues that her actions presented a danger to others and violated the rules."

The Haldeel glanced in Kira's direction. "And did they?"

There was a marked hesitation as the officials shared a look. "Not technically."

"Was anyone injured?"

The woman didn't answer verbally this time, shaking her head instead.

Kira's lips quirked.

Figures. They were leaning in Zepher's direction. Kira had a feeling without the Haldeel's interference, she would have been out of luck.

Now that he was here, suddenly they were forced to see the truth of the matter. She didn't remember the race organizers being this biased, but then most of those races were filled with humans.

"I don't see the issue, then," the Haldeel said.

"It's common sense," the man from Zepher burst out. "They shouldn't have to spell out the obvious."

The Haldeel's expression remained unchanged. "Common sense or not, her win stands."

A heavy thud came from a few feet away. Baran straightened from his crouch.

"You—" Kira mentally cursed.

Baran's lips twitched. "I see you remember me. That's good. It'll make things easier."

Kira hesitated, debating the merits of surrendering.

An object flew out of the stands. Kira caught it before it hit her face. She glanced up to find the person who'd thrown it. A human child around the age of eight or nine grinned at her showing a gap where a tooth was missing. He had freckles spread across his nose and his hair was brown, a little longer than most and shaggy as a result.

"For the show, lady," the boy called.

Kira squeezed the ball in her hand, rotating it to see the words written on its side. "Tomorrow. Same Place. No Tuann."

The words faded seconds later, leaving only a normal ball in her grasp.

Kira sighed. That made things a little more difficult.

Baran smiled. "I'm glad you're not going to make this hard on yourself."

The ball dropped onto the ground as Kira shook her head. "This is going to be so disappointing—for you, that is."

Baran's confusion changed to outrage. He reached for her, but it was too late. She'd already whirled and plunged into the crowd.

EIGHT

THE STANDS ERUPTED at the racer's crash landing—the giddy atmosphere that had been building since the racer began her descent on the tower ignited as the crowd collectively lost their minds.

Any lingering doubts Graydon had had about the racer's identity were put to bed. Not that he'd suffered from any after that maneuver Raider had called the dead man's plunge.

"What now?" Raider asked as the mob surged forward, the racer's call sign of Sparrow being chanted until it was a thunderous roar.

Graydon stood. "We collect what's ours."

Raider tilted his head at the drama unfolding below as the race officials argued with the top four racers, including the one responsible for the current state of affairs. "You think she'll make it that easy for you?"

The racer named Sparrow met his gaze, not even her mask capable of hiding her unease.

"I'm really hoping she doesn't," Graydon replied.

Graydon was quite looking forward to the cat/mouse game they were about to embark on.

"Care to join?" Graydon asked the still form beside him.

Wren stood, satisfaction appearing for the first time since the race's start. "It would be my pleasure."

Below, the little Sparrow couldn't hide her alarm at the mobilization of Graydon and his oshota. Satisfaction filled Graydon. *Now, what are you going to do,* coli?

"Retrieve what's ours," Graydon ordered.

Baran sprung over the stand's railing to drop onto the track below. He and the Sparrow exchanged words seconds before she whirled and disappeared into the crowd.

Graydon grinned. Just as expected.

That's it, coli.

Run. Struggle all you want. You're already caught in the trap I've set.

Raider stretched his legs as he propped his chin on his fist, watching the proceedings with a look of boredom.

"How is it?" Graydon asked.

Wren nodded. "She's moving as predicted."

Satisfaction filled Graydon.

It wouldn't be long now.

While Kira had been occupied with the race, Baran and Wren had worked together to stretch strands of *ki* around the track and surrounding area. The thousands of strands created a web their quarry would be hard-pressed to escape. The more she struggled, the more those strands would wrap around her, making her defeat inevitable.

As long as they could reach her before she left the area or the strands faded, there was nowhere she could go where Wren and Baran couldn't find her.

Graydon stalked toward the exit. "Let's go."

Wren and Graydon's oshota followed, Raider reluctantly bringing up the rear.

Devon sent Graydon a questioning look and got a headshake in return. This kind of hunting was best left to the experienced.

As they trooped up the stairs and toward the exit, the crowd remained in place, too focused on the scene below to take note. Except for one. A small, hooded figure stood and followed, tailing them up the stairs, into the innards of the stadium and outside again.

"We're being followed," Solal informed Graydon.

"I'm aware."

The person wasn't even being subtle about it. They'd made no efforts at going unnoticed nor had they made any attempt to hide their presence.

Graydon found both those facts interesting. For now, they seemed content simply to follow. If Graydon hadn't been planning on re-obtaining a certain troublesome child of Roake, he'd be tempted to allow the person to continue to observe.

"What would you like done?" Solal asked.

"Detain them, but don't hurt them if possible."

There was no sign the person intended harm. They also didn't move in a way that suggested they were a spy. Their actions were too unschooled for that, and there had been no attempt made at being clandestine.

Graydon didn't want to risk reprisal from the Haldeel in the event the person was a citizen simply fascinated by the Tuann.

Jettie had a pretty large human refugee population. Humans had been known to fixate on Graydon's people. Sometimes to an unhealthy extent. As long as their shadow didn't intend them harm, Graydon would respond in kind.

At Solal's silent signal, Noor and Cord fell out of step. As one, they moved to face the person following them.

"Little friend, you'll need to come with us," Noor informed the shadow.

"Graydon," Baran said, sounding like he was standing right next to Graydon. "We have a slight problem."

In front of them, their tail froze.

Noor and Cord didn't move as they waited for the person's next move—whether to flee or surrender. They were prepared for both eventualities.

"I don't know how she did it, but she's gone. I think she had help," Baran continued through the link.

Graydon stopped moving, their follower's presence suddenly taking on a different connotation. Their smaller size. The fact they hadn't acted until Graydon gave the order to pick up Kira.

Only a few people would have an interest in something like that.

As if in confirmation, a familiar voice said, "I'm afraid that option doesn't work for me."

Raider whirled to face the stranger. "Elena."

The hooded figure took off, evading Noor's grasp and disappearing out an adjacent window in the next breath. Raider followed close on her heels.

In an instant, Graydon's quarry changed from Kira to Elena.

"After her," Graydon ordered.

His oshota leapt out of the window.

"What about Kira?" Wren questioned, his reluctance to abandon the chase clear.

"She's gone, but someone just as good fell into our grasp," Graydon answered.

Wren was no fool. He knew Graydon wouldn't abandon the hunt without good reason. Still, Wren's agenda was clear. Find Kira and protect her. As her *seon'yer,* he only cared about her safety.

Wren was a highly respected individual among the Tuann. Even Graydon couldn't force his compliance if he truly objected.

"Trust me. If we catch this person, Kira will come to us."

Wren studied Graydon, his thoughts not easy to read. Graydon waited, knowing no amount of demands would sway him. Wren made a sharp gesture and the three oshota who'd shadowed him like silent sentinels disappeared through the window after the rest.

Good.

That was one problem addressed.

"Follow me," Graydon said over his shoulder.

He left the oshota to chase after the hooded figure, knowing the two of them wouldn't add much value to the pursuit. Instead, they took an alternate route, seeking to cut the other person off.

Yet, every time they came close, the person would veer away.

"It seems our target isn't entirely without skills," Wren observed.

Graydon hadn't expected anything else. The target had been trained by Kira. You could see it in the brash confidence that said they thought they were invincible, even as they showcased moments of extreme caution that made them as slippery as a fish.

The hooded figure led Graydon and Wren's oshota on a merry chase through the city. It was easy to see her familiarity with her surroundings just by the paths she chose.

Weaving in and out of the more heavily frequented tourist areas before trying to lose her tail in the streets and alleys was something only a local would know.

Graydon couldn't help but pause to admire the individual and the person who'd trained them. Kira was the only woman who'd defeated him. It made sense her niece would share in some of her skills.

"Flush her out," Graydon ordered from his rooftop seat.

A chorus of yesses sounded through his link.

They closed in on their quarry, coming at her from all sides and forcing her down a dead-end alley.

Graydon took in the view of the city from where he stood. He loved it when things went his way.

"I didn't think you would give up on Kira," Wren said.

Graydon's smile was brief as he tilted his face to enjoy the mild warmth of Jettie's sun.

"Who says I have?"

Wren's frown said he didn't appreciate Graydon's games.

"Just watch. I think you'll find this interesting."

Wren didn't speak as the minutes passed, the silence deepening.

Eventually, they both caught the sound of furtive movements from below.

Wren tilted his head at the edge of the roof in question. Graydon nodded.

He'd thought she'd choose this route. Good to see she didn't disappoint.

In tandem, they both masked their presence, their breathing slowing as they stood still. An observer would have guessed them to be statues for all the movement they gave away.

As a final touch, they ran *ki* through their bodies, erasing their body heat. Now, no one except a Tuann with a talent for discovery would be able to detect their presence.

Just in time as a set of hands grasped the ledge, a cloaked head appearing next.

Graydon moved, crouching in front of the girl. Her mouth dropped open, and her eyes widened in surprise. She would have shot back the way she'd come if Graydon hadn't been quicker.

With one fast movement, he plucked her off the building's side.

"Damn it, she said you were good." Elena dangled in his grip, a guilty expression warring with disgruntlement as the sound of pursuit grew below.

"You didn't believe her?"

The girl's frown was resigned. "I thought I was better."

At that, Graydon couldn't contain his laugh. "I can see the resemblance between you two."

Like Kira, Elena had no shame. Graydon was pretty sure if asked, the only thing Elena would regret was the fact she'd gotten caught.

With that thought in mind, he deposited her on her feet in front of him.

She bobbed a sarcastic curtsy at him. "Why, thank you, sir. I'll take that as a compliment."

As well she should.

Not just anyone could escape a trap set by the emperor's youngest Face. Had Elena not stumbled into him, this trip could very well have ended in a resounding defeat.

Graydon didn't even remember the last time that had happened.

A sharp inhalation told Graydon that Wren finally saw why he'd changed the hunt's prey.

Wren's gaze was locked on the girl as if she was the only thing that existed in the universe. He looked to be barely breathing.

For the first time since Graydon had known him, he seemed off-balance, losing some of that iron-clad control. To strangers, he would still resemble an unfathomable stone statue, but to those who knew him, his emotional state was clear.

Though moments had passed, he looked like he'd aged decades, seemingly lost and adrift—but behind it all was a thinly veiled hope. As if every wish he'd ever had was standing right in front of Graydon. If he blinked, that mirage might crumble, leaving him cold and alone again.

"Graydon?" There was a question in Wren's voice—tentative, unsure.

"Yes." Even as Graydon inclined his head, there was a warning in his expression. This wasn't the time or place for this conversation.

Wren flinched, catching Graydon's meaning.

Sound from below forced Wren to swallow what he'd planned to say. By the time Raider appeared over the edge, Wren's expression had reverted to his normal stoicism, leaving not even a hint of the turbulence of before.

"Sperm donor, you're quite persistent," Elena teased as Raider climbed onto the roof.

Wren's gaze snapped from Elena to Raider again. "Sperm donor?"

No one answered.

Wren studied Raider for several long seconds before shooting a glance in Graydon's direction. "I submit my name to be considered as his formal *seon'yer*."

"I thought you'd say that."

"Then you accept?"

Graydon inclined his head. "As long as he agrees."

Wren stared at Raider with a determined expression. "I'll see that he does."

Raider ignored the exchange, instead focusing on his daughter.

"Where's your aunt?" Raider asked.

Elena tilted her head, not even the apparent innocence in her wide eyes quite able to hide her displeasure. "Is that how you greet your long-lost daughter?"

Raider froze.

Silence filled the rooftop, only disrupted as Graydon's oshota, Wren's among them, landed arranged in a circle around them.

Elena startled. "How did you do that?"

Amila grinned. "Practice, little one."

"Can you teach me?" Elena asked, channeling a little girl's excitement again.

Amila's chin dipped as she tried to restrain her amusement. "Perhaps one day."

Elena pouted.

"How is this possible?" one of Wren's oshota asked, staring at the girl like she'd seen a ghost.

"Auralyn," Wren barked.

She startled, looking in his direction with a lost expression.

"Not here," he said.

"But—" As if drawn by a magnet, Auralyn's gaze was pulled to Elena again.

"Discipline," Wren ground out.

Auralyn jerked like he'd struck her, but the reminder worked. She closed her eyes and when she opened them again, her expression was composed and still, the previous emotion gone as if it had never been.

Graydon couldn't help but admire their control. But then, he hadn't really expected any less of someone of Wren's status and rank.

"I don't suppose I can trust you to stay put," Graydon said.

Elena flashed him a look, nearly identical to the one Kira got when she thought someone had asked a stupid question.

That was what he'd thought.

Graydon snagged her wrist, sliding a bracelet over it. He pressed his thumb to the clasp, satisfied when a spark of warmth slid into his hand.

"What's this?" Elena asked, shaking her wrist.

"Insurance."

Elena raised her eyes to his.

"As long as you're wearing that, one of us will always know where you are," he informed her.

Her face was a picture of indignant insult as she glanced up at Raider. "Are you going to let him do this to me?"

Raider pinched the bridge of his nose. "I can't believe I'm saying this, but yes, I think I am."

* * *

"What are you doing?" Jin asked as Kira fled past pit crews and dodged around landing racers.

"The contact reached out. We've got a meet."

Baran barreled after her, barely avoiding getting clipped in the head by a returning racer in the process.

"And I suppose they don't want any of our friends butting in."

"You suppose right." Kira ducked under the waveboard of a landing racer. Its heat nearly singed her hair as she rolled away from it.

"Why can't things ever be easy?" Jin asked.

Kira would really like to know that as well.

This wasn't the plan. Graydon wasn't supposed to recognize her. He wasn't supposed to send people to retrieve her. And she wasn't supposed to run from them.

Yet here she was, doing exactly that.

The departure from Ta Sa'Riel could be blamed on Elena and Odin, but this she was doing knowingly and on purpose. You could say she was acting under her own agency.

Jin groaned. "We don't have a choice."

Nope. They didn't.

Their contact was nothing if not difficult. If Kira brought any of Graydon's people, she could kiss goodbye the relationship she'd painstakingly developed.

Elena's future safety depended on her contact's good will; Kira couldn't chance destroying their link.

"I'm uploading a map to your interface," Jin informed her. "Follow it."

A series of broken, floating lines appeared in front of Kira, curving around obstructions before disappearing into the crowd.

Kira plunged after them, her interface calculating and recalculating the best route based on the changing conditions—exactly as it would during a race.

The lines twisted and curved through the landing zone, occasionally disappearing to reappear as a new route opened up.

Baran didn't have the same advantage, but then he didn't really need it. As an oshota, and a persistent one at that, he had his own methods for closing the distance.

"This isn't going to work," Kira said.

Even if by some miraculous chance she managed to evade him long enough to get out of the racing stadium, he'd simply track her down again. Just like he did last time.

She needed to do something drastic and unexpected.

Just then, the sight of a figure caught Kira's attention. It was odd because Kira could only see the woman's back, but there was something Kira recognized in her stance. A familiarity that made the chaos of the race's end fade into the background.

The woman turned her head, her hair covering the majority of her face, except for the smooth line of her jaw.

"Elise."

Kira changed course, starting for the woman.

As if sensing her approach, the woman moved into the tunnel the racers had exited at the start of the race. Her pace was easy and slow, no evidence of hurry.

"Kira, why did you say that name?" Jin asked.

"I saw her. I saw Elise."

"No. You didn't."

Kira didn't have time to argue, the lines abruptly disappearing from her interface.

"Don't do this. You're seeing things you want to see."

Kira didn't respond, picking up her pace as the ground in front of her cleared.

"I programmed the interface to recognize Elise. Standing protocol means it will alert you to anyone matching her description. Did you get an alert?"

That only applied with a face. Kira hadn't seen a face—at least not all of one.

"I'll take a quick look."

The map would eventually recalibrate. Even if it didn't, she'd figure it out. She couldn't see a chance like this and not take it.

How would she face Elise later if she found out she'd come so close only to miss her because she hadn't taken the time to investigate?

"You stubborn, stubborn woman. You're going to get caught."

"It wouldn't be the end of the world."

Granted, it would seriously screw up her immediate plans and put her into hot water with her contact, possibly alienating her fully from the rest, but Kira judged the risk worth it.

If she could catch Elise, all those plans became obsolete.

Elena wouldn't need a caretaker because she'd have her mother.

Kira could finish what she'd started on Roake.

Kira reached the tunnel and hesitated, some part of her remembering caution. Even if this were Elise, there was a good chance she wouldn't be the Elise Kira remembered.

She'd been in the Tsavitee's grasp for a long time. Long enough to be brainwashed and have her loyalties changed.

Kira stretched her senses into the tunnel. The *ki* she'd begun to experiment with floating before her. Nothing seemed amiss except a few racers lingering off to the side where they were tinkering with their boards.

Kira stepped inside, keeping one part of her attention on them in case they presented a threat and the rest on the tunnel ahead of her. A tunnel that held no sign of Elise—or the woman Kira thought might be Elise.

Where did she go?

Kira hurried forward, staying alert.

She glanced into bay after bay, noting the ones with the privacy screen activated. Nothing.

It was possible the person Kira was looking for was in one of those bays. If Kira had the time, she could try to hack them. As it was, Baran was only seconds behind her.

"Damn it," Kira cursed as the sound of running footsteps reached her.

Time was up.

She headed for the building's front entrance. It was the quickest way to the city. Perhaps she could lose Baran there.

Kira made it a half-dozen steps before a hard force latched onto her arm, yanking her into a room.

Kira shifted her balance, already preparing for a fight. The sight of Finn's serious expression stopped her from any reckless actions.

He held one finger up to his lips, a question in his eyes.

Kira didn't hesitate to nod.

He set a hand on her shoulder and closed his eyes. His soul's breath moved within his body, spreading out to hers and coating them both in a thick film, creating a barrier between them and the outer world.

Kira's senses dulled. Their surroundings drained of color, the sounds muffled, until it was the world that felt muted and unreal.

The racing footsteps came closer until Baran appeared outside the door. His pace slowed as if he picked up on the change. He glanced around him in suspicion, even going so far as to peer inside their room. His gaze moved over them like they weren't even there.

Kira held her breath, afraid the slightest disturbance would break the spell and draw his attention.

In the room across from them, a tool clattered to the floor.

Baran spun in time to see a figure that looked exactly like Kira race along the corridor.

Fake Kira disappeared into a hallway as Baran gave chase.

Only when the sound of their footsteps was long gone did Finn withdraw his *ki* and release Kira's shoulder.

Kira didn't move, unable to put together what she'd seen. That fake had been an exact copy. Even down to what she was wearing.

She looked up at Finn in confusion. "How?"

Finn didn't seem to have any idea either, his expression as befuddled as Kira's.

A message appeared in her periphery vision tagged with the sender name—Allfather.

Kira hit play.

Odin's laughter sounded in her ear. "How did you like the present I left Jin? Pretty neat, huh? The holographic projector is of my own design, tailored specifically for the Tin Can. Anyway, I hope you get some good use out of it. Something has come up, but I'll be back for the second round of the race. Don't do anything I wouldn't."

"Odin's gone," Kira told Finn.

The oshota's lack of reaction told Kira there wasn't much love lost between the two.

"Eventually Baran will catch up to Jin and expose the trick," Kira said.

The holographic projector replicated her appearance, but it wasn't actually real. Baran would figure it out eventually. It might take a while, but the first thing he'd do when that happen would be to retrace his steps.

Kira planned to be long gone by then.

"We'll head to our bay and change our clothes then find a place for the night," Kira said, checking the hallway to make sure no one was waiting out there.

Seeing it was clear, she stepped into it before making her way to their bay.

"I thought you planned to rendezvous with Graydon and Wren," Finn said from behind her.

Kira paused in the act of keying in their code.

He was right; she had said that. What's more—she meant it.

"When I go back, it'll be under my own terms."

The privacy screen deactivated. Kira stepped inside, waiting to see if Finn followed. He hesitated on the threshold, studying her.

Kira lifted her eyebrows. "You coming?"

Finn narrowed his eyes. "Yeah. It seems I am."

Kira reactivated the privacy screen. "Good. I'd hate to have to fight you."

Finn slid her a sidelong look. "What makes you think you'd come out the winner in that scenario?"

"You're saying I wouldn't?"

Finn moved further into the bay. "There's a reason Graydon trusted me to act as your lone oshota. Normally, you need at least two shields for adequate protection."

Kira pressed her hand to the side of the mask, waiting as its seal released before pulling it away from her face. She set it on one of the work benches.

"You're saying you're a bad ass."

He lifted an eyebrow. "Whatever made you think I wasn't?"

Good point.

Finn's talent had always been obvious. He held every bit of the skills as any of Graydon's oshota. He was simply a little lower key about it.

If not for the fact his reputation had taken a hit after he left his former sword under less than ideal circumstances, he'd be heavily courted with Tuann trying to get him onto their side.

Instead, he'd agreed to be a nanny/bodyguard for Kira. She still wasn't sure what had compelled him to make that choice.

"What are we doing here?" Finn asked, looking around.

Kira took off her hoodie, throwing it onto one of the tables.

"Change of clothes and to decide our next steps. We'll have to find somewhere to spend the night."

She crossed to one of the unopened boxes, crouching in front of it and sliding off the top. A plain white shirt and a black leather jacket waited inside.

Jackpot.

Below them was an outfit similar to one you'd find in Haldeel fashion. That one she held out to Finn.

"Here, you go."

He took it with a grimace. "Are you serious?"

She nodded at the cloak he still wore. "Unless you plan to lose the armor."

His choice.

To her surprise, he looked like he was actually debating it.

Kira fished around in the box, lifting out a men's pair of pants and a hoody and shirt. She held the outfit out to Finn and waited.

With a marked hesitation, he took them.

They turned their backs on each other, changing quickly.

"Your hair will still draw notice," Finn said when they were done.

Kira's hair was a distinctive color. Anyone looking for her would be able to pull her out of a crowd in seconds. She reached into the box withdrawing a wig with spiky purple hair.

She set it on her head, tucking her real hair away. "Better?"

Finn grunted. "I suppose."

Kira paused to look him over. It was a little odd seeing him out of the armor, almost like something was off in the picture he presented. The clothes fit him well, however.

Except for the en-blade in a sheath at his waist, he could have been mistaken as human as long as one didn't get a glimpse of his ears.

"You'll do." Kira headed for the bay's panel, once again disengaging the privacy mode.

"Where are we going?"

"First, we're going to find a place to stay the night. Then tomorrow, we're going to visit an old friend."

Finn's frown deepened.

"You should be happy. You're about to experience what no Tuann has had the chance to. Tomorrow you get to meet another of your people's lost children."

NINE

A KNOCK PULLED Graydon from his observation of the night skyline outside his balcony.

"Enter."

The door opened and Raider appeared.

"What is it?" Graydon asked when the human lingered on the threshold, seemingly unwilling to step inside.

Graydon took a sip of *keeva,* contemplating the myriad of ways the day had not gone according to plan.

He should really be used to it by now. Kira made a practice of taking his assumptions and then turning them on their head. This was simply the latest in a long line of them.

He'd like to know how she managed to evade Baran, though. His oshota was one of the best trackers among the Tuann. For her to give him the slip was impressive.

When Baran had returned earlier with an update, he'd been beside himself. His frustration had been evident as was the blow to his pride. Graydon didn't even try talking him out of setting out to see if he could pick up her trail.

He knew a waste of time when he saw it.

Baran wouldn't be able to let this rest until he'd redeemed himself.

Graydon had already sent people to watch the station and look for her ship. There was no way she could leave without him knowing.

Though, something told him that was the last thing she wanted.

Her actions during the race gave her inner desires away. If she'd really wanted to go undetected, she never would have taken the chances she had.

He could only conclude she wanted to be found. Eventually, one way or another, she'd return to him.

He simply needed to wait.

Graydon swirled the *keeva* in his glass as he studied Raider. The man seemed more subdued than usual—as if he had a great weight on his shoulders.

When he looked up, Graydon saw his eyes were bloodshot and rimmed with red.

He'd been crying.

Graydon tensed, taking Raider's presence a little more seriously. "Why are you here?"

Raider moved further into the room. He was quiet as he seemed to debate with himself.

Eventually, he put a small data chip on the end table beside Graydon. "There's something you should probably see."

Graydon took the chip, setting his *keeva* down.

Raider didn't look at him, staring out the window instead.

Graydon set the chip on a console.

A video of Kira appeared in front of him.

"This was taken shortly after she and Elena left Ta Sa'Riel," Graydon said after it finished playing.

It was confirmation of what he'd suspected. Her flight from the planet had been unplanned and not entirely of her desire. She would return when she felt the girl was safe.

Graydon didn't think she expected Elena to fall into their hands. It meant the girl's caretaker was likely somewhere on the planet. It was the only conclusion Graydon could make for the sequence of events.

Raider turned toward the door. "You should watch the rest. Start at the beginning."

"Where are you going?"

"I've already seen it." Raider reached the doorway, leaving as abruptly as he'd come.

Graydon didn't dwell on the human's oddity, accessing the chip and selecting the oldest file on it.

A video of Kira formed in the air in front of him.

Everything in Graydon went still.

He inhaled once, then again as he fought to understand what he was seeing.

A gaunt and broken woman looked out at him, her expression dead. She was skin and bones, her eye sockets and cheeks sunken, causing the rest of her features to jut unnaturally under the skin.

Her skin was waxen and pale as if it hadn't seen the touch of sun in years. Her hair hung lank and limp around her face.

But it was the eyes that truly made this horrifying to watch.

The eyes that always seemed to tease and taunt, filled with more personality than Graydon had ever seen in another, were lifeless and dead. All vitality had been snuffed out of them.

Her expression was blank as she stared into the camera. If it hadn't been for the barest movement of her chest, Graydon would have assumed this was a picture rather than a video.

From off camera a voice said, "Kira, you have to say something. How will he understand if you don't explain?"

There was no shift in Kira's expression. Long moments passed before the video ended without Kira speaking a single word.

The next video started to play as Graydon remained motionless, that image burned into his brain.

It took several seconds for him to register the change in her appearance. She no longer seemed so broken. She was still underweight, but not to the same extent.

The way she held herself was brittle, as if she might break at any moment.

"It's been a long time, Raider." A wry smile stretched her lips. The movement seemed unnatural—as if this Kira was out of practice. "At least I managed to say something this time, right? Improvement."

Kira looked uncomfortable. "So, it seems Jin has been keeping secrets. Shocker, right?" She shot a wry glance at the camera. "You're going to flip when you find out."

Kira looked down. "I certainly did." She nodded to herself. "Anyway, Jin says the Consortium is doing a good job of hiding your and the others' whereabouts. Too bad they didn't take those steps sooner."

Bitterness touched her features before disappearing as quickly as it'd come. "It'll take us a little while to track you, but you should know we're on our way and we have something that belongs to you. See you soon."

Barely any time elapsed before a different Kira appeared again in the same seat, a background Graydon recognized behind her. It was the bridge of her ship.

This Kira was covered in blood and had that same dead look in her eyes. Once again, she stared into space for a long while as the minutes slowly slipped by.

"I fucked up, Raider." Kira touched a blood stain on her shirt, her expression threatening to crumble. "I thought if I could get your daughter to you, everything could go back to the way it was. But we can't go back, can we?"

A raw laugh escaped. "I can't even send this message to you now that I've mentioned her."

Kira dragged her hands over her face. Only when she dropped them did she speak again. "Ninety-six. That's how many people died today. Many of them by my hand. I can't even say all of them were trying to kill me either. For some, their only crime was knowledge of your daughter's existence."

Kira rubbed her hands on her legs. "I thought it'd be safe. They were in the war with us. Fought side by side. I never thought the Tsavitee would get close enough to turn them into their puppets. If the Tsavitee learn of Elena, they'd hunt her like they did her mother."

Kira shook her head and looked away. She tapped one finger on her knee before staring directly into the camera. "You're not going to forgive me for the decision I'm about to make. I accept that. Elena's not safe with me. I have a contact but their stipulations insist you can't be involved in her life. They're paranoid like that. Worse than Jin even."

Kira nodded, taking a deep breath as if steeling herself. "I promise you'll have the chance to hate me. I will reunite you with her." Her expression turned wry. "But it won't be today—or likely tomorrow either."

The video shut off, the next one already queued to play.

It was a long time later when Graydon sat and stared unseeing at the wall.

In an abrupt movement he hurled his glass, feeling nothing as it shattered.

Noor entered the room, a questioning look on his face.

"Out," Graydon ordered.

He found he wasn't in the mood for company, not even that of his most trusted.

Noor took note of the shattered glass but didn't say anything, nodding once and disappearing back the way he'd come. Graydon knew several of his oshota were standing guard along the perimeter of his room, ensuring none could harm him even in sleep.

Graydon couldn't remain seated any longer, standing in one sharp movement and pacing over to the balcony.

He stared into the night, struggling to make peace with what he'd seen. One thought stood out in his mind, resisting any effort to bury it. Kira could have died. From the state she'd been in that first video, she'd come very close. He didn't think anyone around her realized just how over the edge she'd been.

The loss of personal connections was viewed as a grievous injury to the Tuann. They had stories of those who'd survived the initial loss only to fade in the end.

Couple that with her repeated use of the Heaven's Wrath, which had likely damaged her *ki* and its channels even further, and it was a surprise she'd survived as well as she had.

Now that he'd seen her in that state, he couldn't make himself forget. It took an insane amount of will power and discipline to drag yourself back into the land of the living. To do so without building new connections was a level of hell Graydon didn't even want to imagine.

A simple tap on the shoulder would have been enough to send her into the abyss.

He'd have never known all that she was. Graydon could have lost her before she was ever his.

* * *

The next morning, Kira and Finn left their temporary lodgings wearing the same thing they'd worn when they'd left the race bay. Finn looked uncomfortable in his hoodie and jeans as the city came alive around them.

Kira's purple wig drew people's attention away from her face. Her jacket protected her from the faint chill of the morning hours as they merged into a crowd predominantly comprised of human and Haldeel. Every once in a while, Kira caught the odd Tuann as well.

The mood was festive, food hover stalls were parked along the side streets, traders among them.

Jin trailed them from the building tops, being careful to stay out of sight.

The battle over whether he'd hide out in her or Finn's clothes had been hard fought. The volume of the argument had ensured they'd need alternate lodging for the night.

When she'd finally conceded, Jin had crowed about his "ninja-like" stealth skills enough that Kira regretted her momentary lapse in judgment.

Although, she had to admit so far, he was doing pretty well in not drawing attention to himself.

"You hear from Odin?" Kira asked as she strolled down the sidewalk.

"Nope. I imagine Odin is doing Odin-like things."

"One of those things better be keeping an eye on Elena," Kira said, studying the crowd.

So far no one was paying undue attention to her and Finn, but it paid to be careful.

Jettie was supposed to be safe. The Haldeel were as uptight when it came to planetary security as the Tuann, but unlike the Tuann they had firsthand experience with the Tsavitee. They knew what to be on the lookout for.

That paranoia and devotion to safety precautions was one of the biggest reasons Kira had left her niece on this planet.

Granted, the current state of affairs opened a gap in their security, but with Almaluk hovering above, Kira didn't think the Haldeel would take any chances.

That still didn't stop her from being wary of a tail.

The person she was meeting today wasn't the forgiving sort. If Kira unknowingly led someone to her, she'd have Kira's head.

Kira picked a direction seemingly at random, meandering from one section of the city to the next. She strolled past water gardens and along canals, enjoying the beauty of the city.

Water and its artful manipulation were one of the most common landscape features. In the short time Kira had been on planet, it had come alive, the trees blooming with lilac-colored flowers as they draped their branches over ponds and lakes.

Kira didn't know if it was truly the time for these trees to be in bloom or if the Haldeel had tinkered with their biochemistry to spark a scene that was sure to be remembered long after the planet's visitors headed home.

Kira stopped in front of a shop's window, using the reflection to check the path behind her. So far, so good. There was no sign of followers.

Finn studied their surroundings with an alert gaze. He'd know the second they procured a tail.

It was now or never. She couldn't keep wandering around the city with no destination. Eventually she'd run into someone who would recognize her even with the wig she wore.

"You sure about this, Kira? She did say no Tuann. Taking Finn could cause problems for us," Jin said as if sensing her thoughts.

"He won't reveal their secrets."

"You and I know that, but do you think she'll believe that?"

Kira was thinking no.

That person was even more paranoid than Kira and Jin. That was saying something.

"If she didn't want an extra party, she shouldn't have let Elena gallivant across the universe," Kira retorted.

"I'm so glad you're going to be the one who explains that the reason you're bringing a Tuann to the meet is because she didn't keep a close enough eye on your niece. I wonder if they sell popcorn on this planet."

"You couldn't taste it anyway," Kira told him.

"You could eat it while you're showing her the error of her ways, and I'll ride your senses. Best of both worlds."

Kira stepped away from the window, heading into the part of the city often referred to by the locals as the refugee quarter. When the Haldeel had allowed those humans displaced by the war to immigrate, they hadn't placed any restrictions on where they could settle on Jettie.

Humans, however, were creatures of habit and often preferred to be surrounded by the familiar. That first wave had stuck together even after reaching the planet, settling within blocks of each other. When the next waves came, they settled around the humans who'd already started their new lives.

Since then, the refugee quarter had grown to encompass a small slice of the various human cultures. From the spicy cuisine of Galileo, to the creamy desserts of Merit and the smart fashion of New Lexington, all of it mixing into a melting pot and emerging as something entirely new.

As soon as you passed into the quarter, you knew. There was a certain atmosphere to the buildings marking their inhabitants as human. It wasn't that the area looked rundown or dirty—the Haldeel were fanatical about such things.

There was a certain charm to the quarter. It was filled with warmth and vitality. This was a place where people lived and loved and laughed.

It was perhaps one of Kira's favorite things about humans. They brought their personality into any space they occupied. Even a Haldeel city. The buildings were as beautiful as the rest of the city, the gardens still plentiful, but everything felt different.

"I'm noticing a theme in this scenario," Kira said as she made her way through the quarter. "I take all the risks while you reap the reward."

"That's how our relationship works. I thought you knew."

A tension in Finn grew as Kira made turn after turn. It was a countersurveillance method designed to expose any potential watchers. Following their meandering path would give the person up.

"We're being watched," Finn said softly.

He was good. She hadn't known if he'd realize or not.

Finn's gaze moved over a pair of children sitting on the edge of a balcony. To a casual bystander, they would appear to be enjoying the ice ball treat they each held.

Only someone as skilled in picking up surveillance as Finn would realize that their vantage point allowed them to see anyone entering or exiting the quarter.

Furthermore, they seemed preoccupied with Kira and her party. Nor were they the first or even second instance of children a little too engrossed in her passage.

"Spare some change, lady?" a young boy asked from the shadows of a porch.

Had he not drawn attention to himself, he and the girl by his side would likely have gone unnoticed.

His hair was even more shaggy than yesterday, a cowlick sticking up like a bird's nest on his head. Clear eyes regarded Kira with a demand.

Next to him, the girl tucked in close as if too shy to interact with strangers.

Finn's hand on Kira's arm stalled her approach. She looked up to find his expression cautious as he stared at the children.

"I've never heard of beggars on any planet belonging to the Haldeel," he warned.

There was good reason for that. The Haldeel had strict rules about employment. To stay on a planet—especially those who didn't have birth citizenship—they had to demonstrate an ability to contribute to society.

If you lost your job, another would be found for you. Should you reject the gifts the Haldeel procured in your name, you would be escorted off the planet.

The only exceptions were for those with injuries or mental health issues who needed time for recovery. Very rarely was an allowance made and usually only if that person had rendered extraordinary aid to society or the Haldeel in general.

Their rules were strict, but it also meant their citizens enjoyed the lowest level of poverty of any planet Kira had visited.

The boy made a tsking sound. "Who's begging? We want some money to buy treats for our friends."

Finn remained unmoved. "What about your parents?"

The boy's expression hardened, showing the junkyard dog he hid at his heart. Physically, he resembled an eight or nine-year-old, but that one glimpse showed the survivor he'd had to be.

Beside him, the girl flinched, her eyes dropping to the ground, but not before her mask slipped. Bright amber eyes, slitted like a snake's, appeared. It was brief, but her eyes nictated, once then twice, before they reverted to a more human appearance, muddy brown replacing the former amber.

Finn's stance stiffened as the children went from cute but harmless to potential threats.

The children above stopped licking their ice treats, sensing the change. Their focus moved to Kira and Finn.

"That child—"

Kira couldn't afford for him to finish that sentence.

She grabbed his arm and yanked him back. "If you want to live past the next few seconds, you'll keep any comments or questions to yourself."

Finn didn't look happy about the order, but he also didn't argue.

Kira approached the two children. "The war left a lot of orphans. Not all of the planets wanted to or could afford to support those they viewed as dead weight during the rebuilding efforts. The Haldeel accepted many of the castoffs and established orphanages for those children who were sent here."

As she explained, Kira held out the wrist with her id chip. The boy mirrored the action, allowing her to touch her wrist to his and transfer credits.

"Jettie's arrangements take into account the children's basic care. They don't go hungry, and they always have clothes, but they don't provide any of the comforts that a child may crave—such as candy or treats."

The boy turned and pressed his wrist against the girl's. She grinned and took off, disappearing into another alley in a blink of an eye.

"The Haldeel turn a blind eye to the orphans' money-raising skills," Kira finished.

The boy aimed a crooked grin at her that didn't hide the sly gleam in his eyes. "The newb doesn't suit you."

"He has his charms."

The boy grunted, unconvinced. "I think a mountain is much more your speed."

Someone had been talking to Elena. That was promising.

Jin had already informed her that Elena's MinMin, and therefore her niece, hadn't slept in her customary bed last night.

Kira wasn't too worried. Odin had already told her yesterday the handoff didn't take place. Elena had likely stayed in a safehouse Odin procured last night.

Nonetheless, the fact she'd passed information to Tommie pointed to the fact she was still safe.

The kid lifted his chin at her before sauntering after the girl.

"You should try the chai," the boy called over his shoulder. "I hear it's to die for."

When Kira looked up, she found the children on the balcony already gone.

"That girl wasn't human," Finn said.

Kira turned, resuming her walk. "No."

"She wasn't Tuann either."

This time Kira didn't answer.

They'd reached their destination, a cafe situated next to a burbling brook that snaked its way through and around the outdoor seating area. The jixy trees provided a colorful backdrop for the cafe goers to drink and enjoy the picturesque scenery.

Kira didn't bother with the hostess, instead crossing the little bridge and taking a seat in the far corner of the patio.

Finn waited as Kira settled into her seat.

He hovered over her, his tense energy interfering with her as she perused the menu.

She jerked her chin at the seat across from her. "Take a seat."

"I cannot protect you from there."

Kira considered him with irritation. Why wasn't she surprised about that response?

His reluctance was understandable. In his mind, she was his responsibility. For him, there was no greater purpose than serving as his sword's shield.

Kira understood. She really did.

But they couldn't continue in the same vein they had. Finn needed to bend and adapt.

Whether he knew it or not, he'd already begun the process. The human clothes he wore instead of his synth armor was the first step. She needed to see how far he could go.

He'd stuck with her through a lot. It was why she was considering letting him peek behind the curtain.

If there was one thing she'd learned over the past few months, it was that people were precious. Once gone, they couldn't be replaced.

Raider had taught her that.

She didn't want to be on the other end of a friend looking at her like she'd betrayed them. Finn didn't have the same history, but he'd shown he could be as stalwart as any of her Curs.

"I hate to break it to you, but I've never been in need of your protection," she informed him.

"Everyone needs someone watching their back."

"True."

Finn watched her carefully, not trusting her easy agreement.

"But if you continue hovering like that, I won't answer your questions." Kira nodded at the chair again. "You'll want to try the chai. The kid was right; it's world-changing."

Finn's hesitance was clear, but he reached for the chair anyway.

Kira took that as agreement, ordering a chai for both of them.

When she was done, she let her gaze drift over her surroundings. It always surprised her how serene and beautiful this place was. Her contact had made a good choice in designating it their meeting point.

"You know when Graydon first put you into my orbit, I thought you'd be easy to manipulate and discard," Kira revealed.

His appointment as her oshota had been as much about Graydon having a spy close to her as it was her safety.

"You surprised me. Not only were you good at your job, but you didn't reveal my secrets even when given the chance to do so." Even when her actions could be construed as a betrayal.

He'd remained steadfast, holding to the values of the oshota, even if she wasn't the sword he picked.

Kira respected loyalty.

It was all the more impressive given Finn's history with his previous sword. It didn't take a genius to know that a woman had left scars on his soul.

In his own way, he was as damaged as Kira.

She knew the cost of abandoning the things you'd built. Perhaps that's why she was acting outside the norm.

"You're leading up to something," Finn said.

A server approached, setting their cups in front of them. Kira leaned forward, cupping her hands around the mug and inhaling. The spicy, slightly sweet scent of chai wrapped around her.

She loved that smell.

Only when the server left did Kira nod. "There are some things I need to clarify."

She took a sip of the chai and closed her eyes at the taste.

When she opened them again, she nodded at the untouched mug in front of Finn. "Not going to try it?"

"I think I'll wait."

Kira shrugged. His loss. This stuff was amazing. The best beverage humans had ever made.

After another sip, Kira set the mug aside. "I need to know under what conditions you would divulge information you've learned."

Finn's expression froze before anger tightened the lines of his face. He glared. Not speaking. Not moving.

She'd expected this reaction. As someone who prided himself on his honor and devotion to duty, he would have seen her question as an insult.

"That you ask that shows how little you understand us," he said in a carefully controlled voice.

"The waters I wade in can't afford such things as easy trust. There can be no misconceptions between us. Your life and many others depend on it," Kira confided, not allowing his affront to shake her. "Before you answer, think carefully. Everyone has a line they won't cross. People they'll protect at the expense of all others. I need to know where your lines are."

Kira didn't have the luxury of trusting blindly. The secrets she held were too important to too many people.

Finn shoved down the anger in a display of discipline that was impressive. Not many would have remained seated after having the very core of who they were questioned in this manner. Most would have already walked away. Probably after ending any relationship they might have had with the person insulting them.

"For an oshota, there is no one higher in our loyalties than our sword. Not a lover, not a parent, not a child. When you pledge yourself as a shield, your sword comes first. Always."

Kira didn't believe that. The Tuann placed a high premium on the emotional bonds they developed. It was a necessity that kept them from going mad.

Most of Kira's current issues derived from the extreme isolation she'd inflicted on herself after the deaths of the Curs. Had she replaced some of those bonds with new ones, she might not have been in her current state.

Finn's definition of an oshota was counter to a Tuann's personality.

"I think you have a small misunderstanding about Tuann society," Finn informed her.

Kira lifted her eyebrows at him.

"You're surrounded by people like Graydon and Harlow who compel the loyalty of their peers. You think all oshota serve a sword. You're wrong." Finn picked up his chai. "In all of Roake there are fewer than forty people who compel an oshota's loyalty."

Kira blinked. That couldn't be right.

There were several thousand members in Roake's House. If Finn's statement was true, the numbers of those considered a sword were astronomically low.

Finn nodded. "Less than ten percent of those who have earned the right to call themselves oshota have swords they serve. Our vows are considered sacred. They're not something to take lightly because in the future, you might have to choose between your sword's life—and your loved ones."

An impossible choice.

Kira had seen such things in war when soldiers had to decide whether to carry out their orders or attempt a return to planets that were already in the midst of invasion.

"Why take it that far?" Kira asked.

"It's an ancient story that has its roots in our escape from the old masters."

Kira listened with interest. She'd already determined that those the Tuann called their old masters were also the ones pulling the Tsavitee's strings behind the scenes.

She'd only met one of their ilk, but that person had left an impression.

"The Tuann admire the strong," Finn started. "There is a reason for that. In the time before our records began, stories tell of those few individuals who fought to free us. Power wise they were no match for the old masters, but they had one thing their enslavers did not."

"Let me guess—the oshota."

Finn nodded. "Though that name didn't come until later. Our people have always been warriors, but in those days, there was no way for a single person to win against the combined might of our masters. Instead, warriors would find individuals who showed superior intellect and skill to pledge their loyalty too—often at great costs to themselves."

Finn leaned forward. "In that time, if their hearts wavered even a little because of external threats to family or life, the person they promised to protect would fall—taking with them the rest of the Tuann."

"I understand the necessity of unwavering loyalty in desperate times, but the Tuann aren't the same group of repressed clans. Why still take the oath to such lengths?" Kira asked.

"You think we're strong?" Finn shook his head. "We're not. We're as fractured and divided as ever. You haven't tasted the darker aspects of our society because Graydon and Harlow have been careful in what they exposed you to."

It took a moment of thought for Kira to put the pieces together. "The infighting between the Houses."

Finn nodded. "Yes. Roake has three blood vendettas with smaller Houses and a blood feud with a major House. Their enemies are many. The only reason Harlow was able to hold the House after your father's death was because of the oshota at his side."

"If an oshota's role is so rigid, then why did you allow Graydon to appoint you as my oshota?"

Except for a rather tense misunderstanding during their first meeting, Finn hadn't known her then. She found it hard to believe he'd make a commitment of that magnitude under those conditions.

"Instinct," Finn responded. "Like recognizes like."

Kira considered him as she played with the handle of her mug.

Finn clenched his hand into a fist. "My previous sword was a selfish, naive woman whose House spoiled her and gave her everything. It took me years to realize the extent of my mistake. Even then, I've never revealed what I learned while in attendance to her. Believe me when I say you're worth far more than she could have ever hoped to be."

Kira wanted to trust his words—if only because it would make things easier. But she knew too much about the human condition and how, when backed into a corner, someone might make desperate decisions they wouldn't otherwise.

Seeing her hesitation, Finn said, "I've been your oshota in truth since the ancestors' room on Ta Da'an."

He placed a hand on her wrist, right over the recently acquired Overlord bands hidden under her sleeves and the inhibitor she still wore. Unlike the symbols that only appeared on her body when in primus form, these remained long after they'd formed. As far as Kira could tell, they were a pair of permanent marks that no amount of scrubbing would get rid of.

She didn't quite understand their purpose, but with the way Harlow and his oshota had greeted their appearance, she was guessing they were of some importance.

Kira remembered the look on Finn's face when he'd first seen her primus symbols. The shock and disbelief. And underneath it all—awe.

"There is no set of circumstances where I would betray your trust. To do otherwise would violate my honor."

Kira drew her arm away, hiding it against her body. "I fear you're promising something you can't deliver."

But—she'd take a chance on him anyway. He'd earned some of her secrets.

Perhaps one of the small ones that wasn't really a secret at all if you knew where to look.

She picked up her chai again. "Children like Tommy and Grace often lack individuals who will ask questions if they disappear. Certain less scrupulous organizations see that as an opportunity. The universe is a vast place with many dark corners. Even if you take away an experiment's primary material, there are plenty of lesser versions of material running around—especially after a war."

Finn did an impression of a statue. "How did you learn of such things?"

Kira's smile was humorless as she took another sip. She'd like to know his reaction if he learned that the genetics those organizations used for their little experiments were derived from the Tuann's own children.

Not so much Kira and Jin's since she'd embarked on a one-woman mission to destroy every sample that existed, but the forty-three hadn't been nearly as thorough.

"You're the one who brought the children to this planet," Finn said suddenly.

Kira paused. Very good. He'd put that together faster than she thought he would. She'd have to be careful with him in the future.

"Why are they being used to run messages and act as spies?" he asked with a sudden scowl.

"Protective. At least you picked the reason for your fall well," a feminine voice said from above them.

Kira sat back in her chair and looked up with an arrogant smile at the woman standing beside her radiating disapproval. "I thought it appropriate given the message you had my niece deliver."

The woman was dressed like a Haldeel. She was covered from head to toe, not a single bit of skin showing. Not even an eyelash.

Her robes were knotted firmly under her bust. They fell in a wide skirt around her lower half. Gloves covered her hands up to the robes' sleeves. She also held a parasol over her head, a length of gauzy material pulled down to shield her face.

From a distance, no one would be able to tell if she was human or Haldeel.

"Dismiss your dog," the woman ordered. "We have business to discuss."

"Do we?" Kira stretched her legs out in front of her as she made herself more comfortable.

"I can always kill you now without giving you the opportunity to explain yourself. Your choice."

TEN

KIRA HELD A hand up, signaling Finn to stay seated and not do the thing he so obviously wanted to do.

He stopped halfway out of his seat, one hand on his en-blade.

"It's a test," Kira informed him. "Don't fail it."

Finn contemplated Kira before shifting his gaze to the woman, torn between two opposing desires. The need to eliminate the threat and the knowledge that she was likely right.

After a moment, his grip relaxed, and he took his seat again, picking up his chai and taking a sip. Surprised pleasure registered as he stared in fascination into his mug.

"Your dog is smarter than I gave him credit for."

"And you're still as rude as ever," Kira returned.

"Then we are a matched pair."

Fair enough.

"Let's go." The woman pointed at Finn. "He stays here."

The woman walked away, gliding smoothly over a bridge and into the tree-lined park next to the cafe.

A protest formed on Finn's lips as Kira stood to follow.

"She's right. Stay here. I'll be back soon."

Kira crossed the bridge to join the woman. To her relief, Finn didn't move from the table as they moved deeper into the park, away from his senses.

"Why did you bring one of them here?" the woman demanded as soon as Kira caught up.

Kira raised an eyebrow. "That's an interesting way of putting it. Are you enemies now?"

"Everyone is a potential enemy. I thought you knew that." There was cold disapproval in the woman's voice as if she couldn't believe how naive Kira was.

The woman's movements were graceful as she strode along the pebbled path, trees covered in lilac blooms framing either side.

"How could you let him come? You know what they would say," the woman asked again when Kira didn't immediately answer.

Yes, Kira had a fairly good idea how that would have gone.

They'd start by ranting about her stupidity, then segue into a detailed list of the danger she'd brought to their door. If she was lucky, they would stalk off in a huff. If she wasn't, she'd be forced to listen to a myriad of threats. Anything stemming from her death to the deaths of those she cared about.

Since most of the people she cared about were already gone, those threats were a little lacking these days.

Finally, they'd issue a warning. Any attempt at sticking to her agenda would be stonewalled. She'd leave the encounter frustrated and out of sorts.

"That's why I'm talking to you, Selene," Kira said.

A sound that was half-frustrated, half-humorous came from underneath Selene's veil.

"You're the one who asked to set up this meet," Kira reminded her. "You had to know he was in my orbit and wasn't likely to let me attend a clandestine meeting all on my lonesome."

While Kira might not have known about the Tuann and their link to her, she wouldn't go so far as to think the others were as in the dark.

She'd elected to retreat from the rest of society, but they'd embedded themselves deep into the different populations. Anything the humans or Haldeel knew would have crossed their path at some point—including the description of the Tuann and their abilities.

It would have been nice if someone had clued her in to those facts before her first encounter with the Tuann. Perhaps then she wouldn't have been taken so off guard.

The fact they'd let her be blindsided was something they'd have to address at a later date.

"What is this about?" Kira asked, struggling to avoid the sense of frustration she always got when dealing with one of the forty-three.

Once, they had been as close as brothers and sisters. Bonded and forged in the same fire. It should have given them common ground.

Instead, Kira couldn't help but feel she was out of step with them anytime their paths crossed. Her reaction to events was always different than theirs. It wasn't easy feeling like an outcast even among the people she should have been closest to.

The Curs had filled that void, providing for a short time the family and sense of solidarity she needed until they too were gone.

"Did you tell him?" Selene asked, coming to a stop at the edge of a small pond, a set of wide, flat stones emerging from its surface to provide a path across.

"I didn't have to. Elena so helpfully delivered the message you and the rest entrusted her with." There was a bite in Kira's tone.

She still wasn't happy about that fact. Bad enough the rest came out of hiding once in a blue moon to make demands on Kira, but she'd be damned if they did the same to her niece.

A heavy sigh came from under the veil. "I was afraid that was what happened."

"You're supposed to keep her safe from that shit," Kira snapped. "She's not a pawn for them to use in their giant game of chess. I thought you understood that."

"You assume your niece is willing to sit safely on the sidelines. She's no more likely to be controlled than you or the youngest." Amusement touched the woman's voice. "Speaking of—where is the youngest."

"Around."

Kira couldn't be quite sure where. It'd been a while since she last saw Jin. Likely, he'd seen something interesting and gone to investigate.

"You've changed," Selene observed.

"People have a way of doing that."

Selene stopped and faced Kira. "Other people. Not you. You've always been fairly consistent. Time was you would never have allowed one of their dogs to watch your every move."

Kira carefully controlled her reaction to that statement. "It's nice having someone to watch my back for a change."

She knew her small dig had landed when the other woman looked away and silence built between them.

Yeah. She thought that might sting.

The forty-three didn't have a lot of ground to cast stones. Kira remembered approaching them and begging them for help after she'd learned Elise's fate.

Never once during the war did she ask for their help. Not when the Consortium was losing. Not when she realized that every use of the burst brought her one step closer to death.

She'd made a deal. She'd honor it.

They had no love for humanity, and Kira understood why. Humanity hadn't done anything for them. Throw in the fact there'd been several humans amid the Tuann and the Tsavitee in that place who were only too happy to hurt them, and it was easy to see why they wanted to exist apart.

When she realized the Tsavitee had Elise, she'd gone to them, thinking this was different. Elise was one of their own in a way she and Jin could never be.

She'd thought this time, they'd help.

Only they hadn't helped. They'd turned her away, leaving Elise in hell and Kira to struggle alone.

"Kira." There was a wealth of guilt and regret in that one statement.

Kira relented. "I know."

Selene was one of the few who'd disapproved of the verdict, but she had demands on her that couldn't be shirked. Too many small lives counted on her for protection for her to abandon them for any reason.

"How are the children?" Kira asked, extending a small olive branch.

"Tommy and Grace look good."

A small huff came. Thin hands came up to part the veil, tucking it on top of the parasol's brim. The heart-shaped face she revealed was a study in perfection, its beauty heightened by the fairy tale-esque setting. Deep, dark eyes that held a serene wisdom peered into Kira's. Over one shoulder a loose braid draped almost to Selene's waist.

Like Kira's, Selene's ears were docked, making her appear more human. The procedure had come much later than Kira's, happening long after her escape and shortly after arriving on Jettie. The more human-like appearance allowed her to blend and meant no one questioned her when she established her orphanage.

Lips painted a deep red parted in a grimace. "I wish they would stop begging."

Kira lifted a shoulder. "I don't blame them. Just because we never had treats doesn't mean they should go without."

"They'll draw attention to themselves."

Kira pretended to shudder. "Oh no, not that."

Selene's frown was repressive. "All it takes is the wrong person noting their differences, and everything we've built will be gone."

Kira rolled her eyes, unable to argue. "Then buy them the treats yourself. Is it money? Do you need more?"

Kira wasn't exactly rolling in it, especially since she'd spent the last months not working, but she could figure something out.

"I hate the fact you get to be the cool aunt who sweeps in and spoils them," Selene said sourly.

Kira grinned. "No one told you to be a den mother."

The woman rolled her eyes.

Kira sobered. "How is the last batch of children I sent you?"

"About as expected." Seeing Kira's concern, she said, "They're adjusting."

The orphanage and the children hiding in plain sight within its doors were the real reason the woman couldn't involve herself in Kira's crusade. She protected the lost little foundlings Kira came across, providing them a safe harbor and ensuring those who'd hurt them would never find them.

Some of the children in the woman's care were human. Most were not.

It was a carefully kept secret even from the rest of the forty-three who would not approve of their extracurricular activities.

"Why are you here anyway?" Selene asked. "You could have dropped Elena on the station and left."

Kira looked away, knowing the answer wasn't likely to win her any points.

The prolonged silence made the other woman's eyes narrow.

"We've found evidence Elise might be here," Kira finally said.

Anger built in Selene's expression. "I thought you were done with that."

Had she really?

"You seem better," Selene explained in the face of Kira's skepticism. "You feel healthy again."

That caught Kira's attention. The woman understood the intricacies of the body much better than Kira did. Her use of her *ki* practically demanded that level of insight.

Most of what the forty-three did with their soul's breath came to them naturally, in the same way moving a muscle would for a human.

If Selene sensed a difference, Kira could only believe she was right.

The treatments with the Tuann and her time near the Mea'Ave were working, restoring some of what had been lost.

"Can't you leave this alone?"

"You know I can't," Kira said. "I owe it to Elena and Elise."

Frustration flashed across Selene's face. "You realize she won't be the woman you knew. If they got their tentacles into her mind, she's their creature now. Are you prepared for that?"

"If that's the case, I'll have a different kind of promise to keep."

Kira hoped it didn't come to that. The act of ending Elise might finish driving Kira over the abyss.

"I can't believe you brought this matter to my doorstep, knowing the lives I protect." Selene's mouth was a thin slash, anger tightening her features.

"You say that like I had a choice in this. I followed her here, not the other way around."

"I noticed you also have your changeling close. You should be careful. Their kind is untrustworthy," Selene said.

"Then they'll fit right in with the rest of the universe," Kira retorted.

She wasn't going to entertain recriminations regarding Odin. Not again. They'd already had this fight, and Selene knew where Kira stood.

A faint screech interrupted them.

They fell silent, each straining their senses to pick up on the disturbance.

Kira didn't hear anything for a long moment. She plucked a tendril of the *ki* that coiled in her center, sending it out into the world. It went easily, no sign of the pain that felt like razor blades sawing at her insides.

It was a small victory, but recovery often was.

For several seconds, Kira caught nothing odd.

Gradually, the sound of many bodies moving in unison reached her. Worse, they were heading directly toward Kira and the woman.

Selene covered her nose with a grimace. "Tsavitee taint."

Kira cast her a sidelong look. When had Selene become so theatrical? Selene would know what she was picking up wasn't an actual scent, though it may have presented as a smell due to her brain's interpretation of what it felt.

Selene glared at Kira. "They followed you."

"We don't know that."

The woman sent her a look that said to get real.

Kira started to respond when she heard her name being called. She frowned. That had sounded a lot like Jin.

Branches rustled. Jin burst into view.

"Kira! We have a little bit of a situation!"

He beelined toward her, a swarm of shriekers erupting from the trees in his wake.

"You're right. They didn't follow you," Selene corrected.

The creatures were humanoid, loping across the ground on all fours, their backs abnormally hunched. Their heads were bald and their skin a mottled color that included violets, greens, and some hard to determine mix of colors that resembled the ponds and lakes Kira had traveled past on the way to the cafe.

The myriad of colors was a camouflage technique and varied for every swarm. They evolved based on their surroundings. Highly adaptive, shriekers bred extremely fast.

Kira hadn't seen any since the war. Typically, the Tsavitee sent them in advance of their first strike. Their purpose was to soften up the ground troops and make it easier for the main invading force. They tended to chew through civilian populations, ambushing from the shadows for weeks before anyone realized they were there.

"What did you do?" Kira shouted as Jin zoomed toward her.

"I don't know," Jin wailed. "I was exploring, and then I was being chased."

"You couldn't have lost them first? Why'd you have to bring them here?"

"Don't you think I tried?" Jin shouted plaintively. "They're exceedingly difficult to shake."

Selene leaned toward her as the shriekers pounded toward them. "Do you think they're here for you or me?"

Kira shook her head. "It doesn't matter either way."

They shared a look.

There was no way Kira could leave Elena here now. Nor would the woman allow her to.

As if obeying some mental signal, the swarm split to circle around Kira and Selene.

"I forgot how much I hate these things." Selene raised her hand, a small distortion in the air beginning a few centimeters away from her fingertips.

It built, growing quickly only to pop like a bubble when Kira pushed Selene's hand down. As much as she appreciated the offer to help, it would be a mistake.

"Tuann who will recognize the use of *ki* are everywhere, to say nothing of Haldeel surveillance. Unless you want to be outed, I suggest you keep your talents to yourself," Kira advised.

Selene's expression softened. "You make it so hard to deny you when you do things like this, little sister."

"Enough jaw jacking; more killing," Jin roared as he threw himself into the midst of the shriekers. Lightning bolts shot from him, hitting several bodies.

Kira grinned as she stepped forward, already sliding into the necessary mental space she'd need for the coming task. A place where mercy was as unwelcome as fear.

"When you see an opportunity to escape, take it," she ordered.

There was no more time to talk after that.

Kira darted forward, palming the small blade she'd hidden on her in the same instant. She'd prefer one of the swords House Roake had given her, but at least she wasn't unarmed for this encounter.

The swarm wailed, rearing upright and slashing at her with their two-inch claws.

Fighting with a knife was different than fighting with a sword. For one thing, she didn't have the reach she would have with a sword. Timing was everything.

Kira stayed light on her feet, dodging in and out of range of the shriekers, as she slashed, each move delivering a precise, lethal blow.

Kira pivoted as a shrieker dove in low. She stepped out of the way, slicing a long line along his spine. It wasn't a killing blow, but she didn't want to chance having her only weapon taken from her if it got stuck in a body.

Movement on her left had her swaying to her right. A shrieker swung at her. Kira blocked with one arm, stepping inside his guard to plunge her knife in his throat.

Hot blood splashed on her hand.

That was three.

She stepped back to find a small circle had formed around her. Her expression turned cold as the shrieker she'd killed folded to the ground.

Kira lifted her head. "Who's next?"

They shrieked and pounced.

Kira became a whirling dervish, never remaining anywhere long as she sliced and hacked her way through them. Blood lust rose until Kira lived for the swing of the blade and the feel of blood splashing.

Shriekers weren't difficult to kill. Their primary danger lay in their numbers. There was a reason they were called the enemy of a thousand cuts. Bring one down, and there would be another to take its place in a never-ending cycle, leaving behind only despair when you realized your fate.

A smart Kira would run, bleeding off their numbers and trying to divert their attention to other victims.

But if she fled into the more densely populated parts of the city, civilians would die. The Haldeel peacekeepers would eventually arrive, but by then, it would be too late.

Kira could take care of herself. Others couldn't.

She danced around, feeling wind scrape by her as she narrowly avoided being disemboweled.

She returned the shrieker's attempt by embedding her blade in his back. The shrieker's scream of agony brought a smile to her face.

That's it. That was what she wanted to hear.

She yanked the blade free, slashing it across the shrieker's throat in the next second.

Kira took stock.

Bodies littered the clearing. Many of them a result of her rampage. A few were Jin's contribution, showing scorch marks.

She pointed her blade at Jin. "This is your fault. Don't think I've forgotten that."

"If you have breath to talk, you have breath to kill faster."

He swooped on a clump of shriekers, lightning bolts erupting from his body.

"How do you like me now?" Jin crowed. "Not the easy opponent you thought, huh?"

Kira killed two more shriekers who decided to test her patience.

"Maybe if you'd done a little more of that sooner there wouldn't still be this damn many."

Jin sputtered. "How do you think I ended up pissing them off in the first place?"

A shrieker padded toward Selene from behind. Selene slid out of its way in one graceful movement, bringing the parasol down hard on his neck. There was a crack, and the shrieker slumped to the ground.

"Perhaps we should focus on the matter at hand," Selene suggested.

"Is that a parasol?" Jin asked. "What is it made of? Steel?"

Amusement touched Selene's eyes as her lips curved up. "Something like that. It's an invention of my own design. This is the first time I've used it. Quite effective I might add."

Instinct warned Kira. She leapt into the air, her body arching as she flipped over the shrieker that had thrown itself into her blind spot.

She landed, stabbing into the base of its neck in the next moment.

"You can handle it from here," Selene said, looking around. "I'll take my leave."

Kira hesitated before nodding in acknowledgment. Selene had stayed far longer than Kira had expected, dealing with more than a few of the pesky bastards. It would be greedy for Kira to ask her to stay to the end and risk exposing her to the Haldeel.

"Maybe stay home until the quorum is over," Kira suggested.

"You worry about yourself. Me and mine know what to do. We're not nearly as likely as you to go tilting at windmills that are already on fire."

With that, Selene glided across the steppingstones of the pond and disappeared into the trees.

Kira and Jin moved to block the shriekers who would have followed, cutting through their ranks with zero mercy.

A long time later, Kira's arms and body screamed. Exhaustion pulled at her, demanding a break. Just a little one. Enough to catch her breath.

Kira felled another shrieker, whirling to meet the next, only to find nothing there.

She panted as she looked around, noting the mounds of dead bodies. Nothing moved except her and Jin. The previously beautiful flowers were now speckled with red.

"I think that's it," Jin said, listing to the side. He sounded weary as he came to rest on a tree branch.

Kira's hand with the blade remained in a defensive position as she weaved on her feet. "Did any escape?"

She held her breath, praying he said no.

If a single shrieker escaped, they'd have to go after them. Otherwise, this would happen again. Shriekers reproduced through parthenogenesis, which was a fancy way of saying they didn't need a partner to multiply.

There was also the small matter that where there were shriekers, there was a handler waiting in the wings. How else would the Tsavitee know when a target was adequately softened.

"No," Jin said when Kira had resigned herself to having to embark on a foot chase. "We're clear."

Kira's shoulders slumped. Thank the universe above for small mercies.

Several seconds passed before Jin summoned enough energy to rise from the branch. "There's at least sixty bodies here."

It wasn't as big as the swarms they'd seen during the war—some of which had reached thousands—but it was much bigger than a swarm on a Haldeel planet had a right to be.

"You think the Haldeel know they're compromised?"

Kira shook her head. If they didn't before, they would now. No way was this going to be covered up. Eventually a civilian would stumble on the scene and report it. There'd be no hiding from the truth then.

"How did they get here?" Kira asked.

The Haldeel were extremely advanced. They had warning systems in place that should have made it impossible to smuggle a shrieker embryo onto the planet.

The fact the swarm was here and had grown to this size was concerning.

Kira started retracing her steps toward the cafe. "Come on. Finn likely is on his way. We should depart before we're seen."

"Too late. Several energy signatures belonging to Haldeel weapons are approaching quickly. The fight must have alerted their peacekeepers."

Of all the luck.

"What do you want to do?" Jin asked.

Fleeing was pointless. The entire area was studded with surveillance equipment. Getting off-planet without the Haldeel catching them was pretty much impossible since they'd still have to use a Haldeel dropship. Leaving now would only make them appear guilty.

"We'll wait and answer their questions," Kira said unhappily.

Finn wasn't going to be pleased that the moment she was out of his sight she'd ended up in a fight for her life.

Kira took out a cloth and began to clean her weapon. Only when it was as clean as she could get it in current conditions did she tuck it into its hiding place.

The rest of her she gave up as a lost cause.

At least none of the blood was hers this time.

She finished just as three Haldeel sped into view, the long, wide skirts of their robes frothing at the quick movement of their appendages.

They stopped abruptly, staring at the scene of the massacre in wide-eyed disbelief.

Kira lifted a hand, smiling at them awkwardly. "Hey there."

The three reacted, leveling weapons that held an uncanny resemblance to a trident in her direction. Kira's welcoming smile stiffened.

It was never a good thing to be on the wrong end of a trident. Depending on its user, the trident had a variety of abilities. She'd seen them fire powerful laser bolts that could rip a hole in a Tsavitee drone. She'd also seen the Haldeel use them as staffs or bury the tips in an opponent and use that opponent as a battering ram.

The Haldeel might prefer peace, but they could be as violent and merciless as any of the other races. They simply hid it better behind a facade of serenity.

Kira held her hands up, trying to seem harmless.

It was probably a wasted effort with the evidence of what she'd done strewn all around the clearing, some of it soaking into her white shirt and smeared across her jacket.

"Are you responsible for this?" The tallest of the Haldeel jerked his trident to indicate the bodies. The base color of his skin was brown and he had forest green markings that encroached on the sides of his jaw and neck.

Kira grimaced. "I guess you could say that, but in my defense, they attacked first."

They took in the many bodies again.

"Just you?" the Haldeel asked.

Kira indicated Jin. "He helped."

Their gazes went from Jin to the bodies whose only evidence of injury were the singe marks marring their flesh.

"Incoming from your three o'clock," Jin murmured.

Finn sped into the clearing, freezing at the sight. A second later, he aimed an accusing glare at Kira.

Her gaze slid away. "I can explain."

Finn's expression didn't shift.

Without hesitation, Kira pointed at Jin. "It's all his fault."

Jin protested.

Kira shrugged at him. "It really is."

"Some friend you are," he shot back.

"In situations like these, it's every person for themselves."

"I'll remember this," he muttered.

"You should. It's your rule."

The leader walked forward, interrupting. "You're going to need to come with us while we sort this out. "

Kira moved slowly, careful not to startle the Haldeel as she withdrew her blade and set it on the ground.

"He needs to come too." The Haldeel indicated Jin.

Reluctantly, Kira nodded. "J1N, power down."

Although Jin would give the appearance of shutting down, in reality he would still maintain full control, aware of everything going on around him.

"I appreciate your cooperation," the leader said.

The Haldeel beside him shifted. "*Za,* I'm still sensing an energy output."

Kira cursed internally. She'd hoped they wouldn't pick up on that.

"Jin has backup systems. That's probably what you're sensing."

Kira held her breath, waiting as the Haldeel consulted each other.

An entire conversation passed without a word being exchanged.

At last, a Haldeel with cobalt markings withdrew a device from a pocket. A buzz invaded her mind seconds before a wall slammed between her and Jin.

The place Jin occupied in her psyche went dark.

Kira flinched, horror and fear rising.

"What did you do?" Kira demanded harshly.

Finn advanced on her, a warning in his face telling her to remain calm.

"Nothing permanent," the leader assured her. "We erected a field around your drone so that its energy output could not affect its surroundings. In the event you are deceiving us and he didn't power down, the field will make any attempts to move impossible."

"He's not damaged, then?" Kira asked, unable to keep the note of fear out of her voice.

The leader inclined his head. "He is not."

For the first time since Jin's presence had disappeared, Kira drew a full breath. She could handle that. As long as she knew it wasn't permanent.

She closed her eyes, concentrating.

Once again, she butted up against that invisible wall. Her mental state trembled.

With an iron will, she gathered herself. He was there. It was faint, almost impossible to register, but it was him.

Kira opened her eyes and nodded. "How does this work? Will there be handcuffs?"

The Haldeel leader considered her with patience. "As long as you don't have intent to bring harm to others or yourself, I think we can forgo such extreme measures."

Kira stared at him. "That's rather nice of you."

Much nicer than the methods that usually greeted her in a situation like this.

The Haldeel's smile was faint as he stepped to the side and gestured for her to join him as his companion moved forward to retrieve Jin.

Finn shot the Haldeel a challenging look. "I'm going too."

The Haldeel leader's lips twitched. "That is acceptable. I suspect before this is over it'll be us who owe you the apology."

Kira contained her snort. That would be a first.

ELEVEN

A VEIN JUMPED in Finn's temple as he fell into step beside her. "Next time, I would very much like to be apprised *before* you do something death-defying."

"Why? You think you can stop me?"

His eyes narrowed to slits. "No, so I can mentally prepare."

"Aren't these kinds of things better as a surprise?"

In his place, she'd rather not have advance notice when the person she'd vowed to protect did something dangerous.

There was a crack in Finn's facade, exposing the boiling anger seething beneath the surface. "No, it isn't."

Kira shrugged. "Suit yourself."

It wasn't like Kira planned this. There was no way she could have known Jin would return with a swarm of shriekers. If she had, she would definitely have invited Finn to the party.

Partners did things like that. They shared in their brushes with death.

"Why were you so late?" Kira asked, eyeing him.

No way did she believe he hadn't heard the fight. Shriekers weren't exactly quiet during a hunt.

"I got hung up. It delayed my arrival," Finn said in a tone that didn't invite questions.

Kira lapsed into silence as the Haldeel marched them along the city streets, drawing stares as they passed. Kira spotted children she suspected of belonging to the orphanage. They watched with fascination before disappearing into the crowds around them.

At least, Selene would soon be apprised of Kira and Jin's survival.

Her hand brushed a spot of blood on her black jacket and drew a grimace.

Now she knew why everyone was so curious. It wasn't often the Haldeel escorted someone splattered with blood through the streets of the city.

The Haldeel turned right at the next intersection, toward the spaceport. Next, they took a left.

Kira was getting a sinking feeling that she knew where they were heading. A place she'd done her utmost to avoid. The Spire. Cultural center of the capital and currently a hotbed of political activity.

If Graydon was anywhere, that was where he'd be.

Her shoulders slumped. The destination made sense. After investigating what happened in the clearing, the Haldeel guards' jobs would be a lot easier if they could immediately turn her over to the higher powers of her race.

Lovely. Just lovely.

Sure enough, soon, they passed the arches framing the avenue. Finn shot her a look that she ignored as they marched over the still water, flowers submerged beneath its surface.

If Finn had been anyone else, perhaps someone less serious, there would have been a pep in his step. And why wouldn't there be? Finn was getting exactly what he wanted—Kira back in the bosom of their people.

The Haldeel leader glanced sideways at them. "You're both Tuann?"

"What gave it away?" Kira asked.

"Just a feeling."

The Haldeel's lingering glance in Finn's direction told Kira exactly who was responsible for that feeling.

Turns out you could take the oshota out of the synth armor, but they'd still be oshota. It was in the way they moved, the hyper-awareness and sense of purpose they carried with them.

They stopped feet from where the avenue ended and a perfectly circular lake began. From its center, an imposing spire rose. At a distance, the spire appeared to be one structure, when it was actually three separate buildings that intertwined like lovers, yet never quite touched. A series of glass walkways connected the structures.

The rest of the city butted up against the lake's edges, surrounding the unexpected oasis of calm and serenity.

The Haldeel waited patiently as the glass-like surface of the lake began to froth. Out of the depths, small flat panels rose until they jutted millimeters out of the water. They interlocked, snapping together one after another.

The Haldeel leader didn't wait for it to finish assembling before he glided onto the pathway, leaving Kira and the rest to follow.

Kira stepped onto its surface, expecting it to be slippery. Surprisingly, it was not. The surface had already dried in the short time since it had risen from the lake. A good thing, too, since there weren't exactly railings to prevent her from sliding off.

The gentle waves caused by the walkway's rise subsided, allowing glimpses of several silvery fish the length of her leg. They darted beneath a wide-leafed plant that looked like the bastard cousin of a lily pad.

"I would advise not falling in," the leader said without turning around. "The lake is filled with the *buka*. They have very sharp teeth and consider Tuann and human flesh a delicacy."

Kira's footsteps slowed. "You surrounded your cultural center with a moat and filled it with carnivorous fish?"

Talk about sending a mixed message.

Kind of like saying "Look at the beautiful things we can create—but beware, our pets might eat you."

No wonder the Tuann were willing to play nice with the Haldeel.

"The *buka* are beautiful. Why would we deprive our guests of their grace?" This time the Haldeel aimed a wide smile at Kira, flashing the sharp, serrated teeth of a predator. "Besides, they're quite tasty."

Kira nodded, feeling like the entire conversation was a bit surreal. "Practical."

But Kira wouldn't expect anything else from the Haldeel. There was a certain poetry in the way they chose to shape their surroundings. They chose beauty and then edged it with thorns.

The thought made her a bit nostalgic for Jin and the quip he would have made in this situation.

She didn't have time to dwell on the feeling as they reached the end of the walkway, passing through the base of the spire. The three structures surrounded them.

From a distance, the spire was impressive. It was even more so when you appreciated it from the worm's eye view.

"Wow," Kira breathed, looking up.

She felt like she was at the bottom of an intricate, twisting well, the sky high above.

She could have stayed right there for hours, soaking in the calm peace that seemed to radiate in this space.

The leader paused in front of a massive opening stretching two stories high. "You're very kind. This way, please."

Kira tore herself from the view, following the leader through the entrance. The building closed around her, muting the gentle sound of the outside world.

Large windows offered a view of the lake and the structure's inner atrium. Shadows danced across the floor giving a feeling of movement and adding to the sense of being underwater, the world hushed and serene.

They crossed the atrium, heading toward a pair of Haldeel standing guard in front of a solid wall.

Like the Haldeel peacekeepers escorting them, the guards held tridents. Their faces were neutral as the leader stopped in front of them, saying nothing. Verbally at least. Standing beside him, she couldn't see what he was saying with his hands, but the reactions of the guards made it clear he was conveying something.

They looked past the leader to Kira, respect filling their expressions.

As one, they stepped aside, tapping the butt of the trident against the wall in tandem. There was a pause as they waited, facing the blank space. A door formed, the wall folding away square by square until it was big enough for all to step through.

The leader turned to Finn. "If you would please wait here."

Finn's body locked.

Kira could already hear his refusal as she patted his shoulder. "I'll be fine."

"You realize the last time you said something to that effect you ended up in a fight for your life against a swarm of shriekers," Finn said through gritted teeth.

Kira saw his point.

"I'd like to say I'll get better about that, but chances are I won't." Kira grinned and winked. "Welcome to the team. Also, I hardly think the Haldeel dragged us all the way here just to kill me. Much easier to do that out there."

"Very wise words." The leader inclined his head in a partial bow.

That answer didn't make Finn happy, but he was also smart enough to know when he wasn't going to win the battle.

They were standing on Haldeel territory—in the very heart of their power. If they wanted Finn to wait here, here Finn would wait. There was nothing either of them could do about it.

"Fine, but try to avoid having anyone kill you while you're gone."

Kira lifted a shoulder as she stepped past the entrance. "I'll try, but my track record isn't exactly the best."

The wall reassembled, blocking Kira's last view of Finn's sour expression.

"I guess that's that," she muttered to herself.

"You will come to no harm in our care, *za*," the leader assured her.

Kira's smile was wry. "I wasn't too worried."

This wasn't her first experience with the Haldeel. She'd found as long as you treated them with respect, they'd do the same to you.

Their politics were a tad warped and vicious, but the same could be said of human and Tuann politics as well.

The leader stopped in front of the entrance to a room Kira could only describe as the nicest conference room she'd ever visited.

White floors were offset by glass windows offering a view of an ornamental garden. Pebbled paths wound through the garden's center, trees not much taller than Kira draped over artful ponds, their fronds reminding her of weeping willows, if a willow's branches were twisted like a braid.

The colorful garden helped offset the sterility of the white room. There was a white table in the shape of a crescent in the center and charcoal gray seats that looked comfortable surrounding it.

It was a far cry from the drab holding cell she'd imagined.

"If you would," the leader gestured inside.

Kira complied, looking around with interest as a Haldeel stepped into the room after her, carrying Jin in one hand. He set her friend on the table before departing.

"Please wait here until we have finished verifying your story." The Haldeel pointed to a basin that had a waterfall of water cascading down into it. "You can clean up over there if you wish."

He didn't linger any longer, touching the butt of his trident to the floor. The door reassembled, cubes crawling into place as they cut off the only exit.

Guess they didn't really plan on giving her an option. Not that she blamed them. If she found someone standing over a swarm of shrieker bodies, she'd probably want to do her due diligence too.

Kira didn't waste time searching for a way to open the door. She already knew she wouldn't find one. Even if she did, where would she go? Chances were the Haldeel had placed guards outside, just in case.

Knowing she was likely under some kind of surveillance, Kira crossed to the table, setting a hand on Jin.

Like this, he almost appeared to be sleeping.

Except, Jin was never this still, and he never slept. It was both his blessing and his curse not to be bound by the same limitations as an organic. He could avoid the time wasted by sleep, but he also never experienced the escape it provided.

Sleep was where biologicals processed their emotions. It offered a chance to allow the psyche to heal and evolve. Without it, people tended to go crazy.

Lucky for Jin, he had his connection to Kira. It allowed him a limited biofeedback that mitigated some of the issues stemming from not being able to rest. Otherwise, she very much would have feared for the stability of his mental state.

It wasn't a perfect solution, but it worked.

"This look doesn't suit you, old friend. You should hurry and wake up." Kira rested a hand on his hard shell, feeling for the spark that was Jin. It was a futile effort, her consciousness bouncing off the same barrier as before.

With a harsh exhale, Kira gave up. It was probably better this way. She could imagine the outcry if she were to break the Haldeel's hold on Jin while standing in their seat of power.

With one last caress, Kira stepped away from his still form. "Rest well. I'll protect us until you can take up the mantle again."

She moved to the basin, cupping her hands under the water only to find it warmer than she expected.

The water turned red as she washed away the blood. She dried her hands and shrugged out of her jacket before picking up a cloth sitting beside the basin.

Too bad there wasn't a mirror to see the extent of the damage.

As if sensing her desires, a silvery oval formed at eye level, reflecting her image.

Blood streaked her cheek and throat, small specks dotting her white shirt. There was nothing she could do about the shirt, but her face was another case.

It didn't take long to clean the blood off her skin and make herself at least semi-presentable again.

She ran the cloth over her jacket. Luckily, it was black and hid the stains she couldn't wipe away.

When it was dry enough, she shrugged into it, knowing it would cover most of the blood.

With one last check in the mirror, she judged that she wouldn't send any kids screaming if they saw her like this.

Good enough for her.

After that she paced around the room, hoping to burn off some of her excess energy. Cleaning the blood off her hadn't touched the adrenaline that had flooded her system.

Being cooped up in this room didn't help. It made her antsy. Not the best feeling when you were supposed to be on your best behavior.

Kira counted her steps. First to one wall and then the next.

"Don't think I'm not going to rub your face in this later," she told Jin. "You're lucky I have nothing to write with, or you'd be covered in graffiti."

The silence that answered her wasn't exactly calming, but the act of talking to Jin, even if he couldn't snipe back, helped settle her.

When long minutes passed and nothing happened, Kira relaxed, allowing herself to soak in some of the tranquility of the garden outside the window. She found a chair, making herself comfortable as she propped her feet on the table and stared out the window.

Time passed, one minute ticking into the next. Eventually, she fell into a form of meditation, one only broken when the door finally disassembled, and a thunderstorm hovered on its threshold.

The sharp, fresh smell of ozone flooded into the room, bringing with it the taste of rain and the wicked bite of wind.

Kira closed her eyes, letting herself bask in the seething energy. The crack of lightning against her senses, blistering hot only to be soothed by the coolness of the storm clouds. A primal feeling that made her lightheaded.

Graydon.

Anticipation rose, fast and furious before Kira strangled it.

"Did they finish their investigation?" she finally asked after what felt like an eternity of silence.

* * *

Graydon held himself in check with a rigid discipline born from the most brutal training a Tuann could undertake. All this time and that was the first thing she wanted to say?

No "how are you", "sorry for leaving", "I missed you".

Fine. If that's how she wanted to play it, he was game. He liked challenges, anyway. They were so fun to conquer.

Graydon prowled across the room, noting the way Kira subtly stiffened at his approach.

Satisfaction rumbled through him.

She wasn't as unaffected as she pretended.

Good to know.

"They've concluded you were in the right," Graydon said, answering her previous question.

Kira dropped her feet from the desk. "I can go then?"

Graydon bared his teeth at her. *It isn't going to be that easy,* coli.

Graydon studied his nails. "They've released you into my care."

He didn't have long to wait.

"What does that mean?"

"I'm so glad you asked. Let me explain." He invaded her space, watching as she barely concealed her flinch at the merciless expression on his face that even his gentle smile didn't fully hide. "It means your ass is mine."

Graydon straightened, enjoying the temper rising behind her eyes. "At least for the remainder of your time on this planet."

"No." The words were clipped, and her movements jerky as she stood from her chair, reaching over and snagging Jin off the table.

Graydon waited until she'd reached the door. "Speak to your niece lately?"

Kira's spine went ramrod straight as she stopped a foot from the exit.

"Because I have," he said.

That got a reaction.

Kira whirled, looking like an avenging goddess as she strode toward him. "We don't speak of her where it's not secure."

A meaningful look at their surroundings made it clear what she meant.

Graydon leaned closer, saying into her ear. "I cut off the surveillance feed the moment I entered."

Kira remained motionless as he straightened.

Graydon found he was rather enjoying that look of impotent rage on her face.

"I wanted this conversation to take place in private," he finished.

Caution entered Kira's expression. "Why?"

"Because there are a few items that need to be clear before you step out of this room,"

Her eyes narrowed. "And they are?"

"We're getting to that," he assured her. "But first, tell me what happened with the swarm."

"Do you really have Elena?" she asked instead, shooting him a hard stare.

Graydon gave a one-word answer, knowing it would get on her nerves. "Yes."

Kira went motionless.

Graydon counted. One. Two. Three.

A harsh exhale left her as she glared out the window.

There she was. Kira hid her anger well, but Graydon could see the frustration and resignation she tried to cover. Mixed throughout it all was love and concern.

"What was Elena thinking?" Kira muttered.

"I imagine she thought she was helping you."

Graydon could sympathize with Kira. She'd gone to great lengths to keep Elena's existence a secret, even kept the knowledge of her birth from the girl's father at considerable cost to her relationship with Raider.

She'd left House Roake in such a way that it could have done extensive damage to the connections she'd tentatively established with them, only for her niece to hand-deliver herself to Graydon within a month.

If he didn't find the whole thing vastly amusing, he'd commiserate with her.

"Nice race by the way. I particularly liked the ending where you crashed."

An uncomfortable look crossed Kira's face as her gaze dropped. "There were some technical difficulties."

Was that what she was calling it?

"I noticed."

Kira's gaze avoided his.

"How angry was Finn afterward?" Graydon asked.

Kira lifted a shoulder. "His anger was somewhat mitigated by helping me avoid your oshota."

Graydon raised an eyebrow. So that's how she did it. He hadn't thought Finn had it in him. Not since the tragic circumstances that had led to the end of his relationship with his poorly chosen sword.

For him to allow Kira to knowingly put herself at risk showed their relationship had evolved—and in a healthy direction.

The bond between sword and shield took trust. One that required a certain flexibility. A sword couldn't always stay within the safety of a shield. Such a sword would be useless if it couldn't slice through their enemies.

The oshota protected, but they also knew when to concentrate on other battlefields so their chosen sword could maximize their forces.

Graydon hadn't thought Finn would ever be able to trust his sword to that extent again.

Kira was showing signs of bonding to her oshota too. If she hadn't trusted him on some level, Graydon had no doubt she would have deposited him on some random planet long before reaching Jettie.

"What I'm more interested in knowing is why you came here—to Jettie, a place you had to know we'd be."

And more important, why she'd allowed her niece to come with her.

For all that she might rebel against the Tuann, Kira had the same overprotective tendencies. If anything, her drive to safeguard her loved ones was even more overdeveloped, likely in part because of her history.

Kira affected a nonchalant shrug. "She wanted to see me race."

Graydon nodded. Uh-huh. Sounded reasonable.

"And it had nothing to do with the woman you were with when the swarm attacked?"

Graydon watched as Kira's expression closed down. It was like a mask descended, not a scrap of the Kira Graydon knew remaining. All emotion was gone, leaving only a blankness his oshota would have envied.

"How do you know about the woman?" Kira asked in a careful voice.

"The Haldeel are as paranoid as we are. But unlike us, they have no sense of privacy and have installed surveillance on all public areas of the city. Let's say I found the video of your battle illuminating."

Interest threatened to crack Kira's mask. "I'm surprised they let you see that."

"Who said I asked for permission?"

A glimmer of respect appeared before it was gone. Her forehead wrinkled. "If they have surveillance on all areas, how did a swarm grow that big?"

"That's what they'd like to know as well."

Kira's expression turned troubled as she fell silent. "The Haldeel have a leak."

Graydon inclined his chin. "That is the likely conclusion."

Kira met his gaze. "This is big. That means the Tsavitee have their hooks in all three races. The Haldeel were the only ones who managed to avoid that fate during the last war."

"That you know of," Graydon corrected.

Kira conceded his point with a thoughtful frown.

"The Haldeel also have a crack in their armor they didn't have last time," Graydon pointed out.

Kira's head lifted. "You're talking about the human refugees."

"Humans do have a history."

Kira slanted him a sharp look. "So do the Tuann."

Everything in Graydon went still as he finally realized the true reason behind her departure from Ta Sa'Riel. He had no problems believing Elena was the architect behind their escape. It was too reckless, even for Kira.

There was no way they would have been able to guarantee they could take Graydon, let alone Harlow, off guard. Add in the obstacle of the defenses, and Graydon didn't think Kira would risk her niece in that manner.

But that didn't explain why she hadn't contacted them to return or why she had chosen to disguise her identity.

She believed there was a mole still in Roake. In the Tuann.

The realization gave him insight into what drove her. For a protector like Kira, no amount of trust or desire would allow her to be reckless with her niece's safety.

In her mind, there was no need to adapt because her niece had already gone this long without an immediate threat. Only by putting Kira's back to the wall and forcing her hand would Graydon have any chance of slipping into her guard.

"She's no one," Kira lied. "Just someone I met."

"You and she seemed pretty familiar for new acquaintances," Graydon said.

It was there in the way they'd fought, as if they'd done this before. The other woman hadn't been flashy, lingering toward the back and only acting when absolutely necessary, but she'd held herself with a readiness that said she was prepared to intercede if necessary.

You didn't get that sort of teamwork without a history together.

There had also been that small interchange at the beginning where Kira had stopped the woman from doing something.

Using *ki* was Graydon's bet.

Kira lifted her chin as if daring him to keep pushing.

Far be it for him to disappoint. "She was very careful not to use *ki* after you warned her."

As if on cue Kira's expression hardened even as her guard snapped up.

"*Coli*, sometimes you are so predictable," Graydon said in a gentle voice. "I have no intention of forcing your friend into the light unless it becomes clear she is in danger." Graydon turned resolute. "But we will intervene should we feel the situation is dire. The emperor has decided to listen. For now. But the Tuann will not suffer the loss of another child."

Graydon waited until Kira met his gaze, letting her see how serious he was. The emperor was giving her and the others a chance to prove this could work in the hopes of bettering the relationship between them, but there were limits to his magnanimity.

To the Tuann, the children were theirs, regardless of what said children thought. If the Houses learned the emperor hadn't moved the stars in an effort to reclaim their progeny, there would be war.

The only reason they were considering letting the children come to them was because Kira was more than anyone had expected. She could take care of herself and held a maturity not seen even in some who had completed their *adva ka*.

There was also the tiny fact that her escape from Ta Sa'Riel—abetted though it was by Graydon—made it clear they couldn't keep her unless she wanted to be kept.

No one wanted to see what would happen if Tuann who held Kira's same level of skill but an even more reclusive mentality were trapped on a planet and told they couldn't leave.

To say nothing of how such an act smacked of something their ancient masters would have done.

Neither Graydon nor the emperor wanted to become anything like those monsters.

"And me?" Kira asked.

Graydon quirked an eyebrow. "I believe you've already made your deal."

An introspective look entered Kira's gaze as she considered.

She nodded. "That's fair."

Graydon felt a pulse of fierce pleasure. Whether Kira knew it or not, she'd already accepted her place among the Tuann. If she hadn't, she would have fought tooth and nail against that statement.

Progress. Slow and frustrating, but there, nonetheless.

Graydon could be patient.

He had a feeling Kira was worth the wait. Her layers seemed endless. A protection she'd needed to survive what she had. But Graydon had a feeling when they were finally pulled back, they would expose a woman with a soul like no other. Beautiful and pure.

Already, she'd given him brief glimpses of that woman when she interacted with her niece and Jin. Those all too brief moments where she forgot to guard herself. The taste was addictive and he found himself utterly enthralled.

Kira rolled her lips between her teeth as she looked like she was debating something. “There’s something you should know.”

Graydon waited.

Kira’s gaze met his. “I think Elise is somewhere on this planet.”

TWELVE

KIRA PRESSED HER lips together as her words hovered in the air. What she wouldn't give to take those words back.

But she couldn't.

They were already out, waiting for the universe to bestow a blessing or a curse. Hard to tell which.

Graydon wasn't the easiest of individuals to predict. He used a veneer of sarcasm and wit that was as likely to draw blood as his sword.

He could very easily use her confession against Kira.

It'd been a long time since Kira had let herself be so vulnerable. She was beginning to remember why she'd stopped.

This feeling sucked.

Handing someone the power to hurt you took bravery. Guts. Both things Kira hadn't felt she possessed in a long time. At least emotionally. Physically, she was just as likely to throw herself into the fire.

Graydon held the ability to crush her and her objective.

Would he though?

That was the question she was hoping to get the answer to.

"You hope to go after her," Graydon stated.

The look he sent her was reflective, as if she'd handed him a piece to some invisible puzzle he was assembling.

"I'm not leaving this planet without her."

Graydon might as well know the truth. She'd sacrifice everything if she had to—even the Tuann.

Of course, she was hoping it wouldn't come to that. If she ever had to fight Graydon for real, she wasn't entirely sure who'd come out the victor.

"It's very convenient for her to appear now. Are you sure it's her?" he asked.

"No, but that doesn't change what I'm going to do."

Graydon stirred, his gaze thoughtful. "The Tsavitee had her for a long time. She might not be the person you remember."

"I've considered that, and if that's the case, I'll do what has to be done."

Kira let herself feel the raw devastation of that thought. She didn't try to hide or pretend. She put it all out there for him to see.

She was going into this with her eyes wide open, knowing she couldn't control the outcome.

All this time she'd been holding onto the slimmest of hopes that when she found Elise, there would be something of the woman she knew remaining. It was her light in the dark, the thing that forced her to pull herself together in the early days after the coma. After all this time, it had become habit to cling to that hope.

But in the back of her mind, she'd always known what she might have to do if Elise had been twisted beyond repair by the torture and brainwashing she might have endured.

It was the nightmare that kept her up nights.

It would be easier not to go looking. To hold onto the memory of who Elise was.

Kira couldn't force herself to do that. It wasn't in her nature to let things go. Even if the hope was small and the chances of failure were great, she'd give everything she was to see this through. Even if it destroyed her in the end.

Graydon could accept that and help her—or he could get out of her way.

"All right," Graydon said.

The sudden absence of tension made Kira almost lightheaded. For a second, she questioned what she'd heard.

Had Graydon, Mr. You'll-Do-It-My-Way, just agreed to her demand? Had the world turned upside down while she wasn't looking?

Graydon's eyes danced at her mistrustful look. "There are conditions, of course."

"Of course," Kira bit out.

How could she not have guessed?

"You're not to make a move without me. No going off alone. No keeping secrets."

His gaze was firm with no room for negotiation.

Kira wondered if that look worked on other Tuann.

"I can't promise you the last one," Kira said. "There are things I know that affect the safety and wellbeing of others. I can't reveal their secrets without their permission."

Graydon waited a long moment before inclining his chin. "That is acceptable."

Kira watched him carefully, not sure if she trusted this magnanimous version of the Emperor's Face. Where were the demands? The rules? This was downright understanding of him.

Graydon's smile widened. "You're not the only one privy to secrets that could move empires. We all must walk a delicate balance."

It was likely as close as Graydon would get to admitting he had secrets of his own he couldn't—wouldn't—divulge.

"Then we're agreed," Kira said.

Graydon straightened, the movement somehow predatory. It was enough to make Kira's insides tremble as he brushed past her.

"Yes, we'll work toward our goals together." Graydon stopped next to her, saying those last words directly into her ear.

Kira shivered at the barely restrained growl in his voice.

Why did Kira have a feeling he had placed an entirely different meaning on that sentence?

* * *

The privileges imbued by rank were made clear during Graydon and Kira's departure. No one tried to stop them as Kira grabbed Jin and they left the conference room. The corridors they passed through as they retraced Kira's steps were empty, not a Haldeel peacekeeper in sight.

If not for Kira's certainty the Haldeel were watching every move they made, she'd have thought they were making a grand escape.

They arrived at the entrance. The Haldeel peacekeeper from before waited there along with two Tuann Kira didn't recognize.

Taller than Graydon by a few inches, the male Tuann had the same powerful build that said he'd spent a lifetime honing his body into the perfect weapon.

A hood with some type of field masked his face, making his features impossible to decipher.

At first glance, it was tempting to assume he was one of Graydon's people from the matte black armor he wore. The protective way he hovered beside the woman, as if ready at any moment to lay down his life in her defense, told Kira that wasn't the case.

The only explanation for why the man was wearing synth armor exclusive to the emperor's people was if the woman was another of the Emperor's Faces.

Kira examined the woman with renewed interest. Where Graydon reminded her of a savage storm, containing the potential to annihilate everything in his path, the woman was his contrast in every way.

She was like a winter's night. Calm, still, a biting chill emanating from her. She didn't wear the synth armor Kira had come to expect among high-ranking officials of the Tuann.

Instead, she was clad in the same intricate style as the Haldeel. Her outfit was built in layers. She wore a silvery, flowing skirt and a cream-colored under top that were overlaid by a dark blue robe fitted with a wide silver belt. It was followed by another sheer robe that hung loose around her body. More intricate by far than the peacekeeper's outer garments, the material was luxurious, a silver pattern shimmering among the darker blue.

It was elegant and not at all suited to moving quickly. If the woman was attacked, it'd be almost impossible to defend herself.

The woman held a kind of beauty that you couldn't help but admire. Hair as black as the void of space was gathered in an intricate tail down her back.

Her eyes were serene as she watched Kira and Graydon's approach.

To Kira's surprise, there was a thread of tension in Graydon at the sight of the woman.

The Haldeel ignored the others to sweep Kira a partial bow. "*Za na ri*, my superiors thank you for your great service."

The waiting Tuann looked with interest at Kira.

She was no less startled.

The most common form of address for the Haldeel was *za*. If they were feeling especially polite or grateful, they'd throw in an extra syllable making it—*za na*.

To be called *za na ri* was surprising.

It was one of the politest forms of address—denoting a respect and acknowledgment that was almost unheard of when speaking to members of an opposing race. To Kira's knowledge no human had ever been called that.

Even Himoto had never earned that honor.

There was only one form of address higher than *za na ri* and that was the form of *za na ri na*—which was almost exclusively used for royalty.

The Haldeel were unique in how they decided their royals. It wasn't based on bloodline and was entirely dependent on a Haldeel's skill and talent. Only the most exceptional among them could reach that status.

They called the climb from commoner to royalty the Ascension. From what Kira had heard, it was a rather brutal fight that more often than not resulted in the hopeful's death along with anyone who helped them.

Kira didn't like the way the Tuann woman was looking at her—like she was a particularly clever pet who had done something interesting.

Leaving the matter aside for now, Kira held out Jin to the Haldeel. "Now that we've settled this matter, fix him."

The woman's slow blink was as effective as a slap at conveying disapproval.

Kira had no problem ignoring her. Jin was what was important right now, and no amount of manners or dancing around the diplomacy bush was going to impede her.

Oddly enough, Graydon relaxed at her comment, regarding the rest of them with the lazy amusement of a bystander.

For the Haldeel's part, he remained unaffected, taking no offense at Kira's abrupt demand. He made a sharp gesture and the same buzz that had preceded Jin's lapse into unconsciousness took over Kira's world.

When it cleared, she could feel Jin's presence in her mind again, right there where he was supposed to be.

"It is done," the Haldeel stated.

The relief at the feeling was overwhelming.

Kira stared at her friend, ready for him to jolt to life. Seconds slid into one another until they formed minutes.

Still, Jin remained unresponsive.

"Why isn't he waking up?" Kira asked, unable to stay silent any longer.

The Haldeel leaned over, taking a longer look at Jin's small sphere. "Hmm. It may take a little time for the residual effects of the field to wane."

"How long?"

The woman stiffened further, her already straight spine going even straighter.

"Not long I think," the Haldeel assured her.

That was good enough for now.

Kira tucked Jin against her body. "I'll be sure to find you again if that isn't the case."

It wasn't a threat so much as a statement of her intentions.

If Jin didn't wake up, Graydon wouldn't have to worry about what Kira did in pursuit of Elise, because he'd have far more concerning things on his mind.

Such as the war she was likely to start.

"You overstep." The woman's stare burned into the side of Kira's face.

Maybe, but Kira always found it best to make one's intentions clear.

It prevented all those nasty little misunderstandings that could result in blood shed.

Jin was her line in the sand. If he saw harm, she'd exact retribution. Simple as that.

This time the Haldeel's bow was deeper. "As is your right, *za na ri*."

Good. He understood.

She so enjoyed when people had a meeting of the minds. It made everything else so much easier.

In this instance, the Haldeel knew Kira would kill him if her friend didn't recover, and she knew he'd defend himself with lethal force if necessary.

Kira smiled. "So glad we agree."

"Indeed."

The woman's expression iced over as Kira swept out of the inner sanctum and into the immense foyer of the building. Shadows danced on invisible waves over the floor as Graydon and the other two Tuann followed her out.

"The *za na ri na* is looking forward to your race in the Pinnacle, *za na ri*," the Haldeel said as the wall sealed behind her.

"How lovely, your little lostling has drawn the notice of royalty," the woman observed in a neutral voice that made it impossible to tell if she approved or disapproved. Her stare was intense as she regarded Kira. "I wonder what chain of events sparked such a rare occurrence."

Kira's expression was blank as she stared back.

To be honest, she'd really like to know that too.

It was never an auspicious occasion when you drew the attention of titans. That was a good way to end up dead or a pawn in someone else's agenda.

"We're being watched," the oshota observed in an undertone.

"This conversation would be best conducted elsewhere," Graydon said neutrally.

The woman's expression grew chillier. "Yes, I couldn't agree more."

Sensing a subtle threat in those words, Kira watched her warily.

The woman didn't say anything further, sweeping toward the exit. Her oshota followed her.

Kira raised her eyebrows at Graydon. "Colleague of yours?"

The corner of his eyes crinkled. "You could say that."

Kira had been right. The woman really was a Face of the Emperor. A beautiful, icy one.

She supposed the name of Face was apt, allowing the emperor to choose the aspects and personalities that best complemented his public persona. Graydon was the brute force that concealed an exceptional intellect. Kira was guessing the woman represented elegance and subtlety.

More and more she could respect this unknown emperor who seemed to make the most out of the people he placed by his side—even as she recognized the threat he could one day present.

The walkway extended over the placid lake. On the other side, several figures clad in black synth armor waited. Graydon's oshota. Kira had wondered where they got to.

Finn waited off to the side, his face expressionless as they approached.

"Yukina may look like a delicate flower, but she's the ambassador to the Haldeel. I'd be careful of her if I were you," Graydon warned as they neared the rest.

Translation—Yukina was treacherous—and knowing the Tuann, deceptively deadly. Qualities that would come in handy for any liaison to the Haldeel.

Her position as ambassador also explained her clothes.

Yukina stopped in front of the oshota, casting a contemplative glance at Kira. "Now that we're out of the Haldeel's seat of power, I'd be interested to know why they refer to you as *za na ri*. They don't even use that honorific when speaking to me."

There were a lot of things Kira could say to that. Most of them insulting. Things like maybe the Haldeel didn't like the woman or that she wasn't as special as she thought.

Kira said none of that. Not with Finn's careful expression warning her to tread lightly.

Diplomacy. Politeness. Blergh.

And the Tuann wondered why she went AWOL.

"You would have to ask the Haldeel. I'm unsure of the reason myself," Kira said in an exceptionally polite voice. She managed a soft smile.

Yukina's expression went cold. "I find that hard to believe."

Kira's lips stayed uplifted in a kind smile, but her eyes were wintry.

Yukina wasn't the only one who could channel an ice princess. Granted, it wasn't Kira's favorite persona to don. She much preferred smashing and bashing her way to victory, but when dealing with someone like Yukina, sometimes you had to fight on their level.

Yukina was the type of person who waged war through sharp words and cutting looks. Kira's least favorite kind of battle.

"You're free to believe what you like," Kira said.

Yukina's smile sharpened. "You're awfully brave. Do you know who I am?"

"Not particularly."

Nor did Kira care.

Yukina's attention shifted in Finn's direction. "You've picked an interesting oshota to have serve you. Are you aware they call him the curse?"

Kira didn't speak as Finn went motionless, his eyes blank.

If Kira hadn't known him as well as she did, she never would have spotted the fine tremble in his hands before he clenched them into fists.

"You're his third sword. The first was killed in battle. Finn was the only one to survive. The second he abandoned. I wonder which fate you'll experience."

This woman played a vicious game. She couldn't make Kira dance to her tune, so she went after the next best thing. Finn.

"I don't think I like you." Kira's voice sounded detached, as if it were coming from someone else.

"I'm heartbroken." Yukina's lips stretched into a feline smile. "Would you like to know another secret?"

Snap. Snap. Snap.

There went Kira's restraint.

"No."

Yukina seemed momentarily taken aback. "No?"

Kira sent Graydon an indifferent glance. "Do the Tuann usually find themselves unable to grasp such simple concepts? It seems like an unfortunate trait in an ambassador. Must cause all kinds of confusion with your allies."

Graydon's oshota stared in shock at Kira as if they couldn't believe her presumptuousness.

Finn looked alarmed.

For a breath no one moved.

A laugh that sounded like wind chimes came from Yukina. "You're very bold."

"And you're very annoying."

Great. They'd now pointed out the other's flaws. Time to hurry this game along.

If Yukina was like the rest of her race, she wouldn't allow herself to be insulted by someone she considered her inferior.

She'd retaliate.

Kira was looking forward to it.

Pressure built in the air between them, ratcheting up until the intensity fairly crackled.

Yukina and Kira stepped toward each other at the same time.

Graydon and Finn blocked Kira's path, Yukina's oshota doing the same to her.

"Move," Kira ordered calmly.

Finn didn't even bother shaking his head.

Graydon smirked. "I don't think so. Not today."

"You don't think I can win."

"It won't matter if you win or lose because you'll take some damage." He quirked an eyebrow at her. "Don't you have other business to concern yourself with?"

Kira hated it when other people talked sense—especially when her skin itched for a good fight and right now there was someone willing to give it to her.

Graydon didn't give her time to argue, addressing his oshota. "Escort Kira to the villa."

Reluctantly, Kira let Finn herd her away, allowing herself one last look at Yukina. "Bummer. It could have been fun."

Amusement touched Yukina's features. "Perhaps another time then."

Amila stepped forward then, indicating for Kira to follow. Carrying Jin in her arms, Kira complied. Finn and Noor fell in behind her as they set off along the avenue. They didn't walk far before Amila headed toward an arch.

They stepped off the water road and onto stone similar to that of the white-gray archways. At this time of the afternoon, the city was busy. Despite the crowded streets, pedestrians moved out of the way when they saw Kira's trio of oshota.

A groggy voice came from her arms. "Why is it the first thing I hear when I wake up is you starting a fight? Can't you play nice for even a few minutes?"

To Kira's surprise, Jin sounded lucid, if a tad sleepy.

She'd felt his mind stirring shortly before Graydon and Finn had intervened, but she'd been afraid to let herself hope in the event she was wrong.

"What? You're not going to answer my question?"

Kira's snort was waterlogged as she forced down the riptide of emotions the sound of his voice engendered.

Jin was her constant.

The ancients of old Earth would have called him her north star. Without him, Kira would have been someone quite different. Someone much darker and more violent. She didn't know if she would have won against her own internal demons if he hadn't been there forcing her to confront her flaws and accept the times she'd failed.

He was ridiculous and temperamental. Childish on occasion. But he was hers, and no one would harm him.

"Aw, you missed me. I knew you would," Jin teased.

"You wish," Kira retorted.

Jin tried to lift out of her arms. He made it only an inch before settling more firmly against her.

"Are you okay?" Kira asked.

"Yeah, I just need a moment to get my bearings." A smacking sound came. "Why does my mouth taste like metal?"

Kira rolled her eyes. Same old Jin. "You don't actually have a mouth so it's probably your imagination."

"Are you sure?" Jin asked as the oshota led Kira across a street.

"No."

They reached the edge of the refugee quarter, its warmth and coziness evaporating as they moved into a more elite part of the city.

This was where the upper crust Haldeel lived and where esteemed visitors to the planet were given a place to reside.

It would be interesting to know whether the Consortium's representatives were ensconced near here or if they'd been relegated to the refugee quarter.

"What did I miss?" Jin asked.

"Not much." If one didn't count the negotiation between Graydon and Kira or the Haldeel using honorifics they had no business using.

Kira brought none of that up. There were too many big ears that might overhear something she wanted kept private. When they were alone, Kira would fill him in.

"Liar."

"Those who let themselves be knocked out are in no position to complain," Kira told him.

"And who's the one who told me to power down?"

Kira glared at him. "Maybe if you'd done an adequate job of shielding your power signature this wouldn't have happened."

"You say that like we weren't dealing with the Haldeel. The same tricks that work on humans aren't going to work on them."

Any response Kira had planned died as Amila stopped in front of a circular gate, its heavy ornate doors spread wide. A narrow waterway framed by leafy fronds led to a second gate. The pathway across was formed by stone blocks jutting above the water's surface.

A pergola with thick vines draping over its wooden slats shaded the water. Through it, Kira caught the barest glimpse of a three-story building, terraces and balconies jutting from its sides.

Seconds later a pair of Tuann blocked her view as they regarded her with flat stares, only a slight flicker in their eyes betraying their uneasiness when they saw the oshota guarding her.

One was a broad-shouldered woman, her face blocky and her hair pulled into a tight tail. The other was male. He was short and stocky and had a pronounced brow.

Neither wore synth armor Kira recognized. It was a deep red with black accents.

"State your business," the woman demanded in Tuann.

Kira glanced at Amila. "Are you sure we're in the right place?"

Amila's chin dipped.

Kira waited, but no further response was forthcoming.

Okay then. It looked like she was on her own. It seemed she'd underestimated how peeved Graydon's oshota were about her abrupt departure.

Not ideal, but good to know.

Kira ignored the regret that moved through her, instead sending Amila a sidelong look. "Really?"

A flat stare was Kira's only answer.

Kira glanced at the stranger, contemplating the best way to gain entrance.

"State your business or move along," the woman ordered.

"Wren." Kira hung her head; she really hadn't meant to say that.

The woman frowned at her, her eyebrows drawing down in suspicion. "What about him?"

Kira exhaled. She'd already pulled the trigger. Might as well see where it went.

"He's my *seon'yer*."

The woman and her partner glanced at each other before looking Kira over.

Kira knew what they saw. A woman of average height—maybe a little short for a Tuann—wearing clothes that no Tuann would ever be caught dead in.

Although they were on guard against Amila and Noor, they'd already discarded Finn as a threat for the same reason.

Kira had always known most Tuann didn't consider her intimidating. She'd seen Graydon and those he viewed as his peers. She lacked their stature and no amount of training would give her their muscle mass. Her delicate bone structure and gray-purple eyes didn't help that impression.

No, it was only after people spent time with her particular brand of crazy that they realized the true awesome of Kira Forrest.

"You? You're his *yer'se*?" the woman asked, not hiding her skepticism.

"Yup, that's me."

Though Kira was betting Wren regretted his decision by now.

Too late. No take-backs.

"Then you must have a token," the woman said.

Kira stared at her blankly for several seconds before she remembered. "Oh, right."

Kira balanced Jin as she stuck one hand down the neck of her hoodie. Her fingers brushed metal, and Kira withdrew a necklace chain attached to a medallion. A creature Kira didn't recognize was stamped on its front. On the back was the crest of Roake—the coiled body of a *lu-ong*, its fangs bared and its mane flared.

Kira held it out to the woman. With apparent reluctance, the stranger took it from her, holding it up so she and her partner could examine the markings.

"It does look like his sigil," the man whispered in Tuann.

The woman turned it over several times as if trying to spot any discrepancies.

"Why is there a hole in it?" the woman asked.

Kira shrugged. "Easier to keep track."

"Why would a respected commander like Wren take someone like you?"

"Perhaps you should ask him."

Kira was sure he'd like that. The woman and her partner, on the other hand, might not enjoy the outcome.

The woman's eyes flashed. "Maybe it's fake."

Next to Kira, Finn bristled. If he'd been an animal, he would have puffed up to double his size in affront.

The oshota, perhaps not realizing the danger they were in, sneered.

Kira shook her head at Finn. As entertaining as it'd be to watch him teach these two a lesson about the perils of making assumptions, she was already in enough hot water.

She nodded at the medallion and held out her hand, making a *give me* motion. "You want to give that back now?"

The woman frowned, holding the medallion closer to her torso as if to guard it.

Don't do it, Kira warned the woman silently.

Kira could brush off the minor digs, ignore the more blatant insults as unimportant. What she could not do was allow the woman to keep what was not hers.

Wren had given that token to her. He'd entrusted it to her. It represented his willingness to guide her in her path to the *adva ka*. It wasn't something to be sullied with these people's greed.

Kira was already being nice enough by letting them set eyes on it.

Should the woman continue down this road, Kira would act. Violently, if need be.

A refusal started to form. Kira could already hear the words *no* on the woman's lips.

The muscles in her legs flexed as she calculated her attack.

Using *ki* directly on them was out. Even with the inhibitor, she couldn't chance killing them. You didn't use a nuclear warhead when a crowbar would do.

"Let her through," a woman ordered from out of sight.

The female oshota scowled, her hand clenching around the medallion. Reluctantly, she held it out to Kira. "Follow us."

The woman and her partner led the way through the gate, their steps echoing on the stone.

Without the obstruction of the wall, Kira had an unimpeded view of the courtyard. Trees and plants crowded the narrow channel of water. Tall walls and the pergola created an enclosed feeling.

The backs of the oshota in front of Kira were tense as they shot several glances over their shoulders at her.

Kira's answering smile was more of a grimace.

"How much do you want to bet those fish are carnivorous?" Jin asked at the same time as there was a low buzz.

The oshota reacted like they were being attacked, their weight shifting as they reached for their swords.

Kira hurled Jin at the woman's face, stepping into the man's guard in the next instant.

She hammered a hard palm against the elbow of his sword arm, preventing him from unleashing his en-blade.

The woman batted Jin away from her face. He flew, hitting the water with a splash and sinking.

Kira backhanded her, sending her stumbling off the stepping-stones and into the water.

Behind her, Kira heard a commotion as Finn and the rest attacked the barrier that hadn't been there seconds before.

Kira didn't spare them any attention, too preoccupied with surviving the unwarranted aggression.

The man recovered while Kira was distracted with the woman, the sharp sound of metal sliding against metal filled the air.

She caught his hand before he could fully bring the sword up, yanking him to the side.

Her *ki* slid through her. She reached, gathering molecules of water and tugging hard. Beads of water crawled up unnoticed onto the stone steps around the man's feet.

He dashed forward, only to lose his balance on the suddenly slippery stone. He hit the ground belly first, his head and left arm sliding underwater.

Kira stepped onto his back, keeping him there, as the water infused with her *ki* closed around his torso and held him firmly under.

The woman snarled and charged her.

Frantic, Kira threw her senses as wide as they'd go, one hand sweeping in front of her. A wave of water shot up to form a barrier.

A shadow dropped from above.

Kira's *ki* snapped back to her, collapsing her makeshift defense. When it disappeared, Kira blinked at the stranger standing between her and the oshota, her back facing Kira. White-blond hair was bound in a tail, its ends stopping between her shoulder blades.

The woman who'd protected Kira wore synth armor decorated in Roake's colors of midnight blue.

The barrier popped, vanishing from existence as Amila and Finn stalked through.

Finn's face was a mask of rage, his en-blade held at the ready.

Noor had a knee to the stone as sweat rolled down his forehead from the effort of destroying the barrier.

"Move. She set off the defenses," the woman in the red synth armor growled.

Kira's protector raised her hand, a black sphere appearing in front of her palm. The air screamed.

The woman drew back in fear. "This doesn't involve Roake."

"That's strange," a male said from above.

Kira glanced up to find another of Roake's oshota leaning against a balcony overlooking the courtyard.

His curious gaze met hers before moving to the red-clad oshota. "House Asanth attacks a daughter of Roake and doesn't think it concerns us?"

There was humor in his expression, but it contained a playful sharpness that said he'd happily dismember the two from House Asanth and sleep like a baby later.

Kira pushed at a lock of hair, her sleeve sliding down to expose the band of tattoos she'd received from the Mea'Ave.

The woman's jaw flexed as a guarded look entered her eyes at the sight.

"I did not realize she held Overlord marks," the woman said stiffly.

Standing in knee deep water, her blade drawn, she looked like she was re-evaluating her recent choices.

Kira's protector finally spoke. "You knew she was the commander's *yer'se.*"

Kira realized this was the woman who'd ordered them to let her through.

The woman from House Asanth lifted her chin. "She carried one of those human abominations through the defenses."

Kira's expression went cold. She'd known the Tuann weren't entirely comfortable with Jin being a drone, but this was the first time she'd heard such strong language in reference to him.

Now, she wished she hadn't held back when they attacked for fear of causing an incident.

"And for this you tried to kill our heir?" the man from above asked.

Kira stiffened. What heir?

It couldn't be her, she told herself. No way would Roake appoint her as heir after the manner of her leaving. Harlow had to know better.

"House Asanth is responsible for the conclave's safety. It would be negligent of us if we hadn't acted," the woman argued.

The man whistled. "Someone's intent on being obtuse."

The man above tilted his head at Amila and Noor who until now had been watching the exchange silently.

"The little heir comes escorted by the emperor's own people." He set an elbow on the railing and gave them a charming smirk. "Or are you questioning their honor too?"

The woman's glare moved from Kira to Amila's neutral expression, taking in the naked en-blade in her hand.

By now it was clear to everyone in the courtyard that House Asanth had overreacted. What's more the woman knew it, but didn't want to admit it at the risk of losing face.

Unfortunately for her, everyone already thought she was an idiot. Every second that ticked by reinforced that impression.

Left with little choice, the woman slid her en-blade into its sheath with a violent motion.

Kira's protector finally moved her attention to Kira. She nodded at Kira's foot where it still rested on the man's back. "Are you planning on killing him?"

Kira considered. As interesting as that would be, it would likely only bring problems later on.

With a disappointed frown, she lifted her foot off the man, withdrawing the portion of her *ki* that enabled the water to keep him submerged and stepped back.

His fellow oshota reached forward, dragging his unresponsive upper body out of the water. She turned him onto his back, hammering a closed fist onto his chest.

The man's body jerked, but his chest remained unmoving.

The woman cursed, joining her hands into one fist and doing it again.

Water splashed out of the man's mouth. The man gasped and choked.

Seeing this, the woman grabbed his shoulders and turned him onto his side to allow him to expel the water from his lungs.

She patted his back even as she glared up at Kira.

"Don't start fights you can't win," Kira advised.

Rage infused the woman's features.

Before she could retort, the water next to her erupted, a dark shape shooting from its depths. The shape hovered in the air, the drips of water droplets loud in the sudden silence.

A heavy layer of algae, pond scum, mud, and a writhing mass of vines covered the creature's misshapen body.

Kira thought she caught the wiggling tail of a fish stuck in the ball of muddy green.

Kira squinted. "Jin?"

THIRTEEN

THE PLANT MONSTER rustled. "Woman, are you trying to kill me?"

"I thought you'd be honored to be the decoy. Aren't you the one always going on about how I never include you in things?"

A garbled sound came from the mass of dead plant matter.

"That is not what I meant at all," Jin roared. "You threw me into water. I'm a machine. Water is my mortal enemy."

Kira waved an unconcerned hand. "Sometimes sacrifices need to be made, and technically I threw you at her." Kira pointed at the woman from House Asanth where she still knelt by her partner. "She threw you into the water. If you're mad, blame her."

Before the woman could prepare a retort, Kira's protector stirred, aiming a bored look in Kira's direction. "Come with me."

She sauntered past Kira as she headed toward the residence, saying over her shoulder. "You two, return to your post. I'd advise you against making any further mistakes."

The water creature vibrated, bits of vegetation falling away until Jin's hard metallic shell was mostly clear of debris. Streaks of mud and green covered his normal gunmetal gray as he joined Kira.

"I can't believe you tried to kill me," Jin muttered.

"You were taking too long to recover your faculties. I thought you could use a little incentive."

"Spare me your kindness in the future," Jin said, aiming his "eye" at her.

Before Kira could respond, the man on the balcony placed one hand on the railing and leapt over it. He fell, landing hard, knees bent, body braced. The water rippled from the impact, spreading out in small waves that lapped the edges of the courtyard.

He straightened and examined Kira.

This close it was easy to see the details Kira had missed before.

A square jaw and bright, curious eyes made the man seem downright amiable. The orange hair that stuck up in tufts around his head added to his approachability.

He was one of the shorter Tuann Kira had met. Although only about her height, he made up for his small size in the width of his shoulders and chest. His forearms and biceps were lined with muscle.

He stroked his chin, looking at Kira. From anyone else, the look would have been considered insulting. With him, he somehow managed to come off as curious and appraising.

"Is this her?" he asked.

The blonde lifted a lazy shoulder as if she couldn't summon the interest necessary to answer with words.

The man didn't pay any attention to her, taking the lack of response in stride as he focused on Kira.

He reminded her of an overgrown puppy. Friendly, eager to play, with a bouncing enthusiasm. Except this puppy had teeth. If his interaction with Asanth was any indication, his bite was way worse than his bark.

He stroked his chin as he looked her over. He nodded to himself as if she'd passed some sort of test.

"Token. Let's see," he ordered, holding out his hand.

Kira stared at his palm before lifting her gaze to his. He quirked an eyebrow at her in expectation but didn't move. The look he gave her said he could wait all day if he had to.

Kira's lips quirked. Friendly but with the same stubbornness as every other oshota she'd met.

Left with little choice, Kira fished out the token and handed it over.

The stranger turned it over in his hands and grinned. "You have no idea how long I've been waiting for this."

Large hands settled on her shoulders before she could react—and she tried. Unsuccessfully.

"Finally. Finally, I'm no longer the youngest," he crowed. His grin was infectious. "Don't worry, little junior. I'll make sure to show you the ropes. If any of these idiots give you a hard time, let me know. I'll be sure to sort them out."

A hand appeared, knocking one of the man's hands off her shoulder.

"Keep your hands to yourself," Finn said stiffly.

The man blinked at Kira's oshota, scanning him. "What are you wearing?"

Finn's expression went cold as the man cocked his head.

Freed, Kira shifted so she was out of the man's reach.

He was good. She'd give him that. He'd been much faster than she'd expected. If he'd meant her harm, she would have been in a little trouble there.

"I mean, really, what are those?" the man asked, his focus entirely on Finn.

Kira discreetly took a step away.

The blonde saw her movement and her lips quirked.

"None of your business," Finn told the man coldly.

The stranger reached out, plucking at the fabric of Finn's hoodie only for his hand to be knocked away by Finn.

"Where's your synth armor?"

Finn's frown grew more pronounced.

"Is this a disguise?" the man asked like it was the most ridiculous thing he'd ever seen.

"It's none of your business," Finn snapped.

The man responded with a sage nod. "You don't want to talk about it. I wouldn't either."

Their interaction pointed to a history between the two—one that wasn't entirely antagonistic given Finn hadn't already tried to kill the other man yet.

"Maksym, are you quite done?" a feminine voice asked.

A woman clad in the same dark blue synth armor as the other two appeared at the end of the stepping-stones, the archway of the house framing her.

Soft-looking, brown hair framed a pretty face that had a small smattering of freckles scattered over the bridge of her nose and cheeks. Unlike many Tuann, her hair was short, only about chin length and formed a soft halo around her head.

Her gaze was chiding as she regarded Maksym. "You'll scare our junior if you continue down this path."

Maksym looked away, the picture of guilt as he rubbed his neck with one hand.

The woman ignored him, aiming a friendly smile at Kira. "I apologize for my friend's enthusiasm. He gets a little carried away sometimes. When we heard Wren had taken a *yer'se,* we were all curious to see what kind of person they would be."

The term *yer'se* roughly translated to disciple as Kira knew from her studies of Tuann.

The woman nodded at the oshota next to her. "That's Auralyn and I'm Zoella. Maksym, you're already acquainted with."

Kira's nod at the three was cautious.

Maksym and Zoella both smiled. Auralyn watched her with an expressionless face that still managed to convey boredom.

A moment passed before Zoella looked beyond Kira to Amila and Noor. "We'll take it from here. You can return to your sword."

The words were polite, but the dismissal was clear. Zoella had just laid a claim on Kira. One that made it clear the other two were considered outsiders.

Amila hesitated, her gaze shooting to Kira before she nodded and spun on her heel.

"Amila," Kira said softly, stopping her.

Amila paused and gave Kira a questioning look.

"Thanks for everything and sorry for the trouble," Kira eventually said after some consideration.

It was as close to an apology for the matter of her leaving as Amila was going to get. It probably didn't mean much, but Kira couldn't stop herself from trying.

She'd enjoyed the oshota's company. The other woman had a subtle humor that she only displayed to those she trusted. Kira had been in that circle once. She regretted that an action she'd taken had destroyed that.

Amila's chin dipped in acceptance. "I'll see you soon."

Lightness spread through Kira.

Amila winked. "Find us if they give you too much trouble."

Not waiting for Kira's agreement, Amila strode in Noor's wake.

Too late it occurred to Kira that she had no idea where Elena was, and it wasn't like she could ask Wren's people.

If they didn't already know about Kira's niece, she wasn't going to be the one to inform them.

Nor was it feasible to search the grounds of the residence. Her encounter with House Asanth made it clear how precarious the balance of Tuann peace was.

Kira had no desire to start fights left and right.

Auralyn strode on. "Follow."

"A woman of few words. Remind you of anyone?" Jin asked.

"Why are you looking at me when you ask that?"

He snickered as they started after Auralyn. "I don't know. What could be the reason?"

Kira shook her head as they moved through the secondary gate, getting their first unobstructed look at the residence where the Tuann were staying.

Greenery encroached everywhere Kira looked, the straight lines of the building softened by the many plants.

Large windows took up many of the walls. The tint on them offered privacy to those inside, allowing them to look out while not allowing visitors to see in.

It was a nice defense feature, Kira had to admit.

It left her wondering if it also had heat-shielding capabilities that would prevent someone with infrared equipment from pinpointing the bodies inside.

The layout was blocky, like someone had taken several rectangle containers and welded them together. Some rectangles lay on their sides, while others stood vertical. Still more were stacked one on top of the other in inventive ways, creating the numerous balconies.

There wasn't much of a transition from outside to indoors as they stepped past a pair of columns. Tall trees with large fronds reached toward the ceiling.

There was no door to knock on as they moved into the entryway, the coolness of the building embracing them.

A stairway led up to their left, and there was a large area with seating overlooking a small garden to their right.

Auralyn ignored all of this, steering them deeper into the house.

"I don't suppose you have any showers around here?" Jin complained.

Auralyn's pace slowed as she regarded Jin. "Didn't you say water was your mortal enemy?"

"What's your point?" Jin asked

Kira's mouth twitched as Maksym squinted at him.

"Won't water destroy your circuits?" Maksym asked, curious.

The sound Jin made was rude. "What type of cobbled together, second rate drone do you mistake me for?"

Kira's shoulders shook as she tried to suppress her amusement. It would be less funny if Jin wasn't serious.

"You're not going to talk sense into him," Kira advised. "Mainly because he has no sense."

Auralyn hummed, looking askance at Kira. Whatever her thoughts, she kept them to herself.

Maksym pointed to one of the ponds visible outside the windows. "Why not use one of those?"

"Do you know how unsanitary those things are? Who knows what kind of bacteria are in there? Not to mention the fish. The Haldeel grow deadly varieties in their ponds. How will you make it up to me if one tries to take a chunk out of me?"

"That's what you're afraid of? Being eaten?" Maksym didn't hide his skepticism.

"Of course not. Those low creatures couldn't even scratch my casing, but that doesn't mean they won't try."

In Jin logic, everything made sense. It was everyone else who had trouble following.

Kira listened, not interfering, more interested in seeing how these oshota of Wren's handled her friend. You could learn a lot by how someone interacted with those they perceived as lower in status.

Most people had some sense of self-preservation. They wouldn't knowingly antagonize a person who was equal or stronger than them—but introduce an entity they thought they could get away with bullying and you saw their true character.

Knowing their reaction would shape how Kira and Jin approached their time with the Tuann.

Jin was pushing the envelope a bit, but sometimes that was when you got the best reactions. Better to know now what they thought of Kira and Jin rather than get stabbed in the back later.

Of course, as always with Jin, there was some level of truth behind his actions.

He really did want a shower to wash off the muck, and he really did think the pond unsanitary for his needs.

Right now, the knowledge that his beautiful casing was smeared with unknown organic material was probably driving him crazy.

In all the time Kira had known him, he had never been one to allow anything to mar his perfection.

Auralyn didn't argue with him as she raised her arm, pressing her fingers near the crook of her elbow. A map slowly formed over her arm.

She pointed to a section that included several rooms. "This is where we are residing." She moved her finger and pointed to a room in the middle. "This is Kira's room. You may go there if you'd like a shower."

Auralyn held the map for a second longer before it faded. "Do you need me to show you again?"

"Nope. I got it." Jin shot toward the ceiling.

"One thing," Auralyn called before he disappeared to the next floor. "I'd advise staying out of the territory of other Houses. If they find you, they won't be as kind."

Jin paused, shifting until his "eye" was focused on Kira in question.

Kira had known Auralyn was dangerous, but her words showed she was also smart.

Her seemingly harmless advice disguised a warning. What's more, she demonstrated how well she understood Kira and Jin, cutting off Jin's investigations of the rest of the dwelling.

Now, if he were caught, he wouldn't have the excuse that he didn't know. It was Auralyn's way of saying obey the rules or there would be consequences.

Kira shook her head once at Jin, telling him without words to give up on exploring. Better not to tip their hand.

If Elena was here, she was under Graydon's care. He wouldn't let anything happen to her niece.

"Understood." Jin disappeared around the corner in the next instant.

Auralyn directed a bored look at Kira. "Shall we continue now that there are no other distractions?"

By all means, Kira thought.

A faint smile touched Auralyn's features as she walked past Kira. "Your *seon'yer* is expecting you. I'm sure you two have much to talk about."

Kira grimaced. That's what she was afraid of.

Maksym clapped her on the shoulder. "Don't worry, little junior. His punishments only hurt your soul and body for a little while."

"Somehow, that's not as reassuring as you might think," Kira said dryly.

"You'll get used to it."

* * *

Their destination turned out to be a gym.

Like the rest of the house, it had a distinct lack of frills, instead making use of clean lines in its designs.

Kira frowned when she saw it. Despite the presence of weights and other equipment, something was missing. There was none of the scent of sweat and blood that inevitably lingered long after a hard training session.

Either the space was a new addition or it had been re-purposed specifically for its guests to work out their natural aggression.

The Tuann walked a treacherous edge. Physical activity helped them maintain a balance that kept them from lashing out in new and unexpected ways.

It was one of the reasons Kira had done so well in the war.

Let her be inactive too long, and she got this itch under her skin. Violence or the adrenaline that came from danger were the only ways to work it out again. Without them, she had to exhaust her body to keep from tearing people's heads off when they irritated her.

She'd always thought those urges meant she was broken inside. It was only recently that she realized it was a normal facet of her species.

Mats lined the floor with simulators on one side for those who desired a more strenuous workout. Any opponent you wished was available along with a wide variety of difficulty levels.

Floor to ceiling windows occupied one entire wall, offering a clear view of the garden and pond outside. Something told Kira if someone wished those windows could easily become a mirror to allow the user to perfect their form.

"Where's Wren? I don't see him," Kira asked as Auralyn ignored her, walking away.

Kira frowned after her. She thought the whole purpose of this jaunt was so Wren could take her to task.

Yet, Auralyn was abandoning her without even vague instructions about where to go next.

Maybe this was all a trap, Kira thought as the other two trailed in Auralyn's wake, leaving Finn and Kira on their own.

"Are they always like this?" Kira asked Finn.

She'd expected many things out of this encounter. Politely being shown to the gym before they went their merry way wasn't one of them. Where was the lecture? The threats?

"They've always had their own way of doing things," Finn said carefully.

Kira shot him a look. Wren had always struck her as a rule follower. Someone who basked in tradition.

Kira, on the other hand, was not. Her way of doing things was considered a little unorthodox—to put it kindly.

That conflicting methodology was why she was hesitant to accept him as her *seon'yer.*

Finn shrugged at her. "You'll see what I mean."

"Why do I feel like I don't understand Wren at all?"

"You're in good company, then. No one truly understands that man."

Kira moved into the gym, noting that it was almost empty except for two figures in the far corner.

"You sound like you're familiar with him," Kira said.

Uncertainty crossed Finn's face. "One of my previous swords was a friend of his."

Kira was surprised he was the one to broach this subject. Since Yukina's revelations, he'd made a point to keep a low profile.

There was something in the careful way he held himself that said he wasn't ready to reopen this wound. Kira could respect that.

From the way his shoulders loosened when she didn't say anything else, she realized she'd made the right decision.

Movement pulled Kira's attention to the tableau in front of her.

An oshota stood guard as a figure not much taller than Kira's waist spun and twirled, executing kick after punch after flip in a short drill Kira recognized.

The figure spun again, showing her the person's face.

Kira inhaled sharply, forcing herself not to move as the oshota tensed, fixating on her like a papa wolf who'd spotted a danger to his pup.

Said pup wobbled as she immediately tried to flow into the next sequence of movements. There was a hitch in her step as she recovered.

Not bad, Kira conceded, but the pup still had a way to go.

Kira stopped several feet from the oshota and young girl. She waited, knowing getting any closer would only escalate the situation. The oshota didn't know who she was. If he perceived her as a threat, he would be within his rights to eliminate Kira.

In the next second, the girl spun, her leg sweeping out in a graceful arc.

She spotted Kira, her eyes widening as she lost focus. Unfortunately for her, her momentum didn't stop. She tripped, nearly face-planting before she caught herself again.

Kira folded her arms across her chest and stared at the waif. "Is there something you'd like to tell me?"

Kira pretended not to see the way the oshota tapped his fingers against the hilt of his sword in clear threat as her niece looked up at her with guilt written across her face.

"Hi, Auntie. Some unexpected things happened."

Kira's eyebrow twitched. "Oh? Do tell."

Elena flinched at Kira's expression.

"I just thought I could help," Elena muttered, deflating.

"Instead, you got caught—and now I'm caught. What have we learned?" Kira asked, not letting herself soften.

They were dealing with extremely dangerous entities. Things had worked out this time because it was Graydon. What if it had been someone else who'd locked onto Elena because of her actions?

Kira's way of speaking might seem harsh—maybe even mean—but she'd much prefer Elena learn with words rather than experience the much more brutal lessons their enemies would teach if they ever caught her.

The oshota watched the two carefully, dropping his hand from his enblade as he concluded Kira wasn't a threat.

Elena answered in a monotone. "Not to act recklessly, or else I'll put everyone in danger."

Kira's smile was humorless. "You don't seem quite convinced."

Elena shot up her head, her eyes widening. "No. I've learned my lesson. I promise."

"Too late." Kira clapped her hands. "Time for some remedial lessons."

Elena groaned. "I hate those."

"Which is why I do them."

Though their effectiveness seemed to be wearing off if Elena's recent actions were anything to judge by. In the future, Kira would need to find a more powerful motivator for good behavior.

Truthfully, she'd been expecting this.

To call Kira and Jin headstrong at that age was an understatement. As rebellious teens go, they were so much worse with Himoto often being left to clean up their messes.

To be honest, sometimes Kira wondered how she and Jin had survived this long.

Elena frowned. "How did you get captured anyway?"

Finn looked away, his shoulders shaking suspiciously.

Kira didn't move, glaring at the pint-sized annoyance. "Are we talking about me?"

Far from the chastened expression Kira was hoping for, Elena's eyes narrowed as speculation filled her face. "No, just surprised is all. You and Uncle Jin almost never get caught."

Kira thanked her lucky stars that Jin wasn't there at the moment. If she had her preference, Elena would never learn how a swarm of shriekers had led to their downfall.

Next to Kira, Finn's shoulders shook harder.

Laugh it up. They'd see who was laughing the next time she decided to go on walkabout. She'd pick a disguise so much more humiliating than the hoodie he currently wore.

A crafty look entered Elena's face as she glanced between the two of them. "Maybe it's the mountain I should be taking lessons from."

"Two lessons."

Horror filled Elena's eyes. "Auntie!"

Kira shot her a look. "Want to make it three?"

"No." Elena's lips held a sulky pout.

"Pick your weapon then."

Elena grumbled to herself as she faced the oshota guarding her. Arms pinned to her side, she bent forward at the waist in a slight bow. "With your permission."

Only the faintest trace of amusement marred the oshota's stoic expression as he inclined his chin.

Kira waited until her niece had turned before aiming a brutal kick to the side of Finn's knee. He easily dodged, stepping out of range.

"It's not that funny," she told him.

"She's a miniature version of you. The universe is just."

Kira aimed her grimace at the ceiling, finally understanding what people meant when they said karma was a bitch. She really should have made more of an effort to ensure her niece didn't turn out like her. Raider was going to have her head when he realized.

"Do you have a preference?" Elena asked as she examined the practice blades on the rack.

Kira waved a hand. "Whatever you choose is fine."

If this had been a real duel, Kira would have chosen for herself rather than trusting someone else to do it for her. Instead, this was a lesson for Elena. It would lose its impact if Kira chose the best weapon for herself.

Elena was solemn as she picked out a practice en-blade before setting it to the side. The second en-blade she spent some time choosing, picking up one and testing it with a few swings before putting it down again. She repeated the movement several times before she found a blade she was happy with.

Finished, she marched over to Kira and handed the second blade to her.

Kira took it, getting accustomed to its weight and feel. Not bad. It was one Kira might have chosen for herself.

She shot her niece a sideways glance. It looked like someone had been paying attention.

Elena waited, her expression hopeful as Kira tested her selection. Anticipation brewed on her face, forcing Kira to smother her smile.

This might have been called a lesson, but it was clear her niece wanted nothing more than to test herself against Kira.

Elena bounced on her toes. "Remember your promise, Auntie."

Ah. Someone had gotten cocky in Kira's time away. She'd have to fix that.

"We're a long way from that. First, a certain someone has to convince me with her actions." Kira sent Elena a pointed stare.

Her niece nodded; her expression serious as she got a focused look in her eyes.

"Remember. No—" Kira wiggled her fingers to indicate *ki.*

Rather than answer, Elena planted her back foot and lunged forward. Kira swayed, barely avoiding the tip of Elena's practice blade.

Elena switched tactics, aiming a kick at her aunt's knee. Kira grabbed Elena's foot and tugged, pulling her niece off-balance.

"That's not what you wanted to show me, is it?" Kira asked with a mocking lift of her eyebrow.

Elena snarled, bounding upright and lunging for Kira again.

This time Kira grabbed Elena's leading arm and hooked a foot around the back of her knee, breaking her stance again. Elena landed on her knees.

"Tut, tut. What did I say about anger?" Kira asked.

Elena planted her hands, lifting in a modified handstand and shooting one foot back and up toward Kira's face. Kira blocked with one hand, grabbing her niece's calf with the other. Kira grinned, right before she picked her niece up and swung her in a circle before gently depositing her on the ground once again.

"Dead," Kira told her.

This time Kira stepped out of reach as her niece rolled onto her back, looking up at her grumpily.

Kira gave her an expectant expression. "Done already?"

Determination shone on Elena's face.

Kira's lips twitched. Good.

She'd be disappointed if this was enough to break Elena's spirit. There were many trials and tribulations facing her niece in the future. Her path, more than most, wouldn't be an easy one.

Not entirely Tuann, not entirely human, but a mix of both with a little extra thrown in. She wasn't likely to be fully accepted anywhere.

Like Kira and Jin, she would have to make her own family and home. If she couldn't figure out how to face adversity now, her future would be a harsh one.

Kira could only provide so much of a buffer. She couldn't be with Elena a hundred percent of the time. Nor would she be able to control the actions of others.

It was her job to ensure Elena had the tools she needed to not only stay alive but to thrive. Kira took that job very seriously. Sometimes you had to be cruel to be merciful. A little pain now would save Elena a lot of heartache in the long run.

Elena stood and dusted herself off.

Kira waited for her niece to take her stance, her blade held loosely at her side.

To her surprise, Elena didn't attack immediately, instead watching Kira closely as she shook one hand out and then the other.

Kira kept her small smile to herself. She was taking the time to assess the situation, just like Kira and Jin had taught her.

Now, niece, what are you going to do?

Elena inched toward Kira, the blade held cautiously in front of her.

She was trying to draw Kira out.

Kira was willing to play. To see how far she'd come.

Kira shifted her weight to her right foot as if she planned to dart right.

Caution filled Elena's posture, but she didn't move.

Very good. She wasn't falling for Kira's bluff.

It was an improvement. A few months ago, she would have.

Kira lifted a hand and made a come-on motion. Caution was all well and good, but sometimes it held you back.

Elena darted forward, bringing her sword down in a standard strike. Kira evaded with a small shift of her weight. This time Elena hadn't committed fully to the strike, so Kira didn't pull her off-balance.

Elena followed up with a feint, advancing as she tried to force Kira to react.

The entire time Kira didn't exchange a single blow with her, instead shifting and dodging, each time with only a fraction of clearance between herself and Elena's blade.

Predictably, Elena's frustration grew, making her more and more intent on reaching Kira.

She lunged forward, an opening appearing in her guard. Kira took advantage, dumping her on the ground.

"Dead again."

Elena spun, sweeping a leg out. Kira hopped away.

"You'll never accomplish your goals with this level of skill."

Elena attacked from a low crouch. Kira swayed to the left, grabbing Elena's sword arm and hauling her closer. She set the blunt edge of her blade against Elena's neck.

"Not fast enough."

Kira pushed her away gently, careful not to hurt her.

"You always attack in the same way. You can already see it's not working. Do something else."

Rather than listen, Elena sprung forward, causing Kira to sigh and shake her head.

She stepped to the side, reaching for Elena's lead arm.

Elena's hand opened, the blade falling. The arm Kira was holding twisted, bringing her closer as Elena caught the blade, and stabbed up under her arm toward Kira's stomach.

It was an unexpected move, designed to force Kira to finally use the practice sword.

Kira's lips twitched. Well done, but not smart enough.

She sidestepped, pushing Elena's arm down to interfere with the path of the sword.

They ended with Elena stumbling a step forward and Kira standing in the same position as before.

"Well done. You finally figured out the handicap," Kira said.

Elena flushed at the compliment.

"For that, you can now use your *ki,*" Kira said. "Show me what you got."

Elena's eyes lit up. Her stance shifted as Kira waited.

Since her time in Roake, Kira had learned about *ki* and how it differed from person to person.

Some, like Auralyn, manipulated *ki* as if it were an external force, manifesting it outside their bodies. Then there were those like Joule who specialized in shields. Kira suspected since his designation was as an earth affinity, he could also manipulate the attributes of materials, a handy talent for anyone seeking the role of protector.

His talent was still raw and unpolished, but Kira had a feeling he would become a force to be reckoned with if guided properly.

And then there were those like Elena who used *ki* internally. Speed, agility, power. All amplified.

This time when Elena attacked, she did so with a speed and force double what she'd used previously.

Kira knocked Elena's sword thrust away. Elena whirled, coming at Kira again and again, her momentum increasing until the thwack, thwack, thwack of their swords filled the room.

Elena jumped and leapt, even her most vicious attacks repelled until sweat dotted her head and her eyes glittered.

Kira waited for her moment, knowing it was coming.

Finally, Elena barreled forward. Kira slid to her right, stepping forward and turning until she was behind her. She poked her niece in the spine in the next second.

"Dead."

Elena gritted her teeth, undeterred.

Her movements came faster and faster. Kira parried easily.

Finally, she swept her niece's legs out from under her, toppling her onto her back. She thrust the point of the blade down, holding it to Elena's neck.

"Dead again, dear one."

This time Elena didn't move, resting with her arms spread.

"Auntie, why are you so good?"

"Practice." Kira tapped Elena on her belly twice with the blade. "Now, chop, chop. You know the rules. Every moment you lie there, you'll take an additional punishment."

Elena rose to her feet with a groan, grabbing the practice sword next to her.

"Remember, it's not always about speed, kiddo," Kira told her. "Sometimes you have to be slow to be fast."

Elena's *ki* made her reactions quicker and her movements faster, but it also made them uneven. Her accuracy fell as a result.

With a normal opponent she'd be fine, but she wasn't up against normal people. They'd take any weakness and exploit it to their own benefit.

Kira stepped aside, taking up a defensive stance and motioning for her niece to continue. "Again."

FOURTEEN

A SHORT TIME later, when Elena landed on her back again, she lay there, panting as she stared up at the ceiling.

Kira bent over her. "Had enough?"

Elena gave her a resigned nod. "I should have known I couldn't beat you."

Kira grinned as she patted her niece's face. "What does this make? One hundred and one wins for me."

"One hundred and seven, but who's counting," Jin said from the sidelines.

Elena and Kira looked over to find he wasn't the only one to join them while they'd been preoccupied. Auralyn, Zoella, and Maksym waited next to him, oshota from other Houses Kira didn't recognize trickling in behind them.

Kira remained crouched as her niece jolted upright with a happy expression. "Uncle Jin! When did you get here?"

Jin headed their way. "Right around the time you hit the ground."

Elena's expression turned sheepish. "You'll have to be more specific. I hit the ground a lot this time."

Jin snickered. "A little while before she let you use *ki.* I have to say you didn't do too bad, sprout."

"It still wasn't enough to make Auntie get serious." One side of Elena's mouth pulled down in disappointment.

"Interesting teaching method," Auralyn observed. "It's rare for the young to train without their *ki.*"

"Auntie says that mastering your body is a crucial first step in any foundation," Elena volunteered.

To Kira's surprise, Auralyn's eyes warmed, her perpetual look of boredom fading slightly. "Oh?"

At the unspoken question in Auralyn's expression, Kira shrugged. "Your young are used to planets with a Mea'Ave. Unless they're forced to the brink, they probably have never felt *ki* depletion."

The Mea'Ave was a semi-sentient entity whose presence allowed *ki* to flourish. A symbiotic relationship that Kira didn't entirely understand existed between it and the Tuann. While it wasn't quite a god in the Tuann's eyes, it did guide many of their beliefs and actions. As a result, the Tuann had grown up in an environment conducive to the replenishment and maintenance of *ki*.

Most were overly reliant on it as a result in Kira's opinion. They trained their *ki* but often neglected their bodies.

If they were always able to fight in ideal conditions, this might be an effective tactic, but in Kira's experience the things that could go wrong would go wrong.

Kira wanted her niece to know how to handle herself when her *ki* failed her. Himoto had taught her to always have a backup plan. It was why she was versed in both the sword and hand-to-hand combat. You couldn't always guarantee you'd have the appropriate weapons when walking into a fight. Those who prepared for the worst-case scenario would have the advantage.

"Also, the gains from *ki* manipulation is greater if her body is already in good shape," Kira finished.

"Smart," Auralyn complimented.

Kira was about to respond when a screech from the entrance to the gym distracted her.

"*Seon'yer*!" Ziva shouted.

The girl had stopped inside the gym, her eyes wide as they fixed on Kira. Joule next to her looked over with interest, the same happiness on Ziva's face showing briefly on his before he buried it.

"Oh boy," Jin said as Kira fought the urge to cover her face with a hand.

Elena sent her a sidelong look as Ziva marched in her direction. "Auntie, you've picked up another one."

"Be nice," Kira told her.

An impish grin flashed across Elena's face. "I'm always nice to your strays."

"Would Tommy say the same if I were to ask him that?"

Elena scowled. "He doesn't count."

"Hmm."

Ziva reached them in the next second.

"Seon'yer," she repeated.

Auralyn slid Kira a look. "Interesting."

Kira ignored her, fixing Ziva with a hard look. "What in all my actions makes you think I'm your *seon'yer*?"

Ziva stopped and blinked. She lifted a hand, pointing at Kira. "Mentor." Next, she pointed at herself. "Mentee."

Finn leaned over. "That is the basic definition of a *seon'yer*."

Kira shot him an accusatory look that said he was supposed to be on her side.

The corners of his eyes crinkled, but otherwise his expression didn't shift.

With no help coming from that quarter, Kira studied Ziva. The girl was a surprisingly difficult opponent. Like a certain other somebody Kira knew, she heard what she wanted and not necessarily what was being said.

Or else how would she have latched onto this ridiculous notion of Kira being her *seon'yer*.

"Joule, please talk some sense into your sister."

When all else failed, appeal to the people who knew Ziva best.

Joule's mouth opened and then shut. He looked from Ziva to Kira, the former's face determined, the latter's frustrated. Many thoughts raced across his face.

Finally, he gave Kira a hopeful expression. *"Seon—"*

Kira pointed at him, her expression sufficiently threatening to freeze the words on his tongue. "Don't even think it."

Maksym doubled over, his shoulders shaking as Zoella looked on with amusement. Even Auralyn seemed to find some humor in the situation, her lips twitching up the barest bit.

Kira focused on Ziva. "You're not old enough to have a *seon'yer*."

From Kira's understanding, one had to be past their *uhva na* to gain that privilege.

"Then you'll be my *seon'yer* at that time?" Ziva asked, nothing in her demeanor making Kira think she had given up.

Kira hesitated with a denial on her tongue.

Ziva was still young. It would be decades before she advanced enough to join any House's selection process. By then, it was possible Kira would be long gone.

Once, she would have even said her leaving was inevitable. Things had changed since then. No one was more surprised than her when leaving Roake proved more difficult than she'd imagined. She felt like she'd left a piece of her behind.

It was an oddly unsettling feeling.

Yet, there it was.

There were things still to be discovered in Roake. She'd be lying if she said she wasn't a little curious about her uncle and the stories he could tell her about her father.

That being said, she didn't want to make promises she couldn't keep.

"We'll discuss it then," Kira finally said.

Rather than adjusting Ziva's expectations in a more reasonable direction, her answer caused hope to shine in the girl's eyes.

Kira hadn't said yes, but she hadn't given an outright no.

For someone like Ziva, who persisted against all odds, it was enough for her to cling even harder to the *seon'yer* she'd chosen.

Kira saw all these thoughts flit across Ziva's face and wanted to close her eyes. Rather than dissuade the child, it seemed she'd only made her more determined.

Story of her life.

One of those who'd been watching from afar approached with a sneer.

"You should reconsider, *zala*. This woman can't even handle fighting a child." His eyes flicked toward Elena in unmistakable meaning. "If you follow a *seon'yer* like her, you'll never amount to anything, let alone pass the *adva ka*."

Ziva spun, a snarl rumbling in her chest. "Shut your face hole, offspring of a *fendrik*."

"Ouch," Jin said. "That's quite the insult."

The man stared at Ziva, his nostrils flaring.

"Well said, little sister." Elena moved toward the two taking up a position on one side of Ziva as Joule raised his hands in the first stance for a shield on the other side.

Ziva's forehead wrinkled as she frowned at Kira's niece. "We're not related."

Elena held up a finger. "Here is your first guidance from your senior. Auntie says family can be chosen as well as born. This means any disciple of Auntie's is also a sister or brother to the rest. Understand?"

Ziva's nod was solemn.

"And I am her first disciple." Elena tapped Ziva's nose. "So, I will always be your elder."

This time Ziva nodded twice, her eyes shining as she soaked in Elena's words.

"What are you teaching that child?" Maksym asked.

Kira's expression was grim. "That is the question, isn't it?"

Kira would really like to know where Elena pulled all that from—because the last part had never come out of Kira's mouth.

Elena's expression was coy as she glanced at the oshota who'd insulted Kira. "Second guidance—don't be as blind as this one."

The man went ramrod straight at that. "Insolent child."

Her niece's lips twisted. "Being young doesn't prevent me from seeing the truth. If you were paying proper attention, you'd have realized that while I used *ki,* Auntie never touched hers, yet she controlled the tempo the entire time. Forget landing a blow. I couldn't even make her take a step back. I wonder if you could do the same." Elena looked him up and down, her expression saying she wasn't very impressed with what she saw. "Would you like to find out?"

Kira stepped forward, inserting herself between the two as she shook her head. "I don't think so. That's enough out of you."

Now she remembered what she'd been teaching her niece. Those comments—especially the last one—was right out of Kira and Jin's playbook.

"Spoilsport," Elena told her.

Kira looked at her. "What did I tell you about picking fights?"

Elena gazed innocently up at her. "Not to get caught?"

"Try again," Kira said dryly.

Elena started to open her mouth but was interrupted by a cool voice coming from the direction of the doorway.

"Yes, I'm interested in hearing this too. Exactly what are you teaching her, Kira?" Raider strode toward them, Wren at his back.

Elena's teasing expression drained away, leaving her quiet and withdrawn.

Kira studied the two of them, not answering immediately.

The oshota who'd insulted Kira looked like he'd bitten into something sour as he caught sight of Wren. Kira's *seon'yer* apparently had a bit of a reputation. A deserved one if his display in the *uhva na* was anything to judge by.

Elena, picking up on her tension, glanced up at her in question.

Kira patted her shoulder, signaling all was well and not to interfere. Whether her niece would deign to listen was another story.

"Is there a problem?" Wren asked, sweeping a gaze over the strange oshota.

Silence lingered until Auralyn straightened. "Nothing beyond the normal. Just a few pests sticking their noses where they don't belong."

The strange oshota bristled but remained silent.

Kira whistled silently. She'd really like to know what Wren and his oshota had done to create such an interesting reaction in another House's oshota.

The Tuann thrived on confrontation and duels. Opposing Houses clashed on a regular basis. She'd never seen an oshota retreat this quickly. At least not before a few blows were exchanged to test the other's mettle.

"And you, *yer'se*? Are you of the same opinion?" Wren directed the question at Kira.

The oshota paled, his gaze meeting Kira's before lifting away.

The oshota probably thought Kira was an easy target. She wasn't well known among other Houses. Of those who'd heard of her, she doubted any would recognize her face.

His unease was reflected in the faces of his companions.

"Yup. No problems here," Kira said, staring at the man who'd thought to ridicule her only to end up being the one ridiculed.

There was a certain poetry there that Kira enjoyed—especially since he'd gone after Ziva to get to Kira.

"In that case, follow me," Wren ordered. "There are things we need to address."

Kira was afraid he'd say that.

A part of her would have preferred to put the coming confrontation off indefinitely.

From the careful control in Wren's expression and the way he seemed to soften when he looked at Elena, Kira had a feeling the thing she'd been most afraid of had already happened.

Wren had guessed at the nature of Elena's relation to him, and it was clear he'd already begun forming an attachment.

If it ever became necessary to remove Elena from the Tuann's sphere of influence, Kira would have a fight on her hands.

Whether her niece realized it or not, her family had grown to include an extremely powerful Tuann.

"Jin, stay close to Elena and get in touch with our friend." Kira tilted her head at Elena. "You know the one."

Jin's sigh was heavy. "I do indeed."

Odin had a lot of explaining to do. He was supposed to watch Elena, not let her get caught by the Tuann.

Elena ignored them in favor of slinging an arm over Ziva's shoulders. "How about I show you my fun moves?"

The Tuann who'd picked a fight earlier, summoned his courage from somewhere. He curled his lip at Kira's niece.

"What would a wet-behind-her-ears infant know about anything? You should let those with something to offer have the floor." He jabbed Elena's shoulder with a hard finger.

Kira, who'd started to walk away, came to a stop.

Did that man just touch her niece?

Kira did an about face. A sweet smile touched her lips, the corners of her eyes crinkling as she took a step toward the oshota.

"Girls, step back. Step back now," Jin ordered, sounding alarmed.

Elena moved quickly, drawing Ziva and Joule with her. "Third and most important piece of advice—never, ever, ever insult someone Auntie cares about."

Ziva nodded with an intent expression, looking like she was taking mental notes.

Joule's eyes widened in understanding and alarm. He, more than his sister, knew what Kira was capable of.

"Someone sure is brave," Kira said in a silky voice.

She'd tried to be kind. Everyone had seen it.

She'd let him off without extracting even the tiniest bit of revenge, but did he learn from his experiences? Did he appreciate her leniency?

No. He did not.

He just had to go and show his ass. Now it was time to learn what happened when you mooned a predator more dangerous than the ones he was used to.

"Kira, do not kill him," Jin warned.

Kira padded closer to the dead man walking.

"I mean it," Jin said when she didn't answer. "Roake is not going to back us in a blood feud if you nuke the oshota of another House."

"Are you sure about that?" Maksym asked.

Blood lust rose off him, matched only by the intensity of his companions.

Auralyn looked at the oshota and those behind him as if they were dog shit she'd found under her shoe. Simply scraping them off would be too kind a fate. Only complete annihilation would do.

Kira noted all this distantly, too fixated on her prey to care.

For the first time since she'd donned the inhibitor, she could feel her primus form crouched in her psyche. A solid wall separated her from it, but that didn't stop the lust for vengeance from seeping through.

The other wanted to rip and tear and, then, howl its supremacy to the sky. It wanted to teach these lesser beings to fear where it trod.

The concept of right and wrong was hazy for that creature. All it cared about was protecting those it considered theirs.

Power flushed through Kira's veins as the primus pressed against the barrier. Pain followed swiftly on its heels; Kira's body unable to withstand the influx.

The inhibitor contracted around her wrist in warning, sending jolts of agony up her forearm.

Sensing the shift, Elena's attention shot to Kira, a cautious look entering her expression. "Auntie. No."

Kira stopped, taking a deep breath to compose herself. Elena was right. Losing herself to the primus would be self-indulgent and reckless.

Only when the pain abated and her *ki* settled did Kira focus on the oshota again. It was his lucky day. He got to live.

Raider threw himself forward as Kira started to speak. He hammered a punch into the other man's face.

Not content to end it there, Raider snapped a kick against the side of the man's knee. The man fell to the ground, catching himself with one hand. Raider didn't give him time to recover, kneeing him in the face.

The man's companions stepped forward with the intention of assisting their friend.

Kira bared her teeth at them. "Do it. I dare you."

She couldn't be sure if they backed down because of her or if it was the way Maksym and Zoella shifted in defense of Kira. Even the oshota who'd been guarding Elena earlier made clear his intentions. If there was a fight, it wouldn't only be Kira and Raider against the other House. Wren's oshota would bloody their hands too.

"Bullying children. I didn't realize House Remie had fallen this low," Wren observed. "I will be sure to let our Overlord know so we can cut ties with such a weakling."

There was something in the way Wren stood that whispered if Raider hadn't acted, he would have.

It was confirmation of what Kira already suspected. Wren considered Elena his, and like all Tuann he protected his own.

What confused her was the fact he'd let Raider act before him. It showed restraint and consideration for the human.

Had the relationship between the two changed so much during her absence?

It wasn't outside the realm of possibility. No one was more acquainted with Raider's abilities than Kira. If the Tuann ever got past their superiority complex, they'd realize not all humans were weak.

Raider was a wolf. People remembered the Phoenix, but Kira would never have accomplished all she had without Raider and the other Curs.

If Wren acknowledged Raider's skills, that would be the best outcome for both Raider and Elena.

"That's enough, don't you think?" Wren asked emotionlessly.

Raider paused, his fist still upraised as he thought it over.

"Any further and you'll kill him." Wren's statement held no judgment. Rather he was making an observation.

Kira was impressed.

Wren already understood the secret to Raider. Try to force him and he'd balk. Persuade him with sweet words and he'd turn those words around on you. Meet him with logic and he'd cool down.

Most of the time.

Raider let the oshota drop. "The sound of his voice offended me."

Kira looked at the man Raider had beaten half unconscious. He'd certainly solved that problem, hadn't he?

Raider straightened, looking neither left nor right as he stalked out of the now silent room. The oshota from the beaten man's House looked green as if they wanted to challenge Raider but were too afraid of House Roake's oshota to do so.

Elena bumped Kira's arm. "That was unexpected."

"You think so?" Kira shook her head. "I don't."

Elena peered up at her with a frown.

Kira slung an arm around her niece's shoulders. "He did what I was about to do."

Elena's confused expression cleared somewhat as she cast a yearning glance in the direction Raider had disappeared in. "You mean he did that for me?"

Kira playfully pushed her head away. "He certainly didn't do it for me."

Elena didn't look entirely convinced, but Kira didn't push. Elena needed to arrive at her own conclusions about Raider's behavior.

She tilted her head at Wren, changing the subject. "What do you think of him?"

Elena narrowed her eyes at the man in question. Noticing her actions, Wren stared calmly at her.

"He'd be a difficult opponent," Elena finally said. "Defeating him would be hard but not impossible for you."

Maksym overheard and made a muffled sound. Next, his shoulders started shaking as Zoella stared at Elena as if she were some odd being from another dimension.

Only Auralyn took the girl's words in stride, not reacting beyond a faint lowering of her eyelids.

Kira coughed. That wasn't what she'd meant, though she supposed it wasn't really a surprise given the type of training she normally subjected Elena to.

Wren's eyes narrowed on Kira. "Follow."

Elena frowned. "He's very authoritative. I'm not sure I like it."

Kira grimaced and patted Elena's shoulder. "Let's leave that aside for now. Stay close and don't go looking for trouble again."

Elena jerked her thumb at Ziva and Joule. "Mind if I show the little sister a few moves?"

Ziva brightened, looking like Elena had handed her a gift of unparalleled worth. In the face of such excitement, Kira didn't have the heart to deny her.

Even Joule seemed eager.

Kira hesitated before nodding uneasily. Why did she have a feeling this was going to bite her on the ass later?

* * *

Wren's back faced Kira as he helped himself to a drink of *keeva*.

Kira was content to wait, letting the silence that had descended during their trip to his private quarters linger.

His surroundings suited his personality.

There was very little clutter to be seen. What furniture there was, was simplistic and minimal. A black coffee table separated a couch and two armchairs.

Though the walls lacked artwork, the space was saved from being austere by the addition of an elegant white rug against dark floors that matched the dark ceiling.

The windows leading out to the balcony added texture and warmth to what would have been an otherwise cold room.

"Do you remember what you told me when I was dying?" Wren paused with his drink halfway to his lips.

Kira froze.

Her silence didn't deter Wren. "You told me my daughter wasn't waiting for me on the other side. You said she was here and that if I wanted to see her, I would have to live."

Kira's gaze dropped. That was the gist of what she'd said.

In her defense, she'd hoped her words would keep Wren alive. In that moment, she'd felt his willingness to slip gently into death and thought it a shame.

It had led to some unwise revelations on her part.

If the forty-three found out, forget about saving Elise, Kira doubted she would be able to save herself. She'd broken the taboo.

Kira's only choice was to bluff. "Did I? Fear has a habit of making you do impetuous things. Who can say for sure what I said then?"

She'd hoped with Wren being so close to death, he would doubt his memory—if he remembered at all. As was always the case, Kira's luck wasn't that good.

"Is Elena my grandchild?" Wren asked.

There it was. A frontal attack as befitting a man like Wren.

"How would you like me to answer that?" Kira asked carefully.

"The truth would be nice."

Kira's smile was fleeting and didn't reach her eyes. "If I tell you yes, will you love and protect her with all the fierceness you couldn't give to your daughter?"

Wren's eyebrows lowered.

"And what will you do if you ever find evidence she has a little bit extra to her?"

Wren's eyes went cold as he picked up on her insinuation.

"What about when enemies come knocking because that little girl is the answer to the riddle they've been struggling with for centuries?"

The Tuann were powerful, but they had one primary drawback.

It took many, many decades for them to fully mature. Trying to build up their military strength took centuries—especially if the former masters of the Tuann had to start with new stock.

Elena had many of the Tuann benefits but aged as fast as a human.

Kira could see Wren's struggle as he wrestled with rage, agony, horror—but not fear.

"How badly were you and the rest treated?" Wren finally asked in a hoarse voice.

"Torture is the proper term. There's a price for everything. The Tuann want their children back so badly they've never considered that their children might have become like the very monsters the Tuann fear."

The things they'd done and had done to them—they weren't easy things to brush under a rug and forget. All of them carried the scars.

"Can the Tuann still love their children if they aren't entirely Tuann anymore?"

Kira knew what it was like to have people's regard. To have them fawn and celebrate her. She also knew what it was like when that adoration was gone—to be reviled as a monster.

That sort of thing had a tendency to leave a mark on your soul, no matter how much you told yourself that you didn't care.

She wouldn't let Elena suffer that fate. Not even from her grandfather.

Wren didn't speak for long seconds. Long enough that Kira was already considering how to extract Elena from this situation.

It'd likely mean burning bridges, but Kira had always excelled at that. Himoto liked to say Kira didn't just burn her bridges, she broke them into tiny pieces and soaked them in gasoline before lighting the bonfire. Afterwards, she'd pull up a chair and roast marshmallows in the resulting blaze.

"I feel I should inform you that you're no longer my only *yer'se*." Wren carefully turned and poured himself another glass of *keeva.*

If he had a purpose for that statement, Kira couldn't see it.

"It's unusual to have two *yer'se* at one time, but the potential you both hold can't be denied."

Kira's eyes narrowed. He was changing the subject.

"I expect you to make every effort to get along with him."

Kira looked around feeling like she was in some alter dimension. How did they go from talking about Elena's lineage to this discussion about another *yer'se* she couldn't give two craps about?

Kira forced herself to play his game. "And who is this *yer'se?*"

Wren set his glass down, his face composed again as he met her eyes. "Raider."

Kira blinked in confusion. "My Raider?"

"I'm not sure he would enjoy being called that."

Probably not. It was more likely he'd try to separate her head from her shoulders.

"I saw your race in the preliminary rounds. It was impressive," Wren said in another lightning fast subject change. "In the future, you will not be so reckless."

Hold on a minute.

"It's only reckless if you get hurt or die," Kira said defensively.

Neither of those things had happened, so from where she stood, all was well that ended well.

The way Wren frowned at her made her feel like he was trying to determine the level of her stupidity.

Despite how it seemed, Kira always had a plan. Granted, those plans were often loosely defined with a high tendency to go wrong at the last minute, but she always came through in the end.

To prove it, she pulled up the hem of her shirt, exposing the under layer she still wore. "I knew this could take the impact. I never would have crossed the finish line that way if there had been risk of serious injury."

Wren regarded her with serious eyes. "You're trying to argue that the *balial* Roake gifted you would have prevented your death if you had miscalculated your descent on the tower."

Kira winced. "Not exactly."

Wren gave a short nod. "Good. Because I know the ballistic resistance of that material. Every bone in your body would have been crushed. If you hadn't pulled out of your dive in time, you would have died."

"But that didn't happen," Kira pointed out.

Wren's face was expressionless as he studied her. "I don't know how you're used to doing things, but you're one of my responsibilities now. I will not allow you to take such reckless actions again. Next time, find a safer way to win."

Kira didn't get a chance to argue before he switched topics again.

"I assume your board was destroyed. Do you need help procuring another one?" he asked.

Kira shook her head. "It's handled."

"Very well. You're dismissed."

Kira stood there for several seconds as she debated the merits of returning to their previous conversation.

He'd never given her a satisfactory answer.

Reluctantly, Kira moved toward the door.

"Kira," Wren said abruptly.

Kira stopped but didn't turn around.

"Thank you for protecting her for so long. The debt I owe you can never be repaid. I'll take over from here."

FIFTEEN

KIRA LET HERSELF out of Wren's room, in time to find Graydon prowling toward her. He was alone—or at least that was how it would seem to outsiders. A man as important as Graydon never went unaccompanied in potentially dangerous territory.

Graydon looked from Kira to the door she'd exited, amusement touching his features. "How did it go?"

There was something in how he asked that and the knowing look on his face that made Kira realize something.

"You knew."

Cunning man. She would never have expected him to put Elena together with Wren. He'd probably known their relation all the way back on Ta Sa'Riel—which meant Harlow was likely aware as well.

"How?"

Graydon stopped in front of her, his expression faintly mocking. "It's true the child doesn't much resemble Wren." Graydon paused, his sly smile widening. "But she looks very similar to Wren's deceased wife."

Kira didn't say anything. She looked away and closed her eyes as she kicked herself for not considering that possibility.

But then, who could blame her? It wasn't as if the concept of parents and lineage was a familiar one. Until her encounter with the Tuann she'd always thought she was a test tube baby designed in a lab.

She and the rest hadn't exactly spared a lot of consideration to where they came from. Surviving had taken up all of their focus in the early days, and later it hadn't seemed important. They'd been more than willing to bury any questions about their origins.

Rooky mistake, Kira.

"I'm impressed you could tell," Graydon said.

It had been difficult. There was a resemblance in their eyes and jaw, but it wasn't until hearing his history and seeing him fight in the *uhva na* that she'd been sure.

Wren and Elise's *ki* felt similar. Nearly identical if she was honest.

From there, she'd gambled that the two were linked.

Kira started down the hall again, Graydon keeping pace. She wasn't surprised when Finn moved out of the shadows, smoothly gliding after them.

As they walked, Kira sent Graydon a sidelong look. "Done with your pretty companion?"

He quirked an eyebrow at her. "Is that jealousy I detect?"

Kira eyed a doorway and then him.

His gaze turned questioning.

Kira smiled at him. "Just measuring to see if your inflated ego would fit through the opening."

Next to Finn, Amila choked on a laugh before hiding her amusement behind her typically stoic expression.

Kira didn't know when the other woman had joined them, but that wasn't odd. Graydon's oshota were among the best. Kira had given up on guessing all they could do.

Graydon didn't react to her words the way she expected. Remaining unaffected, his expression was teasing as he watched her with the focus of a cat that had spotted a particularly interesting mouse.

Kira braced, resisting the urge to slide away. Every time he looked at her that way, she usually ended up the loser in their exchanges.

"Have you spoken to Raider yet?"

Direct hit.

Graydon made a masculine sound that almost reminded Kira of a purr. "Let me know if you need my help dealing with him. My inflated ego and I will be more than happy to run to the rescue."

Kira had had enough of this conversation.

She lengthened her stride, hoping to leave him behind. As was always the case with Graydon, he moved to match her, keeping up easily.

Defeated, Kira resigned herself to having to deal with Graydon for a bit.

"Your exhibition with your niece was quite interesting," Graydon said.

His statement was slow to register, but when it did, Kira sent him a searching look. "You weren't there."

She would have known. Graydon carried this almost raw magnetism that was nearly impossible to miss. If he'd been in the training room, she would have picked up on it. She wouldn't have been able to help it.

Graydon regarded her steadily, his thoughts unreadable. "I have my ways."

Kira's eyes narrowed as she considered him. His ways, her ass. "You're having me watched."

She glanced around, her eyes lingering on Finn before she dismissed him as a possibility. The past weeks had convinced her of his loyalty. If he ever betrayed her, it would be because he considered her a danger to the Tuann's survival and the universe in general. He wouldn't throw away the gains he'd recently achieved to be Graydon's eyes and ears.

"Did you really expect anything else?" Graydon asked, interrupting her thoughts.

Not really. No. In his place, she'd have done the same to a known flight risk.

She and Jin would have to be more careful. Right now, she fully intended to work with Graydon on the subject of Elise, but there were still secrets she didn't feel comfortable revealing.

The need to have an escape route was as embedded in her DNA as the color of her hair.

Graydon and Kira descended the stairs to the first floor.

"I see Joule wasn't lying. You really are back," Devon said, leaning against a doorway as they approached. Spotting Graydon by her side, Devon gave him a serious nod. "*Seon'yer*."

Kira gave Graydon a considering glance. "Really?"

His appointment as Devon's *seon'yer* made perfect sense, considering what she suspected about Devon's lineage.

"You must be pleased," Kira told Devon.

He nodded once. "It was an unexpected reward."

Graydon brushed Kira's shoulder as he focused on his *yer'se*. "How did your preliminary race today go?"

Pride registered on Devon's face as he came to attention. "I qualified for the next round."

Kira was impressed. While the early rounds of the preliminaries weren't exactly impossible, especially for those of her level, they weren't easy either. You needed skill to reach the next stage.

"What position?" Graydon asked.

"Second."

Not bad. It would allow him to advance, but because he was second, he wouldn't draw too much notice from the other competitors.

If Kira hadn't been forced to extraordinary lengths by her awful start, that's the rank she would have targeted as well.

"There was a racer in the round after me that was very impressive. She used the same maneuver on the tower as the racer from yesterday."

Kira didn't move for several seconds, knowing she was the racer from yesterday that he was talking about. "Is that right?"

Devon's brow furrowed before he gave a hesitant nod.

"Did you get the name?" Kira asked.

He shook his head. "They went by the call sign Moonbeam."

Kira's gaze turned distant. Only a few people she knew of could have performed the dead man's plunge without crash landing and killing themselves.

Raider was one. Jace another.

Beyond the two of them, she could count on one hand the rest, and none were currently on the planet.

It was more likely this was a message to her. An act of challenge designed to draw her attention. But from who?

If Elise wanted her attention, why wouldn't she use one of the dozen drop boxes they'd set up for exactly this chain of events?

"Something wrong?" Graydon asked.

Kira shook her head, pushing the questions and half fleshed out theories out of her mind. This would have to wait until she had more information. Until then, any conclusions she drew would be speculation.

Devon's frown had grown more and more pronounced while Kira was lost in her thoughts. "Those allowed on planet are all required to compete in a quorum event."

"You don't know, do you?" Graydon teased.

Devon looked between the two of them in confusion. "Know what?"

Graydon tilted his head toward Kira. "Meet Sparrow."

Devon examined Kira in disbelief. "That's you?"

Kira lifted a shoulder. "The last time I checked."

"Winner of the Dragon Circuit? Two-time champion of the Osiris Belt?"

Kira studied him. Most people knew about the first but not the second. Only die-hard race fans ever remembered that one.

The Osiris Belt was considered boring among most fans. There weren't as many opportunities to showcase fancy skills. Couple that with its location on one of the most remote and unremarkable planets of the Consortium and few had heard of it.

It meant Devon had gone beyond the level of a general fan. His knowledge placed him in the realm of a super fan of the sport. Not something she'd anticipate of someone in his position.

Graydon considered her with interest. "That's quite the reputation you have there."

Footsteps from the hallway forestalled Kira's response.

She looked up to find Joule heading toward her.

He lifted a hand at Devon. "I saw the race. Nicely done."

Devon acknowledged the praise with a nod as Kira watched closely. The two seemed to have grown closer in her absence.

"Are you heading out for your event?" Devon asked.

Joule paused in the middle of peeking at Kira and nodded. "Yes."

"What event did you decide on?" Kira asked.

She'd never gotten the chance to hear when they were on the dropship.

Joule's smile was shy. "Castles."

The quorum ran a gamut of possibilities. From races like the one Kira and Devon had chosen to join, to events featuring various forms of combat, to feats focused on intellect and logic.

Unsurprisingly, most Tuann gravitated toward combat-based games.

The Haldeel, on the other hand, trended to those events that were more mental based. Castle was one such example. Designed to test a competitor's luck and strategic capability, it was a game easy to pick up but difficult to master—and one Kira had never seen played in person.

"Do you mind if I tag along?" Kira asked.

Joule's expression brightened. "I'd like nothing better."

Devon frowned. "I'd like to come too."

Joule nodded, outwardly excited as he led them to the door outside.

Graydon leaned toward Kira. "What are you up to?"

Kira concealed her involuntary shiver as his breath brushed against the sensitive skin of her neck. "What makes you think I'm up to anything?"

"You're always up to something."

Kira couldn't argue with that, so she didn't even try.

"Are you planning to put me under house arrest?" she asked him.

"*Coli*, I wouldn't dare."

Yeah, right. There wasn't much Graydon wouldn't dare. Including locking Kira up and throwing away the key.

To Kira's surprise, Graydon followed them outside.

"What are you doing?" she asked.

"I thought I should join you."

Kira's frown became more pronounced. "Don't you have business to attend to?"

The innocent look he aimed at her wasn't fooling anyone. "What could be more important than supporting the friend of my *yer'se*?"

Ahead, Devon and Joule were careful to stay out of the conversation, pretending not to listen.

Kira shook her head as she bit down hard on the unwise words she wanted to stay. Even a child would be able to see through Graydon's motivations. He hadn't even attended Devon's race, and he expected Kira to believe he cared about Joule's event?

Please. She wasn't that naive.

"Besides, Yukina represents the Face of the Tuann among the Haldeel. I would just get in her way. She'll call me if there's anyone she wants killed."

"So humble," Kira said dryly.

Graydon inclined his chin. "I endeavor to please."

* * *

The sun was completing its descent, twilight deepening into the evening hours as Kira and the rest headed toward the city center.

The streets of Zara were different in the evening. The crowds were denser and the atmosphere celebratory.

Holographic advertisements fought for attention against the smaller game stages known as the stratagem to the Haldeel. The continuous stream of sounds and images bombarded bystanders from several directions.

Unlike Castles, the stratagem wasn't considered an official part of the quorum. There were numerous variations. The more poetic claimed there were as many versions as there were grains of sand.

Winning any of them wouldn't bring the same acclaim or reward as doing well in Castles. Despite that, there was no shortage of visitors wanting to try their hand.

It wasn't unheard of for those who did well in the stratagem to be groomed for greater things. Though rare, there were some who'd won fame and status after a particularly good showing.

It was the Haldeel's version of gambling, only instead of luck, you used talent and skill to win.

Kira paused as she watched a Haldeel ascend the stage to her right. He crossed to the center and the waist-high column waiting there. After a second of perusal he pressed his hand onto it.

Four pillars of light rose around him, forming a square as the solid column in front of him dissolved into the floor. Transparent armor formed over his chest and arms.

His gaze was calculating as he stared at the pillars.

Lightning arced from them. The Haldeel evaded, dancing between the pillars as he tried to dodge the unpredictable bolts.

Noticing where Kira's attention had gone, Graydon paused. "Ever tried?"

Kira started after Devon and Joule. "Once or twice."

Jin referred to that part of her life as her dark period.

She'd found it too painful to be around humans and had landed on the edge of Haldeel territory as a result.

In those days, she'd been on edge. Vicious some might say, hitting back at the least provocation.

That was when she first encountered the stratagem. It filled Kira's need for distraction.

Popular among all ranks of the Haldeel, the stratagem allowed her to lose herself in its world. For a brief time, she'd earned quite the reputation while playing.

"Not going to watch?" Graydon asked, studying her.

Kira glanced over her shoulder, casually assessing the player. "No need. He won't advance to the next level."

As if to prove her right, there was a low hum from behind them as the holographic scene dissolved around the player.

"Good eye." Graydon nodded at a stage set for dual play. "I don't suppose you'd fancy a match?"

"Aren't we here to watch Joule participate in Castles?"

Graydon lifted an eyebrow. "Why can't we do both?"

Kira hesitated, feeling torn.

It had been a long time since she'd played.

Calling her competitive was kind. She'd never been good at turning the other cheek and Graydon was one of those rare individuals who could give her a real challenge.

The unmistakable provocation in his expression made resisting even more difficult.

"Unless you're afraid," Graydon taunted.

He was just asking to have the arrogance wiped off his face. Kira had time in her schedule.

Kira was careful not to let herself appear too eager. "Fine. One match."

Solal and Amila exchanged a look as if they knew something Kira didn't. Finn, on the other hand, seemed worried as Kira and Graydon stepped onto the stage.

"Do you have a preference?" Graydon asked, raising his hand.

The act triggered the menu screen. Several Haldeel icons in the midst of various actions appeared in front of him.

"This was your idea. Your choice."

It made no difference to Kira. She'd played most of them at one point or another.

He gave her a considering look before selecting the icon of a crouched Haldeel, sword held defensively across their body. "Let's try a practice round first."

Kira shrugged to show she didn't care. Practice or not, it was the same to her.

The stratagem Graydon chose was called Barrage. It was a bastardized, simpler version of Castles. Whereas in Castles, you had to take over enemy territory while dealing with the obstacles the puzzle master embedded in the game, with Barrage you only had to defend.

There were two ways to earn points. For every laser beam you destroyed cleanly, you got two points. If you only managed to deflect or damage it, you got a point.

The crux, however, came when you dodged.

A rebounded laser picked up points every time it hit the wall. If it hit the wall once and was destroyed, it brought the gamer four points. Two times and it was six points.

The only catch was every time it hit, it also picked up speed and would change direction, making it a potentially dangerous wild card—especially in the latter half of the game when the number of lasers increased.

Because the game would end when one opponent was struck, most chose to cleanly destroy the lasers so as not to risk ending the game early.

While it was more straight forward than Castles, it wasn't without its dangers.

A transparent blade stretched from Kira's hand, sending a tingle through her palm.

Reflexively, Kira squeezed the hilt, feeling like she was holding an actual sword. As always, she couldn't help but be impressed by the level of sensory feedback. If the sword hadn't been nearly translucent, she would have believed it real.

Thousands of small shapes unfolded from the stage, rising into the air. No bigger than the tip of a pen, they arranged themselves in two fifteen by fifteen squares around Kira and Graydon.

The mini drones shimmered, their colors changing until a box formed around them, their appearance giving the illusion of falling water.

Graydon smirked at Kira through the nearly transparent wall separating them. "Are you ready?"

In answer, Kira fell into a stance similar to the Haldeel's stance of beginning. Her right leg slid forward, the knee bent as she brought her sword diagonal across her body, the tip pointed to the ground with her elbow to the sky.

In his square, Graydon widened his stance, his sword held at his side.

Color bloomed in the water. Beams shot toward them, all three from the front.

Kira dealt with them in three clean moves, Graydon doing the same on his side.

Finished, Graydon took the time to study Kira. "Well, well. Someone is a little more familiar with this game than they led me to believe."

Kira lifted a shoulder. "I never said I was a novice."

It wasn't her fault if that was how he chose to take her words.

Graydon's eyes held a feral gleam that said he was looking forward to this. "This is going to be fun."

Kira hoped so.

Before she could say anything, she caught movement in the audience that had begun to gather along the edge of their stage.

The Tuann who'd taunted Elena earlier stood out from the crowd, the skin around one eye discolored and red with the faintest swelling. He also had a split lip. Other than that, he looked remarkably unharmed after the beating Raider had given him.

Kira supposed there were some perks to being Tuann. Fast healing among them.

He sneered when he spotted Kira.

Walk away; pretend you didn't see me, she told him silently.

He'd already come up the loser in one exchange. Why add insult to misery?

"Friend of yours?" Graydon asked.

Kira rotated the hand holding the light blade as she considered. "I'm pretty sure he sees me more along the lines of an enemy."

Intrigue touched Graydon's face. "You were only in the villa for a couple of hours. How did you upset an oshota from House Remie so quickly?"

Kira frowned at him. "I thought you saw the exhibition with Elena."

"It seems I missed a few parts," Graydon said. "I'll have to pay more attention in the future."

"You know there's a word for people like you." Kira turned away from the audience to face him fully, her expression taunting. "It's called being a stalker."

"Why did you call us over, Niland?" someone asked from the audience below the stage, interrupting Graydon's response. "I thought we were here to watch Castle. Why waste time with stratagem?"

"I've found something much more fun." Niland tilted his head at where Kira and Graydon still stood on the stage waiting for the game to begin again. "Remember the arrogant brat I caught pretending to be a *seon'yer*? That's her."

Kira jerked a thumb at Niland, making sure to keep her voice down. "Is he really an oshota?"

She simply couldn't see it. The oshota she knew weren't this arrogant—or dumb.

Graydon looked like he was trying to suppress his amusement. "You've been spoiled by the quality of Roake, *coli.* Not all oshota are created equal."

That was becoming increasingly clear. Picking fights just for the sake of having someone to push down to make yourself feel better was the act of a bully—a behavior she had never associated with the oshota.

"Wait. I think I know her," one of Niland's companions said. "Isn't she the lost child of Roake?"

Niland's smirk widened. "You're right." He looked over at where Roderick stood stiffly to the side. Not really part of the group except through proximity. "Luatha, didn't your Overlord wipe her hands clean of this one?"

The question was meant to embarrass—whether Kira or Roderick was the question.

Kira looked over to find Roderick frozen in place, looking up at her with a complicated expression like he didn't know if it would be better to interfere or stay quiet.

He'd gotten smarter since the events on Ta Da'an. Back then, he would have cried insult immediately and made the entire matter worse.

Kira took pity on him, signaling for him to wait.

To her relief, he didn't say anything—good or bad.

Seconds later, an arm landed on Roderick's shoulder as a stranger leaned into him. Very slowly, Roderick looked at the hand touching him, his face twisting in a disgust that made Kira struggle to hide her laughter.

"Don't tease the poor man. House Luatha has been through a lot lately. Fighting off an invasion is exhausting work," the newcomer said, sending the others a charming smile.

"Lorcan, you're always so kind," Niland said.

Kira scoffed.

What kindness? The man managed to insult both Roderick and Luatha in a few simple sentences.

Eyes filled with a fiery impatience met Kira's. There was the Roderick she remembered. The hothead who took himself entirely too seriously.

To her surprise, he stayed quiet, his expression aggrieved as he held himself rigid.

Niland smirked at Kira. "Would you be interested in a bet?"

The side-eye Roderick sent Niland was filled with enough rage to strip the man's flesh from his bones if it had contained tangible heat.

"Yeah, Roddy. How about a bet?" Kira said, interfering before Roderick could act on the violence she could see brewing.

Some of the anger faded from Roderick's face as he watched her carefully.

"You're right. The *zala* is cocky." There was a sharp glint in Lorcan's eyes that reminded Kira of Graydon for a moment.

She ignored the similarity, putting on an innocent expression. "You don't have to if you're afraid."

She wasn't entirely sure why she was playing their game. Maybe it had something to do with the careful restraint Roderick was displaying or the way they'd badmouthed Liara.

Kira might not have wanted to be stuck on Ta Da'an, but that didn't mean she'd let other people look down on House Luatha, the birth house of her deceased mother. After all, they were family—and supposedly protecting one another was what family did.

"What're the stakes?" Lorcan asked.

"You're the ones who offered the bet in the first place. Shouldn't you be in charge of the stakes?" Kira asked.

Lorcan's arm dropped from Roderick's shoulders as he straightened.

Triumph flashed in Niland's eyes. He opened his mouth but before he could speak, Lorcan interrupted. "A favor that doesn't clash with either House's interests."

Not bad. The request showed a certain wisdom. Niland and Lorcan were both convinced Kira would lose—and badly. Yet, Lorcan had the presence of mind to protect himself. Not many would be so careful.

It would be enough to make her respect him a little if not for the fact he seemed so intent on needling her.

She just didn't know why yet.

"Done," Kira said as the low hum of the drones warned the game was about to resume.

"You're so confident that you'll win?" Graydon asked as she turned away from the audience.

Kira flexed the wrist that held the blade. "I won't know until I try."

Graydon's chuckle was intimate. "Then how about a side wager?"

Kira paused as ripples spread through the falling water, a prelude to the start.

"What sort of wager?"

Graydon's eyes twinkled. "Same as the one you just made. Loser owes the winner a favor."

Kira debated with herself for half a second. If she refused, it would seem like she wasn't confident in her abilities.

Not that she really cared about that.

The possibility of Graydon owing her one was simply too tempting to pass up. There were all sorts of interesting ways to turn a favor of that magnitude to her advantage.

"All right, you're on," Kira said as a beam of light lanced at her.

Kira dodged, not bothering to destroy the beam, unsurprised to find Graydon doing the same on the other side.

Only when it had hit the wall twice did she eliminate it.

Three more beams shot out right after. Kira danced aside, easily dodging the beams as they hit wall after wall.

From the other square, she caught the *bzzzt* as Graydon destroyed his beams.

Kira didn't pause, evading another wave of beams as they joined the first. By this point, there were seven laser beams she had to avoid.

Not enough.

Graydon was a powerful opponent. She'd need every advantage she could get against him.

Soon, the world faded away as Kira fell into the rhythm of the game. Nothing mattered other than the stray streaks of light that darted around the square.

She didn't bother with flashy moves, each strike efficient.

She wouldn't fall into the trap many players made in the early stages. Arrogance was different than confidence. While the latter would give you the strength to face the difficult things in life, the former would cause your downfall in an instant. There was a reason the saying "Pride goeth before the fall" had endured throughout the millennia.

A lull allowed Kira to catch a glimpse of Graydon. Where she relied on speed, her movements almost elegant, he was a battering ram, destroying the obstacles one after the other.

There was a savage smile on his face as he leapt forward, a sweep of his blade destroying four beams in a move Kira couldn't help but admire.

His eyes met hers for an instant. The same yearning that echoed in her was apparent in his gaze, leaving her feeling like she was balanced on the edge of a blade.

The moment broke as the soft ping of the mini drones fired.

Almost as if they'd planned it, they whirled to meet the next barrage, their movements mirroring each other's.

Faster and faster until sweat beaded on Kira's temple and her chest heaved with the force of her breaths. Her movements were fluid, no hesitation as her blade sliced through the air.

More and more beams joined the rest. Soon, Kira had no choice but to eliminate some. Otherwise, she would have had no room to move within her box.

The near-constant *bzzt* of destroyed beams kept her company as the difficulty level increased. Now, the beams didn't come from only directly in front of her, but the sides and back as well.

Knowing they could come from any direction, Kira flung her senses wide, cognizant of any changes in the environment around her.

Five beams closed in on her at once. Kira pushed off her toes, spinning horizontally in the air. Her light sword whipped out, destroying the two under her, before she completed the rotation, using her momentum to eliminate the two beams above her in the same motion.

The water walls of the cube rippled, mimicking waves. Beam after beam left their depths in a kaleidoscope of color.

The furor in the crowd beyond fell on deaf ears as Kira immersed herself in the game, the only thing that mattered was the next sequence of movements.

Kira swung her arm, destroying a beam that had already rebounded six times. She knew her limits. Once it had touched the walls seven times, she wouldn't be able to keep up. Not with how far into the game she was.

Seeing the light beams converging on her once again, she turned and dashed to the wall, planting a foot and kicking off the wall as she flipped backward over the beams.

When they rebounded toward her chest, she snapped her blade up, cutting through their middles in an efficient, clean strike.

The crowd roared as Graydon flipped over his own set of beams, his big body surprisingly lithe.

He bared his teeth as his blade nearly blurred with his quickness.

Sensing danger, Kira darted forward, her knees hitting the ground as her back bowed. The sleek arrow-like beam passed an inch above her. Completing her slide, Kira gained her footing, knocking two beams away from her.

There was no reprieve, a dozen beams rebounding toward her from several directions. Kira danced away from the first four, her blade cleaving through three of them.

Her back hit a wall.

A warning sparked in her mind. Pink bloomed above her shoulder.

There was nowhere to go with the beams heading for her in an inevitable collision.

Kira spun, her blade breaking two of the beams. If nothing else, she'd try to get as many points as she could.

The pink coalesced, the beam shooting out an instant before the rest would have reached Kira's blade.

There was a high hum as the beams and the stage dissolved around her.

SIXTEEN

A HUSH FELL as the audience waited for the final outcome.

Kira blinked at her chest, expecting to see splotches of white, signaling her demise. Her clothing remained unmarred, its surface still perfect.

Impossible.

Kira twisted, trying to get a glimpse of her shoulder. No white there either.

In disbelief, she glanced at Graydon. His expression held chagrin as he stared at his foot like it had betrayed him.

A spot of white on the tip destroyed the perfection of the otherwise spotless black synth armor.

She exhaled.

It wasn't her. She didn't get the penalty. Graydon had.

A snort of amusement escaped Kira. She slapped a hand over her mouth, her eyes laughing up at Graydon's.

She couldn't help it. His expression was priceless. A little sulky; a lot insulted. It was something Kira had never thought she'd see on the Emperor's Face.

"What happened?" she gasped. "Did one jump up and bite you?"

Graydon rolled his big shoulders as his chin lifted, his dignity already damaged. "Apparently, I misjudged a flip."

Kira lost it, bending nearly double as she could no longer contain her laughter.

"Are you done?" Graydon asked.

Kira paused then shook her head, holding her stomach when it started to hurt.

Graydon leaned down, his jaw brushing her hair. "I'm so glad you're enjoying this."

Kira's laughter dried up at the hint of threat in his tone. She gulped down any further amusement, drying the corners of her eyes.

"Very good." Graydon's smile was slow and decadent. "Let's see who won."

Kira straightened. That's right, the victor hadn't been determined yet.

Although Graydon had fouled out and sustained a penalty, it didn't necessarily place the win in her hands. In the end, it came down to the accumulated points. There was a chance his overall score would still exceed hers.

Kira focused on the holographic score board suspended over the stage they stood on.

The icon for barrage flashed once and then two scores.

The match was hers.

Graydon's hand landed on the small of her back, its warmth burning through the material of her shirt. Kira forced herself not to tremble, her heightened awareness of this man making the moment feel more important than it was.

"I'm looking forward to the favor you claim." Graydon's low voice stirred her hair. "Perhaps it will involve another moonlit swim."

Unbidden, images flashed in Kira's mind. The way Graydon looked with silvery light caressing his skin, his chest bare as beads of water ran down it. The desire when he looked at her. The feel of his lips and skin under hers.

Kira stuffed those images back in their box, forcing herself to seem unaffected as she walked toward the edge of the stage. "I worked hard for this favor. I wouldn't waste it on something like that."

"You never know what the future might bring," Graydon murmured.

Kira rolled her eyes. Somehow, she thought she'd manage to avoid the temptation of his irresistible self.

"You're awfully presumptuous," Kira told him.

Graydon gave her a look of mock surprise. "You think so? I'm not so sure. There's something between us. You can deny it all you want, but we both know this is happening."

"Now, you've made it a challenge. You know how much I love those."

Graydon's expression didn't waver. "That's all right. I've always enjoyed the pursuit."

"Perhaps that's the problem. Not everybody loves being chased."

Sometimes it just made them want to run and hide. Kira wasn't so good at the second, but she'd always excelled at the first.

Graydon's eyes gentled as he reached up, tucking one errant strand of hair behind her ear. The watching audience seemed to fade around them, unimportant for the moment. "It's good then that I prefer what comes after the catch."

Kira held her breath as his fingers trailed along the outer rim of her ear before ghosting over her jaw in a faint caress.

"Whatever type of pursuit you want, I will adjust to match," he told her.

"Why?" Kira's gaze searched his.

She wanted to believe in him. She really did, but something held her back.

Graydon didn't answer as he considered her, his expression enigmatic. "Because a woman like you deserves it."

Kira looked down. "You won't want me when all the truths have been revealed."

Graydon leaned forward. "Bet me. We both know you rarely lose."

He turned his gaze toward the scoreboard. Kira blinked as the list of Allstars scrolled past, their two scores climbing the ranks. They stopped at the number two and three spots.

Murmurs filled the air as those present read the name in first place. It was the same as the second-place name. Sparrow.

"Well played, lovely Sparrow," Graydon said, stepping off the playing stage.

Kira rolled her lips between her teeth, trying to conceal her smile.

They couldn't blame her for their assumptions. They sought to take advantage of a kitten only to realize too late she was a full-grown saber tooth tiger.

"A ringer," Lorcan said.

To her surprise, he didn't sound angry. Instead his voice was speculative as if she'd surprised him in an interesting way.

"You cheated," Niland accused.

Kira's gaze swung toward him. "How so? I never said I couldn't play. You made assumptions, and now those assumptions have bitten you on the ass. As an oshota, you should know better."

Lorcan smothered a snicker, his face smoothing out when Niland glared at him.

"The Emperor's Face allowed you to win," Niland accused.

If he sought death, Kira was only too willing to help him out. With that in mind, she glanced up at Graydon. "He's questioning your honor. Are you going to allow that?"

He sent her a look that said he knew what she was doing, and it wasn't going to work.

"You should teach him some manners," Kira continued, not paying attention to the increasing rage in Niland's face. "I'll wait."

Graydon didn't budge. "But it's so much more fun annoying you than playing with them."

Kira realized she'd lost this game.

With nothing left to do but retreat, she started toward the large entrance Joule and Devon had disappeared into. "Come on, Roddy. Let's go find Joule and Liara."

Roderick trailed after her. "You know my name isn't Roddy, right?"

Kira gasped. "No! Are you sure?"

His glare said he didn't find this nearly as amusing as she did.

Kira sobered. She supposed she shouldn't torture him too much. After all, he had had a hard time of it.

"And to think I've been calling you that in my mind this entire time."

Roderick eyed her with something Kira would call respect if she didn't know better. "You're a difficult person."

She shrugged, well aware of her habits. "How's my cousin?"

"I didn't think you'd care since you broke ties with us."

Kira glanced at him in surprise. "I severed ties only because I didn't want to see them used as a noose to control me."

"And how is that going? You think Roake will let you go?" A harsh snort came from Roderick. "They're even more possessive than Luatha."

"I'll admit there were miscalculations on my part."

How could she know that her father came from an equally significant House or that Roake would cling so tenaciously to his daughter?

She waved a hand. "We've come to a tentative agreement."

Granted, it required Kira jumping through more than one hoop, and she'd be an idiot if she didn't realize Harlow was counting on her wanting to stay at the end of all this.

Roderick regarded her with skepticism. "Does their Overlord know about this agreement?"

"It was his idea."

Sort of, at least.

Despite his clear doubt, Roderick didn't say anything as they joined the teeming mass of people heading for inside.

Spying other Luatha oshota in the stands, Roderick gave Kira a sharp nod. "I'll take my leave."

For a second, Kira debated offering her assistance in case Liara ever needed it. She held back for one reason. Luatha was as proud as Roake. It was within the realm of possibility that such an offer could be seen as an insult.

For now, her actions today were all she could do for them.

Everything she'd said and done would be seen and dissected. The Tuann would realize there wasn't the enmity between Luatha and Kira they had thought. It should give Liara a little breathing room. If not, Kira would have to think of a different way to address this.

Graydon's penetrating stare as Roderick made his way toward the other members of Luatha had Kira tilting her head at him. "What?"

"For a person who fought so hard to escape Luatha's clutches, you went a long way to saving their reputation," he observed.

"I never said I hated them," Kira said, her gaze sweeping over the stadium and settling on the matches taking place on the stadium floor.

The scene was chaotic, over a dozen matches happening at once.

Despite that, it didn't take long for Kira to spot the person she had come to see. When she did, she couldn't help but frown.

Joule stood in the middle of a board that faintly resembled the Go board of ancient Earth, only considerably larger. There were nineteen rows and nineteen columns of tiny squares forming a much larger one.

The objective of the game was to claim territory. To do that, you had to conquer a square on the board. Each one you occupied resulted in a point. However, if your enemy completely surrounded your pieces with their own, you lost the points for that territory.

That's where the similarity to Go ended.

Castles was a game that relied as much on mental strategy as it did physical. Instead of stones to claim a position, the competitor had to wager their own skills. Only by defeating the square's test could they take it over.

Sometimes these tests were similar to what Kira had faced in Barrage—a series of laser fire you had to return or avoid. Other times they were logic problems you had to solve in a fixed time limit.

There was no concept of turns in Castles either. The faster you could defeat the square, the more of an advantage you would have.

If you attempted to conquer a square and failed, you would be frozen in place for a set time, giving your opponent a considerable advantage.

Not only that, but opponents could launch non-lethal attacks against each other. If they scored a direct hit, the square would automatically become theirs.

When a territory was surrounded by the enemy, its ownership would change to that enemy.

From the looks of things, Joule and his opponent were pretty evenly matched. The number of squares each had lit up was comparable.

Kira had always known what Joule lacked in physical prowess he made up for with his strategic mind.

That was likely why he'd elected to lay claim on the section of the board generally predisposed to logic problems.

It wasn't a bad strategy, but if he didn't conquer some of the physical-based squares soon, he'd fall into the trap his opponent had so carefully laid.

Graydon touched her elbow, guiding her toward a set of stairs that led up to the upper echelon where the private boxes of the wealthy and powerful waited.

Kira didn't argue as they left the lower stands, the echo of their footsteps swallowed by the thick carpet lining the hallway.

Graydon stopped at an elegant door, opening it, and stepping inside.

Kira followed, hesitating slightly when she saw who waited inside.

Raider looked up with a frown from where he had claimed a spot on the side to watch the matches.

Before Kira could react, a shape flew toward her.

"Kira! You're finally here!" Jin cried. "I've been waiting so long."

She batted Jin away, hitting only air as he circled her. "What are you doing here?"

He was supposed to be watching Elena. Not gallivanting around where anybody could see and link him to Kira.

Jin put a little bit of space between them.

His tinny voice came to her through their comms. "MinMin is watching Elena. There were things I needed to investigate outside."

Her glare deepened. That excuse failed to explain his presence here.

Jin's feelings of frustration traveled through their bond. "Raider caught me as soon as I exited the villa. The meatsack has gotten smarter. He used Wren's presence to entrap me. If I hadn't come up with the excuse of meeting you here, I think they would have tried dismantling me."

Kira didn't know what to think about Raider's interference. Jin was her eyes and ears. While she drew the majority of attention to herself most times, he snuck around the outskirts, gathering what they needed to destroy those who intended them harm.

It was a partnership that took advantage of people's preconceptions.

They relegated Jin to the role of a mere drone, incapable of separate thought and action.

Most ended up regretting that oversight.

Unfortunately, Raider knew her playbook. Jin was the first person he'd look to if he wanted to disrupt Kira's agenda.

Raider's guarded expression offered her no insight into his thoughts, either.

Stowing her questions for now, Kira took the opportunity to study the other occupants in the room. In addition to Raider, Wren and his oshota sprawled in their seats, observing the match.

In the corner, Yukina and her oshota sat quietly by themselves, their presence unobtrusive.

Furor from below pulled Kira's attention to the matches. Joule walked off the board, defeated.

She didn't think that was what had caused the upset, however. A quick scan showed her a board where one side had managed an overwhelming victory, completely crushing their opponent.

Jin hovered over Kira's shoulder. "What is that?"

Below, the source of the fuss calmly regarded the audience. Its features were smooth, no hint of expression disturbing them. Its eyes couldn't hide the cerulean glow of its processor. Although it had a mouth and ears, no one would ever mistake it for being a biological, not with a metal exoskeleton covering its sexless body.

Yukina put down her tea, her eyes cold as she stared at the android. "Something needs to be done to check the Consortium's growing arrogance."

Graydon hummed an agreement.

"Jin?"

They'd known each other too long for him not to know what she wanted. "There's too much distance. I'd need to get far closer to get an accurate scan."

"Who was the android's sponsor?" Kira asked.

"Zepher," Yukina said, picking up her tea again.

Kira didn't know whether to applaud their arrogance or get busy digging them a grave.

The Consortium had agreed to certain restrictions on avenues of research, among them bioengineering and the advancement of artificial intelligence. With this act, Zepher was not just flaunting the treaty between the Consortium and the Haldeel, they were showing they'd already broken it.

"Himoto's going to have a conniption," Jin said.

"If he doesn't know already," Kira responded.

Having the Haldeel threaten to cut ties could give Himoto the political power he needed to clean house, but that was only if the rest of the Consortium agreed the treaty was worth maintaining.

If that was Himoto's game, he was taking a huge risk.

"I'm surprised the Haldeel haven't stopped this," Zoella said, her expression giving away her unease.

"It's the quorum. They'll allow the humans to hang themselves with their own rope." Yukina's expression was as still as a frozen lake as she surveyed the scene.

Her assessment perfectly summed up the Haldeel's methods. They rarely let you know when you had overstepped until long after you had already waded into dangerous waters and there was no way back.

There was a good bet the Haldeel planned to use the quorum to find out how deep the rot within humanity went.

Only then would they excise the trespassers.

Raider's eyes met hers in a brief moment of understanding.

They could only hope Himoto's faction was smart enough not to get caught up in this.

The moment was broken when Raider's gaze drifted over her shoulder. Confusion gave way to a scowl before his focus snapped back to hers.

Kira glanced at the audience, wanting to know why he was suddenly looking at her like he planned to throttle her.

Odin wove through the crowd, his gaze fixed on the android. As if sensing her attention, he glanced up and smiled. That smile quickly disappeared as he caught sight of Raider.

Alarm registered in his expression before he dove back into the crowd.

"Same old Kira," Raider said, his tone scathing and practically dripping with derision. "I can't believe I let those videos twist my thinking."

Kira frowned. What was he talking about?

"This isn't the place, Raider," Jin said, dropping into Japanese in the hopes the rest of those present wouldn't know the language.

Raider's laugh was mocking. "According to you two, it's never the time and place."

"I know you're angry but not here," Kira said in Japanese.

She'd let him rage and yell all he wanted. Just in private, where certain things wouldn't be in danger of slipping out.

Raider acted like he didn't hear her. "That person is supposed to be dead."

Kira's gaze was steady, not betraying a flicker of her worry. "You want to do this now? In front of them?"

"This is the only time I can get the truth out of you," Raider returned with a snarl. "It's funny. I used to think death permanent. Now, every time I turn around, someone else is coming back to life."

"You don't understand," Kira said.

Not that it was his fault. She'd kept many things to herself—even back then.

"I understand enough." His lip curled.

"You don't know when to quit, do you?" Jin said in disgust.

Raider snapped, pointing at Jin. "You be quiet, Tin Can."

"If only you could make me, Meatsack."

Kira inserted herself between the two of them. "Enough."

Raider sent a mocking look at Jin. "The Phoenix to the rescue once again."

"We'll see who needs rescuing, Meatsack," Jin snarled, edging around her.

Kira had known something like this was bound to happen sooner or later. Raider wasn't the type to let bygones be bygones.

In this, he and Kira were alike. When someone trespassed against them, they hit back twice as hard.

Odin being alive when Raider knew Kira had orders to kill him long ago was simply the flame that lit the bonfire.

Electricity shot from Jin to Raider, narrowly avoiding the human.

Raider sucked in an audible breath, rage filling his face.

"Crap," Kira muttered.

She needed to stop the coming confrontation. Otherwise, they'd destroy the private box. It had happened before.

If Kira saw Raider as a brother, the same could be said for Jin. Like brothers, the two had no trouble throwing down when the occasion called for it.

Kira stepped forward, hoping to halt the fight before it could go any further. She got a fist to the face for her trouble.

Pain lanced through her cheekbone as she staggered.

Raider and Jin froze.

Seconds later, Raider blanched as Jin rapidly backed away, putting as much distance between him and Kira as possible.

Kira ignored both of them, raising a hand to probe the spot where Raider's blow had landed.

"Kira," Raider started, holding up his hands.

Kira's smile would have been called sweet if not for the fact it appeared a little deranged and a lot bloodthirsty.

"You hit me," she said.

"It was an accident."

"This will be too," she informed him.

Raider's eyes widened as he cursed. He turned to run, but not fast enough.

Kira yanked him toward her. He shoved his hand against her face, trying to hold her at arm's length.

Well then. If that's how he wanted to play it.

Kira twisted, sinking her teeth into his wrist.

"What did I say about the biting?" Raider screamed, grabbing a fistful of hair.

Kira's eyes smarted from the pinpricks of pain, but she refused to let go.

"I'll yank it out. I swear I will," Raider threatened.

Kira released him.

He'd do it. It wouldn't even be the first time.

Raider's shoulders relaxed.

He didn't think he was getting off that easy, did he?

Kira kicked him in the shin, feeling smug satisfaction at his answering howl.

"Damn it, Kira!"

"You're a million years too young to get away with punching me in the face," Kira shot back.

Raider knew what that meant. No mercy would be forthcoming. Not until she had her retribution.

Perhaps that's why he didn't waste time running and instead charged. He wrapped her in a bear hug, trapping her limbs.

"That's fine," he snapped. "I have a score to settle too."

Kira's grin was vicious. "Good. It seems we're on the same page."

She'd tried to be respectful, knowing her actions had hurt him.

But in the end, a knockdown, drag-out fight had always been the way they settled things.

"No regrets," she told him.

"Same to you."

With that said, Kira reared, slamming her head against his chin.

A muttered oath was her reward.

Jin circled them as they wrestled back and forth, stumbling into the wall.

Raider had the advantage, his arms pinning hers.

Not to be outdone, Kira planted a foot on the wall and shoved, sending them staggering back several steps.

"Yes, Kira! Knock the asshole out of that idiot," Jin crowed.

"Shut up, Tin Can. This is your fault," Raider shouted.

Around them, Kira was vaguely aware of Wren telling them to stop, but neither Kira nor Raider were in the mood to listen. This had been a long time coming.

Kira twisted in Raider's grip, stomping on his foot. Raider grunted.

Stubborn.

But then, had she really expected anything else?

This was Raider after all. The only person who was nearly as muleheaded as Kira. They were a matched pair, each too ornery to get out of their own way sometimes.

Only—Kira had once considered Raider a brother. Like all good sisters, she knew every one of her brother's weaknesses.

She reached back, pinching his side then twisting.

Raider cursed again, his hold loosening.

Kira slithered free.

The next minutes passed in a blur. An honorable fight it was not, consisting mostly of open-handed slaps, pinching, hair pulling, and yes, biting.

Mostly on Kira's end.

"That is enough," Wren roared.

There was a loud clap and then an invisible hand forcibly shoved them away from each other.

They both lay where they landed as Wren glared, looking angrier than Kira had ever seen him.

"You're acting like children," Wren spat.

Over his shoulder Amila and Graydon's oshota looked like they were fighting to keep their composure, their shoulders shaking.

Kira pointed at Raider. "He started it."

Raider lunged for her.

Wren made a motion and Raider flew backward, landing on the floor again with a pained grunt.

Wren didn't say anything, simply regarding them with that intense stare that said he was inches from disposing of them to save himself time and headaches later on.

Raider sat up, looking the worse for wear. There were multiple scratches on his face, and blood oozed from his neck. His collar was ripped, and she thought she saw a slight darkening around his eye where she'd elbowed him.

Judging by the minor aches and pains on her face and torso, she was guessing she looked about the same.

Now that the adrenaline from the fight was fading, she could feel the way her cheek and eye were beginning to swell. Chances were she'd have a nice shiner tomorrow.

To say nothing about her tender scalp. Her hair likely resembled a bird's nest from all the hair pulling.

"I don't care what problems you have with each other. This ends here," Wren said, sounding like he was reaching for his last shred of patience. "Settle this. Now."

Kira and Raider looked at each other, before squinting up at Wren.

"Not possible," Kira started at the same time Raider said, "Fine."

She stared at him in surprise. "Fine?"

Since when was Raider the type to listen when someone told him to drop it? Not even when they were friends could she get him to obey.

Raider's eyes narrowed as he spoke in Japanese. "I'm only going to ask this once. Lie to me, and we're done. For good this time."

His expression was serious. Something told her that he'd follow through on his threat.

She'd thought she'd braced for the pain and hurt that would come when he found out how much she'd kept from him. Turned out even she didn't anticipate the devastation that would follow.

No matter how angry he was or how fractured their relationship, she'd always held out some hope that they'd somehow find their way back to who they'd once been.

Now, however, she was beginning to realize how difficult of a task that really was.

Raider lowered his voice, still speaking in Japanese. "Is Sunshine alive?"

The moment stretched between them.

Kira knew Raider was already aware of the truth, but until she confirmed it verbally there would always be room for doubt in his mind.

Elise was too important to him to leave even the smallest thread of ambiguity over her fate. By confronting Kira directly like this, Raider could cut through all the bullshit and get to the heart of what mattered.

After what felt like an eternity, Kira jerked her chin in a nod, unable to force herself to speak the words aloud.

Raider rose from the floor, dusting off his pants.

"That's it?" Kira asked as he turned to go.

He slid her a look. "What else is there?"

She leaned on her hands. "Honestly, I thought you'd be a little angrier. Where's the ruthless asshole I know?"

When it came, Raider's smile was crooked and carried a little of her old friend. That smile reminded her of a time when she'd thought they'd always have each other's back. When nothing and no one could come between the three of them.

If Elise shared in some of the darkest parts of Kira's life, Raider was with her for some of the best.

"I remembered something."

Kira frowned, not sure she trusted this new, reasonable Raider.

"What's that?"

"You're not the person I'm truly angry with."

That wasn't the response she expected. The resentment that had been hiding beneath the surface was entirely gone.

Raider could hold a grudge like no one's business. That slap fight they'd had wasn't enough to clear the air and fix all their issues.

He should be angry. Furious even.

He wasn't.

Why?

Ignoring her confusion, Raider bent his arm, examining his wrist. "Did you have to bite me?"

"You know the rules," she said slowly, still trying to catch up with the sudden shift in his mood.

Raider dropped his arm. "Need help getting up?"

In answer, Kira climbed to her feet on her own, muffling an internal groan. By no means had it been a one-sided fight. He'd gotten in as many good hits as she had.

"That was an interesting display," Graydon remarked, observing them with a faint amusement.

"The Curs don't use closed fists to settle arguments," Raider answered when Kira remained silent. "At least not when outside a ring."

"Why?" Amila asked, looking intrigued.

"Because they're trained to kill people," Jin answered. "Killing family is forbidden."

"Unless they're trying to kill you," Raider and Kira said at the same time. Neither looked at the other.

It felt strange to hear that sentiment established over a decade ago echoed in the here and now.

Kira's chin lowered as she sent a sidelong glance in Raider's direction, only to find him staring at her. They considered each other for long seconds.

Kira was the first to turn away. "I'm tired from all this excitement. I'll head back first."

No one tried to stop her as she left the room, Amila and Finn slipping out behind her. To her relief, they both kept their distance, careful not to intrude on Kira's privacy.

"Jin, check the ship's logs to see if any messages were sent," Kira murmured in a low voice.

"Why?"

"Just a hunch."

Raider had let something slip that she hadn't paid attention to in the moment. Now that she was thinking clearly again, she had time to follow up.

"Pay attention to my past logs," Kira added after a moment of consideration. "Particularly those in my hidden files.

Kira made it to the stadium floor. By now, officials had congregated around the android and the human controlling him.

With one last probing glance, she headed for the exit.

"You were right," Jin said at last. "Kira, all of your video messages meant for Raider were sent."

Kira closed her eyes. "Elena."

She was the only one who had the motive and knew all of Kira's passwords. Not even Odin would have been able to hack the system Jin created to send those videos out. Not without alerting them in the process.

"What are you going to do?" Jin asked.

"I'm going to have a chat with my niece."

SEVENTEEN

THE NEXT AFTERNOON Kira held still as Auralyn tugged and pulled at the interlocking sections of armor currently being fitted to her body under Auralyn's supervision.

"You know you don't have to do this," Kira said for the third time. "My old armor works just as well."

Auralyn's hands paused as she pinned Kira with a hard stare. "I doubt that."

With that, Auralyn returned to fitting the armor, adjusting as needed in an impressive display of skill.

Armor like this cost a small fortune. Kira could easily see families treating it as a priceless heirloom to be passed down through the generations.

While a few notches below synth armor, it was nonetheless one of the most impressive pieces of technology Kira had ever seen—comparable to the old battle armor she wore during the war.

Only this armor weighed much less, and she could already tell it would be easier to move in.

Although lightweight, it still felt substantial.

If she crashed while wearing this, there was a good chance she'd survive.

Even if Kira had salvaged a thousand Tsavitee ships filled with priceless technology, she still wouldn't have been able to afford the arm of this armor.

Members of Roake had given Kira valuable gifts before—but none of this quality.

She couldn't understand it—and what Kira didn't understand generally left her feeling antsy.

Something no one wanted.

"You're not good at accepting gifts," Auralyn observed.

This wasn't a gift. This was a priceless treasure shoved at Kira whether she wanted it or not.

"Wren accepted you as his disciple. That means you're one of us now." Auralyn tapped a few buttons, watching as the armor elongated and then contracted.

"You're awfully quick to pass approval," Kira said unhappily.

"Not the trusting type, are you?"

Kira acknowledged the statement with a twitch of her eyebrows. "Not really. No."

"You'll have to learn."

Not likely.

There was a reason for the saying "not to trust those who came bearing gifts."

Reading Kira's rejection, Auralyn's gaze sharpened. "The connections between Tuann aren't so easily dissolved. No matter where you go in this life, you will always have a home with us."

"That's a lot of faith you're placing in me."

"You've already proven yourself." The significant look Auralyn cast over her shoulder at where Elena watched them with a bored expression left Kira with no doubt as to what she meant.

Kira didn't have a chance to discuss boundaries with her niece last night. By the time she'd returned, Elena had already been asleep.

"Be very careful in whatever you say next," Kira warned.

Kira didn't care if Auralyn gifted her armor worth millions. She'd destroy the woman in a heartbeat if she thought she was a danger to Elena.

For the first time, the boredom in Auralyn's expression faded, leaving warmth and humor behind.

"You don't need to fear. She is ours, just as you are." Auralyn stepped back, nodding once to herself before turning to pack up the case she'd used to transport the armor.

Kira watched her go.

Auralyn paused at the door. "My sister would have been proud to know she had such a granddaughter." Auralyn finally looked at Kira. "And she would have given her life for the woman who protected her all these years."

Kira's lips parted as she caught Auralyn's meaning.

Auralyn inclined her chin. "I'm looking forward to seeing you race."

She stepped through the privacy screen before Kira could respond.

Elena lifted her head to watch her go. "What was that about?"

"It seems you have more living relatives than we thought."

"You mean that lady is related to me?"

"It's possible," Kira conceded, not wanting to get her niece's hopes up.

"What would she be?" Curiosity filled Elena's expression as she stared up at Kira.

"An aunt, maybe?"

Elena relaxed into her bored pose again. "I already have several of those."

True. Even if none of them shared blood with her.

"How about a grandpa?" Kira asked.

Elena perked up as her feet dropped to the floor. "I've never had one of those before. Who is it?"

"You'll have to wait for that answer," Kira said, crossing the floor to her niece. "Instead, I want to discuss why you sent those videos to Raider."

The flash of guilt on Elena's face confirmed she'd been the one responsible.

"If you'd been anyone else, we wouldn't be having this conversation because I would have already cut ties with you," Kira told her.

Elena winced but didn't speak.

"Those were private. They were never meant to be seen by him."

Jin had verified that the video files meant for Raider were the only ones Elena had accessed. A relief since there were other recordings on her ship that held the potential to hurt Elena.

What had started as a genuine attempt to reach out had evolved into a type of therapy for Kira when her demons felt overwhelming. Some of those recordings had been intended for Elise—and not all of them were kind.

"I know," Elena said, sounding lost.

"Then why did you send them?"

Elena ducked her head, her eyes glossy.

Kira steeled herself. She couldn't let her niece's pain keep her from doing what was right. Elena had stepped over the line. Kira let her get away with a lot to make up for the fact that she couldn't be there all the time, but she'd be doing her niece a disservice in the long run if she didn't address this here and now.

"Deep inside, you carry a pain that never fully goes away," Elena finally said, reaching up to fiddle with MinMin where he clung to her shirt. The silver turtle lifted its head, knocking it against Elena's fingers. "When I look at the sperm donor, I see the same pain. I know Mother has a lot to do with that. I thought if I could make him understand, you could both heal."

Kira felt herself softening. In a perfect world, Elise would have been able to give her daughter everything they hadn't had growing up. A family. Warmth. Love. Security.

Instead, Elise and Elena's fates had been twisted. Elena had to rely on Kira—a pale imitation of the real thing.

It was natural for Elena to wish for a reconciliation between Kira and the father she'd always yearned for.

Kira reached out, dragging her niece into a hug, ignoring Elena as she wiggled and squirmed in her embrace. Kira rested her chin on the top of Elena's head. "Sometimes I forget you're just a sprout who still doesn't know anything."

In response, Elena planted her hand on Kira's face and shoved.

Her attempt was largely unsuccessful, only managing to dislodge Kira partially.

"I'm not feeling the love right now, child of my sister," Kira said in an injured tone. "Is it that you think you're too old for my hugs?"

Kira let out a gusty sigh and faked wiping a tear on Elena's hair.

"Your armor is uncomfortable," Elena complained, using both arms to try to push Kira away. "Let go."

Kira held firm, her expression the picture of hurt. "You must bear with it. Soon this time will pass and you will wish you hadn't been so stingy."

"Auntie, we both know you only give out hugs when you're being tricky." By now, Elena had managed to put a couple of inches between them, using her whole body to fight free.

Kira fought her smile. It seemed her niece could see through her.

"Alas, woe is me. Even my own niece doesn't love me anymore," Kira continued in a sad voice.

"I get it. I get it. I was wrong. I won't do it again," Elena yelled.

Kira pulled her in for another hug, being sure to smoosh Elena's face in the process. She dropped one final kiss onto her niece's hair and then stepped back.

"If you understand, don't let it happen again in the future," Kira said, the facade of sadness dropping from her in an instant.

Elena smoothed her hair, grumbling as she trailed Kira out of the bay.

"Did you have to be so annoying?" Elena asked.

"I have more of those hugs in me. Want to experience them?"

Elena's eyes widened. "I just remembered. Wren got me a seat in the stands. I'd better get over there before the race's start."

"Wise choice," Kira waited for her niece to scamper off toward Auralyn. The oshota dipped her head toward Kira before the two disappeared toward the audience entrance.

Only then did Kira step into the tunnel, heading toward the race's start line where her waveboard and the rest of her pit crew, such as they were, waited.

The transition from tunnel to track was seamless, her eyes adjusting quickly. The starting area teemed with bodies as the competitors conducted last-minute checks.

Kira skirted the edge of the crowd as she headed for her team's designated area.

Though it was only a semifinal, you wouldn't know it by the crowd in the stands. Today, the number of spectators wearing synth armor had nearly doubled from her previous race with Roake and Luatha dominating. Despite that, Kira caught the synth armor of numerous other Houses and knew news of her participation in the races had spread.

No doubt, the other Houses were here to investigate this strange child of Roake and Luatha and see how she measured up to their own offspring.

"This is quite the crowd," Kira said as her gaze caught on familiar faces.

Liara, Roderick beside her, watched Kira with a focused intensity.

"You don't know the half of it," Jin said over the comms. "Look to your right and up."

Kira followed his direction, scanning but not finding anything that stood out to her. She didn't have Jin's abilities to parse thousands of pieces of information in a single second or a camera for eyes that enabled him to blow up even the smallest of images for study.

"Not yet. Keep going," Jin said without prompting.

Kira looked up and up. Past the common spectator stands to the private boxes. Unlike the one she'd stood in last night, these were on a whole other level. Several of them hovered several feet above the top of the stands.

"Is that a royal?" Kira asked.

"It would seem so."

"What is one of them doing here?"

Haldeel royals were different than human royals. They weren't decided by birth but rather by achievement. The tests to join were rigorous and quite dangerous. Assassination attempts and sabotage were considered par for the course and not illegal. It was a vicious fight to the top, and one not many humans knew about.

Most humans assumed the Haldeel weren't violent, and this was true for most aspects of their society. They relied on technology to gain an advantage over their enemies. However, succession and social advancement was as bloody as any struggle of the same on old Earth. The Haldeel were just a little more civilized about it.

They'd stab you in the back with a smile while thanking you for being their stepping-stone to the next level.

It was a dichotomy that had always fascinated Himoto, who likened it to the power struggles in the ancient empires as families fought for supremacy.

As a result, the royal family was not related to each other by blood, but by shared experiences.

Humans assumed because of that they would be easily divided.

Surprisingly, that wasn't so. The Haldeel empire was tens of thousands of years old. They would never have lasted that long with a system that had such obvious flaws.

To be honest, Kira hadn't thought she'd see one of them until the finals. While it was normal for the royals to watch the events of the quorum, they usually only made their presence known for the latter half when the stakes were higher.

Even more concerning was the presence of Graydon and Yukina in the royal's box. The royal in question was keeping a low profile. From where Kira stood, she couldn't see their face.

"I don't know, but you have more pressing concerns right now," Jin responded.

At his words, Kira headed in his direction.

Finn's large body was easy to spot even with the number of people between them. It was only when there was a brief lull in the crowd that Kira saw what Jin meant.

Odin bent over the monitors, making last-minute adjustments to her board.

Kira's pace sped up as she made a beeline for him.

Odin's eyes narrowed as he looked up.

His features were more feminine than the last time she'd seen him. Gone was the shadow along his jawline.

Kira's gaze moved to his ear, catching the twinkle of a green stone.

Odin had assumed the female persona again.

Kira was a little surprised. While the hacker rarely stayed the same gender for long, Odin typically tried to stay consistent during a mission.

It made it so much easier to slip through the nets of law enforcement when they were looking for one gender while Odin became the other.

The transformation was so thorough that even scanning Odin's DNA wouldn't expose the deception.

It was a useful talent, but only if no one ever suspected. It made Odin as slippery as an eel and was one of the reasons Kira had so much trouble tracking the changeling that first time.

Finn watched Odin with suspicion, likely picking up the same change Kira had but not knowing what it meant.

"If you kill me, everyone will see. The Haldeel will arrest you, and you'll lose this race," Odin said as soon as she arrived.

"Do you think I give a shit about this race?"

"Probably not, but you might change your mind after what I tell you."

Kira narrowed her eyes at Odin. "I'm waiting."

"The Tsavitee have something planned for the race. I want to know what, and the only way to learn that is by competing."

Finn glanced at Kira. "We should inform Graydon."

"And say what? Hello sir, this person wanted by half the universe says they think the Tsavitee are here and plotting?" Scorn filled Odin's expression. "Do you think they'd believe that?"

Finn's jaw flexed. "It will be our fault if something goes wrong."

"It's more likely you'll scare them off. Then what? It could be years before we draw them out again," Odin argued.

Finn ignored Odin, his eyes never leaving Kira's.

She gave him a sharp nod. "Do it. Inform Graydon."

Odin made a rude sound. "What happened to 'at all costs'?"

"I made a promise," Kira said, reaching for patience. "Also, it will only benefit us in the long run to have Graydon in our corner."

"They could be monitoring our communications," Odin said sulkily as Finn touched his arm to open a channel.

A humorless smile came from Finn. "Not these."

"Being cocky will only lead to destruction," Odin said.

Jin snickered. "Oh ho, someone gets a little touchy when they're overruled."

Odin regarded the drone with a flat stare. "Careful Tin Can, or we'll revisit exactly how touchy I can be."

Jin spun toward Kira. "Why is this menace here? We already know we can't trust her."

"Odin is here because she has a unique set of skills that no one else can replicate," Kira forced herself to say.

"And also because you need someone with a pulse to act as the controller since the officials won't recognize a pile of nuts and bolts as advanced enough to trust with someone's safety," Odin added in a chipper voice.

"Shows what you know. I don't have a single nut or bolt in my body. I'm way too advanced for that," Jin sniffed.

While the two were arguing, Finn moved closer. "Graydon said that without more concrete information, the race officials won't delay the semifinals."

"Told you," Odin sang.

"He will, however, deploy his oshota to keep an eye on the crowd," Finn finished in a cool voice.

"It's already done," Kira warned when it looked like Odin was going to argue. "And don't think we're not going to have a conversation about Elena later."

Odin's mouth snapped closed. "Fine. Do you want to know about your competitors?"

Kira made a gesture to continue. Data scrolled across Kira's optics. Names were attached to photos, along with their finish times during the qualifying races, and their preferred tactics.

Kira scanned the files quickly, sorting them into those who might present a threat and the non-threats. Unlike last time, there were quite a few strong contenders.

"Most of the field aren't much better than trash," Odin said. "Their skills are mediocre, but they could be annoying if they banded together."

And because of Kira's actions in the last race she was probably first on their list to target.

"From the information I gathered, these three will likely be the ones to cause the most trouble on this section of the race."

Images formed in front of Kira's right eye courtesy of the small lens Odin had given her. Unlike other lens computers Kira had tried, the images on this were crisp.

"Do you see them?" Odin asked.

"Yes."

"Good. The one on the left is the former disciple of the current champion. There was some type of falling out, but I couldn't find out over what."

"I'm surprised. Is the great Allfather slipping?" Jin taunted.

"Should I tell you a story then?" Odin teased. "I don't mind, but I thought you wanted to stay focused. My mistake. I didn't realize you were such a glutton for gossip."

"You shape-changing bastard," Jin hissed.

Finn's gaze met Kira's for a brief second.

"Don't suppose you could do anything about those two?" she asked.

If she had to listen to endless arguments during the race today, it would drive her crazy. No one wanted a homicidal Kira on a waveboard.

Finn's smile held menace. "It would be my pleasure."

Kira immersed herself in studying the dossiers, not paying any attention even after the loud crash and subsequent grumblings of the other two.

"There won't be any further issues," Finn informed Kira happily.

She paused on two dossiers she found interesting. "Devon and Raider are in this race?"

Odin sent a sulky expression toward Jin. "See what you did? You ruined my big reveal."

"Maybe next time you shouldn't get so distracted," Jin retorted.

Finn coughed. The two retreated to opposite sides of the table.

Kira flipped through the rest of the dossiers, only finding one other of interest. The one Devon had said used the same technique as her. Moonbeam.

The only image included in the file was one where the racer's face was hidden by a mask similar to the one Kira used.

As she finished up, Raider joined them. Like Kira, he wore flight armor—though his wasn't as advanced as hers.

He cut a fine figure in it. He had a sort of roguish appeal. A little bit dangerous and a lot dashing. He had the sort of charm that made him easy to love, even as you kind of hated him too.

He flicked a look at Kira. "This is who you've chosen to work with? Are you being serious right now?"

"Odin has her uses," Kira said.

Raider scoffed. "That changeling tried to kill us."

Odin held up a finger that was slightly longer and slenderer than a human's. "Point of fact—I did no such thing. If I'd wanted you dead, you wouldn't still be breathing."

Kira knew enough about Odin's methods to guess she was probably speaking the truth. It was the biggest reason Kira had let her live, even going so far as to stage the other's death to help her escape from those who'd held her leash.

"There were mitigating circumstances," Kira revealed.

Raider shot her a disbelieving stare. "She was working with the enemy."

"You don't know anything, *kithiw*." Menace rolled off Odin as she glared at Raider from the brim of the cap she wore to shield her face.

Raider didn't back down, if anything looking even more murderous.

Kithiw was a term the Tsavitee used for humans. Extremely derogatory, as most Tsavitee terms for outsiders were, it translated to fodder/food, something Kira had always found interesting given the way the Tsavitee divided their ranks and the fact half of them couldn't even operate without someone controlling them.

Kira caught Raider's arm, preventing him from stepping any closer. "Not everything is as it seems."

The tension in his arm under her hand remained for several long seconds before he relaxed and shrugged her off. "I hope you know what you're doing."

Raider didn't wait for a response, walking away without another word.

Odin busied herself with removing the cables attached to the waveboard, pretending not to notice Kira's stare.

"Using that word was a mistake," Kira said softly.

It was a trigger for any human who'd fought in the war.

Odin's hands slowed. "I know."

"Don't let it happen again." With her warning, Kira let the matter go, knowing Raider's accusation was a trigger for Odin as well.

In some ways, Odin was very like Kira.

The changeling's early life was controlled by people who only sought to use her. Kira's interference had saved her from that fate, but it didn't save the rest of those Odin cared about.

Everything Odin did now was in service to one goal—freeing those left behind.

Odin finished the preparations and handed the board to Kira.

"There aren't going to be any issues like last time, are there?" Kira asked.

"Not unless the Tin Can made a lot of useless upgrades again."

"Good." Kira set the board on the ground, stepping on it and activating the drive chain.

She listened to its throaty rumble with satisfaction.

While the drive chain in the board she'd used in her last race was still intact, the rest of the board had been pretty thoroughly destroyed.

It had necessitated Odin finding her a new one. From the sound of its engines, it looked like Odin had gone above and beyond.

"Is this a Blair class 500?" Kira asked.

"It's the 503." Odin leaned a hip against the table, her expression one of satisfaction.

"Those just came out. They're still pretty rare."

Odin lifted a shoulder. "I have my ways."

There was never any doubt of that.

Odin straightened and moved behind the monitors. "The race is starting. You'd better get out there."

Kira nodded. "Jin, you're point. Finn is support, and Odin can help as needed."

"Roger that."

Not wasting time, Kira pointed her board toward the starting line where her fellow opponents were beginning to gather. The friendly banter died down as anticipation and nerves took hold.

Beneath it all, excitement bubbled.

For some, this race was the culmination of years of hard work. For others, it was a chance to prove their worth to the powers that be. For Kira, it was simply a means to an end. Win or lose, it didn't really matter in the grand scheme of things.

"Stay alert, Kira," Jin advised.

"Understood," Kira responded as she took a look around.

Several racers were between Kira and Raider. He had a relaxed stance as he watched the rest with a bored look.

When his gaze landed on her, she brushed her hand along her shoulder, showing him three fingers. It was an old hand sign meant to warn the other to keep a wary eye out because danger was close.

His expression didn't even flicker before he looked away again.

Kira continued her scan, noting Devon ahead and to her right. Skye, in a bright pink race suit, was next to him.

Unlike Kira and Raider, they'd elected to jockey for position in the front row. Not a bad plan unless another interfered with their start.

It was one of the reasons Kira preferred to stay at the rear of the pack where it wasn't as crowded—less opportunity for someone to sabotage her so early on.

Kira turned her attention to the rest, not immediately spotting the person she was looking for.

Someone jostled Kira's shoulder, pulling her attention to them.

To her surprise, a racer in faded blue armor stood next to her. A helmet covered their head, hiding their features.

Even with the change in mask, Kira recognized the person. Moonbeam. The mysterious racer that no one seemed to know much about.

Kira didn't have time to study her longer as a Haldeel appeared from the box next to the royal's. His robes fluttered as he stepped off its edge, looking like some otherworldly being as he slowly descended.

The Haldeel regarded the racers with a placid expression, the sleeves of the robes draping artistically over his arms.

The Haldeel were a fan of showmanship, and never had that been more on display than now. He looked like a figure out of a fantasy. Impossible and dream like.

As if that wasn't enough, crimson petals began falling from the sky as if out of nowhere. Some of the racers reached out, trying to catch the soft-looking flowers only to have them dissolve into glittering sparks as soon as they touched them.

"Why are there so many theatrics for a semifinal?" Odin complained.

"I don't mind it," Kira said, absorbed in catching her own petal. "It's kind of nice."

"You've got to give it to them; they certainly know how to make a statement," Jin said.

The petals fell until they created a carpet of bright red along the starting lane. Only when the last petal had fallen did the Haldeel before them speak. "Today, you bring glory to yourself and those who support you. Go and show us what you're capable of."

Those Haldeel present among the racers whistled in approval.

Next to Devon, Skye punched her fist into the air, her expression determined. The humans and Haldeel were quick to follow suit until over a hundred racers had raised their voices in challenge.

The Haldeel official gestured and the racers quieted, crouching on their boards as an electric feeling filled the air.

The Haldeel raised his arms, and as if that movement had summoned them, the crimson petals rose too, swirling in the air.

At a sharp movement from the Haldeel, the front line of racers shot forward, the petals leading their way.

The race had begun.

"It's time, Kira," Jin said. "Conditions are clear. You are a go."

Directly in front of her, a racer bashed his board into another's, the sharp crunch of metal warning that neither was likely to continue in the race.

Kira eyed them "Exactly what criteria are you using to call that clear?"

"Aren't you the Phoenix? The mythical being who rises from her own ashes?" Odin teased. "So rise, little firebird. This should be nothing for you."

"Do a couple of stupid things in your youth, and you never hear the end of it," Kira muttered, stomping the heel of her back foot down.

The board roared to life, its rumble vibrating in her bones, bringing with it a sense of homecoming.

"Looking good across the board," Odin said. "No signs of stress. All systems are well within the green. You are clear for your run."

Kira started to shift her weight forward when movement on her left had her veering abruptly.

"What the hell? Did that racer just try to dethrone me?" Kira shouted.

Moonbeam's board roared as she lifted off.

"She didn't just try; she nearly succeeded," Jin said. "That racer's got skills."

Kira cursed and followed.

In seconds, she cleared the snarl in front of her, weaving back and forth through the struggling bodies.

She passed under the Haldeel official, noting how his gaze seemed to follow her. Then she was free with no more time to worry about others.

Kira followed the efficient movements of the other racer.

"How far behind the lead am I?"

There was the sound of clicking. "Eighteen seconds."

Kira whistled. "They're booking it."

"Do you blame them with you on their tail?"

Not really.

"You've got company," Jin said in the next moment.

Kira looked over, finding Raider closing in on her port side. In front of her, Moonbeam slowed way down, nearly clipping the front of Kira's board.

Kira dove right, swinging wide for the next obstacle.

"Damn it," she cursed when Moonbeam and Raider followed.

"They're trying to shut you down and hamper your movements," Jin warned.

Unless Kira could create enough of a space around her during the ascent, she wouldn't be able to use the dead man's plunge maneuver on her way down.

"We knew that was a risk." Kira leaned left, using the curve of the berm to pick up speed. The other two matched her, refusing to allow her to widen the distance.

"It's strange. They make a surprisingly good team," Kira observed as she shot over the rhythm section, trying to stay as close to the ground as possible.

Raider remained right on her tail, using her as a wind draft to conserve energy.

"Put space between you and them," Jin warned.

"Don't you think I'm trying?"

Raider wasn't like the other racers. He knew all her tricks—some he'd even taught her. This other racer was just as tenacious.

"I thought he forgave you last night," Jin grumbled.

"That doesn't mean he'll take it easy on me."

He wouldn't be Raider otherwise.

"Contact right. Break," Jin warned.

Kira flipped her board, shooting under the laser fire with barely any space to spare. The world spun, and Kira caught sight of Raider and Moonbeam doing the same.

Unfortunately, the racer behind them wasn't as lucky and took a direct hit. His board flared, his altitude dropping.

Odin cackled. "Nicely done. Show them true terror."

"Yes, because that's our real purpose for being here," Jin said in a sarcastic voice.

"There's no reason we can't do two things at once," Odin pointed out.

Kira ignored them as she closed in on a piece of track that doubled in on itself, diving through a tunnel as the laser fire flashed almost in slow motion. She burst into the sunlight, heading immediately into the next section, the last one before the tower.

"Protect your rear flank. That Moonbeam looks like they're about to dump you," Jin advised.

Kira reacted quickly, sliding out of the way, only for Raider to try to bump her board from the other side.

Kira shoved at his shoulder. He didn't go down, but then, she hadn't expected him to.

In retaliation, he grabbed her arm. Kira twisted it, slipping out of his grip.

The tower approached, along with the backs of the pack leaders. Skye and Devon jockeyed for first place, the young Haldeel muscling ahead of the Tuann for the first part of the ascent.

Kira hit her thrusters, shooting past Raider and the other racer. Wind whipped around her as she fixed her eyes on the beacon high above that marked the turnaround point.

By this time, the race had led them far outside the city, lakes and ponds spreading beneath as the course wound lazily between them.

Gravity pressed on Kira as she started her ascent, the board whining under the pressure.

A third of the way up, Odin's voice came across the comms. "I'm picking up something strange. There are weird power fluctuations I can't pinpoint."

"Alert Graydon and block all comms," Kira instructed.

She had no sooner said the words when a rocket launched from the city, screaming across the sky.

"Incoming," Jin shouted.

"Trajectory."

"It's heading for the lead racers."

The rocket's altitude climbed as it shot toward Devon and Skye

Cursing, Kira hit her thrusters, trying to climb. Her board shot up but not fast enough. She already knew she was going to be too late.

Ki shot across the sky, striking the rocket, and nudging it to the left.

"Where did that come from?" Kira shouted.

"I don't know," Jin responded.

The rocket overshot, already in the process of turning when it hit the beacon and exploded.

Kira dodged the burning debris, her heart in her throat as the two hoverboards above collided.

Devon grabbed for the other racer and missed. His board, already damaged, tilted. Smoke trailed him as his board, unable to take the abrupt movement, started to spiral.

Devon and his board bumped into the updraft of the tower, launching in the opposite direction almost instantly.

Skye dropped like a rock, plummeting toward the ground.

"He's not going to be able to recover," Kira said, feeling a sense of creeping dread as she watched events unfold.

"There's an issue with the safety team," Jin said, sounding frantic. "They're having trouble getting off the ground."

Damn it.

Kira cut acceleration. Gravity reclaimed her, pulling her toward the surface.

"You won't be able to save him," Odin warned, understanding what she wanted to do. "You'll likely die in the process."

Kira twisted, pointing the nose of her board toward the ground.

"Kira, what's more important than your goals?"

"Many things."

Starting with a war between the Haldeel and the Tuann. In that scenario, no one won.

If Devon died here, the future would be bleak. The Haldeel and the Tuann would expend themselves against each other, leaving the Tsavitee free to waltz in and destroy whatever remained afterward.

Then, there was the personal element to all this. The part she hadn't yet found the time to tell Jin about.

"Jin, there's a few things I need to tell you when this is over."

And she had no idea what his reaction would be.

To date, he'd shown zero interest in locating his biological family. Kira still didn't know if that was because he was ashamed to show them what he'd become or if he genuinely didn't care.

Either way, she could no longer put off telling him of her suspicions.

"It's a promise, Kira. You'll come through this safe and sound."

Kira couldn't help but feel warmth at his statement—as if by making that claim it would come true.

Kira plummeted, already working through the current problem. She needed more speed, and the only way to get it was through drastic measures.

"What's the plan?" Jin asked.

"First, open a line to Raider."

Jin was quiet. "Please tell me you're not thinking what I think you're thinking."

Kira grinned into the wind. "I'm going to do exactly that."

"Do you know how dangerous that is?" Jin cried.

"Yup, that's why I need Raider."

A frustrated sound came from Odin. "Standby, I need a minute."

"I thought this would be child's play for you," Kira responded.

"As pleased as I am about your faith in me, I'm not a magician. Miracles take time."

Kira glanced in the direction of the two racers, one falling straight down while the other arced across the sky. Time was the exact thing they didn't have.

"Patching you through now."

There was a brief pause before Raider's voice came over the line. "Is there a reason you're playing chicken with me?"

"There is."

A gusty sigh sounded in her ear. "Fine."

"I'll take Devon; you catch the girl."

"Try not to die," he advised. "I don't feel like dealing with the whining from the rest of your House if you screw this up."

Kira sneered. If either of them screwed this maneuver up, chances were, it wouldn't be her.

Twenty feet. Ten.

Raider flipped so the underside of his board faced her, Kira doing the same on her end.

Seconds before impact, Kira hit the thrust as hard as she could, praying she'd done the calculations right.

The Curs had discovered, quite by accident, that when two antigrav fields came into contact they could create an almost magnet-like effect. The only catch was you had to be exerting the exact same amount of force, otherwise one antigrav field would overwhelm the other and catastrophically repel the weaker field.

With anyone else, Kira would hesitate to undertake this course of action. Raider was the only one, other than her, crazy enough to even make the attempt.

The antigrav fields met, clinging together. Even with her inertia dampening shields at maximum, she felt the jolt in every bone in her body.

Her quads and knees buckled, threatening to give out. Kira flooded the muscles with *ki,* strengthening them the slightest bit. Enough so that she didn't destroy her legs.

"Here. We. Go," Raider snarled, wrenching them sideways and aiming Kira in the direction of Devon.

He stomped on his thrust, sending their balance out of whack. Like a cannonball fired from a cannon, the polarity reversed, firing Kira at Devon.

The board under her feet flexed, bits of its exterior breaking off as the forces of gravity threatened to snap it in half.

Out of the corner of her eye, she saw Raider recover. Seconds later, he shot toward Skye.

"Your trajectory is good," Jin said. "Prepare for collision in ten. Nine. Eight."

Kira braced. This was going to be rough.

"Four. Three. Good luck, Kira," Jin said. "Brace, brace, brace."

EIGHTEEN

"FIND ME THE location of that attack," the *za na ri na* ordered, looking at the master of her guard.

Unlike other Haldeel, this man wore clothing appropriate for a warrior. His garment fit closely to his upper torso, faithfully outlining his chest before stopping at his shoulders. It left his forearms and biceps seemingly bare, exposing the violet markings set against skin as black as ink.

At his waist, the garment fell in a series of panels that resembled a skirt. Only unlike normal skirts, the slits in the bottom half would allow his lower prehensile appendages complete freedom of movement.

Such a consideration would enable him to use those appendages as a weapon against an enemy.

It was lucky for the rest of the galaxy that not many Haldeel chose the warrior's path, preferring disciplines linked to intelligence instead. Those who did were exceptional even by Tuann standards.

Their prehensile appendages could grow back, giving them a considerable advantage. Couple that with their tendency to wind their appendages around the limbs of their opponent to immobilize them, and they were a headache to fight.

"Security has been dispatched to the origin of the attack," the Haldeel Master of the Guard informed the royal. "In addition, I've instructed the remainder of our force to spread into the surrounding city to lock down potential conspirators. Anti-ballistic systems have gone online and will shoot down any further attacks."

There was no explanation of how a rocket had managed to slip past their defense system in the first place. This incident would tarnish the perfect reputation of the Haldeel.

Above, the two lead racers managed to veer to avoid the rocket, crashing into each other instead. The resulting uproar from the crowd nearly drowned out the *za na ri na's* next statement.

"Deploy our recovery forces."

The Master of the Guard's expression tensed. Seconds later, he glided forward, bending to whisper in the royal's ear.

"What?" she asked, sounding shocked.

One racer fell, their body limp in a way that signaled unconsciousness. The other spun into the updraft of the tower, hitting it before careening wildly in the opposite direction.

The oshota standing behind Yukina took a step forward.

The atmosphere around him warped.

Graydon moved quickly to intercept, putting his hand up to stop the other man. "If you go there now, you will create an incident."

Whether he successfully saved Devon or not, it wouldn't matter. There would be consequences.

The rules under which the Tuann had to abide while on Haldeel territory were very strict. Intervening without permission would be considered a violation.

That wasn't the only danger. The man's simple presence here would cause an uproar even Graydon and Yukina would struggle to contain.

Yukina stood in a graceful movement, her robes settling around her. "Little storm is right, Torvald."

The oshota turned his head slightly, a flash of gold shimmering in his eyes before disappearing again.

"You know what I will do if he dies."

"I do," Graydon responded.

The man before him had already lost one child. If he lost another, the universe would be bathed in blood.

"Then I will wait—for now."

The atmosphere around the man settled. The warping of before was gone, as if it had never been.

"What is the child doing?" Yukina asked, sounding puzzled.

Graydon looked up to see Kira speeding toward another racer in what looked like a headlong collision.

He blinked, expanding the scene. He recognized the racer Kira was charging. Raider.

"She's trying to save him," Graydon said in realization.

"How?" Yukina asked.

"I don't know."

To most in the audience, Kira's actions seemed counter-intuitive. She wasn't rushing to where Devon was wildly spinning out, but rather straight for the ground. She wasn't even diverting to catch the racer who'd collided with Devon.

Yet Graydon had no doubt rescue was what was in her mind.

For her, the potential danger didn't matter. She saw a problem and knew she had a solution. He'd seen it before. Many times. Kira placing herself in jeopardy with reckless disregard for her own safety.

He didn't know how her Curs or Jin had managed all these years. It took someone strong to allow themselves to care for a person so reckless, knowing at any moment they might willingly thrust themselves into death's path.

Graydon found it a loathsome feeling he was in no rush to repeat.

This was the byproduct of caring for someone. In the good times, you shared in their happiness and success. In the bad, you stood idly by wishing you could take their troubles onto your own shoulders, while knowing it was impossible.

Elena reached up to take Auralyn's hand. In her eyes, Graydon caught the deep-seated terror only someone who had lost a parent would understand.

Her attention shifted to Graydon, her gaze pleading.

Graydon rested his hand on her head. "Steady, *zinyai*."

Graydon sent a meaningful look at Auralyn. As much as he wanted to act, his first priority was ensuring Elena's safety.

If anything happened to her, it would break Kira.

Having Elena watch the race with them in the box was a calculated risk. Sometimes the best place to hide someone was in plain sight.

By all appearances she would seem like any other Tuann child visiting the quorum with their elders to widen their world view and gain experience.

"No matter the pressure, the Phoenix always rises," Himoto said from where he'd nearly been forgotten during the drama.

They were words of comfort, serving to steady Elena's emotions as her shoulders relaxed.

Himoto's gaze lingered on Elena as she drew in a deep breath. When she released it, she seemed like a normal child again. Her gaze wide and innocent. Someone you'd easily dismiss as a threat.

You'd never tell from looking at her, just how scared and worried she was.

Wren and Auralyn had a note of pride in their expressions as they looked down at her.

"You have too much confidence in that woman," Admiral Kent murmured.

Those who heard had varying reactions.

Graydon caught the faint movement as Elena squeezed Auralyn's hand a little tighter but otherwise didn't react.

Good girl.

Kira's influence on her showed.

Elena had all the arrogance of youth—that indestructible notion that she'd always come out of any situation all right—but she acted with the caution and cunning of someone much older.

It was a trait that would benefit her well in the future.

On the human side, Jace was an impassive rock, watching everything that happened from behind a blank mask.

Himoto was the one who surprised Graydon the most. Though it wasn't obvious, Graydon thought he caught the flash of frustration and impatience at the other admiral's words.

The Consortium was growing more and more fractured. Without a common enemy, the natural tendency of humans turning on their own was beginning to show.

The Tuann and the Haldeel shared that weakness. The only difference between them and the humans was that the Tuann and Haldeel could withstand such internal pressures. Humanity was a fledgling race that likely could not.

If they didn't fix that weakness, a crafty foe such as the Tsavitee would find a way to take advantage of the division.

Himoto's eyes met Graydon's briefly before lifting to focus on Kira again.

Graydon might have believed the facade if he hadn't caught the break in his mask seconds ago.

Himoto cared for Kira. Much more than he let on.

What Graydon found interesting was the lengths he'd gone to conceal that care.

"*Za na ri na,* since your people are having difficulties, I think it only fitting as your guests that we offer our assistance," Admiral Kent said.

What a waste, Graydon thought, shaking his head.

Raider's abilities already proved humans were stronger than the Tuann had previously thought. Even Himoto and Jace showed promise. They were respectful while still not losing themselves.

If they had the proper backing, they would both go far on the galactic stage. It just was too bad the rest of their party didn't understand the subtle intricacies of diplomacy on this level.

Graydon would be tempted to ignore such a short coming—if only for Kira's sake—if humans weren't so short-lived.

Kent's offer of assistance was impertinent and far too obvious an attempt to incur a sense of obligation on the Haldeel's part.

The Haldeel had been part of the fabric of power in the universe since long before humans took their first step into space.

If they accepted now, it would be tantamount to admitting they couldn't handle their own affairs. They'd lose face in a very public manner.

The admiral had to know this.

"That's not necessary, Admiral." Though the royal's tone was mellow and her expression hidden behind the veil she wore, her posture spoke of reproach.

"*Za na ri na*, I understand you want to keep control of this matter, but if the culprit is not caught, it will reflect poorly on your people," Kent said.

From the stands, awed gasps erupted as Kira and Raider flipped so the bottom of their boards were facing each other.

In the next moment, Kira burned across the sky at a speed considerably faster than before.

"The Rocci's split," Jace murmured.

Elena's breath shuddered in excitement.

Himoto and Jace shared a glance.

"It looks like we'll have to update the record books again." There was the faintest curve in Himoto's cheeks that spoke of relief. His gaze was gentle as he focused on Kent. "The Haldeel have no need for our services now."

Kent's teeth clenched at the unspoken rebuke in Himoto's words.

Himoto bowed toward the *za na ri na*. "I apologize for any offense my companions have caused. I am sure that wasn't their intention."

The *za na ri na's* stance relaxed, speaking of acceptance. "No apologies are necessary. We understand tensions are high."

"If that is all, I will take my leave," Himoto said. "All of this excitement has made me tired."

Graydon saw through Himoto's motivations. Excusing himself now gave him the time to investigate the attack without interference from his own people.

While the Haldeel wouldn't allow any of the parties present to actively interfere, they also wouldn't stop them from looking into this matter.

Graydon doubted the rest of the humans, with the exception of Jace, understood Himoto's intentions.

The *za na ri na* did, though.

The motion she made to her master of the guard wasn't one Graydon had seen before. Most Haldeel in high positions developed their own set of motions only understood by their close confidants. A secret language, if you will.

"My guards will escort you out," she said.

Seeing an opportunity, Graydon motioned to his people. "My oshota will go too. They have their own matters to address."

Auralyn and Zoella nodded, escorting Elena out of the box, Noor and Solal taking up defensive positions around them.

They'd take the child somewhere safe in the event this was a misdirect and the Tsavitee were after Elena.

A commotion from the stands pulled Graydon's attention to Kira. His heart dropped as her board collided with Devon's.

"Lord Graydon, my people have dropped the barrier protecting the stands," the *za na ri na* said. "You have permission to act."

Graydon gave her a sharp look.

Seeing it, the *za na ri na* tilted her head. "Restraint should be rewarded."

She stepped forward, her voice lowering and developing a vibration that would ensure no one listening would be able to hear. "Besides, neither of us want to see such a precious treasure damaged."

Graydon eyed the royal with suspicion, only catching the faint impression of a smile behind the veil.

"Go," she urged.

Graydon didn't wait to be told again. "With me."

Torvald launched himself over the balcony, creating a streak of light as he raced unaided by technology toward the two racers.

Graydon and Wren sprang after him, leaving their own trails of light.

Be safe, Graydon urged, even knowing they'd never make it in time.

* * *

Kira hit Devon with enough force to rattle the teeth in her head. Multiple bones in her body protested.

Thank every power in the universe Auralyn hadn't listened when Kira had tried to reject the gift. Without the armor, she would have taken considerable damage just now.

Kira wrapped her arms around Devon, activating the magnetic feature in her armor. Without it, she would have bounced right off him and wasted this opportunity.

Unfortunately, the collision had worsened the tailspin he'd entered. The horizon careened wildly around them.

Her vision tunneled as the spin sent blood rushing to her legs from the g forces. Much more and her body wouldn't be able to take it.

Kira bared her teeth. Not going to happen in this lifetime.

She was a Cur. A few measly g's wasn't going to be the reason she went into the long night.

She tensed her legs and abdomen.

"What was that?" Jin asked as a piece of shrapnel shredded the side of her board.

"It's nothing."

Kira cursed. As always, his instincts for knowing when a situation had taken a turn for the worst were on point.

"Then why is your board smoking?"

Kira worked to steady them; her efforts largely wasted. They were going too fast and her board wasn't ideal for carrying additional weight.

"A small piece of debris collided with my board."

Jin gasped. "Abandon him right now."

Kira rolled her eyes. He was always so dramatic.

"Kira!" Jin wailed.

Rather than answer, Kira hit the thrust on her board, trying to slow their spin and guide them onto some type of stable flight pattern.

Their speed dropped but not enough.

"How's Raider doing?"

"He's already recovered the second racer," Odin said.

"You'd better not die or he'll hold it over your head for the rest of eternity," Jin added.

Kira ignored his last statement. "Do you have a line to Devon yet?"

"It's open now," Odin responded.

"Devon, can you hear me?"

"Yeah."

Finally, something that had gone her way.

"My board's not responding at all," he said. "I've run through every recovery procedure I know. Nothing is working."

In the next second, his board went silent. The drive chain powering the engine going dead.

That wasn't good.

"Don't panic. I'll get you out of this," Kira told him.

How was the question.

First order of business was to dump the extra weight.

"I'm going to need you to kick off your board on my mark."

Devon shook his helmet. "Your board won't support both our weight."

"Let me worry about that."

Sensing his refusal, Kira bashed the faceplate of her helmet against his. "You do what I say, when I say, and there's a good chance we both survive this. You continue playing the martyr, and we'll probably die."

Something she said must have gotten through to him because he nodded.

"Got that?" she asked.

"Yes."

Good. She didn't have time for hand holding. Even with her skills, they weren't going to make it out of this unscathed. She put their chances at fifty-fifty.

"Unlatch."

Devon hit the controls that would enable him to detach from the board.

It fell away from him.

Kira wasted no time, stomping down hard on the thrust. Alone, correcting for the tailspin would not have been outside her capabilities.

As it was, the extra weight of Devon's body only served to unbalance her every time she thought she'd gotten the hang of it, sending her into a new spin.

That wasn't the only problem. They were still going entirely too fast.

With the damage from the shrapnel, her board wasn't as responsive as it had been before.

The seconds to impact were ticking by, and she still hadn't solved this problem.

If technology wasn't going to work, what about *ki*?

A shield might disperse some of the force from the crash. Only problem was that with the inhibitor she was still limited on the amount she could draw at once.

If this were before, she could do it. It'd cost her, but she'd be alive at the end.

Removing it wasn't an option either. Jin had done some research during the journey on the *Wanderer*, but still hadn't found a way to unlock it.

Surprisingly, Odin had run into the same obstacle.

Wait. Just because she couldn't use it the way she wanted didn't mean Devon couldn't.

"Devon, expel your *ki* behind you at my command," Kira said.

"Are you sure?" he asked.

"We're kind of out of options."

If this didn't work, one of them was going to have to jump and hope for the best. Since her armor was better than his, it was more likely she'd survive the crash.

"You ready?" Kira asked.

"Yeah." Devon's answer showed his nerves.

"Three. Two. One."

Ki the color of sunlight burst out of his back briefly giving the image of two wings before the flare became impossible to watch.

At the same time, Kira stomped on the thrust.

Miraculously, the board jerked before correcting. Their flight was unstable and wobbly but infinitely better than the tailspin.

At least now she could steer.

Kira scanned the terrain, her lens computer assisting. Potential spots for a crash landing expanded and contracted, dismissed one after another.

Kira locked onto a glint of blue. There. That could work.

Landing in water wasn't without its risk. At this speed it would feel like hitting concrete. If they survived, they'd have to worry about drowning.

If Kira's armor had been heavier, she would have dismissed the possibility. As it was, she thought she could drop their speed enough to live past the impact.

As long as neither lost consciousness, they would be fine—theoretically.

Kira shifted her weight, the board whining as it adjusted their direction. By now, smoke was spewing in a trail behind them. Kira could feel the heat under her feet as flames licked up its sides.

As if things weren't bad enough.

The lake neared. Five hundred meters. Four hundred.

She could do this. It was the same type of maneuver she'd practiced a thousand times.

She flicked her eyes up and to the right, glancing at her speed.

It was still much too fast.

Kira tapped Devon's shoulder. They both leaned back, pointing the bottom of the board in front of them.

The board coughed once then sputtered, its rumble abruptly silenced.

Just what she needed. Another dead board.

Left with no choice, Kira kicked it away. "Shield."

Two shields, one golden and one a violet-blue snapped around them.

The ground rushed up to meet them.

Kira braced. This was going to hurt.

An invisible hand squeezed, popping the shields.

Fear touched her seconds before a shape surged out of the depths of the lake.

A long serpentine body armed with a head filled with very sharp teeth launched itself at her.

With no board and no way to change their trajectory, Kira could only watch as those teeth got closer.

The *lu-ong*'s mouth closed around them, swallowing Devon and Kira whole.

***

Graydon surged forward, instinctive denial filling him.

Massive with a teal fringe and a scar running across its snout, the *lu-ong* twisted, aiming toward the lake.

Graydon's *ki* surged as his form seemed to almost disappear as he shot toward the *lu-ong*.

If the *lu-ong* disappeared into the water, they wouldn't be able to save Kira and Devon.

He knew even as he fought for every bit of speed he was too far. There was no way of stopping this. No way to avoid what was coming.

The inside of Graydon's mind went silent and cold. The same way it had when news was brought of his parents' deaths.

It was a place that lacked warmth. Stark and sinister. Reality was stripped to its bones.

Graydon's future stretched before him. Empty and dull. Centuries upon centuries unbroken in their tedium.

Gone was Kira's smile, her fearless energy.

The moment passed, too slow and too fast all at once with Graydon a bystander. All his power rendered useless.

Blink—the *lu-ong* dove. Another blink and its head entered the water. Waves cascaded away from it.

A last blink and its tail disappeared beneath the surface.

Helplessness tried to rise; Graydon shoved it down ruthlessly.

She wasn't dead.

He could still feel her.

There, burning as brightly as before.

He simply needed to retrieve her.

Tragedy had a way of showing you what was important.

To him, Kira's worth couldn't be measured. He refused to let this be the end.

Graydon poured every bit of his *ki* into going faster. More and more, until only Torvald could keep up with him, his desperation matching Graydon's. Physical manifestations of *ki* flickered in and out of existence around his form, creating a brief halo.

It was a rare side effect, only happening when a large amount of *ki* was used in a short amount of time.

Pressure built in Graydon's body as he fed his power from his own personal well. If he went much further, he would court *ki* burnout.

Graydon judged the risk as acceptable against the potential loss of Kira and Devon.

Ahead, the ripples in the lake disappeared.

Graydon condensed a hard shield made up of air and *ki* in front of him as he prepared to hit the surface at full speed. He hadn't sensed a large output of *ki* from the *lu-ong*. Such a thing would mean it had jumped planets. As long as it remained here, he had a chance.

The lake wasn't that big, especially for a being as massive as a *lu-ong*.

Graydon didn't have more than a second to spare on the question of why the creature hadn't already made the jump or what it was doing here.

Right now, all that mattered was Kira and Devon and their safe recovery.

Seconds before Graydon prepared to dive, the *lu-ong* from before breached the surface.

Graydon veered away from his path, avoiding crashing into the ground only by chance. He circled quickly, a spear of black *ki* condensing in front of his palm.

Before he could attack, the *lu-ong*'s neck bent and its mouth opened. Two slimy forms were spit out.

"They're out. It's Kira and Devon," Wren shouted through their connection.

"They're not safe yet. Secondary attack from our right," Torvald instructed in a calm voice.

"Scatter bombs," Amila spat.

"Little Storm, Wren take care of the bombs," Torvald ordered. "I've got the rest."

Graydon was already acting before the first word was out of Torvald's mouth, the black spear he'd prepared for the *lu-ong* arcing toward the two silvery streaks.

It destroyed the first of the scatter bombs, disintegrating it until only microscopic pieces of debris remained. Unobstructed, the spear shot past, grazing the second of the bombs.

It impacted the ground with a dull roar, the shock wave hitting a second later.

If Graydon and the rest hadn't raised a *ki* shield they would have been knocked to the ground.

A nearly transparent wall of gold formed between the prone figures on the ground and the blast seconds before it reached them.

Wren flew past Graydon, his *ki* bursting out of him to destroy the second of the bombs. His actions weren't as flashy as Graydon's, but they were precise.

"Stay focused. There's no guarantee there won't be another attack," Graydon ordered before peeling off and heading for Kira.

***

Kira hit the ground hard, Devon right beside her.

Kira lay still, processing the fact she wasn't dead or being digested in a *lu-ong*'s stomach.

Devon groaned.

"You alive?" she asked.

"Somehow."

Kira pushed herself up to sitting, trying to figure out what happened. She remembered kicking away the waveboard in preparation for the crash. Then the gleam of teeth as they were swallowed. Afterward, there was only darkness and the feeling of being dipped in an electric hot bath akin to what she felt from the Mea'Ave.

She had no idea how it was possible, but it was clear the *lu-ong* and the Mea'Ave were linked in some inextricable way. She simply didn't know how.

By rights, even if the *lu-ong* had leapt out with the intention of catching them, they should still be dead.

Their bones should have shattered when the *lu-ong* swallowed them. Kira was very clear on their possibility of surviving, despite what she'd told Devon and Jin.

Honestly, she considered the fact she was still breathing a bit of a miracle.

All she remembered in the seconds the *lu-ong*'s mouth had closed around them was *ki* wrapping around her like a blanket, somehow cushioning her from damage.

Even her muscles and bones felt better than they had before. An invisible energy filling her up to the brim.

She clenched and unclenched her hands, catching sparkles darting in and out of her vision.

"What happened?" Devon reached up to touch a spot on the side of his neck. His helmet unfolded, revealing his face.

Kira shook her head, still occupied with the way *ki* seemed to be rising out of her armor in tiny flares before sinking back in.

Devon's gaze fell to her hands as a small exclamation left him. "That's manifestation."

"What is that?" Kira asked.

Devon reached over, his hand hovering over the tiny flares. "It's when your *ki* communes with the universe."

"That's quite the poetic description," Kira said.

As was her habit when things felt out of control, she retreated to sarcasm.

Devon didn't take offense. "You're like a pot boiling over, but instead of the water spilling, it is putting on a brilliant light show. We simply don't have the eyes to see except in rare circumstances."

"Kind of like what you get with the aurora borealis," Kira said, thinking she understood. "How is this possible if I'm wearing this?"

Kira raised her wrist with the inhibitor.

Devon touched it lightly. "The inhibitor doesn't drain your *ki*. It simply puts a wall between you and it. The potential is always there whether you can touch it or not."

His explanation was similar to what the Tuann healers had given her.

The inhibitor didn't stop her from using *ki*. Rather it was like slowly opening a faucet.

At first, the flow of *ki* was like a trickle, the opening gradually widening as she grew stronger, healing the *ki* channels she'd nearly destroyed through her misuse.

A massive shadow fell over them before Kira could ask any other questions, the sense of being watched unmistakable. She stiffened, afraid to turn her head and see what was waiting.

Seeing her expression, the awe on Devon's face faded.

His hand moved slowly to his waist.

Kira shook her head once. "Don't."

Any blade he drew would be useless anyway.

Inch by excruciating inch, Kira lifted her gaze until she was staring up at the giant *lu-ong* behind them. Its body half-submerged in the lake, small mounds of its serpentine form visible in places.

The *lu-ong*'s eyes were wise and knowing as he waited for her gaze to reach his.

He had a scar along one side of his jaw and over his snout. His whiskers almost made him seem like a wizened old man with a mustache and beard. The color of dawn, they were the longest Kira had ever seen on a *lu-ong*, almost brushing the water. Against the black of his body they were even more vivid.

His mane was sleeked back, indicating he was at ease. If it had been flared, they likely wouldn't have lived through the next few minutes.

Kira was careful not to move, holding still as she gestured for Devon to do the same. He listened, his breathing slightly faster as he stared at her, not daring to look back.

Kira moved to face the *lu-ong* more fully, ignoring the way her shoes squelched and the long strings of saliva still clinging to her.

"I suppose we have you to thank for our lives," Kira finally said after what felt like an eternity of staring.

Her previous encounters with the *lu-ong* had led her to believe they were highly intelligent.

A deep chuckle reverberated through her bones. *Wise child.*

The *lu-ong*'s amusement brushing against her senses felt a lot like sandpaper, abrading but not painfully so.

"Great one, why did you swallow us?"

You looked in need of assistance.

Kira couldn't argue with that. She bowed, her arms held away from her body, as if in doing so she could limit the amount of saliva that would get on her. An impossibility given every inch of her was coated in it.

Kira contained her shudder. She had a thing about bodily fluids—as in she didn't want them on her.

She held her revulsion in, knowing it could be construed as an insult. If it was this or possible death or maiming, she'd take the saliva, even if it didn't lessen the ick factor.

Approval pressed in on her.

Straightening from her bow, she took a moment to observe him in more detail, noting what she hadn't before. Silvery white threaded through some of his scales.

He was old. Much older than the ones she had met before.

"This is the second time a *lu-ong* has saved me," Kira said.

She didn't know whether to be concerned about that or not. Her debt to these strange creatures seemed to grow every time she turned around.

"Why?"

From what she'd inferred from Harlow and others, the *lu-ong* were treasured by the Tuann in the same way a god might be. They were worshipped from afar but didn't have much interaction with the Tuann.

She found it strange that they'd concern themselves with her small existence.

You still have a task to complete. It would be a shame if the machinations of others got in the way of that.

"What does that mean?"

The *lu-ong* lowered its head until an eye as large as her body was directly in front of her. For a moment, Kira caught the impression of galaxies in its depths.

In your heart, you know what I mean. Not everything will remain true when put into the crucible.

Kira's forehead furrowed. He might think she knew what he was talking about, but she was as lost as she'd been before this strange conversation.

The *lu-ong*'s attention shifted to over her shoulder. *The rot has grown. Soon it will need to be excised.*

A heavy thud came from behind her, followed quickly by a second one.

The intensity of the *lu-ong*'s stare froze Kira in place in much the same way a snake did a rabbit right before it struck.

One evil deed does not make a person evil. Nor does one good deed make a person good.

"Well, that's cryptic," Kira said.

The *lu-ong* sank into the lake. Light skimmed beneath the water's surface. When it was gone, the heavy weight of the *lu-ong*'s mind disappeared too.

"Kira!" Graydon's powerful strides carried him over to her.

Before she had time to react, she found herself enveloped in his embrace. His hand landed on the back of her head, pushing her head more firmly against his chest.

At any other time, Kira would have protested and done considerable damage at being manhandled without her permission. It was only because she felt the tremble in his hand and sensed his disquiet that she fell silent, letting the embrace lengthen.

Graydon's smell, one that spoke of a summer storm, surrounded her.

"You are bad for my heart," Graydon said into her ear.

Kira's response was muffled against his shoulder. "Now you get it."

Graydon's cheek brushed hers. "You make up for it in other ways."

Kira's smile was brief. He said that now, but what about in the future when it became clear she wasn't going to stop?

"If the *lu-ong* hadn't spit you out, I would have gone in after you."

Kira slanted him a sideways glance. "And what good do you think that would have done?"

They would likely have both perished at that point.

Graydon's grin was roguish. "I'm sure I could have figured something out."

Somehow, Kira found it hard to doubt him.

"The boy?" Graydon asked, focusing on business again.

"Safe." Kira tilted her head at Devon and the oshota who'd landed next to him. "You can have a look for yourself."

A wail came from a distance. "Kira!"

A muscle in Graydon's cheek jumped.

Kira stepped aside in time for a round shape to barrel into her.

"I thought you were dead!"

Jin burrowed into her chest, stray bits of electricity pinging off his casing and zapping Kira.

She winced but didn't push him away.

"You should know I'm tougher to kill than that."

Jin made a rude sound. "You got lucky."

He knew better than anyone else how bad it could have gone. They'd seen the aftermath of numerous waveboard crashes. They weren't known for having high survivability rates.

In a sense, the *lu-ong*'s intervention was the best outcome they could have hoped for.

"Not everyone can be swallowed by a *lu-ong* and survive," Kira pointed out.

Jin held very still. She knew the exact instant he put together the fact she'd been in a creature's mouth with the substance he could see on her clothes.

Kira's arms closed on him the moment he tried to dart away from her.

She laughed at his struggles to escape.

"No! What is this stuff? Why did you let me touch it?"

Kira's chuckle was evil. "Don't you want to share in my fortune?"

"No!" Jin broke free, landing on the ground where he rubbed all sides of himself against the dirt.

Instead of removing the sticky substance, he simply mixed the dirt in with the saliva.

Kira's head dipped, her shoulders shaking as Wren and the rest of

Graydon's oshota landed nearby.

The pitch of Jin's voice rose. "Are you laughing?"

Kira shook her head frantically, unable to stop her grin from breaking over her face.

Jin snarled, darting toward her head. Kira dodged as Jin chased her around Graydon.

"You shouldn't be so mean to someone who was just in a *lu-ong*'s belly," Kira shouted, avoiding another of Jin's swoops.

Graydon stood still, letting them have their fun.

"I'm so glad you find this amusing," Wren said in a neutral tone of voice.

Kira and Jin shared a look as they stopped and faced Wren and the rest.

The oshota crouched beside Devon drew her attention. For the first time the field in his hood wasn't activated, allowing Kira to see his face.

Like all Tuann, he had an ageless quality to him that made it impossible to guess his age. Whether he was a hundred years or a thousand, his face would never age, except for the weight of experience in his eyes.

Despite the lack of clues regarding his number of years, he had a calm reserve that said he was much older than he looked.

His face was the sort that stayed with you long after its owner had dismissed you as unimportant. His hair was short and cut close to his head.

His gold eyes were striking against the backdrop of his light brown skin. They were the first thing anybody would notice about him. Those eyes made you feel like there was no escape. They saw everything.

For someone used to her secrets, that wasn't necessarily a good thing.

Seeing him next to Devon, it was impossible to mistake their resemblance.

There was a trace of awe and relief on Devon's face as he looked up at the man.

Jin moved closer to Kira. "Who is that?"

Seconds passed as Kira studied Jin, surprised he needed to ask. Did he really not know?

Devon and the man's features held enough similar characteristics to those of Jin's original form.

After a moment, Kira mentally sighed.

Perhaps it wasn't so surprising after all that he didn't recognize the link between himself and them. It had been decades since he'd had that form.

The memories were no doubt hazy. It wasn't like they'd spent the time in the camps admiring their reflections. Kira couldn't recall a single time she'd looked at a mirror in that time. If she took all that into account, it was almost understandable Jin didn't see what Kira did.

"You really don't know?" Kira asked.

"Should I?"

Kira started to scrub one hand down her face and paused, eyeing it in distaste. Her hand dropped.

"You find nothing familiar about that man? Nothing at all?"

"No?" Jin made the word a question.

For someone so smart, Jin could be awfully obtuse at times.

He inched closer to Kira when she didn't say anything else. "Are you going to tell me?"

Kira debated with herself for half a second. She'd prefer to make this sort of revelation in privacy, but knowing Jin, now that he sensed something, he wouldn't let the matter drop.

Kira did something she rarely did since their comms were so much easier to use and caused less side effects later on. She reached out with her mind to project her thoughts at him.

"Think of me and Harlow." She sent him a pointed look.

Jin's puzzlement flooded the link, suppressing Kira's emotions.

This was the biggest reason they didn't use this method of communicating often. It tore gaping holes in the boundary between their minds, making it hard to distinguish where one started and the other left off.

"You mean you think he's my uncle?" Jin said, choosing to use the comms rather than their mental link.

"Close."

Kira waited for the pin to drop. When several seconds passed and Jin seemed no closer to the answer, she shook her head.

"I'm not certain but I think he might be your father."

Jin's eye swung toward the two. "Kira, there's at least an eighty percent chance that he and Devon are related, judging by the similarities in their features."

Kira folded her arms. Now he got it.

"No." He drew the word out.

"Yup."

"Not possible."

"Only it is," Kira assured him.

"I can't be related to that idiot."

Kira gave him a flat stare, reverting to normal speech. "Make me say yes one more time. I dare you."

Jin didn't get another chance to deny it as Wren drew his en-blade, and Maksym erected a *ki* shield.

"Incoming," Amila barked.

NINETEEN

THREE DOTS APPEARED against the backdrop of the sky, details becoming clearer as they neared. More elegant and refined than Kira would expect from a rescue vessel, the trio held more in common with pleasure crafts.

Sails that looked like butterfly wings jutted from the main hull. Their design put Kira in mind of a vibrantly colored dorsal fin on one of the deadly fish the Haldeel stocked in their ponds.

Like those predators, the vessels cut through the air with an efficiency that was as reliable as it was deadly.

Jin retreated to Kira's side as the ships prepared to land. "Look who finally shows up when the fun is already over."

Kira allowed the change in subject, knowing he'd talk when he was ready. Truthfully, she was grateful the revelation went over as well as it had.

"Let's keep our thoughts to ourselves," Kira told him. "We can't afford to offend the Haldeel."

While Kira's actions had been necessary to preserve Devon's life, they could also be seen as presumptuous. Kira didn't want to be made the scapegoat in the event the Haldeel needed to save face.

Jin grumbled but didn't say anything else as the first of the ships lowered in a gentle landing.

"Is that a royal cutter?" Kira asked, feeling slightly sick as she caught sight of Haldeel soldiers wearing the armor of the royal guard.

She took another look at the cutter, picking up on the details she had missed earlier. The sails were a pink so deep and vibrant it verged on crimson. Violet tinged its edges as black lines wound throughout.

Not just that. Though the material of the hull mimicked the look of wood, she caught a shimmer that suggested it was coated in a substance that would make it extremely resistant to long-distance projectile and energy weapons.

With a glance she noted areas on the hull which housed several weapons, including energy cannons of force distributers.

She gave Jin a sidelong look.

As always, he read her mind. "They're armed to the teeth."

To say nothing of the way the other two were currently circling the area. Kira recognized the pattern. Those two ships had set up an overwatch.

Any enemy stupid enough to attack would easily be taken care of from there, leaving the grounded ship plenty of time to recover their people and get airborne.

Those weren't the actions of somebody sent to retrieve a pair of unlucky racers.

"Did something else happen? Are they expecting another attack?" Kira asked.

The attention of the oshota next to Devon moved to Kira. A thoughtful look settled on his face, even as he remained silent.

"The perpetrator was caught," Graydon said, distracting Kira.

She looked at him in surprise. The Tsavitee weren't normally so inept.

Kira didn't have time to ask any more questions as the Haldeel official who'd overseen the start of the race disembarked from the cutter.

He glided toward them, sinking into a deep curtsy by flattening his lower appendages against the ground. For a Haldeel, the act of ensuring one's head was below another's was considered one of the highest forms of respect.

Kira had only seen it once when a Haldeel was seeking an audience with a puzzle master.

It wasn't the type of action offered to someone outside their race who also had little to do with their empire.

By doing this, the Haldeel was making it clear they were in the wrong.

It was a strong stance to take in a forum such as this. If she were an unscrupulous individual, she could use his action to extort a lot of benefits from the Haldeel.

There was surprise on the faces of the oshota around her.

"This humble one apologizes for his tardiness and begs for your forgiveness," the Haldeel said, not rising.

Kira wavered, unsure what to do.

Diplomacy wasn't one of her strengths. She much preferred the straight and easy solution. If it involved the extreme application of force, even better.

Still, it was clear the Haldeel wasn't going to move until Kira made some sort of statement.

"Name?" she asked, buying time.

"Khartor."

Kira nodded as her gaze strayed in Graydon's direction. He looked passively at her as if telling her what she did next was entirely her choice.

Kira was afraid he'd say that. There was nothing like having all of the pressure on your shoulders.

It was times like these that she missed her peaceful life as a salvager. It was lonely, but at least then if she made the wrong decision, the only one to pay the price would be her.

"There's no need for all this fuss," Kira finally settled on saying. "No lives were lost, and the damage from this matter is minor."

Though if Devon had died, that wouldn't have been the case.

Given how protective the Tuann were of their young under normal circumstances, it would have been a disaster if he was injured or killed. Throw in his relation to the man next to him, who she suspected was the Tuann's emperor, and you could magnify that by several factors.

If she wanted to make a big deal of this, she could, but Kira judged it would be more beneficial to downplay her role.

The Haldeel weren't blind and they weren't stupid. Her actions would endear her to them more than if she had blown this matter up.

They'd owe her a favor for this. The Haldeel had a reputation for paying their debts.

Kira was also aware the matter needed to be settled here and now. As soon as the other Houses became involved it would no longer be so simple. Even with the risks she'd taken to save Devon, the incident could be magnified to significant proportions in the right hands.

Kira didn't want that. The Tuann and Haldeel needed to stay allies.

A wedge between them would only benefit the Tsavitee.

The Haldeel rose. "The Haldeel owe you a great debt and the Tuann an apology for our oversight."

Kira waved her hand, not interested in either. "It's impossible to protect against every eventuality. Where there is a wall, people will constantly seek to scale it."

It was the nature of the beast.

Khartor bowed at the waist. "*Za na ri*, you are ever kind and wise."

Kira didn't think either attribute had ever been attached to her name before.

Khartor stepped to the side and gestured at the cutter. "If you'll allow me, I've been instructed to escort you back."

"Your kindness is appreciated," Kira said.

They'd flown quite far off course. With Kira's board trashed, it would be a long walk back.

Speaking of her board.

Kira sent Jin a pointed look. She didn't care about the board itself, but the drive chain was extremely important to her. Falling into the wrong hands wasn't so much of a problem unless the other party was a hacker as good as Odin, but that didn't mean she wanted it getting lost either.

Jin ignored her pointed stare, drifting closer to Devon and the man beside him.

"Jin," Kira warned as the two watched him.

Devon's gaze was open, more curious than anything. Kira didn't know if he had been told about Jin's contributions to breaking them out of the memory loop they'd landed in during the *uhva na.*

She and Jin had left immediately afterward, making any interaction between the two brief.

Despite that, Devon didn't hold any of the unfriendliness many Tuann had upon meeting Jin.

The man Kira suspected as his father—and the emperor of the Tuann—was a little more guarded. Not hostile, exactly, but not welcoming either.

Understandable considering all that had happened.

Khartor inclined his chin, drawing her attention. "We've dispatched people to recover your belongings."

Convenient—especially since a certain drone was ignoring her orders.

Left with no reason to delay, Kira headed for the cutter.

She boarded with the rest of the Tuann following. Jin stuck close to Devon and the oshota, his "eye" focused on them as he kept the barest of acceptable distances.

Perhaps Kira had been hasty in assuming he was handling the possibility of his relation to them well. The last thing she needed was for her friend to be accused of being a stalker.

That would be the cherry on top of this shit show.

As they flew closer to the stands, Kira expanded the view of the leader board in her optics.

It wasn't surprising that the race had continued despite Devon and Skye's mishap. Crashes, while tragic, were an inevitable part of the sport.

The racers who'd finished in the top three would continue onto the finals in two days when the rest of the semifinals finished.

Raider and Kira were the only two racers who'd lifted a hand to help. While their actions had disqualified them from the race itself, Kira couldn't bring herself to care too much.

Winning had never been her goal. She'd only entered to have a reason to stay on the planet. Since Elena had already been discovered, there was little reason to continue.

There was also the fact that reuniting with House Roake and Wren now meant she had a sponsor whose backing could allow her to remain even after the loss.

"Looks like that racer with the ridiculous name of Moonbeam, the one who came close to dethroning you, came in first," Jin observed.

Moonbeam's name was the only one she recognized on the leaderboard. The other two were unknown to her.

Kira's eyes narrowed as she considered Moonbeam's ranking.

There was something familiar about the person and the way they rode, as if they were trying to get Kira's attention. From the dead man's plunge on the qualifying race to the jockeying at the start of today's race.

One incident Kira could discount. Racers were an arrogant and cocky lot. Two? That was pushing it.

"Find out what you can about this Moonbeam," Kira ordered.

"I'll get Odin on it."

"No. You do it."

Jin paused and turned his "eye" on Kira.

"Understood," Jin acknowledged.

Kira's clenched fists loosened.

She'd thought he'd argue—or at least ask questions. It was a relief when he didn't pry further.

Kira couldn't explain why she'd made that order.

Kira trusted Odin, but only up to a point. Odin had her own goals for their partnership.

For Kira, locating the Tsavitee home worlds was only important if Elise was on one of them. That was where Odin's goals diverged from hers. Without the star maps Kira had secretly downloaded from Luatha's nexus on Ta Da'an, Odin had no hope of liberating what remained of her people.

While Kira still planned to help Odin even if she found Elise on Jettie, there was no certainty Odin would believe in her promises.

Odin's issues with trust were multifaceted and made Kira look well adjusted.

The cutter began its descent as it prepared to land on the strip of flat ground in front of the stands.

The race had long since ended, and the participants cleared from the finish line.

In their place, a phalanx of guards in Haldeel armor stood in formation, Raider and Skye next to them.

Kira noted all this at a glance before her attention locked on the figure standing resolutely in front of the rest.

She had the poise of a ruler—elegant and regal even under so many watchful eyes.

Her gown was the color of amethyst with silver embroidery woven throughout. Its neckline would be considered a halter in human fashion, exposing her slim shoulders. From behind her extended a long train in the same design that attached to the silver collar of the dress.

Her face was concealed by a veil that stopped at her chin.

"A royal greeting you personally," Graydon said. "You seem to have made quite the impact."

Kira flicked him a look. Why did she have a feeling he found that prospect highly entertaining?

"As the highest-ranked here, you should handle this," she suggested.

Graydon's lips curled. "Oh no, I wouldn't dream of taking this honor from you."

Some honor. All this would bring her was unnecessary attention.

From the sympathy in Devon's expression and the way he made no moves to intervene, Kira could already tell there was no way out of this. You'd think after saving his life on two separate occasions he'd be a little loyal.

But no. He was as willing to cast her to the wolves as Graydon and the rest of his oshota.

Traitors. All of them.

Graydon leaned closer. "Besides, we're not the one she wants to speak to."

There was a tension in the air and a hushed atmosphere as Kira disembarked, followed by Devon, Graydon, and the rest.

Kira may not have won the race, but her dramatic actions during the rescue had overshadowed the rest.

A loud cheer from those still waiting in the stands marked their triumphant return.

Wren and Maksym flanked Kira, in an unmistakable gesture of protection. If anybody tried to snipe her from a distance, one of them would intervene first.

It was only when she neared the royal that they fell back a step, allowing Kira to close the remaining distance with only Graydon at her side.

"I see you haven't fixed your habit of rescuing lost souls," the woman said in a warm tone that carried over the sounds of celebration.

Kira paused in mid-step.

"Kira Forrest, Scourge of the Tsavitee, the protective Phoenix of the Consortium, and now prodigal daughter of the Tuann. Don't tell me you don't remember me."

Kira sucked in a harsh breath, finally able to place where she'd heard this voice before.

Eight years ago. The edge of Haldeel space at an often-overlooked outpost.

She'd hoped her actions there had been forgotten. To be truthful she was kind of counting on it.

What she did on that outpost should have seen her arrested and dumped in a deep dark hole as soon as the Haldeel realized she was the same person who'd orchestrated the destruction of several of their most elite ships.

Of course, if they did that, they'd also have to arrest the person standing before her. The real reason Kira had gone to the lengths she had.

"Ah, you do remember. I was worried."

Kira felt the side of her face burning from the heat of multiple stares. Graydon, Raider, Wren. The oshota standing next to Devon whose face was once again hidden behind a disrupter field.

Pretty much anyone who had just overheard the royal's statement.

"My cherished *za na ri,* there is no cause for such concern. I simply wished to greet my friend again."

Kira didn't respond, struggling to reconcile the individual in front of her with the one she'd once known.

Back then, Tierni had been about Elena's current age and height. She'd worn her fear and poor self-esteem in the same way she'd worn the ratty clothes she'd used to cover her body.

At the time, she'd been malnourished and barely surviving. The rare genetic disorder that caused her blindness in a society whose technological advances could cure damn near anything, isolating her far better than any cell ever could.

"Come now, will you not greet an old friend?" the royal said, startling Kira out of her thoughts.

Kira knew behind her veil, Tierni's eyes would be a milky white, the nerve fibers that would have routed behind the retina in another Haldeel missing.

What should have been a handicap had turned into a strength for the other woman, allowing her empathic senses to compensate. Tierni didn't perceive the world in the same way other Haldeel did.

In the short time Kira had known Tierni, the other woman had discovered how to use those senses in a way that gave her the advantage.

Deceiving her was impossible. She could read feelings like they were an open book.

Not only that, but as long as someone was around her, she could use their perception of the world to navigate, "seeing" it through their eyes.

In the time since their last encounter, it seemed Tierni had managed to rise to one of the Haldeel's highest positions.

Tierni's veil fluttered as her head tilted, recalling Kira to the present.

She'd been rude.

As surprising as Tierni's new status was, Kira was happy to see the scared little girl she'd once known succeed in a way Tierni hadn't been able to conceive of when Kira first met her.

Kira let that feeling flush through her, the pleasure and warmth. The joy and pride. The happiness at seeing her friend again.

"Tierni," Kira said softly, holding those feelings close.

"You do remember."

"Yes."

Tierni's gaze swept up to where Jin hovered above Kira's head.

"Little Jin, I see you're as dapper as always," Tierni said.

"And you are wearing much nicer clothes than the last time I saw you," he responded.

Tierni inclined her head. "This is true."

With a deliberate movement, the royal turned, sweeping her train out of her way in a practiced gesture.

"I'm glad we got to meet again," Tierni said before she disappeared into her crowd of guards.

The leader of those guards remained behind as the rest marched away, giving Kira her second shock of the afternoon.

She blinked at the Haldeel, noting the familiar markings on his arms and face.

His lips lifted in a smirk as he made a gesture that when translated would mean her legs were showing. To a Haldeel, the saying was the equivalent of the human saying that she was wearing her emotions on her sleeve.

"When it rains, it pours," Jin said, almost more shocked than Kira.

Neither expected to see Lieven here. Though they should have.

Lieven had been Tierni's companion all those years ago, protecting her in the darkest circumstances. He was the reason Kira understood the nuances of the Haldeel language, both verbal and nonverbal, as well as she did. He'd been the one to undertake the painstaking process of educating her.

"Lady. Lord." Lieven greeted both of them. "You look well."

Considering their last encounter had ended with Kira half dead, that wasn't saying much.

"You seem calmer. Steadier. This pleases me greatly," Lieven continued, making the gesture for relief and happiness.

Lieven sobered as he left behind the past in favor of that of the present, adjusting his position so he was partially facing both Raider and Kira.

"The Haldeel wish to extend their sincerest gratitude," Lieven started.

At the same time, Odin's voice came over the coms. "Kira, you're never going to believe this."

Kira tried to split her attention between the two.

"Although the quorum's official celebration won't be held for several days when it has reached its conclusion, we'd like to invite you to a small banquet tomorrow on Almaluk as a token of our esteem."

"It's Elise. They caught Elise."

Kira went still, feeling like she couldn't draw breath as the rest of Lieven's words descended into a mass of sound as the world froze around her.

Sensing her disquiet, Odin rushed to assure her. "I've examined all the feeds. It's her. I'm sure of it."

Kira ducked her head to hide the movement of her lips as she spoke in as silent a voice as possible. "Where?"

"I'm tracking them now. From what I can tell, they're heading to Almaluk."

The same place this banquet was going to be held.

Seeing a watchful look descend on Lieven's face because she hadn't spoken in so long, Kira smiled, her lips feeling stiff. "We'd be honored to attend."

At that, Raider frowned at her in surprise.

He knew how much Kira detested such things. Normally she would refuse unless forced.

"One question," Kira started. "I hear you apprehended the person responsible for the attack. What is going to happen to them?"

Kira very much doubted it was actually Elise they'd caught, but she couldn't take the chance she was wrong.

Lieven gave her a probing look, no doubt sensing some of her feelings. "We can discuss that tomorrow night at the banquet."

In other words, unless she attended, she could forget setting up a meeting with the culprit.

Well played, Lieven. Well played.

With that, he strode in the wake of the rest, leaving Kira standing with a bunch of Tuann who had a plethora of questions she didn't want to answer.

Graydon's warm palm landed on the small of her back as he guided her in the opposite direction, his oshota and Wren falling in around them. Raider trailed in their wake.

Graydon leaned close. "I think you owe us some of those answers now."

Kira didn't answer for several steps.

"Not here. This isn't the sort of thing that can be discussed in such a public setting."

Not when it came to matters as delicate as this.

"Later then."

Left with no choice, Kira nodded.

The inflexible set of Graydon's jaw told her arguing at this stage would only hurt her cause.

She only hoped they delayed the interrogation until she'd rid herself of the remnants of the *lu-ong*'s saliva.

* * *

To Kira's eternal regret, her worst fear played out.

She'd barely stepped inside the Tuann residence when she was intercepted by Yukina.

"With me now."

Yukina had already swept away before Kira could open her mouth.

Seeing the frustration on her face, Graydon smirked as if to say she had only herself to blame.

Kira narrowed her eyes at him, dragging one hand down her leg before slapping it on his shoulder and rubbing.

Graydon's lip curled in faint disgust.

What could she say? Fucking with others always put her in a better mood.

Kira dragged her eyes up and down his body, ignoring his wide chest and clearly defined muscles, as if to say he didn't have much room to complain.

He was covered with saliva from his earlier embrace with Kira. Granted, not to the same extent as Devon and her, but he was by no means pristine.

Amila and Solal smothered their grins at the interchange.

Graydon recovered quickly, lifting an eyebrow as if to ask if she was brave enough to keep Yukina waiting.

It turned out the answer was no—but Kira had no intention of telling him that.

Instead, she sauntered in Yukina's wake, not commenting as the Emperor's Face led her upstairs and through several hallways before arriving at a door located a fair distance from the entrance.

Kira slogged inside the room Yukina had chosen, trying to ignore the thick and clingy substance that had somehow managed to work itself under her armor.

She stood awkwardly in a corner, not wanting to dirty the pristine monochromatic furniture as Graydon, the oshota Kira was pretty sure wasn't an oshota, and Wren entered.

Devon tried to follow but found his way blocked by Graydon.

"You should get cleaned up."

Devon's alarmed gaze found Kira. "I'm your *yer'se*. Shouldn't I be present?"

"Perhaps next time."

Raider slipped through as Graydon shut the door in Devon's face.

Yukina pointed at him. "Leave."

"Raider stays," Kira corrected. "He needs to hear this too."

Yukina pressed her lips together as her eyes flashed. "Only if he swears to keep anything he hears from the Consortium."

Raider threw himself into a seat, his expression that of a cat who'd just swallowed the canary. "What kind of person would I be if I promised to keep important intel from my own people? Would you trust such an individual?"

The answer was no, and they all knew it.

Someone capable of betraying their own kind once could be convinced to do it again.

Before anyone could raise an argument, Raider waved a lazy hand. "But I will tell you I've been instructed not to share anything I learn unless it directly pertains to the security of the Consortium."

The room fell quiet as all eyes turned to him.

Even Kira regarded him with a somber expression.

"There's a power struggle in the Consortium," Graydon guessed as he joined them, finding a seat across from Raider.

Yukina and the rest remained standing.

Raider didn't speak, but then, he didn't have to. The cause was clear.

If Himoto had given that order, it was because he feared any information Raider gleaned would fall into the wrong hands.

Better for everyone if it didn't make its way to the Consortium's ears at all.

"Who is the rebel faction?" Graydon asked.

Raider regarded him with a lazy expression.

"Zepher is leading it, if I was to guess," Kira supplied, not looking away from Raider.

His smirk said she was on point.

"Kent is part of the faction," Kira went on.

Another twitch of his eyebrows; another confirmation.

Kira rubbed her forehead. Such twisted webs Himoto wove.

"I'm willing to set the issue of the Consortium aside, but you will explain your history with the Haldeel," Yukina said with a direct stare.

Jin hummed. "Someone is a little confident. If we didn't know better, that would sound like a threat."

Yukina's stare turned arctic. "That's because it is."

Jin whistled. "Kira, pay attention. I think we're going to learn some things."

Kira's mouth quirked but she refrained from commenting. She'd be lying if she said she wasn't a little curious about what this so-called threat entailed.

Yukina's gaze moved between them. "You think I'm bluffing? I'm not. I've worked for years to foster a relationship with the Haldeel. I'm not going to let you jeopardize that."

Jin let out a guffaw. "Hate to break it to you, but the Haldeel see you as a distant acquaintance, nothing more."

The pupils of Yukina's eyes dilated as the air around her body got colder. "Test me and I'll have you sent to the Manth sector. You'll do nothing but chase pirates for the rest of your lives."

Dead silence came after her words.

"Kira!" Jin whispered.

"No."

"But—"

"Don't do it," Kira warned.

Jin made a sound as high pitched as a tea kettle as his spherical body vibrated with excitement. "Pirate hunters. We're going to be pirate hunters."

Damn it. She'd lost him.

Jin bobbed up and down, looking like a jack in the box. "I never say this, but be yourself, Kira, and we can realize our lifelong dream."

Jin screamed to himself as he careened in a circle. "We'll get a big fancy hat and an artificial leg. This is going to be great.

Kira tilted her face up to the ceiling and sighed.

She knew the reasoning behind Jin's overblown antics was to draw attention away from her. He was an old hat at playing the fool to give her space to work unobstructed.

Perfect teamwork as always—except for one thing.

There were those in this room who easily saw through their schemes.

"Quit teasing her," Wren ordered.

Just like that, Jin settled down, turning serious in an instant. "Fine, but next time, if you're going to threaten someone at least make it something they fear."

To Yukina's credit, she was able to ignore Jin's distraction, instead focusing on Kira. "What is between you and that royal?"

"I'm curious to know as well," the oshota next to her said.

Graydon stretched one arm across the back of the couch. "You were somehow involved in her Ascension, weren't you?"

Yukina collapsed onto the opposite end of the couch from Graydon, some of her arrogance dimming.

"I don't know if I'd go that far," Kira started.

"If we were, we had no idea," Jin added.

At the dubious looks that asked how that was possible, Kira said defensively, "When we knew her, Tierni wasn't royal."

Yukina reclaimed some of her poise. "We're listening."

"I don't know if you realize, but Tierni is blind," Kira started. "She was born with a rare genetic mutation. Essentially the optic fibers that pass through the back of the retina didn't develop in a way to translate sight."

"I've heard of this. Only one in several million are born with this condition," Yukina said. "Tierni caused quite the stir during her Ascension. Most born with the mutation are given to the Vertier order to raise."

"Yeah, I've met some of that order." Kira's lip curled as she snorted, scorn and derision written on her face. "They're little more than exploitative assholes."

The order was considered sacred among the Haldeel. Those who joined were kept cloistered, spending their time in meditation and service—at least that was what was written on the brochure.

Those of the Vertier that Kira had encountered were little more than abusers and bullies, content to prey on those who'd been entrusted to them for their own greedy purposes.

"Not all. I've known many who embodied the ideals of the order," Yukina murmured. "But what you said is true enough. There are some who abuse their position at the expense of those who rely on them."

"When we first met Tierni, she was on the run after her creche gave her over to them," Kira said.

On a human world, the act held some similarities to adoption. Only instead of being able to age out of their care, she'd be a permanent dependent. The order would assume responsibility and authority over her for the rest of her life whether she wished it or not.

"Lieven got her out, and the two were on the run until we—"

"Excuse me," Jin interrupted.

"I," Kira corrected, "interfered."

"She means to say she picked a fight with the order," Jin said in a chipper voice.

Kira grimaced. That was an accurate assessment.

A million ways she could have handled it and she'd chosen the most explosive.

It was about half a year after she'd woken up from a several years long coma. The war was over. Her remaining friends scattered, most of whom no longer held favorable views of Kira.

She still hadn't known about Elena, Jin judging her mental state as too fragile.

To say she was looking for a place to die wouldn't be out of line. The only thing that kept her from doing anything she couldn't take back was the knowledge of how her fallen friends would be disappointed in her if she took the quick way out.

"I was occupying myself in the gauntlet of the stratagem." It was a series of round-robin challenges. It wasn't usually considered deadly unless you were on a perimeter planet not exactly known for having peacekeepers of any sort.

Kira's smile was self-deprecating. "I ran across Tierni and Lieven there."

"And you interfered," Graydon guessed.

Kira nodded. "You could say that."

"If by interfere, you mean she scuttled two chariots in the process," Jin added.

Kira sent him a cool look.

"What? They said they wanted the truth," Jin argued.

Kira shook her head, aware of how the rest of them stared at her like she'd sprouted two heads.

"I didn't know a Haldeel chariot could be destroyed. That class of ship is said to be indestructible," Wren said.

"Not if you work from the inside," Jin said. "And if you want to get technical about it, we only destroyed one. The second simply got too close to the first."

Jin said it like it was no big deal, but they'd barely escaped with their lives.

The chariot class ship had earned its reputation. Both had belonged to a faction in the Vertier order. When they'd taken Tierni, Kira had gone and gotten her out.

She'd bitten off a little more than she could chew, but the ending had worked out, even if it was a bit flashy for Kira's tastes.

"I don't know how she ended up a royal or when her Ascension was," Kira confessed.

That hadn't been anywhere on their radar then.

After they'd destroyed the ships, they left Tierni and Lieven somewhere safe and skedaddled for fear the Haldeel would try to arrest them for wanton destruction of property.

Yukina's head lifted. "Eight years ago? In the Fieri sector?"

Enlightenment filled Graydon's expression. "If I remember correct, wasn't that the source of a minor scandal?"

Yukina's stare drilled into Kira. "Yes, a Haldeel higher echelon family was caught trying to pass the offspring of a distant branch as a candidate for the Ascension using the scores of another."

Yukina's lips curled in a smile that didn't reach her eyes. "When the deception was discovered, the child responsible for those results deposed the imposter. It was a bloody affair, I'm told."

That would explain Tierni's current position—and perhaps some of why Kira and Jin weren't arrested for their actions.

"Your royal made quite the splash on her return. Her first act was reforming the laws around the Vertier," Yukina added.

"She's garnered a reputation since her Ascension," Torvald said, sounding approving.

Yukina's stare drilled into Kira. "You're lucky you didn't die. The Vertier has a warrior sect within it."

"I'm aware," Kira said.

They'd sent those warriors after Tierni and Lieven. Never again did she want to face a Haldeel in battle.

"What could have possessed you to be so reckless?" Wren asked.

Kira lifted a shoulder. "It involved a child."

For her, that was the only reason that mattered.

She could never walk away from a child who needed her help. It was a weakness she knew the Tsavitee might one day try to take advantage of. Even so, she had no desire to fix the chink in her armor. It was what made all the rest bearable. It made her feel clean.

Ignoring Tierni's situation had been impossible—especially in those days.

Raider stretched one arm across his armchair and leaned back. "You found Tsavitee meddling, didn't you?"

"There was the suggestion of their hand in the mix," Kira allowed. "No proof however."

Just her gut feeling.

While the Tsavitee gave the appearance of defeat after the war, it was a cover to launch a much more insidious attack—one that sought to take advantage of the fact everyone believed them gone.

"It's obvious from the royal that whatever Kira's actions, they were seen as legitimate by the Haldeel," Yukina said after a projected silence. "We have no reason to reject their invitation to tomorrow's banquet. Kira will attend with the rest of those who've distinguished themselves today so as not to insult our hosts."

She sent a hard look in Kira's direction. "There will be no surprises during this banquet. No fights, no scuttling of ships. Nothing. Am I clear?"

Kira really wanted to know exactly what sort of person Yukina thought she was. It was almost like the Emperor's Face didn't trust her.

Seeing Kira didn't have an argument, Yukina flicked her fingers toward the door and sat back. "You're dismissed."

Kira excused herself, Raider following.

Kira headed toward the room Auralyn had shown her to last night.

Two corridors later she finally looked at the man at her side. "Is there a reason you're shadowing me?"

Raider stuck his hands in his pockets. "Just waiting."

"For what?"

"To see if you'll keep your side of the bargain."

Kira's footsteps came to a halt as she watched him out of the corner of her eye. "It looks like there's no need for that since you already know."

Raider smirked but said nothing else.

Seeing Elena rocket around the corner, Kira started toward her. "No matter what, make sure you're on the station tomorrow night."

Raider sent her a startled glance. "You have a plan?"

Kira made a *mmm* of agreement.

"Will it start a war?" he asked.

"Don't be ridiculous. Even I know better than that."

Seeing Elena's suspicious gaze as she slowed in front of them, Kira reached out to ruffle her hair only for her niece to duck away with an expression of disgust.

Kira's hand froze in midair as she stared at it, feeling a similar repulsion. It wasn't that she'd forgotten she was covered in saliva—it was far too repulsive for her to do that—but she'd put it on the backburner until seeing Elena's expression.

"I'll leave the two of you to get caught up. I'm going to get a shower," Kira said.

Kira walked away. Despite her assurance to Raider, Kira wasn't entirely sure what she'd do if the Haldeel rejected her offer. One thing was for sure—she wasn't leaving the station until she talked to the woman who wore Elise's face.

TWENTY

AN HOUR LATER, Kira climbed out of the shower. Steam escaped from the stall, curling around her body as she reached for one of the fluffy towels on the counter.

Her motions were quick as she dried off.

She paused as she caught her blurred reflection in the mirror. The condensation that had formed distorted Kira's image, veiling her features until they were indistinct.

With one smooth movement, she wiped the moisture away.

Her eyes stared at her. Penetrating and deep. Their color hard to pin down. They were a shade between gray and purple, seeming to change based on her mood and clothing.

Once upon a time, those eyes had set her apart, making her feel like a freak.

Then she met those from House Luatha and found out they weren't that original after all.

Strange how things had changed in such a short time.

What had set her apart was now something, if not ordinary, at least not unique.

"Not alone anymore," Kira told her reflection.

Her gaze dropped to Luatha's mark on her forearm, three crescents over a circle with smaller lines joining those crescents.

The mark of her mother's people.

She rubbed a thumb over the band of tattoos rimming each wrist, only the inhibitor she wore hindering her movements.

The Overlord bands. The mark of her father's people. At least one of them anyway.

Kira raised her head. "One more night."

Time and the full strength of the Haldeel royal guard were all that separated her from answers.

Impatience thrummed beneath the surface of Kira's skin.

Maybe when she was young and reckless, she would have chosen to act without thinking of the consequences.

This Kira, however, was older and wiser. She knew the taste of defeat, the hopelessness of loss.

She'd learned patience. She'd absorbed the lesson of endurance.

"You've waited this long," Kira told herself. "You can wait a little longer."

No mistakes. Kira couldn't afford them.

Turning from the mirror, Kira dropped the towel and grabbed the long, silk robe she'd found mixed in with her belongings after she'd returned.

It was a work of art, far nicer than anything she'd ever owned. Made from the silk of *zanti* worms, it was beautiful and made her feel feminine.

The color of the midnight sky in the brief moments before night changed to dawn, it was a deep blue. Silver accents made it glitter.

Despite being made from a fabric delicate enough to make the wearer fear they would accidentally shred it, the robe was surprisingly sturdy.

It slid against her skin, cool at first before Kira caught a faint tinge of warmth.

With her body still slightly damp, it clung to her curves.

Like this, Kira opened the door, stepping into her room.

She came to an abrupt stop at the sight of Graydon's big body draped over her couch.

The appreciation in his expression quickly changed to laughter when he caught sight of her hair.

It seemed when *lu-ong* saliva dried it became hard and unyielding. Getting the stuff off her body had taken some work.

She'd given her hair up as a lost cause after three rounds of shampoo hadn't been enough to wash the saliva away. It was now a stiff, hard helmet around her head.

Worst-case scenario, she could always chop her hair off and let it regrow.

"Laugh it up," Kira warned in a mild voice as she headed toward him.

She'd like to see him keep laughing while she strangled him.

Graydon straightened on the couch and beckoned her toward him. "Come here."

Kira sent him an arch look.

"What are you doing here?" she asked.

"I had a feeling you'd have trouble with the *lu-ong* saliva, so I'm here to offer my services."

Kira studied his sincere expression before snorting.

"I know you don't think I'm that dumb," she told him.

The fake sincerity dropped from his face leaving the self-satisfied warrior behind.

"Come, let me help you with your hair while we talk," Graydon ordered.

Kira narrowed her eyes but complied.

Her hair had always been a source of nuisance for her. Privately, she often referred to it as a tentacle monster because of its refusal to be controlled.

That was why she tended to keep it short, cutting it anytime she lost patience with it.

Right now, it was longer than it had been in years because of all the distractions with Luatha and Roake.

That being said, she had no true wish to be bald.

Kira padded toward Graydon, the edge of her robe dragging along the floor behind her and exposing her legs below the knee.

Another woman would have felt self-conscious wearing nothing but thin fabric held together by a tie and a belt.

To Kira, it was no big deal. The robe covered all the important bits.

Her sense of modesty had long since vanished.

When you lived in close quarters with your fellow soldiers, the things that once mattered no longer seemed so important.

Kira only needed to come back from one two-week training exercise to lose any remaining scraps of reticence regarding nudity. When it felt like the skin was going to crawl off your body because of germs and dirt, you made do with what you had. Even if it was a six-person shower with a ten-minute time limit that needed to accommodate thirty women in that short period.

Add in a childhood where her keepers found such things to be a hindrance to their training, and Kira had long since been conditioned not to care.

At least that was what she'd always thought right up until the moment she caught Graydon watching her like a hawk who'd just spotted a juicy rabbit.

There was a dark awareness in his eyes. A sensual decadence that made her chest get tight and her breathing a little heavier.

It was as if the very molecules that formed the epidermis of her skin could sense his presence and were doing their own tango of delight.

Why? Why was it this man out of all the rest?

Kira had had partners before. They were rare and always consisted of one-night stands. She'd never been willing to make herself vulnerable to another in an emotional way.

After seeing what happened to Raider and Elise, she was even more determined.

Yet, here she stood.

Danger circling.

Not the type to steal her life. No, it just wanted her soul.

"Aren't you going to sit?" Graydon asked when she remained standing.

Kira didn't mistake the challenge in those words that were nothing short of a dare.

Never one to back down, Kira took a seat next to him, turning from him to give him access to her hair.

He tugged at a lock, the gentle pulling sensation sending tingles rocketing through her.

Get a hold of yourself, Forrest. He's just a man. A potent, alluring man, but a man, nevertheless.

Even as Kira scolded herself, she knew it wasn't that simple.

Graydon was like a drug, tempting her into addiction.

Maybe if there hadn't been admiration mixed into this craving, Kira would have had a hope of resisting.

She knew better now the trials Graydon dealt with on a regular basis. The Houses weren't easy to control. They were rife with infighting capable of toppling the Tuann if allowed to go unchecked.

Only someone like Graydon could keep the balance without turning into a tyrant.

He was harsh when protecting what he loved, but Kira didn't see cruelty in him.

All she needed to do was look at the oshota around him. They loved him. They would die for him.

Not just anyone could engender that type of loyalty in another.

"Was it you who got Elena out of the audience?" Kira asked.

Graydon hummed as he prodded at another stiff chunk of hair.

"Why?"

With his duties, she would have thought he wouldn't have the time to safeguard her niece.

"She's important to you."

Such a simple answer.

Yet the words felt emblazoned on her soul.

Had anyone besides Jin ever understood her in this way?

Even Elise had been held at a distance. Kira had seen Elise as a sister, but she never let down her guard. Not fully.

Now here was Graydon. Able to see through her so easily.

Kira had a feeling if she let him, he could wreck her, destroy her beyond all recognition.

Fear and desire melded, creating a cocktail of emotion that threatened to drown her.

As if sensing her preoccupation, Graydon went to work on her hair, his light tugs on her scalp feeling like they had a direct line to her libido.

"*Lu-ong* saliva is rather special. It has a hardening agent that reacts to heat and air."

Kira frowned in realization. The substance coating her hadn't become unmanageable until right before she climbed into the shower.

"There's a trick to getting it out," Graydon continued.

His *ki* enveloped her skin, an invisible caress that sent shivers through her.

Graydon used gentle movements to run his fingers through her hair. Each pass softening the strands a little more.

"The *lu-ong* are made of soul's breath." Graydon's voice was an intimate rumble in her ear, his breath stirring the hair on the back of her neck.

The skin around her breasts tightened as she sucked in a shaky breath.

Mentally, she upgraded his threat level.

If he could draw out this type of reaction from her when he hadn't even really touched her, she'd self-combust if they ever had sex.

"Is that how one ended up on this planet?" Kira asked, trying to distract herself.

Graydon made a sound of agreement. "They're not constrained by the same laws of physics. The *lu-ong* are wanderers. They follow the paths of the universe and always have."

Kira felt like this was important information Graydon was giving her, but she couldn't concentrate enough to put it all together.

"It's rare for them to show themselves on a planet without the Mea'Ave, however."

Kira twisted, her hair sliding out of Graydon's grip. "Why is that?"

Graydon reached for her hair again, playing with the ends as he sent *ki* through the strands. "They're linked through a symbiotic relationship. If one were to disappear, the other would decline as well."

It wasn't a far jump from there to realize hurting the *lu-ong* would also cripple the Tuann.

No wonder they were so sensitive when they found some of their own hunting them.

It made it all the more curiouser for a *lu-ong* to expose its presence like that to save Kira and Devon.

"Your father's family and the *lu-ong* have always been intertwined,"

Graydon said, guessing where her thoughts had gone. "There has always been a representative of the *lu-ong* choosing to act as an intermediary between their race and ours."

Kira looked out the large windows into the night beyond, her forehead creased in thought.

From what Harlow had told her, her father had also shared a connection with the *lu-ong*.

Nearly a century had passed since then. That was a long time to go without a connection between the two.

"The *lu-ong* are even more long-lived than the Tuann. The passage of a few years is a blink in the eye for them," Graydon explained.

"You're saying they went out of their way to save me." Not Devon.

Kira twisted in Graydon's arms to see him better.

His expression was complicated. "That does seem to be where this all points."

"You don't look happy about that," she observed.

"That's not the right word for it," he said after a moment. "More like it worries me that after being content with the seat empty for so long, they're suddenly driven to fill it."

"Almost like they know something is coming and are busy fortifying their defenses," Kira said softly.

Graydon nodded, his eyes not leaving hers. "And I suspect you're the lynchpin behind their plans."

Kira's frown was troubled as she stared beyond him, barely noticing when he resumed playing with her hair.

The room was silent as they each descended into their own thoughts.

It was several minutes later when Kira slid him a look. As important as this information was, it didn't demand his presence here.

No, he was after something else.

A look at his intent face had Kira revising that statement. Perhaps more than one something else.

Their gazes met, anticipation descending.

Kira was the first to break the stare, looking down and fiddling with the edge of her robe. "I know you didn't come here just to tell me all that."

Graydon's fingers moved to the hair at her temples.

Kira closed her eyes under his ministrations, the gentle combing turning into a scalp massage.

Lethargy stole through her limbs as she leaned toward him, feeling like a stray comet caught in the gravity well of an inescapable star.

Her eyes snapped open, and she sat back.

He smirked but didn't pursue her. "I wanted to know what else you were holding back."

Kira had a feeling it was something like that.

In their short acquaintance, it had become clear that Graydon knew her better than those who'd been with her far longer.

Kira lifted her chin. "What makes you think there's something else?"

Graydon's smile was sly. "Isn't there?"

Kira turned her head, giving him access to a new section of hair.

A few weeks ago, she would have kept Elise's possible capture a secret.

She would have gone it alone.

No Raider.

No Graydon.

No backup except for Jin.

"The person the Haldeel caught—she wears Elise's face."

Graydon's hands paused.

"You sound uncertain," he resumed his slow, careful movements.

Kira shook her head. "The only thing I'm sure of is that underestimating the Tsavitee would be a mistake."

"Wise words." He nodded. "Does this mean you don't think it's actually her?"

"I want it to be," Kira admitted. It would mean an end to all these years of struggle and uncertainty. "It's all I've thought about since I realized she survived Rothchild."

"But you're scared at the same time."

Kira set her chin on her knees.

He'd caught the crux of her problem.

"The Tsavitee are skilled at making you think one thing when another is true," Kira said.

Who was to even say this woman was the one she'd been looking for?

"It could be a clone," Graydon allowed.

While the Haldeel, Tuann, and Consortium had strict laws against such things, the Tsavitee weren't constrained by the same ethics.

Cloning and genetic manipulation of sentients was considered old hat for them.

It was impossible to tell what could come out of their labs. Kira only knew it was rarely good.

"What if Elise isn't Elise anymore?" Kira whispered.

It was her biggest fear.

A clone could be dealt with.

Mental manipulation would be a lot harder.

For the first time in a long time, Kira felt utterly lost—caught between yearning and fear.

To come this far, to get this close, only to find the very thing she wanted more than anything was a mirage. She couldn't think of a more horrifying ending.

Yet, she couldn't stop herself from walking toward the inferno, even knowing she could very well end up consumed in the flames.

"You want to talk to her," Graydon stated.

Kira nodded.

It was the only way to know for sure.

Graydon released her hair and sat back. Kira dropped her feet to the ground.

"The Haldeel are restricting access to the prisoner," Graydon said with a considering look on his face. "We're in Haldeel space. Even as the Emperor's Face, I don't have enough power to get you an audience."

The barely formed hope in Kira curdled.

"There is one way," Graydon said, sending Kira's heart pounding. "Earn a boon from the Haldeel. Impress them, and they may let you speak to her unobstructed."

Kira stared at Graydon unblinking; her thoughts scattered.

He cupped her chin, his thumb brushing across her lips. "You seem surprised, *cheva nier*."

Kira leaned forward before she could talk herself out of it. Graydon acted fast, pulling her against him. In the next instant, she found herself straddling him.

Graydon yanked her lower body closer to his hips, fitting his hardness against her bare core.

Her robe had long since parted, giving him access.

Breath hissed out of her as his palms cupped her bare ass.

Kira tipped her head back, relishing the feeling of warm lips as they trailed across her throat.

It no longer mattered that common sense warned her away from him.

One touch sent reason fleeing. Desire replaced it.

This time there were no oshota to remind them of their duties.

It was just Graydon and Kira and the heated expanse of skin.

"You're mine," Graydon whispered against her neck.

His hips moved, thrusting up and causing Kira's eyes to roll back. It was as if he wanted to imprint himself so deep in her bones, she'd never be rid of him.

Kira sank her fingers into his hair. "Only if I want to be."

His chuckle sent vibrations tingling through her.

Damn man. It was like he had a direct line to her sensitive bits.

His talented hands delved under the robe that had fallen loose. They wrung a moan from her as they explored each curve, lingering on the places where she was most sensitive.

Kira rolled her hips, feeling a fierce sense of satisfaction at the way his hands clenched on her waist and a groan slipped free.

His eyes were wild as he reached over, tapping a command into his forearm. Kira watched greedily as his armor peeled off, revealing bronze skin.

He didn't give her time to explore, his hands sweeping along her sides and cupping her breasts. Kira jumped as he pinched her nipples, soothing the sting seconds later.

His eyes held hers in a silent dare as one hand trailed down her belly, past her navel, and to the apex of her thighs.

Kira huffed as those fingers changed direction, drawing patterns on the sensitive skin there.

Graydon's smirk deepened as he continued to play, increasing the anticipation until it was almost unbearable.

Kira's eyes flashed in warning.

She sat forward, attacking his neck with a string of kisses as her hands slid lower.

They reached the edge of his armor just above his hips. Her fingers danced along the smooth skin.

"If you want to play, I'm game," she said with a smirk.

In answer, Graydon speared one finger into her, his thumb rubbing against her clitoris at the same time.

Kira's breath caught as her eyelids fluttered.

Oh, that felt good.

"Be careful not to awaken something you can't handle," Graydon warned.

Kira skated her nails up his chest, pressing lightly. Not hard enough to draw blood or do damage, just hard enough that he could feel it.

This time it was his turn to suck in a shaky breath.

"You should be cautious of the same," she told him with a teasing grin.

Kira didn't have long to gloat as Graydon's fingers started moving again.

Soon, warmth pooled in her lower belly. Tension climbed as she felt her body approaching the precipice.

Not without him.

If she was going to get lost in this madness, she wasn't doing it alone.

Kira dipped one finger beneath his armor but could go no farther.

"Take it off," she said around a breathy moan.

His chuckle was warm. "Are you sure about that?"

Her eyes pinned him with a look.

His grin widened seconds before the armor that had obstructed her disappeared, leaving her hands on flat smooth skin.

She'd always wondered if the Tuann wore anything under their synth armor. It appeared the answer was no.

Graydon's warm length spilled into Kira's hands.

He pressed his head against the back of the couch as she cupped him and ran her hand along him.

Air hissed between his teeth as his jaw flexed.

Kira drew one fingertip along the tip, entranced by the sensation.

Graydon sat forward in an abrupt movement. His fingers bit into her waist as he lifted, his eyes holding hers in an unmistakable question.

In answer, Kira reached between them, guiding his length to her entrance.

Both of them shuddered at the feeling as she sank onto him.

Kira went slow, savoring the sensation.

Graydon held still. If not for the way the muscles in his chest jumped and his nostrils flared, Kira would think he was unaffected.

Kira didn't move for long seconds, letting herself adjust to him.

Finally, she lifted up in a small movement before sinking again.

Pleasure speared through her at the sensation.

Graydon clenched his hands on the couch, his gaze never leaving hers as he let her take the lead.

They stayed like that, Kira torturing him, Graydon enduring. Until finally, he couldn't anymore.

His hips speared up, seating them more firmly together.

Kira laughed as he leaned forward, setting his lips on her chest, nibbling the flesh there as their pace increased.

A spring drew tight in Kira, pleasure and sensation mixing together until everything was tingling.

Warmth and madness spilled through her until it felt like she couldn't take it anymore.

Kira opened her eyes, catching sight of her skin. It glowed as her markings appeared one by one as if written by an invisible hand.

Alarm jolted through her.

"Graydon—"

Even with the fear that she'd lose control and hurt Graydon, it was hard to resist the seductive pleasure.

Graydon looked at her, appreciation glinting in his eyes. "You're not the only one."

He took one hand and set it on his chest. Sure enough, faint marks had appeared on his skin. Their number growing until they matched the amount Kira had.

She looked at him in wonderment.

His pace picked up and soon she didn't have time to think about anything but the sensation within.

The world whirled as Graydon changed their position. Now, it was Kira pressed against the cushions, Graydon above her.

He looked like a conqueror as his markings flaring brighter and brighter.

Kira lifted her hand to one. It was like touching an electric socket, pleasure so sharp it was almost pain nipped through her.

She didn't know when their *ki* had joined the party, but it flirted and danced along their skin, melding and tangling much as their physical bodies did.

Graydon spoke in Tuann, his words fast. Kira was too distracted to translate, only catching a smattering of words and phrases.

Kira detonated, her inner muscles clenching around him as she found her release.

Graydon roared seconds later as he followed her.

It was a long time later when Kira came back to herself. Her head hung over the edge of the couch. Graydon was sprawled on top of her, his head lying on her chest.

Neither of them had the energy to waste on speaking as they both struggled to slow their breathing.

"What was that?" Kira asked, staring upside down at the other side of the room.

Graydon shifted, creating a little space between their upper bodies. At the same time, he withdrew from Kira.

Aftershocks of sensation made her skin feel sensitive, as if the slightest breath could have her quivering for more.

She was exhausted, yet energized at the same time.

Never before had she felt this tangle of confusing desire.

"It's called resonance," Graydon said, settling himself on his side and drawing Kira more firmly to him.

She shivered as he traced the afterimage of her marks.

Ki nipped from his fingers, sending a bolt of lightning to her core.

Kira slapped his hand away. As fun as that was, she was pretty sure it'd kill her if they did it again so soon.

She was still recovering from the first time.

Graydon's lips tilted, and he ducked his head, placing a scattering of butterfly kisses on Kira's upper chest and shoulder.

"Essentially, our *ki* had a little melding of their own," he said after several moments.

Kira's forehead creased. "Does that happen with all Tuann?"

Graydon hid his face against her shoulder, but she could feel his lips move in a smile.

She grabbed his head, tugging until he was forced to look up.

"No, it's rare."

Kira's eyes narrowed. Why did he look particularly pleased about that fact?

Graydon's smug look deepened. "It's considered quite flattering."

"If you ever want to be flattered in that way again, you'll tell me why exactly you seem so happy about this."

Graydon chuckled, scooping Kira into his arms and turning so she was lying half on him, half on the couch.

"It's considered a sign that partners are highly compatible."

Kira drummed her fingers on his chest, waiting. She knew there had to be more.

"It also shows a deep trust."

Kira reared back.

"You trust me," he teased happily.

Kira struggled to sit up, Graydon's arms closing around her before she could. Though there was strength in the way he held her, it was simply an illusion.

They both knew if she wanted to, she could force the issue and he wouldn't stop her.

A thought occurred to her.

"Wait, your *ki* resonated too." Graydon had been right there with her the entire time.

Graydon arched an eyebrow. "I never said it didn't."

Her face was pensive as she let her weight settle more firmly against him. This bore consideration.

Kira rested her head on his chest, rubbing her cheek against him. She didn't know what to think about this new information, so she shunted it to the back burner.

"Why don't the Tuann like artificial intelligence?" Kira asked abruptly.

Graydon's hands paused in their stroking. "We have a dark and painful history with them."

Kira lifted her head to peer at him. "Oh?"

His smile this time didn't quite reach his eyes. "I'll admit the machines from that period all had a bit of extra mixed in with them."

Kira went still, feeling like there was a nagging sense of importance in his phrasing.

"We called them the soul bound," Graydon said, not taking his eyes off hers.

Kira controlled her reaction, burying the recognition that term brought and the flood of worry afterward.

She had a sinking feeling she knew exactly what that phrase was intended to convey.

"They were the reason our former masters retained such control over us for as long as they did," Graydon continued.

His gaze was penetrating, as if he were trying to peer through Kira's defenses.

Not wanting to give him the chance, she hid her face in his shoulder, staring at the couch.

"The way you call them makes it seem like there's more to the story," Kira ventured after several moments.

She needed to know exactly how much danger Jin was in.

"You'd be correct," Graydon pressed a kiss onto the top of her head. She felt him pick up a strand of hair to play with. "The masters have always been obsessed with immortality. I'm not talking about the way Tuann can live for long years unless they're killed either. They wanted true immortality. The kind that never fades and can never be destroyed."

"And these soul bound are part of that?"

"In a sense," Graydon said. "The masters created machines and then they separated the souls of their slaves and bound them to those machines."

Kira could see how someone who cared nothing for moral or ethical boundaries would venture down that path.

Inserting their consciousness into machines would get rid of the inherent weakness of a body that would eventually die and decay. A machine could constantly be modified and fixed as long as its programming remained untouched.

"What was the result of these experiments?" Kira asked carefully.

"Failure due to the complete and utter madness of every single being the binding was used on."

Kira held herself rigid, almost afraid to breathe.

Jin wasn't insane. Cocky, yes. Immature, at times. But crazy? No.

Despite that, Kira could see why those former soul bound had gone mad. The potential was there in Jin. Without the link between them, Jin very well could have descended to those depths.

"Their madness didn't stop the masters from finding a use for them," Graydon continued. "They lacked a conscience or any sense of right and wrong, but they still possessed enough cunning to serve as the masters' guard dogs. A side effect of the process made them much more obedient to the masters than the rest of us."

"What happened to them?" Kira asked, lifting her head.

"We put them down when we escaped," Graydon informed her. "Every last one."

They stared at each other as Kira came to a realization.

"How long have you known?" Kira finally asked.

Graydon brushed her hair behind her ear, his expression gentle. "Since the *uhva na*."

So long.

Kira pressed her lips together, not sure what to think.

Graydon was the Emperor's Face. This wasn't the sort of secret he could keep—not without drawing accusations of treason.

"Why haven't you told anyone?"

It was clear to her that even with his suspicions he hadn't made a move. If he had, Jin's welcome would have been much different.

It was likely they both would have been arrested and tried before being sentenced to death.

Graydon exhaled softly. "Despite what our records indicate, I see no sign of madness or cruelty in Jin."

The tight feeling Kira's chest loosened at that statement.

Jin was her dearest friend. She wasn't sure what she would do if there was a serious threat to his wellbeing.

She did know she wouldn't walk away from him. If the Tuann and Roake couldn't reconcile themselves to his existence, there would be no future for Kira among them either.

"How did it happen?" Graydon asked.

Kira shook her head. "I don't know."

To this day, she wasn't exactly sure how Jin's soul had ended up in a machine. Her memories of that night were hazy and indistinct.

She remembered almost dying. Then the next thing she knew she woke up in Himoto's arms, Jin clutched to her chest.

It took her days to realize the drone she'd refused to let go of was the boy she thought had perished.

They'd been inseparable ever since.

"That's interesting," Graydon said, his thumb drawing soothing circles along her shoulder blade.

"Why?"

"To my knowledge neither the line of Roake nor Luatha possesses the ability to draw out the true essence of something and insert it into another material."

Noting the look on Kira's face, Graydon went still. "What?"

"My line might not possess that ability, but I do."

Graydon sat up, taking Kira with him. His gaze was penetrating. "That's impossible."

"It's how I saved Wren."

He'd been mortally wounded. There wasn't enough time for help to be summoned, so she did something she'd thought she'd never do again.

She took the destroyed form of Jin's avatar and broke it down to its base self. Only when she'd extracted the essence did she insert it into Wren, using its energy to repair the extensive damage to his body.

Graydon's eyes widened. "Only one line possesses that trait—the emperor's."

Kira didn't need him to tell her how bad it would be if news of this ability got out.

"Kira, you can never do that again," Graydon warned.

Kira didn't answer, pressing her lips together instead.

His hand caught her chin, raising it, so she met his eyes. "I mean it. They will execute you. I won't be able to stop them."

Knowing he wasn't going to drop this until she conceded, Kira nodded.

"Do you know why I can do this?" Kira asked.

"I have a few theories," he said in a grim voice.

So did Kira, and they started and ended with Jin.

TWENTY-ONE

SUNLIGHT STREAMED INTO the bedchamber, summoning Kira from sleep.

Her eyes still closed, she stretched, enjoying the feel of the sheets against her skin. Her bare skin.

Her eyes popped open as the memory of last night came to her.

Kira tensed then relaxed when she found herself alone in the bed, Graydon's side long cold.

It would be easy to have regrets about last night. Letting Graydon breach the diamond-hard walls she'd kept around her innermost self made her vulnerable in a way that she hadn't ever been before.

Still, Kira couldn't quite bring herself to feel that way. What they'd done felt as necessary as breathing

He'd lit a soft flame inside that no amount of pragmatism could extinguish.

Come what may, she was glad they'd had that moment.

She was even open to experiencing it again.

He made her feel safe and filled with possibility. Both things she'd thought she'd lost long ago—if she ever had them at all.

However, as nice as their interlude had been, she needed time to process those feelings.

She'd been solo for so long. She didn't know if she knew how to take someone else into account—or if it was even possible.

A flashing beacon on the nightstand caught her attention. She reached over, the system responding to her movement.

Graydon's disembodied voice came over the line, bringing a smile to her face. "Kira, I had to attend to some matters. Breakfast is on the table."

Kira climbed out of bed, snagging the robe from where she'd tossed it last night. She drew it around her body, securing it at the waist before making her way to the table.

An energy field covered the plates of food, keeping it at the perfect temperature. It powered down at her approach, the tantalizing smells that escaped making her stomach rumble.

The cup of chai caught her eye first, steam still rising from the frothy goodness.

"How in the world did he know?" she murmured, touching the mug gently.

The breakfast was a thoughtful action. Even more so with the addition of the chai.

She could tell by looking he'd chosen food consisting only of items she'd enjoyed while on Ta Da'an and Ta Sa'Riel.

Graydon had paid much closer attention to her than she previously realized.

Kira picked a cube of blue fruit up and popped it in her mouth. It was tart and sweet, a perfect balance of flavor.

She'd never realized how amazing food was until she'd lived with the Tuann. Before them, food was a necessity. Something she had to eat to survive.

Simply put, only a small microcosm of human food suited her palate. The rest either made her sick or tasted awful.

Kira had found enough options never to go hungry, but she also didn't go out of her way to eat.

Furtive sounds from the window drew her attention.

Jin rose into view as he used a plant to shield him from the sight of those below. His "eye" was focused on the garden.

"What are you doing?" Kira asked, picking up her chai and moving toward him.

The transparent barrier separating her room from the balcony swished out of the way, allowing her to step outside.

She peered past the plant Jin was using as a hiding spot to find Devon and Joule practicing their sword play.

"Gathering information," Jin said grudgingly.

AKA spying.

Kira took a sip of her chai. "Is that where you were last night?"

He'd disappeared after they'd returned from the races and she hadn't seen him since.

Jin's answer was a grunt.

Kira settled against the balcony, watching the two below with interest.

"You're wrong about Devon," Jin suddenly burst out. "I've been studying him. I don't see a resemblance. At all."

"Ah," Kira hummed.

So it was to be denial then.

Not entirely unexpected. Kira had gone through a similar phase herself. With Jin, it would likely be more pronounced. He had always been way more stubborn than her.

"We have nothing in common," he argued, swinging his eye to face her.

"What are you basing this on?" Kira asked, curious.

"Looks."

Kira's eyebrows climbed as she fought to hold in her laughter. "You remember what you look like?"

"Not really, but I know it's nothing like him." Jin dipped in Devon's direction.

"Anything else?"

"I'm also not nearly as annoying. Our mannerisms are nothing alike."

"I agree with that last part," Kira muttered into her chai.

"He's an ass," Jin said flatly.

Kira smiled. "I'd argue you can be one too on occasion."

Jin sputtered as Kira poked him.

"Also, he hasn't displayed any ass-like qualities since the *uhva na* on Ta Sa'Riel," Kira pointed out.

"Only because you saved his life. I'm sure he'd still be an asshole otherwise."

Perhaps, but Kira thought it was more from how close he'd come to being kidnapped by the Tsavitee. Something like that tended to change a person's outlook.

Whatever the case, neither of them had spent enough time with Devon to make an accurate judgment on his personality one way or another.

"There's no way he's my brother."

That had Kira looking over at him. "His eyes are the same as yours were."

Jin made a dismissive sound. "Eye color isn't a deciding factor. Many people could have that eye color."

Kira gave up, knowing no amount of argument was going to solve this today. "You're stubborn."

Jin twisted one way then another, his emotions spilling into their bond. Anxiety and apprehension mixed with unease. Beneath it all, the smallest kernel of longing.

"I don't want to open myself up to hurt down the line," he whispered.

Kira's expression softened. She could understand that. Wasn't it at the core of why she had so much trouble accepting Harlow and Roake?

It hurt to get your hopes up only to have them dashed in the end.

Rejection in any form was corrosive. It ate away at the person you were.

Both Kira and Jin had been conditioned to expect the worst out of people. It was damn near impossible sometimes to remember the universe wasn't always a dark place.

"How would they ever accept what I've become?" Jin asked. "The answer is they wouldn't, and you know it."

Kira's expression was contemplative as she set the cup of chai on the railing.

The conversation with Graydon pointed to the truth of Jin's words. Still, she didn't want her friend to turn away just because he was afraid.

Jin had always been fearlessly himself, not caring what others thought he should be.

It was one of the things Kira loved most about him, and she wouldn't see it change for anything.

"Perhaps you're right," Kira allowed. "But I think I remember it was you who said it couldn't hurt to learn a little more about these people before we reject them."

"This is different."

Kira propped her chin on her hand. "I believe I said that too."

Jin's eye turned to Devon as he fell silent.

She straightened and bopped him on his casing again before he could argue further. "I never said you had to reveal yourself to them, but I also don't want you making decisions without having all the facts."

Kira picked up her chai again. "If you want to ignore this possibility, you can. I'm on your side. Forever and always. Remember that."

Wren stepped into view below, catching her eye. He jerked his head in an unmistakable summons.

"Better go before your *seon'yer* remembers everything we've gotten up to without his permission," Jin advised.

"We wouldn't want that," Kira said before heading inside.

It took only minutes to dress in the clothes she found in one of the dressers. Made from the same ballistic proof material as the ones she received on Ta Sa'Riel, she admired the cut of the fabric before heading out.

Kira's jog slowed as she found Wren waiting at the bottom of the stairs for her.

"Something the matter?" she asked.

"In light of your revelations yesterday, I thought it would be appropriate we spend some time together."

Kira descended the last steps, wondering how she got so unlucky.

Wren quirked one eyebrow at the grudging look on her face. "Unless you have something else to do?"

Not unless he counted investigating the waverunner who went by the call sign Moonbeam.

Truthfully, Odin and Jin would be more useful for that.

Kira shrugged, giving into the inevitable. "I don't have any plans until the banquet."

Which was still hours from now.

"Good." Wren set off at a brisk pace, heading for a room adjacent to the training room she'd visited two days before.

So much had happened since then that it was hard to believe so little time had passed.

The room Wren entered was empty except for Maksym who waited in the middle of the space with his arms crossed over his chest.

Before him was a table, various size spheres arranged before him.

"What's this?" Kira asked, looking them over.

Wren stopped next to Maksym. "Your little adventure has cut into my duties as your *seon'yer*. I thought we'd take this time to fix that."

Kira ran her eye over the spheres, not hiding her skepticism. "With balls?" She looked up at Wren again. "Are we going to play a game?"

Maksym's cough didn't entirely conceal his choked laugh.

Wren looked like he was struggling for patience. "I've learned some things about you since your time away. Your problem with *ki* doesn't lie in its use or manipulation. If anything, the amount you are capable of accessing is too much. You lack control. Without it, you will only land in the same situation as before."

He nodded at the inhibitor she still wore.

Kira touched it lightly, wondering how he had come to that conclusion. Not that she could argue with his assessment. It fit her thoughts as well.

"You use *ki* like a hammer when a scalpel will do just as well," Wren continued.

Those words and the disproving look he sent her seemed studded with a double meaning.

Kira's eyes narrowed, wondering if he'd somehow managed to uncover some of those files Himoto had gone to a lot of trouble to bury. Specifically, those records pertaining to the burst.

"What do you want me to do?" Kira asked.

Maksym picked up a sphere the size of a tennis ball and held it in his hand. A faint glow lit it up from inside. Moments later it lifted an inch off his palm where it hovered.

Gradually, the glow diminished, and it plopped back into his palm.

Maksym nodded at a sphere the size of a watermelon on her left. "Start with that one."

Tentatively, Kira picked it up, surprised to find it was much lighter than it looked.

Maksym touched the ball. "Now, push your *ki* into it."

Kira frowned but didn't argue, focusing on the sphere again.

Ki, Kira had learned, was something that existed both within and without.

The Tuann were like a glass and the world around them an ocean. They could only use what was in the glass but the ocean would refill the glass over time.

Since building a friendship with Joule and spending time on Roake, she'd learned there were set stances and patterns of movement that could help draw out the *ki* within and give it form.

What Maksym asked of her was a bit different than what Finn and Joule had showed her on Ta Sa'Riel. Closer in line to how she'd always used her soul's breath. More reliant on instinct and feeling around in the dark as much as anything else.

She pooled her *ki* within before feeding it into the sphere.

A loud pop startled her as the sphere burst, its shards embedding into her palm and arm.

Kira sucked in a harsh breath but the cuts and the blood that should have been there were already gone.

The sphere had attributes similar to a hologram with some type of sensory feedback, Kira realized.

Maksym doubled over in laughter. "You might be blessed with an abundance of the good stuff, but your control is shit. It's even worse than Wren told me."

Wren's lips twitched with amusement.

"What was that?" Kira asked, glaring at the two.

"A test," Maksym said, straightening and wiping the tears away from his eyes. "One you failed pretty spectacularly."

Kira pressed her lips together as she waited, silently counting to ten in her head. When that didn't work, she started again.

Must not try to strangle her *seon'yer* or his oshota.

"It's nice to be on the opposite end of one of Wren's extreme training methods, for once," Maksym continued with an easy grin.

"I'm sure." Kira's voice was flat.

Maksym didn't seem bothered by her irritation, tapping Kira's palm. The sphere expanded again, growing out of her hand like it was some type of mutated flower.

"What the—"

Maksym's eyes crinkled. "Let's try again, shall we?"

Kira frowned at him but concentrated on channeling her *ki* into the sphere.

This time it burst almost immediately. Kira flinched as small streaks of pain whispered across her skin, only to leave her hand whole and healthy again in the next moment.

"Wren thinks pain helps us learn faster." Maksym studied her hand with a clinical detachment. "I'd argue if he wasn't right."

"How long am I expected to do this?" Kira asked, forcing patience into her voice.

"Until you can channel your *ki* into that without breaking." Wren pointed to a sphere the size of a golf ball.

Seeing her objection, Wren sent her a chiding look. "I've seen your niece's training. It's quite intense. Are you telling me you're unwilling to learn in the same fashion?"

Kira pressed her lips together hard.

There was a lot she could say to that statement. Most of it sarcastic.

She kept silent for one reason. He was right. She couldn't expect excellence from Elena if she wasn't willing to persevere against her own weaknesses.

If this would make her a better warrior, keep her healthy once the inhibitor came off, it was worth the small frustration and fleeting pain.

Approval shone in Wren's eyes at her acceptance. "Good."

Elena stuck her head into the room as Kira lifted her hand again. "Auntie. Finally. I've been looking everywhere."

Elena walked toward them, looking at the table and its spheres with curiosity. "What's that?"

"Training." Kira grinned. "Want to try?"

Elena stopped, keeping her distance. She shook her head several times. "No, thank you. I've already had my fill of that man's training."

Wren met Elena's irate stare with a bland expression.

"Why were you looking for me?" Kira asked.

Reminded of her mission, Elena bounced forward. "Your *yer'se* and some of the others wanted to go sightseeing."

Kira stopped what she was doing and gritted her teeth. "For the last time, she's not my *yer'se.* I'm not her *seon'yer.*"

Elena shrugged, not bothered by Kira's denial. "That's between you and her. Honestly, I don't think you're going to win this one. Ziva seems like the sort to wear you down."

Kira's sigh was loud. "Is that what you came to ask for?"

Elena shook her head, folding her hands in front of her as she tried to appear as innocent as possible. "Nope. I wanted to go with them. I know Jettie better than them. May I?"

Kira hesitated.

Elena's upbringing had been untraditional in the extreme. Oversight hadn't really been a thing.

Selene had many children who needed her attention, and Jin and Kira had to be careful in their visits.

As a result, Elena was used to using her own judgment and going where she wanted, when she wanted.

For her to ask permission like this showed Elena felt some guilt over getting caught by Graydon because of her own arrogance.

It was her way of making it right with Kira.

And under normal circumstances, Kira would have already said yes. Jettie had always been considered safe because of the Haldeel influence, but with the attack yesterday on Devon and Skye all that had changed.

"I'll keep an eye on her," Wren promised, reading her hesitation.

Elena's gaze darted between the two of them, her expression almost pleading with Kira to say yes.

Kira wavered. Wren and his oshota had proven their motivation in protecting Elena yesterday when they'd gotten her to safety after the attack.

She could trust them with this.

"All right," Kira said finally. "You can go."

Elena let out a yip of excitement as she bounced on her toes.

"But—" Kira pointed a finger at Elena's face. "You will listen and obey him and his oshota. If there's another incident like what happened on the *Wanderer* or like when you got caught, you're going into lockdown. Nothing and no one will be able to save you then. Understood?"

Elena nodded quickly.

She bounded forward, giving Kira a quick hug before racing out of the room with a high-pitched squeal. "She said yes."

Kira glanced at Wren. "I'm trusting you."

He bowed his head. "I won't let you down. I promise."

Kira watched him set out after her niece, feeling torn. She wasn't used to relying on others anymore.

She, Jin, and Selene had been the only ones invested in Elena's safety for so long.

The worry of what could happen if the Tsavitee ever got their hands on Elena gnawed at her in the depths of night. It lurked in the back of her mind at all times.

"You did a good thing," Maksym said.

Her gaze met his, reading the sincerity there.

"His wife's passing and daughter's loss broke him. You've given him a chance he never thought would come. Thank you."

Kira's eyes dropped, feeling the urge to hide from his words.

She'd face the possibility of death a thousand times before she willingly dealt with someone else's emotions.

Just the thought made her want to retreat to a remote part of the galaxy.

Instead of running, Kira forced herself to respond, knowing his words deserved an answer. "He will be good for her too."

She couldn't see any downside to having more people willing to safeguard her niece.

As choices went for relatives, Wren was a pretty good one. He was a powerful warrior and more importantly knew the devastation that came with loss.

He'd do what was necessary to make sure it didn't happen again.

"Now, shall we start again?" Maksym's smile said he was looking forward to hours of torturing her—for her own good, of course.

* * *

A long time later, conversation ebbed and flowed around Kira as she sipped from a glass of *keeva*.

The training with Maksym had been slow and tedious. By the time she'd stopped for the day, she'd only managed to push her *ki* into a sphere one size smaller than the one she'd started with.

Her gaze dropped to the hand that held the glass. She knew at a thought she could activate the sphere again.

It was a little gift Maksym had given her so she could practice any time she had a moment.

Oh, joy.

Kira tapped her finger against her glass as she studied the gathering.

Her position along the edge of the banquet gave her an excellent opportunity to observe her surroundings without having to interact with them.

The room she was in was one of the most impressive she'd ever seen. With a transparent ceiling and walls offering an unobstructed glimpse outside, the chamber felt like an enclosed bubble nestled in the heart of the station.

The unique towers of Almaluk rose around them, unfolding like a flower to offer a glimpse of space. Trillions of stars decorated the sky like tiny jewels only overshadowed by the planet Jettie rising off the port side.

It was breathtaking. You could visit a hundred worlds and travel the galaxy for decades and never come close to matching this view.

It was a fitting backdrop for the high-stakes discussions taking place around Kira.

It had only been half an hour since she'd entered the celebration, but she had already learned so much.

From the small faction of humans interested in mineral rights on a planet whose ownership was highly contested to the group trying to broker a marriage alliance between two powerful, opposing families.

Take into account, the two previously unknown alien races she'd just encountered for the first time and the possibilities were endless for wheeling and dealing.

The outfits of those present ran the gamut. Ball gowns and military uniforms were side by side with synth armor.

Even Kira had gone out of her way to dress the part. For the night, her hair had been swept to one side to spill over her shoulder in seductive, glossy waves she couldn't help but admire.

Dramatic makeup highlighted her eyes, the colors making them more violet than gray.

Unlike many of the women, Kira hadn't opted for a ball gown, instead choosing an outfit that would be easy to move in.

Militaristic in design, it consisted of a formal overcoat with buttons marching down the front. Silver embroidery lined the edges before branching out into a complex pattern that covered her upper body.

The only glimpse of skin came from the keyhole over her chest.

The coat fit closely through her shoulders and chest before flaring over her hips and dropping behind her to form a small train.

Soft pants tucked into knee-high black boots completed the look.

It was the perfect balance between dressy and convenient.

Movement on the far side of the room attracted Kira's attention as humans wearing the uniforms of the Consortium entered. They were accompanied by seven-foot-tall figures covered in long cloaks.

Odin emerged out of the crowd. "I was wondering if they'd show up."

Kira looked around, making sure no one was watching them. "How did you get in here?"

The guest list for the night was highly restricted. In addition to politicians and some of the most powerful people in the galaxy, only those who'd distinguished themselves in the quorum were invited.

Odin didn't fit either of those categories.

Odin swirled the glass of champagne she was holding. "You should know by now I have my ways."

"I'd very much like to hear about those ways."

Odin lifted the glass and sipped from it. "A lady never reveals her secrets."

Not giving Kira a chance to ask any more questions, Odin took an interested look around. "Where's the Tin Can? Don't tell me you left him behind."

"He has his own matters to take care of."

Odin's lips curled. "You mean he's spying."

That was exactly what Kira meant.

Odin didn't make any more comments about Jin's absence, instead focusing on the trio whose presence had attracted quite the crowd, all of them humans.

"What do you think of our friends?" Odin asked.

Kira folded her arms and tapped one finger against the rim of her glass. "I think their presence here is remarkably interesting. Last I heard, the Consortium was decades away from such an advancement."

Humanity had made great strides in the field of artificial intelligence and robotics before the treaty with the Haldeel, but since then, their research had stagnated. They shouldn't have been anywhere close to achieving a breakthrough.

"They're the newest model. The latest and greatest." Odin tilted her head, peering at them with an interest that was a little too pronounced.

In the middle of the floor, Admiral Kent held court over the group that had formed around the cloaked figures. Zepher's military representatives were among those present.

Himoto and Jace stayed in the background, patiently observing the group.

Feeling her gaze, Himoto made eye contact and gave her a cordial nod.

Kira looked away, not reacting outwardly to his greeting.

"The Consortium hopes their new toys will put them on even ground with the other powers in the universe," Odin said with a twisted smile.

"You don't sound approving."

"They should be careful not to let their arrogance lead to their destruction." Odin drained her champagne, setting the glass on a passing drone carrying a serving platter.

Kira was quiet as she watched their hulking figures. A part of her couldn't help but wonder if these constructs could solve Jin's problem—at least partially.

At an order from their handler, the androids removed their cloaks, facing their audience with blank expressions.

On first glance, their bodies seemed modeled after that of a human, with a set of legs and arms, a torso, neck, and head.

It was only upon closer inspection one realized how different they were.

Their faces were strange. The designs etched on them making them seem eerie. Black lines trailed under each eye, adding an illusion of emotion. A series of circles connected by squares and additional lines were embedded on their foreheads.

The androids lacked noses. Their necks were elongated and protected by a series of heavy metal interlocking plates.

"I know what you're thinking," Odin said. "It won't work."

"Why not?"

Odin plucked another champagne glass from a passing drone server. "As advanced as they are, they still can't achieve biofeedback. I already checked."

Kira sighed in disappointment. If that was true, there was no point in pursuing this line of thought.

The act of moving Jin's soul from one thing to another was inherently dangerous. A big part of that stemmed from the fact they didn't really know how to do it.

If they were to take the risk, Kira wanted it to be worthwhile. They wouldn't get a second chance if things went wrong.

Simply exchanging one shell for another didn't justify the effort. Without all five senses, Jin would still be living a half existence, reliant on his link with Kira.

After last night, Kira was conscious of how dangerous this was for him. The goal of finding him a body had never been more important or felt further away.

At that moment, Jin arrowed out of the crowd, circling them before taking his customary spot over Kira's shoulder.

Odin nodded at the androids. "What do you think of them?"

"The further I can stay away from them the better. They give me the creeps."

"Is it because you're afraid they're better than you?" Odin teased.

"Please." Jin blew a raspberry. "This form is already the epitome of excellence."

"How would you know unless you give theirs a try?" Odin asked.

Jin went silent. "I know what you're trying to do."

Odin arched an eyebrow. "Oh? Do tell?"

"You won't trick me that easily this time."

Craftiness settled on Odin's features. "Are you sure?"

Jin moved a foot back. "I don't know why you named yourself after the Allfather. The name Loki suits you much better."

"It's because I know all."

While the two verbally sparred, Finn stepped closer to Kira from where he'd been keeping watch a short distance away. "The rest of the delegation has arrived."

Kira had been expecting the news, but even so she felt a flutter in her chest.

Trying not to be obvious, she scanned the crowd, stopping on a familiar face. Graydon.

It was like being punched in the chest when you least expected it.

His hair was styled away from his face. Because of that there was nothing to distract from the brutal beauty of his features.

Unlike their previous encounters, Kira now knew exactly what that armor hid. It didn't matter how lovingly it clung or how well it fit, it would never do credit to the body beneath.

Today, his armor was a little different than normal. More fitting to an event of this caliber.

Although still a matte black, it had silver trim throughout, creating a complex pattern that only amplified Graydon's physique.

That wasn't what drew the eye, however. It was the cape Graydon wore. A fiery red, it was flung back from his shoulders, its length sweeping the ground behind him. Metallic gold was interwoven throughout. Every time it caught the light it looked like a fire had sparked in its depths.

Kira blinked at it, feeling off-balance.

Seeing her, Graydon prowled in her direction. "You don't seem happy. Weren't you the one who said you wanted to see me in a cape?"

Kira found herself hard-pressed to respond.

The thing was she'd said something exactly to that effect on Ta Sa'Riel when Roderick had shown up in a cape. Kira hadn't been able to resist teasing Graydon about having one of his own.

Never in a million years had she expected him to comply. Let alone that the mere sight of him in one would render her speechless.

"Tongue-tied? *Cheva nier*, there's no need to be shy." There was a playful look on Graydon's face.

"Shouldn't you be with the rest of your delegation? Working?"

Kira sent a significant glance to where Yukina held court among the various Houses vying for her attention.

Her gaze lingered on the group of Tuann who had bet against her during the stratagem. The looks Niland and his friends kept sending Kira's way made her feel like they were talking about her.

"What are your plans for them?" Graydon asked noticing where her attention had gone.

That's right. Niland and Lorcan still owed her a favor.

"As long as they keep their distance, I won't do anything to them."

However, the moment they stepped in Kira's way; she'd be merciless.

She frowned as she caught the look that passed between Graydon and Lorcan. Before she could decipher it, Lorcan smirked at her, raising his glass in a silent toast.

She wasn't imagining things. There was something between him and Graydon.

The only question was whether they were allies or enemies who simply knew each other well.

Knowing the Tuann, it could be either.

"Where's your *yer'se*?" Kira asked, not seeing Devon in the party that had accompanied Graydon.

"He remained behind with your imp and the rest of the younglings who've made you their hero."

"And you let him?" Kira could only imagine all the trouble Elena could talk Devon and the rest into.

"I think learning from your imp wouldn't be the worst thing for him."

It would certainly give him another perspective on life, Kira conceded.

As they circled, Liara, with Roderick beside her, caught her eye. Liara offered a gentle smile but made no attempt to approach.

"Not going to go over there?" Graydon asked.

"It would probably be best to wait," Kira responded.

Liara had her own matters to attend to.

The invasion of Ta Da'an had weakened her House's position among the Tuann. There was time later for the two of them to reconnect.

"That reminds me. Where's Raider?" Kira asked. "He should have been here by now."

Graydon snagged a drink from one of the hovering drones. "He's around somewhere."

Before Kira could ask more, the crowd started to move toward the raised dais Kira had noted before but hadn't paid much attention to.

Holding a lot in common with the Mayan pyramids of ancient Earth, the dais stood at least a hundred feet tall, stairs leading from the pavilion on top to the banquet floor.

In the space above the dome, a small fleet of ships approached, hovering protectively around the ship at their center.

As they neared the dome, the other ships stopped as the smallest ship continued, penetrating the membrane of the dome.

Two banners unfurled on either side of the pyramid. This time there was no mistaking the presence of a royal.

The banners carried their insignia. Stark white against an amethyst background, the crest of this royal was modeled after a creature that looked like a cross between a snake and a Betta fish.

Long, elegant fins trailed behind it. A counter to the deadly looking spines along its back.

As a symbol it was very effective in demonstrating the concept of an elegant glove wrapped around an iron fist.

Waves of Haldeel dressed in the uniform of the royal guards filed out of the ship carrying ceremonial tridents.

They glided down the stairs of the dais in two uniform lines. When the first reached the bottom, they came to a stop. As one they faced inward.

All attention turned to the ship.

Tierni stepped into view, pausing on the threshold as she regarded those assembled. A headdress added several inches to her height, long chains framing her face.

The dress she wore was elegant in its complexity. Interwoven metal chains hung in a gentle arc over her chest. Her shoulders were bare but similar chains clasped her biceps before transitioning into sheer sleeves that hung nearly to the floor. A slit in the front of her sleeves made it so she could still use her hands.

The rest of her gown flowed in a line down her body, a chain belt clasped around her waist.

The banquet was silent as she made her way to a throne set on the edge of the platform.

Only when she had taken her seat did her companion descend two steps and stop.

"Esteemed guests, the *za na ri na* of the Haldeel gives you her greeting and bids you welcome," the man began.

Graydon made a thoughtful sound next to Kira. "That's intriguing. I never expected to see a human entrusted as a Haldeel royal's voice."

Kira's expression was faintly troubled as she stared at the man. "Yes, it is quite the surprise."

In more ways than one.

"What is Alexander doing here?" Jin hissed through the comms. "Did Selene tell you about this? Why didn't you tell me? You know the last time we crossed paths with him, he nearly killed us and warned you never to come close to him again. What if he tells the rest of them what we're up to?"

Kira could only guess as to why Selene had failed to inform them of this development. Most likely, it was the same clandestine bullshit as usual.

"Do you know him?" Graydon's expression was curious as he looked at her

"You could say that," Kira said after a pause.

"This isn't good, Kira," Jin warned. "The forty-three never bring anything but trouble."

Not able to respond without alerting Graydon, Kira sent soothing thoughts down their link.

It didn't matter why he was here, or how he'd ended up as a trusted aide to Tierni. All they had to do was remain focused on their own goals. The rest would sort itself out one way or another

Graydon didn't pry further as he studied the man with interest.

Kira should probably do something about that, but somehow, she couldn't bring herself to act. While it had never been her intention to draw Graydon's notice to the man, she also didn't feel particularly motivated to distract him either.

Alexander had made it quite clear his affairs were his own. If he wasn't confident in his facade, it was his business.

Even if she did intervene, he wouldn't thank her. Instead, it was more likely that he would find a way to put the blame on her.

With that thought in mind, Kira tuned in as the man was finishing his speech.

"A few of you have the rare chance to participate in the Harkening. It's a time-honored tradition. Those selected will have the chance to display their potential before the galaxy."

As if answering an unseen signal, three Haldeel stepped out of the crowd. They lined up at the base of the pyramid before facing the rest of the banquet.

"You sly man, you expected this," Kira said softly.

This was what Graydon had meant last night when he said to win their favor and impress them.

Graydon's eyes gleamed in answer.

"I present three of our most talented masters," Alexander said. "They will be your opponents for today. Each will select one individual whose performance has impressed them over the past week. Be warned—while this is a great honor offering you an opportunity to ascend to the heights, it also holds the potential to dash you into the rocks. Accept their challenge at your own risk."

Murmurs from the crowd announced the rising tide of excitement. Whatever anyone claimed, this was the true prize of the quorum.

"Three. That's an interesting number," Graydon said. "Usually it would be two."

One for humans and the other for Tuann.

The Haldeel on the far right stepped off the stairs. He made his way toward the clump of Tuann in the center of the banquet, stopping in front of Yukina.

He folded his hands in front of his chest in a gesture of inquiry. "The Haldeel challenge the Tuann. Please choose a representative."

Yukina moved forward with a serene look on her face. "Very well. I will answer your call."

The Haldeel dipped his head and led Yukina to a section of the room that had been kept conspicuously empty. The floor rose, transitioning into a hovering platform as they stepped onto it.

When it was several feet off the ground, it stopped. Its height allowed those standing in the back of the room an unobstructed view.

The Haldeel extended a hand in summons. The golden sphere in the middle shot forward, stopping over their heads.

The Haldeel inclined his chin. "I look forward to your performance."

The Haldeel moved to the edge of the stage, where he clasped his hands at his waist, his sleeves falling forward to cover them.

The sphere sent out blasts of golden light. One after the other, the speed and frequency picking up, until, with an audible crack, the sphere shattered.

Golden specks rained down, catching the light and glittering like stardust.

They froze in midair around Yukina.

From all around, the sound of a solo flute began to rise. Its cry was lonely and poignant, echoing somberly throughout the room.

Yukina lifted a hand, holding a golden fan the length of her forearm. There was elegance in the simple motion.

Before long, Yukina began to dance within the shattered flecks of the sphere, careful not to disturb them as she moved.

"Not bad," Kira said, impressed.

The puzzle was much more difficult than it looked.

The person had to dance as they deciphered the pattern of the specks while determining a course out of the middle. Misjudge even a little and you would find your path forward cut off.

To complicate things further, falter or hesitate and the puzzle would fail.

In essence, you had to be decisive and also perceptive.

"There's a reason Yukina is a Face," Graydon said. "She is one of the emperor's most accomplished Faces."

Kira regarded Graydon with some surprise. That had almost sounded like a compliment.

He picked up on her thoughts. "You should be careful not to rile her too much. She's the oldest of us."

"Is that the only reason you want me to be cautious?" Kira asked, glancing at Yukina's oshota.

He stood on the right side of the stage. Despite his face once again being concealed by the disrupter field in his hood, Kira couldn't shake the feeling he was watching them rather than his Face.

Graydon's expression didn't change. "Sometimes it's better not to ask questions."

On the stage, Yukina slid into a low lunge before extending her arm and the closed fan out before her.

The fan snapped open. Yukina leaned back before leaning forward again and sweeping the fan before her.

This set off a chain reaction as it collided with the flecks, sending them dancing in a hundred different directions.

They revolved around her as she straightened.

Her dress swirled as she gracefully turned, her arms coming up and around as she bent and dipped, advancing in a steady fashion.

Every once in a while, the fan snapped open as she spun, snapping closed again in the next instant.

The tempo of the music picked up, several string instruments joining the flute.

Yukina never hesitated, one movement flowing into the next until she stood before the Haldeel.

Behind her, the specks of light rotated in several different directions, creating a pattern in a pattern. A flower took shape as a sphere spun around it.

Yukina sank into the final pose, the fan open and held in such a way that it hid the lower half of her face.

Applause broke out at the sight.

The Haldeel on the stage broke into a smile, his posture announcing his pleasure in the outcome.

"The Tuann have impressed us with their elegance and sincerity," Alexander announced.

The platform lowered.

As soon as Yukina and her challenger cleared the way, a second Haldeel disembarked from the pyramid.

He strode across the floor, stopping in front of Himoto. As the first one had, he bowed. "Honorable guest, I have come to challenge you."

"The Consortium answers your challenge."

At a nod from Himoto, Jace moved forward.

"Don't be so hasty, Admiral," Kent said. "Such actions would lead our hosts to believe you speak for all of us."

A hush fell.

"Is he really that much of an idiot?" Jin hissed.

"I'm going to go with a yes."

Why else would he do such a stupid and pointless thing?

The way the Haldeel had approached Himoto made it clear how highly in their esteem they held him. Challenging their decision in such a public forum was not only disrespectful to the host but could also affect the standing of the Consortium as a whole if the Haldeel chose to take offense.

"He strikes me as the sort of man who allows ambition to cloud his better judgment," Graydon observed.

"Should we intervene?" Jin asked.

Kira hesitated, studying Himoto.

"No need," she said, shaking her head.

Something told her Himoto had this well in hand.

"The rear admiral isn't the only one who has performed well during this quorum," Kent said in a chiding tone. "Come. Allow others to make a name for themselves."

The crinkles around Himoto's eyes deepened. "I don't remember you having the rank or privilege to question me. Know your place, Admiral, or be put in it."

The words were a harsh rebuke delivered in a pleasant tone.

Kent bristled, but even he wasn't stupid enough to push back. He didn't have the rank to question Himoto. Any further actions would result in removal from his station. It wouldn't matter how many powers supported him from the shadows in that case.

"Rear Admiral Skarsdale," Himoto said.

Jace snapped to attention.

"Please show our hosts the extent of our fighting spirit."

"With pleasure, Admiral," Jace said.

Jace and the Haldeel made their way to the platform. As before, it started to rise as soon as they stepped onto its surface.

"I've chosen the sphere of color for you. May the tides be in your favor," the Haldeel said.

His summoned sphere shot toward Jace, stopping at the last minute.

It flared, a prism of colors surrounding Jace in an incomprehensible three-dimensional image of a cube.

Every few seconds the colors switched, the pattern in front of him shifting in an endless permutation.

Each third shift, the cube contracted.

If Jace didn't solve it, the cube would eventually restrict his movements to nothing. At that point, he would be considered the loser.

Jace paid no attention to the contracting cube, instead studying the patterns.

"Finally," Jin said as Jace began.

Jace selected then flicked away the smaller cubes one after another, the pattern shifting quickly as he made changes. Each movement was assured, speaking to his confidence.

While the rest of the gathering was distracted by the display on the stage, Himoto took the opportunity to join Kira and Graydon. "The knight you trained has progressed. He's barely recognizable from that impetuous and headstrong boy you first introduced me to."

Knowing it was Kira Himoto wanted to speak to, Graydon touched her wrist. "I'll be waiting over there."

"Such a polite killer," Himoto observed as Graydon walked away.

Kira arched an eyebrow at him. "Be careful, old man. My patience is even worse than it used to be."

"So protective. I'm surprised you'd choose someone like him."

"You're as fond of double-speak as ever," Kira stated.

On the stage, Jace won an advantage, the cube expanding several steps.

"There was a time you'd never have considered giving your heart to a man whose loyalties were split. Why else did you never favor your knight?"

"You know why."

Jace had a savior complex.

There was nothing wrong with that—Kira had one herself. But she was smart enough to know two people with the same issues would never last in a relationship.

There was admiration between Jace and her but nothing else. Any other feelings that might have sprouted between them had long since fallen to the wayside.

"Have you made any progress on that matter Jace and I discussed?" Kira asked, changing the subject.

Himoto's eyes lingered on Kent as a mysterious smile crossed his lips. "A little."

Kira was smart enough to read between the lines.

Kent had mis-stepped tonight when he sought to interfere with the Harkening. He'd shown his allegiance to Zepher's faction. Something Himoto would never allow in the upper ranks of the Consortium's military.

Knowing her former mentor, he'd use this opportunity to lure out those supporting Kent.

If he stayed true to character, Himoto's next step would be to eliminate those responsible with extreme prejudice.

The next months in the Consortium would be a bloodbath as Himoto cleaned house.

"Don't worry. I won't let what happened then, happen again."

Kira sent him a hard look. "You'd better not. It's not just me waiting for humans to stumble anymore."

Himoto inclined his head but didn't say anything else.

"Do you need help?" Kira asked abruptly, not knowing what compelled her to make the offer.

Maybe it was the years of history centered around this man. Perhaps it was the knowledge she'd long be dead if not for his actions.

Whatever it was, she found she couldn't simply leave him or humanity to their fate.

He was once very dear to her. Still was, if she was being entirely honest.

The bonds forged between a lost and traumatized child and the man who rescued her from hell weren't so easily severed.

There would always be a part of her concerned with his wellbeing, even if she didn't show it.

If he needed her—truly and deeply—she'd be there.

"Kira-chan, you're so kind. Always so concerned for this old man."

Kira snorted. "I don't see an old man here. We both know you can take care of yourself."

"Yes," he agreed with a radiant smile that warmed his eyes.

Cheers resounded from the gathering as Jace finished the puzzle. Colors swirled, forming a prism before they were sucked into the sphere.

Himoto turned to go. "I am glad to see you looking healthier. Perhaps my betrayal was worth it. Yes?"

Kira pressed her lips into a flat line, reminded of something unpleasant. "That's right. We never did address the issue of my resignation since you hung up like a coward."

Himoto chuckled. "I'll do my best to make it up to you."

Fat chance of that. Just remembering the way he'd thwarted her plans had her seeing red.

It was only because she knew how adept he was at gaining the upper hand over opponents who lost their tempers that she held back.

Himoto lifted a hand as he moved away. "Give my regards to Raider later."

Jin hovered over her shoulder as they watched Himoto leave. "That man is as difficult to deal with as always."

That was an understatement.

Jace stepped off the platform as the humans in the crowd started clapping. He smiled and held up an arm as the cheering grew louder.

"You'd think he had returned from battle with the way they're acting," Lorcan said as he joined her where she stood.

"I believe the Haldeel consider this a form of battle," Kira said.

She was quite popular tonight, drawing the attention of powerful people left and right.

She didn't know whether to rejoice or cry.

This wasn't exactly the type of notice she'd hoped to attract while here.

At that thought, Kira glanced at the top of the pyramid, making eye contact with Alexander. Seeing her gaze, he frowned.

Noticing where she was looking, Lorcan said, "Humans have come quite far from their humble beginnings. Who would have thought one would ever be trusted to act as a Haldeel royal's voice."

Kira finally faced Lorcan. "The Tuann's greatest weakness is their tendency to underestimate others. One might even say you and the Tsavitee have that in common. I'd be careful of that. It could get you killed one of these days."

Kira stalked away, not giving him the chance to respond.

"I'll keep that in mind, lady," Lorcan's sly voice followed her.

Alexander clapped his hands, drawing the attention of the guests once again.

Kira stopped walking and looked up.

"Friends, we have one final entertainment for you tonight. A puzzle from our newest and youngest master."

At that, the last Haldeel standing at the base of the pyramid walked into the crowd.

Shorter than her two companions, the Haldeel was young to be considered a puzzle architect, let alone a master.

As she got closer, Kira realized she knew her. It was the racer Raider had saved. The one Kira had met that first day. Skye.

On her shoulder perched her *ilsa*.

A sense of inevitability filled Kira as the girl bypassed many other important guests, her path leading her straight to Kira.

She stopped in front of her, raising her eyes at last. "Kira Forrest. I challenge you."

TWENTY-TWO

SKYE'S WORDS FELL like little stones into a pond, causing silence to ripple around them in ever-widening circles.

The first two challenges issued were expected. Some might even say they were half the reason for the quorum.

However, Kira's challenge was different.

She was a nobody. Even when she'd been the Phoenix, not many knew her face. She was a call sign they brought out when the situation turned dire.

If they reassigned that moniker to someone else, Kira doubted anyone would even realize.

She was famous and nondescript at the same time.

Kira disregarded the shock from those around her, staring up at the top of the pyramid and the royal sitting there.

"A puzzle master who doubles as a waverunner. That's an unexpected combination," Kira observed in a bland voice.

Especially for a Haldeel.

Skye fidgeted with her sleeves. When she realized Kira was watching her hands, she dropped them and straightened.

"The *za na ri na* says the depth and breadth of a master's experience can only enrich the flavor of their puzzles," Skye said stiffly.

Jin hovered over Kira's shoulder. "Didn't you say something similar to Tierni once."

Out of the corner of her eye, Kira caught Yukina's approach.

Her lips quirked as she kept her focus on the adolescent Haldeel before her. "I wasn't nearly so poetic. I believe what I said was more along the lines that one never knew which odd skill they picked up by chance would come in handy when faced with danger."

At the time, Tierni had questioned Kira's preoccupation with the stratagem and the way she focused on each version and skill until she mastered it.

Tierni had implied it was a waste of time since Kira had no intention of making her fortune as a stratagem master.

Kira had never seen it that way. Every skill or stray piece of knowledge she picked up was another weapon in her arsenal. Yes, the purpose behind them might not be immediately clear, their use unknown, but she believed they'd come in handy one day.

Case in point—the current situation.

"Do you like being a waverunner?" Kira asked.

Skye's expression was serious as she met Kira's eyes, as if she understood that her answer affected the outcome of this request.

Slowly, she dipped her head in a somber nod. "I do."

"Why?"

Skye hesitated before lifting her chin. "It makes me feel free."

The truthful answer made Kira like the girl a little bit more. She reminded Kira of Tierni at that age. Both were willing to step out of the boxes others placed them in.

Tierni wasn't willing to go quietly into a life she hadn't chosen. Skye yearned to be more than what she was.

It was obvious she was a genius. The Haldeel took the title of puzzle master serious. There were many trials and obstacles one had to overcome to earn the label.

It was nearly unheard of for one so young to be elevated to that rank.

Yet she'd participated in a race that was thoroughly human. It showed her thirst for excellence wasn't only limited to her own people's culture and ideals.

Among the Haldeel she'd likely be considered a strange one.

Kira was starting to see why Tierni had included Skye in this banquet, and why she'd allowed this challenge despite the forum.

The corners of Kira's eyes crinkled. "Me too."

Hope brightened Skye's expression. Her eyes glittered with excitement and anticipation.

"All right then, do it properly," Kira instructed, ignoring Yukina's soft protest.

The girl took a step back before forming a fist with her right hand and setting it on her flattened left palm. She thumped herself in the chest with them then bowed.

"Esteemed lady, please hear this humble one's request. It would be my greatest honor if you deigned to undertake my latest offering."

The words were different than the other challenges. Those had been to the Tuann and humans as a whole and part of a greater narrative. This was to an individual. It was up to Kira whether to accept or not.

In a way, it was much more intimate than the other two challenges.

For someone who'd likely just achieved the title of puzzle master, Skye would lose face in their society if Kira refused.

On the other hand, if Kira tried and failed, she'd be the one they looked down on.

It was a carefully balanced game of give and take.

"You should walk away from this," Yukina advised in a thinly veiled order.

Kira ignored her and grinned at Skye. "Now, was that so hard?"

Stepping past the girl, Kira headed toward the floating stage.

Skye's head popped up. "Really?"

"Sometimes it's best not to ask too many questions," Jin warned. To Kira, "It's been awhile since we participated in something like this."

"Let's hope we don't make utter fools of ourselves," Kira returned.

Otherwise the opportunity Tierni had so kindly arranged to have dropped in her lap would go to waste.

"What made you choose me?" Kira asked as the girl hurried to keep up.

"The human told me you're the one who directed him to save me," she answered as they approached the platform and the Haldeel waiting there.

"You decided from that?"

Kira studied Lieven carefully where he waited by the platform, his hands clasped behind him; his expression calm.

That was an unexpected addition to the event—especially in light of the fact he was considered a master at this. Last time they'd gone head-to-head, Kira only beat him by the narrowest of margins.

Chances were he'd gotten better in the time since. Whereas Kira had only played on the rare occasions they stopped on a planet or station that had a stratagem present.

"They've brought out the big guns. Looks like they don't plan on making this easy," Kira muttered.

"Nope," Jin responded.

"I know you're the reason behind the *za na ri na's* return. I've heard the stories of how you saved her," Skye said.

Kira frowned. For Tierni to have told Skye about those events, it meant the adolescent was closer to the royal than Kira previously assumed.

A relation of some kind perhaps?

Kira had been under the impression Tierni destroyed her family upon her rise to power.

Yukina hovered next to Kira as Skye broke away to talk to a Haldeel standing on the sidelines. "Do you have any idea what you're doing?"

"Nope. I thought I'd wing it."

Yukina's expression tightened.

"She'll be fine," Graydon said. To Kira, "Won't you?"

There was a faint pressure in the way he asked that. Kira suspected if she supplied any other answer but yes, he'd drag her off this platform and stash her somewhere safe.

For that reason, she forced her lips into a semblance of a smile. "Of course. Would I accept if I didn't think I would win?"

Jin blew a raspberry through their comms. "Absolutely."

"I'll be fine," Kira reassured them again.

Now if only she could make herself believe it too.

Kira stepped onto the platform, Jin following.

"The drone must stay here," Yukina objected.

Lieven stirred. "That won't be necessary. *Za na ri* Kira and *Za na ri* Jin are considered one soul in the eyes of our people. I would consider their participation an honor."

At that, Kira gave Lieven a cocky look. "You sure about that? You know we kicked your ass last time."

A broad grin spread on Lieven's face. "Has the smack talk portion of the challenge started?"

Kira didn't answer verbally, instead making a gesture that roughly translated to "bring it."

An evil chortle came from Lieven as he paid no attention to the disbelieving looks of their audience.

"I will make sure to humiliate you before your ancestors," he said after some thought.

"Come, come, you can do better than that," Kira moved to her side of the stage, taking her position as the remaining sphere moved into place above them.

The taunt awakened his competitive spirit.

"Such boasting. One would think you're afraid." He gave her a pronounced frown. "It's been a while for you, after all."

Jin crowed. "That was a good one. Good job."

Lieven's expression thawed into a real smile. "I would wish you fortuitous tides, but this time I intend to crush your soul."

Kira sketched him a half bow. "May the best one win, then."

Curtains of golden light threaded through with umber and midnight blue flashed around them, forestalling any further conversation.

Piece by piece, a multi-level maze made up of glistening strands of light formed around them.

"Five stories." Jin spun around as he studied the transparent structure. "They've really pulled out all the stops for you."

Kira pressed her palm against the nearest translucent wall, unsurprised when she met firm resistance.

The walls of the hologram looked fragile and easily broken, but they were as hard as the wall of a real room.

Kira tilted her head to take in the impressive hologram of the labyrinth. From this angle, the pattern that formed its structure was impossible to decipher.

Like her, Lieven was locked in a tiny room at the bottom of the labyrinth. The only way out was to climb the levels and find the exit.

"What a pain," Kira said with a grimace.

"You could have refused," Jin sang.

"I know." Kira sighed.

The sphere pulsed, and a sheet of light enveloped Kira and Lieven.

Armor built from light particles enclosed her limbs and protected her chest.

With a light push of thought, she directed those particles into the shape of a staff.

Midnight-blue light coalesced until Kira could feel the weight of the staff in her hand, solid and insubstantial at the same time.

On Lieven's side, the curtain of light fragmented and shattered around him. Interwoven around his chest and limbs was a ceremonial armor the color of burnt umber.

It was different than Tuann armor, consisting of plates set one on top of another to allow freedom of movement.

Kira thrust her staff forward, fracturing the panes of light. The Haldeel weren't the only ones capable of showmanship.

"Kira, look!" Jin spun in a circle, showing off his own set of interlocking armor that hovered an inch off his sphere.

His crazy swoops resembled the antics of a toddler hyped up on sugar.

"Was creating your own set of armor really necessary?"

Jin stopped in front of her and sniffed. "Why should you get armor if I don't?"

Kira prodded his armor with her spear. "Because I have limbs and other things you don't."

"The Haldeel are thoughtful—unlike some."

"You're ridiculous."

"You mean ridiculously awesome," Jin corrected.

The beat of several drums echoed around them, first slow but picking up tempo.

Lieven crouched, his lower appendages spreading out from his body with the staff held parallel to the ground.

"Get ready," Jin warned, abandoning Kira to take a position above her and to her left.

Kira didn't argue, adopting a stance of beginning. She lowered one knee to the floor and planted the other foot.

Time for a little flair.

Kira twirled the staff twice before setting it flat against her arm and holding both parallel to the ground.

Just in time as the drums went silent, only to be replaced by the lonesome cry of a wind instrument.

Kira inhaled once, then twice.

It was time.

The drums started up again.

Lieven was the first to his feet, gliding across his room in a set pattern as he sought the exit.

Kira remained in place, studying her surroundings

Being the first out of the labyrinth wasn't enough.

For a puzzle like this, she needed to up her game. Not just win but do it as elegantly and prettily as possible. Form and function, two halves of the same whole. They were the foundations Haldeel society was based on.

Lieven paced in a circle, the butt of his staff pointed toward the ground. From his movements, Kira assumed he had almost found the way out.

Instead of hurrying to start, Kira remained in place, waiting as the music built in intensity.

The pattern would show itself. She just needed to wait.

Kira tapped the butt of the staff against the floor in time with the drums, each tap sending out flares of light that spread like ripples on a pond through the ground below her.

The ripples met the wall and cascaded, exposing a small distortion in their pattern.

There.

Kira moved, darting forward and sliding through the small opening next to the floor in an instant.

Jin dove after her, barely escaping before the exit was concealed again.

Kira straightened from her crouch before rotating the staff in a flashy figure eight. First with one hand then the other, switching off in a continuous movement.

She spun, her staff a whirling dervish before her as she danced on light feet across the floor.

She dodged as a section of the wall sailed toward her, avoiding it by millimeters.

She planted the butt of the spear against the ground, using it as leverage to launch herself into the air. She twisted, flipping over the pit that had suddenly opened up.

With cat-like grace, she landed on the opposite side, only to sprint forward and run up the next wall.

Kira grabbed the opening to the next floor and pulled herself up.

Jin hummed as he followed her onto the second level.

Burnt umber slashed at her. Kira bent backward, barely escaping Lieven's staff. She straightened, blocking the next attack.

Sparks flew as their staffs collided.

In the next second, they spun away from each other as a transparent wall popped up from the floor. Kira turned on her heel and sprinted in the opposite direction.

Several similar exchanges played out over the next minutes as they fought their way to the third floor.

They broke through the barrier at the same time. Abruptly, the floor pitched below her, rotating around the edge of the labyrinth.

Kira raced counter-clockwise to the floor's movement. It took only seconds to realize her actions wouldn't offset the speed.

She kicked off one wall, then the next, using them to keep her forward momentum before diving onto the next level.

Once again, Lieven and Kira reached the next floor within seconds of each other.

By now, they were both breathing hard, the labyrinth pushing their limits.

Despite that, there was no time to rest.

Kira barely avoided falling through the floor as it dissolved under her feet. There was no choice but to race ahead. A single moment of hesitation would send her back a level.

The traps came faster, testing Kira's reaction time until it was all she could do to keep up.

Jin hummed in time to the music as he found his own way, sometimes ahead of Kira, sometimes slightly behind.

Soon, Kira made it onto the fifth and final floor.

Her breath burned her lungs.

By now, instinct and muscle memory were the only things guiding her movements as the labyrinth shifted, its walls and floor changing position every other second, their transformation coming faster with every iteration.

Kira persevered, waiting for her moment. That tiny break that would lead to her salvation.

She waited, her breathing getting choppier as her body begged for respite.

It flashed, there and gone in a split second.

Kira didn't hesitate, bursting through the instability in the wall.

At the last second, she grabbed for the blue ribbon of light as she plunged toward the ground. She caught it, using it as leverage to slow her descent.

With one last push, Kira leapt away from its wall, flipping and landing with a flourish.

When she straightened, she wasn't surprised to see Lieven holding his own ribbon of light having landed within seconds of her.

In the same second, they both touched the end of their staffs to the ground.

Light ignited. Blue for Kira and burnt umber for Lieven.

A third color, silver, raced to join them, following Jin's flight path.

Awed murmurs came from the audience as the colors spun around each other, following each flip and twist they'd made during the labyrinth until the light ended in the exact same place they had begun.

"Impressive as always," Lieven said with an admiring stare at the work of art they'd created.

"Not bad for someone who has been out of the game awhile," Kira prodded.

The faintest of teasing smiles touched Lieven's face. "Had you not let your skills lapse, it would have been your clear win. As it is, you can barely consider this a draw."

Kira's mouth popped open as she sucked in a sharp breath to protest.

She'd totally aced the challenge.

Lieven touched his hands to his heart and then his chin, in a sincere gesture at odds with his previous words. "It was a pleasure competing with you again."

Kira forgot her irritation. "I guess I should thank you for being a good teacher."

"You were my best student."

Kira let herself feel how much those words touched her, knowing he'd pick up on the emotions.

His guidance during that time in her life and Tierni's need had pulled her from the darkness she'd fallen into upon waking from her coma.

They'd reminded her of what was important and that although she'd lost more than anyone ever should, she could still make a difference. Maybe not in the same way as before, but a difference nonetheless.

It was only after she left them that she started pulling herself together. It was why Jin finally trusted her with news of Elena.

She owed so much to Lieven and Tierni. She didn't think she could ever fully repay them.

Kira allowed her gaze to wander over their surroundings as the crowd stared at the work of art she and Lieven had created, impressed all over again.

While the Haldeel were known for their intricate architecture and exquisite stations, there were still pockets that didn't live up to the rest.

Selt was one such pocket. It was a grim and dark place where every day was a fight for survival.

Almaluk and its many wonders suited Tierni and Lieven much better.

"I'm glad your fortunes turned," Kira said.

Lieven's stance shifted to one that denoted pleasure. "Me too."

Before Kira could say anything else, Skye darted in her direction.

"It's beautiful," the girl said, her eyes wide with wonder as she stared at the ribbons of light as they wound around each other, the shimmering gold of the labyrinth acting as a backdrop. "More than I ever dreamed."

There was a wealth of emotion in Skye's voice. She acted as if Kira had handed her a priceless gift beyond her wildest expectations.

"It has the same feeling I get when I'm on a waveboard," Skye said.

Kira looked away, uncomfortable. It was true she had Skye's words in mind when she'd planned her movements. It was just an extra touch, not anywhere near as special as Skye was making it out to be.

Kira's eyes caught on Alexander as he descended the pyramid and crossed the floor toward them.

Noticing her preoccupation, Lieven asked, "Do you know each other?"

Jin made a low sound. "We wouldn't dare."

Kira frowned at him in warning as Skye looked between them. She was smart enough to keep her questions to herself as Alexander approached.

Jin grumbled to himself but didn't argue further.

Alexander reached them, focusing exclusively on Kira and acting like Jin was no more important than the drone he pretended to be. "Follow me."

"Of course." Unable to fully resist being a snarky asshole, Kira added with a taunting smile. "Why wouldn't I want to listen to such a kind invitation?"

Skye rolled her lips together to hide her smile as the man's eyebrows twitched at the jab but remained stoic.

Lieven stepped into the awkward silence. "Our apologies *za na ri* if this seems abrupt. The *za na ri na* anticipated your request and has already made the necessary preparations."

Kira couldn't hide her surprise.

She knew damn well she'd never shared about Elise all those years ago. Her mental state had been too unstable for one, and she'd been more interested in losing herself in the challenges than exposing her deep emotional wounds.

Seeing her confusion, Lieven's expression softened. "We knew you had a difficult history and didn't feel it appropriate to force you to talk about something that was so obviously painful. That didn't stop us from making inquiries after the fact, however."

"Yes, the Phoenix and her Curs are rather famous. How could they not realize?" Alexander's tone was bland, but Kira could sense the disapproval lurking beneath the surface.

Kira forced herself not to react. It was what Alexander wanted. Why live down to his expectations when irritating him was so much more fun?

"Please lead the way," Kira said with a stiff smile.

Alexander set off, crossing the room with powerful strides.

Kira lowered her voice. "Locate Raider and make sure he meets us outside."

If he missed this chance, it would be hard to get another one. Kira didn't want to think how he would react if that happened.

He might finally kill her if that was the case.

"I already sent the message."

Kira released a breath. Good. One less thing to worry about.

With that, she stepped off the platform and followed Alexander, battling conflicting feelings of anticipation and anxiety.

It had been so long, and she was so close to the goal she'd made the day she learned Elise wasn't as dead as she'd assumed.

Now she could only hope she was ready.

* * *

Kira didn't mind the oppressive silence as they traveled through the station, instead using it as an opportunity to study the man next to her.

At first glance, he was nondescript. Everything about him, from his wire-frame glasses to his conservative clothes, went toward projecting the persona of a scholar. Someone easily overlooked except when it came to the depth of their knowledge.

He was tall but lean, lacking the muscular physique of the oshota Kira was now used to.

While not handsome, he had the sort of features that inspired trust in others. Because of it, he likely made new acquaintances without difficulty.

It was easy to see how he rose to his current rank. In a society where skills and talent outweighed wealth and family status, someone like him would go far.

Yet for the life of her, Kira couldn't figure out what he was doing here.

Such a high-profile position was the complete opposite of what Alexander had gone after in the past. He was someone who preferred remaining in the background, letting others weather the eye of the storm while he slipped along the edges.

Alexander stopped. "If you have a question, just ask it."

Kira considered before shaking her head. "I wouldn't be so presumptuous."

He started walking again.

"I have a colleague I wish to join us," Kira said seconds later.

Alexander peered at her, his glasses helping to hide his emotions. "Do you think that's wise?"

Kira's smile was fleeting. "Everyone keeps asking me that."

"Then perhaps you should take the hint."

"I can't do that."

Alexander sighed. "No, you never could."

They reached another corridor, turning left and heading toward the center of the station where security was much more stringent.

Kira debated bringing up Raider's presence again when Alexander interrupted her. "I've already sent someone to escort him to our destination in advance."

Relief caused Kira's shoulders to loosen.

"You don't have to worry we'll ruin this thing you have going," Kira assured him. "As soon as we've finished our business, we'll be gone again."

Jin was a silent observer as Alexander looked from Kira to Finn where he shadowed them from a few feet away, giving them the illusion of privacy.

"I don't think you ever intend to cause trouble, Kira. Yet somehow, that's always what ends up happening," Alexander said at last.

Touché.

Kira could have argued, but what was the point? Alexander had long since made his mind up about her. No amount of discussion would change that.

He had his opinions; she had hers. They simply had to agree to disagree.

They approached a Haldeel checkpoint and were quickly waved through.

"What are you doing here anyways?" Jin asked. "I thought you and yours had a policy of noninterference."

"Jin," Kira warned. "You know the rules."

"Aren't you the least bit curious?"

Maybe, but she didn't want to have this conversation with Finn present.

Alexander wasn't like Selene. If any important secrets were to be exposed in Finn's hearing, Alexander would try to kill him.

Kira wasn't sure he'd succeed—Finn wasn't exactly a pushover—but the damage would be done. She'd like to avoid that sequence of events if possible.

"It doesn't concern us," she said firmly.

In fact, the less they knew about the forty-three and their plans, the better.

Jin sighed. "Fine. Fine. Forget I asked."

Alexander stopped in front of a door. "We're here."

Kira stared at the door in question but made no move to walk through it.

She'd always thought when she finally caught up to Elise, she wouldn't hesitate. That she would seize the opportunity to fix the mistakes she'd made in the past.

Yet standing here, all she felt was the fear of failure and the yearning for what was.

A decade of planning. Endless nights of grief followed by days where it took everything she had to crawl out of bed.

All of it leading up to this moment.

It didn't feel real.

At her hesitation, Alexander adjusted his glasses. "It's not my place to say, but I think you're making a mistake."

"You're right. It's not." Kira pressed her hand against the door, unsurprised when it opened under her touch. "You gave up that right long ago."

When he and the rest had refused to consider trying to save Elise.

Kira stepped into a darkened room, barely taking notice of the others standing there. All that existed was the woman seated at a table on the other side of the viewing window.

Elise.

It was really her.

Kira had prepared to be disappointed, yet there she sat, looking the same as all those years ago.

Her hair was drawn into a messy bun, tendrils escaping to curl around her face. Her eyes held the same bright curiosity Kira saw in Elena's.

Thick, dramatic eyebrows, high cheekbones, and full lips lent her expression a playfulness even when she was trying to be serious.

Kira felt like a hand had reached into her chest and squeezed her heart. Like a floodgate had been released, all the emotions Kira had repressed from that time surged forth. The grief and heartache, the pain and rage.

Kira didn't fight it, immersing herself in those emotions and letting her feel their entirety.

She allowed herself five breaths to experience what she'd spent years trying to ignore.

Only then did she stuff all those emotions into their mental box, nailed a lid down on them, then set the box back on its shelf.

After she finished, she finally looked at Raider.

He leaned against the mirror, his hands stuffed in his pockets, never looking away from the woman who wore Elise's face. "I didn't expect it to feel like this."

"Did they tell you what she did?" Kira asked.

She couldn't afford a Raider who acted emotionally. Just because this looked like Elise, didn't mean it was her.

"They did."

"Do you want to go in, or should I?" Kira finally asked.

A tired laugh came from Raider. "I'm surprised you'd ask that."

Kira avoided his eyes, knowing she deserved that. "You loved her as much as I did."

She didn't regret the things she'd done or the secrets she'd kept, but she did regret the hurt she'd caused.

As difficult as it was, if Raider needed this, Kira would do her best to give it to him. It was the least she owed him.

Raider pushed away from the window and straightened, the previous exhaustion and grief falling away as if it had never been. Composed, he studied Elise.

"I don't think I could be objective right now," he admitted.

Kira patted him on the shoulder as she moved in the direction of the door and the Haldeel standing guard there.

If she was being honest, she didn't think she was going to be any better.

Still, she couldn't force herself to step aside and assign another the task. She'd risked too much for this chance. No one knew Elise better than her.

The Haldeel looked from her to Finn. "Only one inside at a time."

Kira shook her head at Finn as he opened his mouth to protest. "It's fine. Stay here."

Finn's frown was grumpy.

It was clear her assurances didn't hold much weight with him. Considering the last two times she'd said something to that effect had ended with her life in danger, she could see why he thought that way.

Undeterred, Kira pointed at the viewing window. "You can watch me from there. As you can see, there are no exits except for this door. The likelihood of me finding trouble is practically nonexistent."

"I've heard that before."

"You're much too handsome to be so suspicious," she said.

"I wonder if Graydon would think the same."

Kira's mouth dropped as she sputtered. "What does he have to do with this?"

Finn sent her a look as he made his way over to the viewing window. "You forget I stand guard outside your room."

Kira made a strangled sound as Jin reacted like he'd been touched with electricity.

"Say what? Did something happen that you forgot to tell me about?"

"Nope." Kira shook her head in denial. "Not at all."

Before Jin could fixate, Kira faced the Haldeel and pointed at Jin. "It's fine if he comes with me, right?"

The guard hesitated, glancing at Alexander to ask permission. Receiving it, he stepped to the side and opened the door.

"You only have a few minutes," he informed her.

Kira didn't answer, her attention already on the woman inside.

"Her biorhythms are consistent with Elise's," Jin said, using the comms so the woman wouldn't hear.

His words woke her out of her daze. Kira slowly made her way over to the table and took a seat.

Elise's gaze followed her the entire way.

A less suspicious person might have assumed the woman was feeling the same cocktail of emotions as Kira.

Unfortunately, Kira's rose-colored glasses were destroyed long ago.

"You've come all this way. Aren't you going to say anything?" the Elise lookalike asked when Kira didn't speak.

"Do you recognize me?" Kira asked through numb lips.

A pang of recognition went through her at Elise's crooked smile.

"It hasn't been that long," Elise said.

"Thirteen years."

"Twelve and four months." Elise winked. "But who's counting?"

"Why are you here?" Kira asked, not letting herself get pulled into the other's pace.

"I missed you."

"You have a funny way of showing it."

Elise flicked a dismissive hand. "You can't blame me for that. I knew you'd save them. You always do."

Instead of the expected anger, Kira felt herself relax. "I'll give you this. You almost had me fooled."

Elise watched her carefully. "You think I'm a fake."

"I don't just think. I know. You wear her face and have her mannerisms, but you're not her."

Kira stood and made her way over to the door.

"Red balloon."

Kira froze as Elise sent her a coquettish look.

"Do I have your attention now?"

Kira didn't answer, feeling rooted to the spot, her chest tight and her gaze unseeing.

"Not enough?" Elise tapped her chin. "Then how about the hawk jumped over the crow."

Kira flinched.

"Still think I'm fake?" Elise asked.

Feeling like she was in a nightmare, Kira took in the woman who knew things only Elise would.

If it was just one code, Kira could have passed it off as coincidence. Everyone had a breaking point, and Elise had been in Tsavitee hands for over a decade.

It was a given she would have broken under the torture.

That's why she and Elise had come up with the second code. It was supposed to be a failsafe.

"You're really Elise," Kira said through numb lips.

"Bingo. You're finally getting it."

"Where have you been all this time?" Jin asked, speaking aloud for the first time.

"Tin Man, it's been so long, and that's the first question you're asking?" Elise made a tsking sound. "Where's the outpouring of relief and happiness? If I didn't know better, I'd think you'd both be happier if I were dead."

Kira and Jin didn't respond as they stared at Elise like they had seen a ghost.

"Why don't you and Nixxy have a seat so we can have a proper reunion?" Elise invited as she tilted her head at the seat across from her.

Her wrists were locked to the table with force cuffs preventing any movement in her arms.

"Kira," Jin started.

"I know."

Elise looked between the two of them with a small smile playing on her lips. "I missed this—the way you two can have an entire conversation with a few words. I always thought it meant you had an otherworldly connection."

Alexander and Selene were right. This was going to bring Kira nothing but heartache and grief.

Kira forced herself to the table, taking a seat and projecting a calm she didn't feel.

"Answer Jin's question," Kira ordered. "Where have you been?"

Elise ignored Kira's words, staring at Jin in a way utterly unlike any in the past—like he was a science experiment she was trying to figure out the answer to.

"I've always wondered. Do you feel?" Elise asked Jin.

Under the table, Kira's hands clenched.

She's trying to get into your head. Treat her like any other enemy. This Elise isn't the one you knew, Kira told herself.

"You must," Elise continued. "Otherwise, you'd go crazy, right?"

"I think we're done here," Kira said.

Jin was her line in the sand. She wouldn't risk him or his safety.

"Did I hit a sensitive spot?" Elise asked, faking contriteness. "I did, didn't

I?”

The question helped clear Kira’s mind, washing away the feeling of being off-balance as logic reasserted itself.

This wasn’t the way Elise did things. Words that hid sharp blades designed to draw blood. Barely veiled taunting.

Elise had always been direct. She wasn’t as sarcastic as Kira, but she’d never backed down from a fight.

They’d butted heads on more than one occasion, and never once had Elise used this subtle verbal sparring to make her point.

“Why did you attack the race?” Kira asked.

Seeing she’d failed to elicit the reaction she’d intended, Elise made a moue of disappointment and sat up. “Who said I did? I’m an innocent bystander who got caught in the commotion.”

“Do you really think I’ll believe that?” Kira asked.

If the Haldeel had arrested her and arranged her transfer to Almaluk, they were sure of her guilt.

Kira simply didn’t understand the why behind it.

Until she did, there was no point in continuing this conversation.

“Where are you going?” Elise asked as Kira made to stand. For the first time there was a hint of concern in her words.

“I’ve learned what I need to know,” Kira said.

“What about Rothchild?” Seeing Kira’s hesitation, Elise chuckled. “Didn’t you ever wonder why the moon exploded?”

Common assumption was that the miners had set off the charges to ignite the smaralta which caused a massive chain reaction in the tunnels under the moon’s crust.

What no one except for Kira, Himoto, and Jin knew was that those charges had failed before they ever saw use.

Her superiors had been in the process of ordering her to use her burst, when the moon unexpectedly exploded early.

In Kira’s nightmares, she sometimes wondered if she’d somehow unknowingly used her burst, directly causing the deaths of the people she cherished the most.

"We both know you didn't do it. You were too busy playing savior. Haven't you ever wondered who was responsible?"

A sick feeling filled Kira's stomach as Elise gave her a cruel smile.

"Someone had to do what you weren't willing to."

Kira shook her head. "You couldn't have."

Kira had reviewed the recordings from Rothchild a hundred times. There was no way. Elise had been too far away at the time of detonation.

"Sister dearest, you're not the only one able to use the burst. Granted, mine is only a fraction of yours, but a small spark was all that was needed."

Kira couldn't reconcile this woman with the one she'd known.

There was no emotion in those words. No care for the fallen.

It was like they didn't even matter.

"Why?" Kira ground out.

"Himoto." Elise's playfulness turned spiteful. "I tried to tell you a thousand times he was linked to the camps, but you never wanted to listen. He saved you which meant you were willing to ignore everything else."

Kira opened her mouth to respond when the station bucked around them.

"What was that?" Kira asked as the station shuddered again.

Glee spread across Elise's face. "The show has finally begun."

"A Tsavitee fleet appeared next to Jettie's moon." Jin sounded distracted as he tapped into the communication network of the station.

Jin's horror flooded their link. "Kira, they've started bombarding the planet."

Kira felt like she was hearing those words from a great distance. Fear she hadn't felt in years welled up.

"I hope you don't have any friends down there. Chances are they won't make it," Elise crooned.

Stricken, Kira's gaze met Elise's. Elena was still down there.

Before Kira could recover, Elise yanked her hands out of the force cuffs and hit the deck.

Kira reached for her *ki* as a warning screamed across her instincts.

An explosion ripped through her world, sending her body spinning. She crashed into the window behind her, cracking it.

Darkness slammed into her brain.

TWENTY-THREE

THE CONCERN ON his First's face pulled Graydon's attention from the tedious boredom of the conversation he was currently trapped in.

It wasn't like Solal to interrupt during a gathering as influential as this one.

Solal was the first oshota to pledge himself to Graydon. As a result, the two knew each other better than anyone else.

Whatever had put that look on his face was important.

With a conciliatory smile at the Haldeel in front of him, Graydon excused himself.

Solal stepped up to his side and bent his head toward Graydon. "There are concerning reports from our ships. Unknown transmissions have been detected on Almaluk and surrounding space."

"Inform our people," Graydon ordered, sweeping his gaze over the crowd. "Assign Cord and Isla to escort Yukina and her oshota to their ship. I want them off the station as soon as possible."

It should be extraordinarily difficult to penetrate Haldeel space, but nothing was impossible.

The quorum had opened a hole in Haldeel defenses. A wise foe would seek to take advantage of the influx of people to stage an attack.

Graydon's face grew grim at the possibilities.

Just then, his attention landed on Jace as he leaned down to speak into Admiral Himoto's ear in much the same fashion Solal had with Graydon.

Himoto's expression didn't shift, remaining stoic. He turned his head, hiding his mouth. Jace nodded at whatever he said before straightening.

Not looking left or right, Jace moved away at a quick clip. When he was gone, Himoto stood and made his way over to Graydon.

Curious, Graydon waited for him.

In the dealings Graydon had had with this human, he could see the man was different from the rest of the Consortium. Graydon even held a measure of respect toward him.

Himoto was a man of principle and duty—devoted to the greater good rather than the lesser few.

Such a man would be admired as a leader but hated by friends and family.

It took a strong person to endure the recriminations of others when they were forced to make the difficult choices that would ensure the safety of so many.

In this, Graydon thought he understood Himoto better than Kira.

Her first instinct was always to save everyone. Himoto was more pragmatic. He'd save who he could and silently bear the burden of those he couldn't.

"We meet again," Graydon said in greeting as Himoto reached him. "To what do I owe this pleasure?"

Himoto didn't beat around the bush. "Judging from your actions, you've been informed of the same thing I have."

Graydon didn't confirm or deny, waiting to see what Himoto would do.

The human didn't disappoint. "What you may not know is that I have intel that an attack is imminent."

"You're sharing this with me why?"

"We have something in common. We both care for the same woman," Himoto said simply.

Graydon bared his teeth in a smile more suited to a dragon. "Are you sure that's the only reason?"

A man like Himoto always had more than one reason for doing things.

Graydon believed he really did care for Kira and wanted only the best for her. That didn't negate the fact Himoto had other motivations for sharing.

"There are some concerning developments on my side. I thought it best to reach out," Himoto said with a faint smile.

In other words, he no longer trusted his own people.

After the display by Admiral Kent, Graydon couldn't say he was surprised.

Seeing Graydon's acceptance, Himoto lowered his voice. "They'll go after Kira first. Under no circumstances can she be allowed to fall into their hands."

Graydon's eyes sharpened. "Why?"

"That is an old story that would take too long to tell."

Before Graydon could ask anything more, the floor under their feet bucked and rolled as explosions rocked the station.

Screams sounded around them as a second explosion made people stumble.

"Those were internal explosions," Himoto said.

It was the worst nightmare of any station master. Fear of sudden depressurization was one of the reasons projectile weapons were universally banned in space.

Most ships wouldn't even let you on board with one.

The frame of the station was self-repairing, but it wouldn't prevent loss of life from those in the immediate vicinity of the explosion.

Movement above pulled Graydon's attention upward.

"It looks like that's the least of our problems," he observed as dozens of Tsavitee warships dropped into orbit around the planet.

With no time for anyone to react, bright beams of light erupted from the ships as they immediately started firing on the cities below.

"This ambush is exceedingly well planned," Graydon admitted with a dark look.

They'd waited until the strongest warriors were on the station before attacking, increasing the likelihood of landing a decisive blow against those remaining.

"The Tsavitee have always been good at striking when you're at your weakest." Himoto's face was creased in deep thought as he stared at the attacking ships.

Graydon detected no fear in the human general. It was as if the specter of death and defeat held no sway, his mind already devising scenarios likely to lead to optimal outcomes.

"You two are very alike," Graydon murmured.

Kira got that same look on her face when she was up against the wall. When others would lose themselves to panic, she always had this calm about her, as if by taking in the different variables of a situation she'd find a way through.

Himoto sent Graydon a questioning look.

Graydon shook his head, ignoring it. Now wasn't the time to be caught up in such things.

"I find it strange the station's defenses haven't come online yet," Solal remarked.

"It's likely the first explosions targeted those systems," Himoto said. "It's what I would do in their place."

Above, the Haldeel had finally scrambled a response to the threat, several cruisers firing at the enemy as they arrowed toward them.

The smaller size of the Haldeel ships against the massive frames of the Tsavitee ships made it seem like they were minnows up against a shark.

Defeat was inevitable. The best they could hope for was to delay the bombardment and buy time for the rest of the fleet to intervene.

"Isn't this an interesting development," Torvald said, joining Graydon and Himoto, his eyes on the stars and the battle taking place there.

Graydon scowled at him. "Shouldn't you be with Yukina?"

"It's so cute how you thought I'd obey such an order."

It would certainly make Graydon's life easier if he had.

Forget it. The man had always been capricious and only did what he wanted. Nothing Graydon could say would change that.

"How delightful, the enemy has decided to come and test us." Torvald sounded happy as two of the Tsavitee ships broke off from the bombardment to head in their direction.

"Most wouldn't find that a cause for celebration," Himoto observed as the previously stunned crowd finally woke up to the danger they were in.

They stampeded for the exit. The Haldeel guards who'd remained after the royal's departure immediately following Kira's exit tried to maintain order.

"Admiral, shouldn't we leave too?" one of Himoto's aides asked.

"You could try, but I doubt you'll make it out." Torvald stepped forward as the Tsavitee ship spun, lining up their cannons. "Your toys have blocked the exit."

The Tsavitee ship fired.

Torvald raised a hand, golden *ki* snaking up his arm and spilling out of his palm. It shot up, spreading across the bubble in a split second.

Light seared the eyes of those present as the shot from the Tsavitee ship impacted.

"You're a thousand years too young to challenge the great me," Torvald shouted with a cruel grin.

"You look like you're having fun," Graydon drawled.

Torvald's eyes sparkled. "Of course. It's been ages since I played."

Because the rest of the Tuann no longer dared entertain him. They'd already learned their lesson, Graydon added privately.

Above, silvery ribbons swarmed out of the ship, darting toward the station. They moved as if they were organic, their patterns hard to predict as they slithered in a sinuous glide as if they were swimming through space.

"Strigmor eels," Himoto supplied, sounding unruffled. "If even one reaches the station, they'll eat through the hull and burrow into the electrical systems. Once that happens, it'll only be a matter of time before this station dies."

"That's the least of our problems," Solal said, his focus on the room's exit where those who'd tried to evacuate were being forced back by Zepher's androids.

Pools of blood painted the floor, prone bodies sprawled next to them guarded by androids.

Their faces were eerily blank, and the gunmetal gray of their bodies was splattered with streaks of red as Kent joined them.

Humans wearing the insignia of Zepher stood behind him.

It was obvious from their body posture who had ordered the androids to act.

A wide circle grew around the interlopers.

Graydon looked around, finding it curious some Houses who'd attended were now missing, including Remie and Asanth.

Those who had remained had fallen in on each other, their oshota working together to set up a small perimeter.

A short distance away, Liara and her people weren't panicked. They'd already taken up defensive positions to safeguard those who had attended with them.

Liara caught his eye and nodded, saying without words they were ready for anything that came.

Faint approval filled Graydon. The Overlord had grown into her position nicely.

Himoto moved toward Kent, stopping on the edge of the crowd and regarding the human calmly. "I always warned you your ambition and greed would lead you into disaster, but I never thought it would come so soon."

Kent sneered. "I've done what you weren't brave enough to do. The alliance brokered with the Haldeel only hampers our evolution. We cannot become what we were meant to be when another holds our leash. I'm simply rectifying the mistakes of you and the old guard."

"By working with an enemy who wants to drive us to extinction?" Himoto asked.

Kent drew himself up. "The Tsavitee's methods are harsh, it's true, but sometimes you need to go through a crucible to achieve your true potential. Our race must become strong. Don't forget, you're the one who taught me that sometimes sacrifices need to be made for the greater good."

While he was speaking, Graydon sent several hand signals to his people, warning them to get ready.

Solal and Amila touched their sides where their en-blades were hidden. They watched intently for their moment, their stance defensive.

Himoto's expression was pained as he closed his eyes and shook his head.

"You stupid boy. You had such promise."

There was pity in the way Himoto watched his fellow human. His gaze held a kind of ruthlessness that made it clear he wouldn't hesitate to sacrifice the other man, no matter their prior relationship.

Graydon and Torvald exchanged looks.

"What do you say we go a little wild today?" Torvald asked.

Very well. If the man wanted a little excitement in his life, who was Graydon to deny him.

"Leave the small fry to us," Graydon instructed. "You concentrate on those ships."

Torvald's bloodthirsty smile faded. "Why do I think you got the more interesting task?"

Despite his obvious disappointment with his task, Torvald was already moving to take care of those outside. His hands flowed swiftly through several runes.

Pressure built in the air. The molecules around them seemed to scream as with a clap Torvald finished his formation. He threw a hand toward the scene above. Dozens of lights arced up, spearing the approaching strigmor eels.

"I'll take care of the trash," Graydon said, starting toward the androids and the humans around them.

Kent's face contorted at the destruction taking place above. He looked over his shoulder at an android. "Kill him."

Graydon moved before he'd even finished speaking the order. His en-blade drawn in one second and the android's head falling onto the ground in the next.

"What's that you were saying?" Graydon asked. "I didn't quite get it the first time."

Kent snarled, backing away as the two remaining androids charged.

The bzzt of a *zuipi* split the air, killing the androids instantly.

Jace walked into the room. "Sorry I'm late. I got a bit hung up."

Torvald raised an eyebrow. "Why does that weapon seem familiar?"

"This?" Jace held up what looked to be a modified version of the *zuipi*, only smaller and much more compact. "It's an invention of Blue's; it's the first of its kind. Raider passed me the schematics a few days ago. Isn't it fun?"

"That's one word for it," Graydon said, his predatory gaze turning to Kent.

The human stumbled back, fear and the self-preservation that had been missing earlier finally returning.

Too late now.

"What should we do with him?" Graydon asked.

"Take him into custody," Himoto answered, no mercy on his face. "Death is too good for him after this betrayal. He should be given a trial, his rank stripped, and live in shame for the rest of his days."

The words seemed to give Kent a backbone as he stopped and straightened. "I'm not the only one who believes the Haldeel are a threat as great as the Tsavitee."

Himoto ignored the words, glancing at Graydon. "I also want the chance to interrogate him to root out the rest of his followers."

Humor touched Graydon's expression as Kent stiffened at the revelation.

"We can help," Torvald said, peering over Graydon's shoulder. "The Tuann have many interrogation methods."

Himoto's eyes gleamed. "I look forward to exploring the possibilities." To his people, he said, "Take him into custody."

They moved toward Kent. He didn't resist as they reached for his arms.

"You are a disappointment who doesn't deserve your rank," Himoto told him as the humans secured his wrists behind his back.

The stamp of many sets of feet announced the arrival of reinforcements.

Anticipation and a ruthlessness twisted Kent's expression.

Jace grimaced. "I thought I took care of those."

"Looks like there were more," Graydon told him.

"What are your orders?" Torvald asked.

"I'm up for killing them all," Graydon said.

Then when they were done, they could address the betrayal by the human admiral and all those who'd helped him

Jace pointed the *zuipi* at the androids. "Can't argue with that."

Graydon cracked his neck. He'd be lying if he said he wasn't looking forward to this.

He grinned at the androids, a dangerous light in his eyes. "Now. Who's first?"

* * *

The world slid in and out of focus, pain and the percussion of the blast making it difficult for Kira to keep her eyes open.

Dim shapes climbing through the smoking hole in the wall. The sound of shattering glass as Finn launched himself through the window Kira had damaged.

Raider appearing above her a second later, his mouth moving but his words not penetrating the tinny ringing in her ears.

The station shuddering around them every so often.

As if in a dream, Kira reached up to feel her temple. Her fingers came away covered in blood.

So that's why her head hurt so much.

Raider was gentle as he pulled her to sitting, his gaze frantic.

He should go after Elise, Kira thought, her eyes sliding closed again.

"Can't let—" Kira trailed off, struggling to focus.

She blinked as the figures around her wheeled, a strange shape with many legs launching itself from the ceiling. It wrapped itself around one of the figures.

Her mind finally made sense of what she was seeing. It was the Haldeel guard. His lower half restrained his foe as he separated its head from its shoulders.

The body didn't crumple, not until the Haldeel ripped the limbs from its torso.

The android's companions screamed, the metal panels protecting their heads and necks flaring like the hood of a cobra. Their mouths dropped open, letting beams of light blast toward the Haldeel. He spun his trident, diffusing them.

Finn moved to intercept, his en-blade carving a path through the androids.

The world snapped into focus.

"Kira, we have to go," Raider shouted.

"Jin. Where's Jin?" Kira asked, shoving her way toward her feet.

She stumbled and would have fallen if Raider hadn't caught her.

She didn't see Jin anywhere. More concerning, she didn't feel him either.

"Elise took him."

Stunned, Kira could only stare at Raider. She didn't understand. Why would Elise take Jin?

"And you let her?" Kira knew it was wrong even as she made the accusation.

Raider dropped her arm. "There was no "let" about it. She grabbed him and leapt out of the hole. These things attacked right after."

Finn put distance between him and the last few androids, his left arm sweeping in an arc. *Ki* blasted from him, lifting the androids and flinging them into the wall.

They hit with a crunch, collapsing to the ground.

"That should be the last of them," Finn said with an approving nod.

When he faced Kira, there was a look of condemnation in his eyes.

Kira couldn't even summon the energy to move as she leaned against what remained of the wall where the window had been.

She took a look around the room, noting its complete destruction.

The table was on its side and in two pieces. The place where she'd sat had scorch marks from the blast.

Things could be worse.

If she hadn't summoned her *ki* to strengthen her body just then, she would probably have looked like that table.

"Don't say it; I already know."

In her defense, no one could have predicted that Elise's accomplices would blow a hole in the wall.

Frankly speaking, it shouldn't have been possible. This room was located in a secure area and access was restricted.

Elise's accomplices shouldn't have been able to get anywhere close.

Glass crunched under Alexander's feet as he walked into the room, surveying the damage with an impartial gaze.

"Should I go after the prisoner, *Za na*?" the guard asked him.

Alexander shook his head. "We have more important worries at the moment. The station is under attack both internally and externally. The lives of those within take priority over chasing that prisoner."

Kira ignored him, pushing herself away from the wall and staggering toward the hole. If that was the way Elise had gone, Kira would follow.

Raider blocked her.

"Move."

His expression only got more stubborn. "No. You can barely stand."

Kira snapped. "Raider, she has Jin!"

Raider's flinch brought Kira back to herself.

Shame had her taking a step away. She wasn't the only one who'd suffered a blow. Elise was the woman Raider loved. As difficult as this was for Kira, Raider would be even more devastated.

"I'm going after him," Kira said in a calmer voice.

"I know," Raider responded. "And I'm going with you."

"Idiots, the both of you." Alexander stabbed a finger at Kira. "You can barely stand. What do you think you can do?"

"I'll figure it out. I always do."

Despite the brash words, Kira knew she was in bad shape. She suspected she had a concussion and judging by the sharp pain anytime she tried to move her left shoulder, her collarbone was broken.

Alexander looked up at the ceiling. "Do you know where she's gone? What she plans? How many of those monsters are with her? Who's helping her?"

There was nothing Kira could say to any of those questions. She didn't have the answers, and she wouldn't pretend.

She was still going.

"Stubborn as always," Alexander said.

Kira took that to mean he wouldn't stand in her way. A fact she was grateful for.

Every second was precious if she wanted to recover Jin. If Elise got off the station with him, her chances of ever seeing her friend again were nearly none.

Alexander was motionless as Kira started for the hole Elise had fled through. With the expectation he would let her pass, Kira dropped her guard, her mind already on what needed to be done.

It was why she didn't immediately react when he grabbed her shoulder and drove his fist into her stomach.

Kira curled in on herself, fighting to inhale against the sudden constriction of her lungs.

Fire spread through her, originating in the place where he'd hit her. Everywhere it touched, warmth followed.

Kira raised her head only to find Finn holding his en-blade to the side of Alexander's throat.

Alexander sent him a dangerous look. "Get that thing away from me."

"Finn," Kira cautioned, straightening gingerly.

To her surprise her injuries hurt much less now. Where before they would have been a seven or an eight on the pain scale, they were now a three or four.

Her shoulder moved easily, too.

The forty-three weren't trained in *ki* in the same way as most Tuann, but that didn't mean they hadn't learned to use their innate abilities. From what Kira had seen in her short time with the Tuann, their methods of mastering their soul's breath were different but just as impactful.

Unlike Kira, they'd had each other to learn from, sharing their discoveries along the way. Perhaps that was why they didn't suffer *ki* poisoning in the same way she had. Perhaps it was because they'd formed bonds between themselves, keeping them from withering in the same way Kira had.

Or maybe it was neither of these things.

Kira had always been powerful—abnormally so when compared to the rest. She was stronger, faster, more intuitive.

Could be where their foundation could handle the influx of *ki*, hers simply couldn't.

Whatever the answer, it didn't matter now.

Finn sheathed his en-blade but didn't step back, hovering protectively near Kira as Alexander started for the door, the guard following him.

"Alexander—" Kira started.

"I didn't do it for you," he interrupted, not looking back. "I did it for her. She seems to find some meaning in the children you bring her. She'd be sad if that ended."

Kira snorted as he walked away. "As dishonest as ever."

Though it did answer the question of whether he knew about Selene's extracurricular activities. From his actions, she could infer he had no plans of interfering or informing the rest.

When he was gone, Raider moved closer. "You going to tell us what that was about?"

"Nope, and you're not going to ask."

From the cautious way Finn looked from Kira to where Alexander had disappeared, she could tell he had his suspicions. As long as they remained just that, Kira could keep pretending.

Raider raised his hands. "You don't want to talk about it. That's fine. We can focus on what's important instead."

"I couldn't agree more," Kira said, crouching next to one of the androids to study it.

It was the one the guard had dismantled. Its eyes shifted to meet hers, making Kira pause in the act of reaching for it.

"Isn't that interesting," Kira said softly to herself.

"What is?" Raider asked.

Kira didn't answer, immersed in deciphering the energy she could feel pulsing in its chest. It felt similar to Jin's but more chaotic.

Kira's fingers hovered over the spot where that energy was anchored. Bracing herself, she bridged that last gap and immediately wished she hadn't.

She'd been mistaken earlier. This was nothing like Jin.

Madness and darkness lurked within, coupled with a powerful thirst to destroy everything. The only thing keeping it in check was a series of commands Kira couldn't quite decipher.

No wonder Jin said they felt creepy.

"You poor thing," Kira whispered.

She reached deeper with that same sense that allowed her to pull the essence out of matter, hoping for a connection that would lead her to the ones who'd taken Jin.

She found nothing but isolation so stark and deep it had warped the soul of whoever this had once been.

"Soul bound," Finn said from the opposite side of the android. "It must be destroyed."

Kira didn't move, her fingers separated from that chaotic mass by a few millimeters of metal.

"It wouldn't be a mercy to allow it to live," Finn told her. "It will never rest. Never feel. All that lies in its future is endless madness. It can't be saved."

"I know." *Ki* streamed from Kira's fingers, wrapping around the ball of energy and smothering it.

It struggled, its energy fluttering against her senses as it fought to survive.

With a final flex of her *ki,* Kira ended it.

She rose, her face carefully blank as she tried not to think about what she'd just done.

Killing in that fashion was different than when you ended someone with a blade or laser fire.

Her hands clenched as she took a deep breath, pushing the feeling aside to be examined later.

"What was that?" Raider asked as she walked past him toward the hole in the wall.

"Tuann stuff."

Raider glanced at Finn's stony face.

"We call them soul bound. They are mad creatures deserving of our mercy."

"Soul bound, huh?" There was speculation and an understanding Kira refused to acknowledge as Raider stared at the side of her face.

Kira ignored the two, carefully listening for any signs of hostiles before diving through the hole. She landed, on guard for an attack that never came.

There was a thud, then a second one as Raider and Finn ducked out after her.

Raider nodded his head at a prone body to their right. "What do you want to bet they went this way?"

Kira started forward with a sense of resignation. "There's no point in betting when it's a sure thing."

Raider jogged after her, Finn next to him.

"Really wishing I had a weapon right about now," Raider muttered.

Kira snapped off the dangling gem in her earring and pressed a button. A long thin blade extended out of it, forming a knife.

She tossed it to Raider. "Happy now?"

"Ecstatic."

* * *

A short while later, Kira held up her hand as they reached an intersection. She looked down one corridor and then another without the faintest clue which direction to take.

More than anything, she wished Jin was here. She wouldn't even complain about his smart-ass comments or his ridiculous antics.

At least he'd have some idea what to do, which direction to take. He'd hack the security feeds or use any one of a dozen methods to get a lock on Elise.

"Which way do we go?" Raider asked, turning in a circle.

This time there wasn't a handy body left behind that they could use as a compass.

"I don't know."

"Do we split up?"

"I don't know!" Kira yelled.

She took a deep breath immediately after.

Focus, Kira. One foot in front of the other until you accomplish your mission. Losing control won't help anyone, least of all Jin.

Raider paced, his movements almost frantic. "You go that way. I'll go this way."

"We can't split up," Finn objected. "The enemy is too powerful. None of us stand a chance if we meet up with them alone."

And by none, he really meant Kira and Raider.

"We don't engage then," Raider argued. "We hang back and notify the others."

Finn sent a pointed look in Kira's direction that seemed to mock that suggestion. Noticing the look, Kira could only shrug. Even she knew the chances of that working were small.

It wasn't just her. Raider was as likely to run into the fray as her.

"We don't have a lot of options," Raider said, unwilling to back down.

Static filled Kira's comms.

"—tie."

Kira frowned and pressed a finger against her ear.

"Auntie, are…there?"

"Elena." Kira closed her eyes in relief.

At Elena's name, Raider took a step toward Kira.

"Is that Elena? Is she okay?"

Kira held up a hand as she moved further into the hallway in the hopes of strengthening the signal. By now, they had to be out of the protected section of the station. That had to be why she was suddenly able to hear Elena.

"I've been trying you forever," Elena burst out, sounding close to tears.

"I know. Some things happened. The place I was in must have blocked unauthorized signals."

"Do you know what's going on down on the planet?"

Kira started to answer but paused.

"Where are you?" Kira asked.

"About that—" Elena drawled.

"You're on the station," Kira answered for her.

Elena's silence was answer enough, her guilt traveling down the line as clear as her voice had.

It made perfect sense. The channel Elena was using wouldn't have reached the station from the planet, especially with the interference from the bombardment and the signal blockers that were standard procedure for the Tsavitee when they launched an attack.

"You did say we could go sightseeing," Elena finally offered.

Elena knew this wasn't what she'd intended. Trust her niece to take a mile when she'd been offered an inch.

It was a trait she'd inherited from Jin and Kira, both of whom were known to twist the meaning of words to find a loophole when it suited them.

"Not on Almaluk." Kira pinched the bridge of her nose.

"She's here?" Raider asked. "Let me talk to her."

"Why not? You know how hard it is to find this place at any other time," Elena argued. "Besides, Wren and Devon were interested in seeing the *Wanderer*."

Kira bet they were.

She twisted away as Raider tried to reach for her ear.

"Stop that. You know my comms are embedded in my ear canal," Kira snapped.

"Are you with the sperm donor?" Elena asked, brightening. "Hi, sperm donor."

Kira rolled her eyes but passed on the message.

"Why is Uncle Jin being so quiet?" Elena asked.

Kira caught her breath against the unexpected stab of pain.

"Auntie?"

Kira stared unseeing down the corridor as the words to explain clogged her throat.

"Auntie, what aren't you telling me?"

Kira knew she needed to say something. Continued silence would only exacerbate Elena's fears.

Her niece was surprisingly sensitive. Hiding things rarely worked with her.

"If you're not explaining, that means something happened," Elena said slowly. "You're in a secure section of the facility. One of the perpetrators was caught yesterday."

"How do you know that?"

Elena ignored Kira's question, intent on following the logic. "You'd only be interested if that person was someone important to you. My mother. Judging by the fact you haven't mentioned her and Uncle is now missing, I can only assume Mother did something and took Uncle Jin."

Kira wanted to bang her head against the wall. Damn Jin for teaching Elena that trick.

"Auntie?"

Kira rubbed her head. "Yes."

Elena was quiet for several seconds. "Is it really my mother?"

"I don't know."

There was a moment of silence where Kira thought she'd lost the connection.

"It doesn't matter either way," Elena said finally. "If you have a choice between Mother and Uncle Jin, you need to save Uncle Jin."

Kira glanced at Raider before ducking her head, not wanting him to see her expression.

"Elena—"

"You and Uncle Jin are my family," Elena said loudly, drowning her out. "I won't trade either of you—even for Mother."

Despite Elena's firm words, Kira could sense the turbulent emotions her niece choked down.

"If it's really Mother, she's lost to us anyway," Elena said, her voice breaking.

The hardest thing Kira had ever learned—and something she had never mastered—was knowing when to call it quits.

It seemed her niece was a little more advanced than her in that respect.

Kira leaned her head against the wall and closed her eyes. "You're a good kid, do you know that?"

"I know," Elena said.

Kira took a deep breath and straightened. "Raider, if you had staged an attack and stolen something, what would be your next move?"

"I'd find a way off this station," he said.

Kira glanced at Finn to see him nodding in agreement.

Her lips tilted up in a half smile. "Me too."

Finn accessed the interface on his forearm. "They'll want to take the quickest path to the docks. Let me see if I can find a map."

"Auntie, I want to help," Elena said. "I love Uncle Jin too."

Kira quelled her instinctive rejection.

As much as she wanted to wrap Elena in a bubble, she could already tell it'd be futile. Kira knew what it felt like to feel powerless while the people close to her were in jeopardy. It was the worst feeling in the world.

She didn't want that for Elena. At the same time, she had no intention of placing her niece at risk.

"Before you say no, you should know I'm not alone," Elena said.

A chime sounded in Kira's comms accompanied by a notification in the upper right corner of her optics. Kira clicked on it, and a holo video of her niece appeared.

Elena swung the camera to capture Wren's serious expression, his oshota, Auralyn, next to him.

They weren't the only ones either. Devon, Joule, and Ziva stood to the side.

"Are you kidding me?" Kira asked. What was this? A fieldtrip?

There was some comfort in Wren and Auralyn's presence, but not much. To attack Almaluk like this, the Tsavitee would have a lot of tricks up their sleeve.

Even warriors as accomplished as that group could be overwhelmed eventually.

Before Elena could answer, Kira's gaze locked on the silver turtle clinging to her collar. The creature's head lifted as it yawned before curling into a ball.

"MinMin," Kira said softly.

"What was that, Auntie?"

Why didn't she think of that before?

MinMin could be considered part of Jin. Not just in a metaphysical sense through *ki,* but also through an actual physical link that could be traced.

Kira dismissed the thought almost as soon as it occurred to her.

As talented as Elena was, she lacked the skills to perform such a complicated task. Kira would need a hacker for that, something Elena wasn't.

Jin could—or Odin.

"I've got the map," Finn announced. "We need to take the corridor to our left."

"Elena, standby." Without waiting for an agreement, Kira put the call on hold, switching to search mode. "Please. Please, still be on the station."

"Kira, we need to get moving, or we'll lose them," Raider warned.

Kira stayed silent, sifting through her contact list. Jin always made this look so easy.

The name Allfather popped up. Kira hit it.

"Odin, are you there?"

Silence stretched.

She waited, feeling more and more hopeless as the moments passed.

Finally, there was a click.

"You do have an interesting knack of timing," Odin said grumpily.

"Odin, thank God," Kira said as Finn and Raider lost patience and set off.

Kira's pace was much slower as she followed.

"Your comm almost got me caught by the Haldeel. Do you know what they do to people they find hacking their most sensitive systems—especially during an invasion?"

"Listen to me," Kira interrupted. "The Tsavitee have Jin."

Dead air echoed through the comms.

"What do you need from me?" Odin asked, sounding grim.

"There's some type of interference preventing me from using our special connection."

Not that Kira had ever tried using their link in that fashion. Jin could ride Kira's senses, and they could each feel each other's emotions, but tracking the other? That had always been Jin's ball of wax.

"Can you use his avatar to pinpoint his location?" Kira asked.

"He's started playing with those?"

Kira picked up her pace, keeping Finn and Raider's backs in view. "Just answer the question."

"Yes. Yes. He would have established some type of feature so he didn't lose track of the avatar. I should be able to reverse track his location from there."

That's what Kira wanted to hear.

"I'll need the avatar though."

"Can you get to the *Wanderer*?"

Kira had no way of knowing how bad it was in the rest of the station. According to the Tsavitee's way of doing things, their forces should have already infiltrated with the help of the androids. That was in addition to the attacks they were launching from the outside.

Kira wouldn't risk Elena's life—even for Jin. He wouldn't want her to either.

The *Wanderer* had the advantage of some of the most advanced tech coupled with the fact it was probably the safest place right now. Her security measures ensured any infiltrators would have a hell of a time breaching her defenses. If things got really bad, they could unlatch from the station and flee.

Odin didn't hesitate. "I'll find a way."

The comms clicked as Odin signed off.

Kira activated her link with Elena. "Head for the *Wanderer*. Odin will rendezvous with you."

"Auntie," Elena protested.

"This is how you help me," Kira interrupted. "It's more important than anything. Odin will use MinMin to find Jin, and then I will go get him."

Kira took Elena's silence as agreement.

"Wren, I'm trusting you to protect them," Kira said, knowing her *seon'yer* would hear.

Wren didn't hesitate. "With my life."

Kira felt relief at that promise.

"What will you do?" Wren asked.

"What's necessary."

TWENTY-FOUR

KIRA AND THE rest left the warren of hallways behind, bursting onto the level of the main station. Signs that a battle had recently taken place lay all around them. In the distance, they could hear a fight still in progess.

"A few androids wouldn't have been enough to do all this," Raider said, studying the blackened marks on the floor and wall.

"The soul bound are different. Besides, I don't think it's just a few," Finn said. "They had help—a lot of it."

If the Tsavitee had made it onto the station, it could explain the difficulties the Haldeel were having. She didn't know what had possessed them to make this move.

Even with the blows struck to Almaluk, it was only a matter of time before the Haldeel took control again.

Finn pointed to their right. "The map says to go this way."

Kira hesitated, torn between continuing to follow the map and waiting for word from Odin.

Finding the nearest port off-station sounded like a good idea in theory. For a station the size of Almaluk, the port would be humongous, and with all the ships currently docked for the quorum, it would be impossible to search all of them in time.

Also, the port wasn't the only way off Almaluk. Kira didn't want to overlook something because she was too impatient.

She needed to balance the desire to close the gap between her and Elise with the knowledge that making the wrong choice would put her too far behind the other.

"Come on, Odin," Kira urged.

Finn waited patiently. Raider less so.

There was a certain frenetic urgency to his movements that screamed of his need to act until he was practically vibrating in place.

"Kira, I think I've narrowed down the location," Odin said suddenly through the comms. "It's not precise yet, but I have a general direction."

"Where?"

"They've headed for the lower decks in the Day Lily sector. Sending the map to Muscles now."

Finn jerked like someone had stung him.

Odin's ability to hack the interface in his synth armor was surprising. The use of *ki* in the Tuann's networks made their technology nearly impenetrable to traditional hackers.

It was like being on two separate networks that had no way of talking or even hearing the other.

It figured Odin would find a way around that eventually.

"Patch Raider into our comms in case we get separated."

Raider touched his ear and then nodded at Kira to say he'd received Odin's message.

"Everyone ready?" Kira asked.

Finn and Raider nodded with serious expressions.

"From here on out, we go silent unless there's an emergency." Kira didn't want to risk alerting the enemy of their approach.

"Finn, you're our compass. I'll take point. Raider, protect our back."

Their formation was different than what an oshota would prefer for their sword, but it was necessary. With Finn preoccupied by the map, he wouldn't be able to pay as much attention to his surroundings.

Most importantly, this formation fit Kira's personality.

"Let's go," Kira said, taking the lead.

The other two chased after her, careful to keep their movements as silent as possible.

They raced through the station, Finn tapping her shoulder every now and then before indicating where to go.

In this fashion, they advanced, diverting around the small pockets of fighting they encountered every now and then.

Nearly twenty minutes later, Kira and the other two slowed as they neared the docks. The area they found themselves in was adjacent to the port and contained a maze of shipping containers stacked until they nearly reached the ceiling two stories above.

Along one side was a massive opening, the atmosphere inside contained by a thin membrane that allowed the entrance and exit of freight.

"You're getting close, Kira. I can't narrow his signal any more than this," Odin said softly into her ear. "I'll see if I can access the feeds, but it'll be difficult from here."

Kira tapped behind her ear twice, knowing the sound would carry to her comms to show she understood.

To Finn and Raider, she sent them a hand signal to be on guard.

The two spread out, moving cautiously as they made their way through the stacks of containers.

A surge of energy crashed through the space.

Instinctively, Kira dove for cover, rolling until her spine fetched up against a container. Her heart pounded as adrenaline flooded her system.

The spot where she'd just been standing had been turned into a crater.

She scanned her surroundings, relieved when she spotted Finn and Raider behind their own container.

"Well, well, look who we have here." Niland walked out of the shadows. "A weaponless human, a misguided Tuann, and the reject who led them to their deaths."

Across from her, Raider rolled his eyes at the posturing by the oshota from House Remie. "Kira, have you ever noticed how the weaker one of these guys are, the more they like to pontificate?"

"What are you doing?" Kira mouthed.

"Go," he mouthed back.

Kira shook her head.

"Yap all you want, human. You'll soon be dead."

There was a loud thud as if Niland had leapt onto one of the containers.

Identical thuds came from several different positions in the warehouse.

Finn looked around Raider's shoulder and dipped his chin once, his eyes grave.

"You have to," Raider mouthed.

Even from this distance, Kira could see the emotions he was suppressing. Adrenaline clashed with anticipation and fear.

"Find another way," she mouthed at him.

Finn tapped Raider's shoulder, and with one last glance in Kira's direction disappeared into the shadows surrounding the containers.

Kira's nose burned as she shook her head at Raider again.

This wasn't necessary. They could deal with these people together.

Raider's eyes were suspiciously wet as he gave her a bittersweet smile and touched his chest over his heart.

No, he wasn't doing this. Not for her.

Kira reached for her *ki,* summoning every bit she could. The desperate pull caused her *ki* to sputter and flame out.

It was like trying to suck an ocean through a straw in a second, only to have the straw collapse under the stress.

A tear ran down her cheek as she clawed at her inhibitor. If she could just get it off.

"Kira, I forgive you." A roguish grin split Raider's face. "For real this time."

There was no time to stop him as he broke cover, standing tall. His expression was carefree, as if the danger never even registered.

Confused, Niland stopped his advance.

"My father always told me arrogance will destroy even the most powerful of men." Raider took a long look at Niland's companions. "I hate to admit that man got anything right. It really burns my ass, you understand?"

Niland ignored the question as he drew his blade.

Raider heaved a sigh. "Like really bad. To the point I want to dig out my brain so I don't have to think about it."

Niland cocked his head. "You talk too much."

Raider winked at him. "I'll let you in on a little secret. There's a reason for that."

The blood drained out of Niland's face as he sucked in a breath to warn his fellow oshota.

Too late.

Red sniped from the shadows, cutting one of the oshota in half despite the protection of his synth armor.

Finn dropped into their midst.

Raider let out a battle cry, barreling forward.

Kira dug her nails into the flesh of her palms, sheer willpower the only thing keeping her in place. The hardest thing in this world had never been the pain and suffering she'd survived; it was watching someone else sacrifice themselves in her stead.

It was something so anathema to the core of who she was that it felt like her soul was being torn asunder to stand by and do nothing.

It wasn't the first time she'd experienced this.

She'd been here many times before. The mission took precedence—every time.

Only, unlike then, there were no orders, and the objective was personal.

Don't spit on their sacrifice, Kira told herself.

It took a considerable amount of discipline to force herself to slink away like the basest of cowards, bypassing the fierce battle and using the containers as cover.

Kira reached the edge of the shipping yard when she stopped abruptly, staring at the man blocking her path.

"I don't suppose you'd let me call in my favor," Kira tried as Lorcan stepped out of the shadows.

Even as she spoke, she knew the chances of that happening were zero. His presence here said he had already made peace with the idea of betraying his own people. No amount of personal honor would affect that.

Kira's weight shifted as she prepared to attack.

She never got the chance. A whip of *ki* split the air, too fast for her to even react.

She didn't even have time to brace for the inevitable pain.

A sharp bark of agony came from behind her.

Lorcan's stare was enigmatic even as mirth tugged at his lips. "Consider us even."

"Only if you don't hurt Finn or Raider," she said.

She could already tell Lorcan was different from these others. That whip of *ki* had come too fast for her to dodge. If he'd wanted to, he could have ended her right then and there.

"You should hurry, or you'll be too late."

Kira couldn't move, an unknown pressure making it hard to breathe.

"I wish you luck," he whispered, his passage revealing several bodies strewn behind him, all wearing the synth armor of House Remie.

She bit her lip and whirled.

The shipping yard was empty. Lorcan gone.

The only thing remaining that pointed to the fact he'd once been there was the body of the Tuann who'd tried to attack her from behind.

His eyes stared unseeing up at the ceiling, the edges of the gaping wound on in chest still glowing from the heat of the whip.

A clatter to her right made Kira look up.

Elise stared at her in surprise, Jin held in her hands.

"Elise," Kira started.

Elise's eyes dropped to the body of a Tuann from House Remie where it lay dead at Kira's feet. Her eyes widened and she spun, darting away.

"Stop, Elise!" Kira shouted, before rolling her eyes at herself.

Like the woman would listen in this kind of situation. Kira certainly wouldn't.

With a muttered curse and a glance in Finn and Raider's direction, Kira gave chase. Sometimes there was no choice but to trust in your companions.

This right here was why she'd tried so hard not to get anyone else wrapped up in this business.

These kinds of decisions were the sort to haunt you later. She hated the idea of sacrificing anyone, yet here she was doing exactly that.

Kira gritted her teeth and reached for more speed.

Elise rounded a shipping container, Kira fast on her heels.

Elise fled through a small gap before leaping onto the top of another pallet. Kira grimly followed.

Abruptly, they burst onto the docks.

To their left, a cavernous opening led into space, the battle being fought outside visible.

A walkway extended as far the eye could see, ramps branching off it leading to the ships nestled on either side.

Kira sprinted after Elise. If Elise made it to her ship, it was game over.

Kira narrowed the gap between them.

Just a little bit more.

Now.

Kira leapt, tackling Elise hard enough that she lost her grip on Jin.

They hit the ground hard and rolled. The walkway disappearing under them.

They fell, coming apart.

Kira hit the deck on her side, the landing knocking the breath out of her. Pain spread through her as she blinked at the ten-foot drop above her.

The belly of a ship blocked her view of the ceiling.

They'd rolled off the walkway and landed in one of the berths.

She lifted her head, seeing the landing gear of the ship.

With a groan, she flipped onto her stomach. From the quickly growing pain, Kira knew the boost Alexander had given her was wearing off.

She needed to finish this before it was entirely gone.

Elise was in the middle of crawling back onto the walkway as Kira forced herself to her feet.

She leapt, snagging the edge of walkway and pulling herself up as Elise stood.

Kira snapped out a kick, sending Elise sprawling.

"You've never beaten me in a foot race," Kira told her. "What made you think that had changed?"

Elise crab-walked away from Kira.

The bittersweet pull of regret mixed with love and guilt was gone. Kira felt dead inside as Elise pulled herself to standing, watching Kira warily.

Kira should have felt hurt with the way the woman she'd once considered a sister was looking at her—like she was a venomous snake.

Instead, she felt nothing but emptiness.

Elise yanked a knife from her boot.

Kira reached out, merciless as she grabbed Elise's hand and twisted. "Don't play with me, Elise. You know I'll win."

There was a crack as Kira broke Elise's wrist.

She watched dispassionately as Elise fell to her knees with a cry. Her head sagged, her hair covering her face as she cradled her wrist.

"That's always been your problem, Nixxy." Elise raised her head and glared at Kira through her hair. "You're sentimental. It makes you do stupid things—like fall into simple traps."

Elise raised her other hand, hitting a button on the palm-sized device that she'd kept concealed until now.

Agony stole the breath in Kira's lungs as she doubled over.

Elise rose. "How stupid of you. Did you really think it was chance you stumbled onto me here?"

Kira was too preoccupied with the pain to respond. White hot, it hollowed out her insides, leaving behind nothing but ash.

A scream ripped from her.

"Poor, poor Kira. You fought so hard only to fail in the end."

Kira moaned as strange runes materialized on the skin of her arms as if an invisible hand wrote them. A pale purple-blue light emanated from them.

She covered one with a hand, fear coating her throat.

Primus.

Her primus was trying to rise.

"I see you understand what is happening." Elise held the device up to admire. "Nifty little toy, isn't it? Something the masters developed. I'm told a forced shift to primus is quite painful."

Kira curled in on herself, trying to force her primus down. There were too many civilians around, and no one to help her contain the damage if she let it out.

Right now, she couldn't sense any rationality in her other half. Just pain and fury.

It would slaughter anything and everything in its rampage. Not just the enemy but allies too.

Elise knelt and petted Kira's head. "Look at you trying so hard."

The primus bashed itself against an invisible barrier. Every failure to escape resulting in further madness.

"I'll let you in on a little secret." Elise reached down to touch the inhibitor Kira still wore. "Repressing the primus leads to insanity followed by an extremely agonizing death. But don't worry, Nixxy. Our masters won't let it get that far."

Elise stood. "My orders were to start a war between any of the three races."

Kira struggled to think as her very body started rebelling against her.

"Your little stunt during the semifinals may have saved the life of the Tuann emperor's son and the niece of the Haldeel royal. You may even have delayed the war we'd planned to start between them—for now." Elise lifted a foot and pressed it against Kira's hand, pushing down.

Kira barely felt the pressure, too preoccupied keeping her primus and *ki* from rioting.

"That's okay though. The Tsavitee have plenty of backup plans. As we speak, the androids the humans brought are launching an all-out assault against the Haldeel. Do you think the Haldeel will keep a race who betrays them around?" Elise's grin was menacing. "I don't."

Kira shivered, holding in her scream as her skin attempted to split apart.

"The Consortium's alliance with the Haldeel will fall. The deaths of your Curs on Rothchild only delayed the inevitable. Soon, things will go back to the way they were."

"What do they want?" Kira managed to force out.

Elise's looked down at her with a detached expression. "What else? Total domination."

"Cliché," Kira gritted out.

"Yeah. I will say they're quite curious as to how you managed to create a soul bound that retained its sanity. They have so many plans for the two of you."

Elise's smile was the last thing Kira saw as her consciousness faded.

* * *

Graydon grabbed an android's arm, ripping it away from its body and tossing it to the side. Next, he stabbed upward with his en-blade.

It entered beneath the android's jaw, spearing into the "brain".

Sparks flew, but the light in its eyes didn't die. Graydon channeled his *ki* into the blade, ripping it out as the android blew apart.

Mist rose from its body, dissipating in the next second.

Graydon's lip curled at the pathetic creature.

It seemed the Tsavitee's masters knew no limits, trespassing into the realm of life and death.

This was the reason for the Tuann's hatred of them. This was why the Tuann had strict rules when it came to artificial intelligences and why they didn't trust humans.

Binding an unwilling soul to such an existence could result in a powerful army at the mercy of their creator's will, but it was also dangerous and abhorrent.

There were going to be consequences because of this attack.

The Consortium thought they were restricted before; they had no idea how merciless the Tuann could really be.

It wasn't out of the realm of possibility for the emperor to decide to wipe them out because of this—or at the very least knock them back into an age where space exploration was nothing but a dream.

It had happened before to those the Tuann perceived a threat.

Torvald dropped the body of a Tsavitee lower form at Graydon's feet. Horns jutted from the creature's forehead and it had an underbite that exposed inch-long fangs meant for ripping the flesh of its enemy from their bones.

Torvald stepped over the creature with a look of distaste. "This has grown quite tedious."

In answer, Graydon buried his blade in the chest of a Tsavitee who had thought to take advantage of Graydon's distraction by attacking his back.

Blood spewed as Graydon yanked his blade out. The Tsavitee dropped to its knees, falling face first on the ground.

"Agreed," Graydon said, taking a moment to observe the battle.

The stench of blood and smoke clogged the air.

Around them, his oshota continued to fight, the humans providing cover where they could.

Finn's presence flooded Graydon's mind.

"Report," Graydon ordered.

"We're betrayed. House Remie has joined the enemy. I don't know how many other Houses have followed their lead."

Grief and resignation touched Torvald's face. There could only be one fate for such a House—complete annihilation.

It was a step the Tuann didn't often contemplate, saved for the most egregious of transgressions.

For a House to ally with the enemy like this and endanger their peace with the Haldeel, they would have to deal decisively to prevent other Houses from following suit.

Neither Torvald nor Graydon relished the coming task, but they'd ensure its completion for the sake of the Tuann empire.

They'd leave no weaknesses for their old enemies to exploit.

"And Kira?"

"She's gone after the woman. We're holding the line for the moment."

"Do you need reinforcements?"

There was a grunt and a tendril of pain that Finn locked down almost as soon as it invaded the link. "It wouldn't hurt."

"I'll see what I can do," Graydon told him. "Send me your location."

Getting someone to Finn and Kira would be hard.

The fighting from the banquet had spilled into the rest of the station. Most of the civilians had already fled, leaving only Graydon's oshota, Himoto and a few of his people, along with the Haldeel guards who'd gotten caught in the conflict.

They were holding their own, but if Graydon abandoned the line to go to Kira, there was a chance they would fall.

The primal part of him urged him to do exactly that. The only things that kept him fighting here was the oath he'd taken to the emperor and the knowledge Kira would hate him if he let others die in favor of saving her.

The solution then was to kill every single enemy between him and her.

Noting the cruel twist of Graydon's lips, Torvald switched his grip on his en-blade. "Youngsters these days are so passionate."

"Will you do it?" Graydon asked.

Ki swirled around Torvald, building in size and intensity until it was a massive ball. Torvald plunged his blade into the floor. Acting as a conduit, the blade channeled the *ki* directly into their surroundings.

Torvald's eyes held a faint glow as he bared his teeth. "I've protected our immediate area."

Graydon rolled his shoulders, opening himself to the *ki* inside. Without Torvald, this would have been dangerous, likely causing irreparable damage to Almaluk.

Color drained out of the world as black *ki* condensed around Graydon's hands. An invisible force fought him as he pushed his hands closer together, his arms shaking from the effort.

With a roar, he sank all his strength into those last few inches.

Black *ki* shot out in a wave.

It snuffed out the glow of life in the androids and they dropped like puppets whose strings had been cut. The Tsavitee fared no better. The wave cleaving them in two.

Graydon fell, Amila catching him before he could hit the deck. Noor stepped toward him as the rest of the humans stared in stunned disbelief. Only Jace and Himoto acted like it was nothing out of the ordinary, understandable given their close relation to Kira.

"Graydon," Noor said, concern on his face.

"I'm fine." Exhaustion from burning all that *ki* pulled on Graydon as Amila steadied him.

Distracted, none of them noticed the way Kent's expression deadened or the foam that spilled out of his mouth until too late.

"Take cover," Himoto yelled suddenly.

There was barely any time to react as an explosion tore Kent apart.

Amila pushed Graydon down, her body covering his. Noor moved to intercept the blast, his hastily erected *ki* shield crumpling like paper.

He took the brunt of the explosion as the ground rocked.

Graydon struggled up, careful to support Amila's body as those around them started picking themselves up off the floor—those who could still move at least.

"Amila?" he asked, fearing the worst.

His oshota moaned as she shifted. "I'm alive."

They both stilled as they caught sight of Noor's body at the same time. The explosive device Kent had installed in his torso was effective, shredding Noor's synth armor.

The last time Graydon had seen anything like that had been during a battle with the pirates that plagued the Tuann's borders.

The grief and sorrow in Graydon was reflected in the face of the oshota around them.

To lose any of them was always difficult. More so when the enemy used such a cowardly tactic.

Perhaps if Graydon hadn't drained his *ki* and reacted in time or if the explosion had happened a few feet further away.

Either scenario would have led to a vastly different outcome.

"Those who can move take a headcount," Himoto ordered from where he propped himself up against the wall.

The admiral's face was unnaturally white; blood stained the ground around him.

The two humans who'd been tasked with guarding Kent were dead, their remains scattered in several pieces.

"The rest of you, quit gawping and fortify our position," Himoto ground out as Jace went to his side.

Himoto tried waving the other man away. Jace didn't listen, breaking open a first aid tube containing coagulant which he sprinkled on Himoto's wounds.

"You need to go. All of you," Himoto told Graydon and his oshota.

Graydon didn't answer. The inside of his head was cold and silent. There would be a reckoning for Noor's death later, but for now he had compartmentalized.

Noor gave his life for Graydon and Amila. Graydon wouldn't throw that sacrifice away by wasting the gift on rage and revenge.

The only way they survived was by staying clear headed.

The sound of more enemies echoed along the corridors of the station.

"This isn't their final game," Himoto said, holding out his hand to Jace.

The rear admiral glared at it before giving in to Himoto's expectations and helping the admiral up.

"They didn't bring enough forces to take over the planet and station," Himoto said when he was standing again. Pain carved grooves into his face.

Around them, those humans who had survived were already lifting tables and anything they could get their hands on to block the avenues of attack.

"This is all just smoke and mirrors designed to distract you from their true objective," Himoto said. "You can't let them win. Go. Kira needs you."

"You won't make it," Graydon said.

Already the other man could barely stand.

Himoto's smile was more of a grimace than anything. "Maybe not, but humans had a hand in this mess. We need to help clean it up."

Himoto's eyes were steady in a way that said he'd already made his peace with the possibility of death.

He didn't fear its advance. He would meet it on equal footing come what may. He wouldn't run. He wouldn't shirk his responsibilities.

There was nobility in the way he held himself.

"He won't be alone," Jace said. "My people and I will stay with him."

Himoto tried to glare before giving up, too tired to expend energy on pointless things. "I don't remember inviting you to this party."

"Try to stop me, old man."

Graydon's hesitation lasted only a moment. Time was of the essence. Finn's last message made Kira and her situation seem dire. He couldn't afford to linger here.

Graydon's gaze paused on Noor's body where Amila knelt beside it. Her head was bowed and one hand rested on his chest.

Sorrow and grief echoed through their bond. All of his oshotas' bonds.

Graydon's throat grew tight as loss pulled at him despite the urgency of the situation.

"We'll take care of him," Himoto promised.

"I'm trusting you to do exactly that," Graydon forced out, starting to turn away.

The thought of leaving Noor to strangers wrenched at him with a sense of wrongness. It went against everything Graydon believed in to not see Noor to a proper resting place, but war wasn't kind. It didn't leave you the time to mourn.

Sometimes you paid your respect to the dead by surviving.

Today he'd repay Noor's sacrifice by ensuring Kira lived and the Tsavitee didn't get what they wanted.

Resolve fed his anger, burning like a banked fire in his chest.

"Tell Kira—" Himoto cut himself off. His shoulders rose as he took a deep breath. When he spoke again, he was the admiral. "Take care of her."

Graydon stared after Himoto as he limped away supported by Jace, finally understanding what he hadn't before.

Jace's eyes caught his as he turned away. The human inclined his chin in a gesture of respect.

"I understand what Roake's heir sees in them now," Torvald said from Graydon's side. "They possess unexpected depths."

"Yes." Graydon turned on his heel. "With me."

Liara looked uncertainly between the two groups before taking a deep breath. "We'll stay."

Torvald's eyes narrowed, but he didn't move to interfere.

"Are you sure?" Graydon asked.

Liara offered him a faint smile. "She cares for these humans, and they need help. I would be letting her down if I abandoned them."

She moved toward where the humans were fortifying their defenses.

"Let's go," Graydon ordered before racing in the opposite direction.

I'm coming. Wait for me, Kira.

* * *

Curled on her side in the fetal position, Kira fought to stay present as her mind threatened to buckle. All that was in her line of sight were her clenched hands and Elise's legs.

Unable to move, Kira could only listen as there was a pained grunt above her.

Elise dropped to her knees, the light in her eyes dimming. There was a gaping hole in her chest the size of a fist that didn't belong there.

Kira barely had time to react before Elise toppled onto her side, her head bouncing off the deck.

A person wearing black, calf-high boots, the kind racers tended to favor because of the support they provided to their ankles, stepped over Elise's prone body.

She walked toward Kira and knelt beside her. The thunk of metal against metal told Kira she had set something down outside her line of sight.

The stranger reached over, rolling Kira onto her back.

Even through the madness courting Kira's thoughts, she recognized the individual. This was the waverunner from the semifinal race, the one who'd nearly knocked her off her board. The person who felt familiar and strange at the same time.

Her faceplate reflected Kira's image. A sense of dread filled her as she watched the strange violet lines that formed her markings crawl up her neck and across her face.

The stranger reached up, removing her helmet and setting it to the side.

Familiar eyes met Kira's.

"Little sister, you've gotten yourself into quite the predicament this time," Elise said in a gentle voice.

This Elise was different than Kira remembered. Sorrow and the pain of time had chiseled lines into that once familiar face. Her eyes were haunted, and even when smiling, she seemed sad.

"E-Elise." Tears squeezed out of the corner of her eyes.

Elise stroked Kira's forehead. "Yes."

"You're really you," Kira managed to get out.

Elise's eyes glistened. "In the flesh, pippy bunny."

A broken sound came from Kira.

The third code.

It was really her.

"Wh-where have you been?"

Elise continued to brush her fingers across Kira's forehead, the movement soothing some of the agony currently splitting Kira apart.

"Here and there." Elise shook her head at Kira. "Don't ask. I won't explain."

Kira's back bowed at a new surge of agony.

Elise reached for the inhibitor cuff, ignoring Kira's moan of warning. "I've never deserved you, my dearest."

The cuff unlocked under her fingers, falling away from Kira's wrist.

The barrier that had kept the weight of her *ki* from crushing her as she recuperated on Ta Da'an disappeared.

Kira screamed as soul's breath surged up from her core, burning a fiery path through her *ki* channels.

"Shh," Elise soothed. "Your body is adjusting to the sudden influx. This'll pass soon. Ride the wave, little sister."

A man's legs moved into view behind Elise. "You can't stay. They'll be here soon. We have to go before that."

Her thoughts swamped with a pain that threatened to incinerate her,

Kira barely registered the fact he spoke in Tsavitee.

Elise looked to the side and nodded. "I know."

The tendons in Kira's neck strained as her body was pulled tight, her muscles clenching so hard she feared they'd snap her bones.

Cold spread from where Elise touched her, taking away some of the pain and letting Kira think again.

"Stay," Kira begged.

"I can't," Elise confided. "They need me."

There were people here who needed her too.

Elena. Raider. Kira.

Elise leaned forward, pressing her forehead against Kira's. "I can't abandon them. They remind me too much of us."

"Time is up," the man said in an emotionless voice.

Elise straightened, her gaze going distant. A misty smile touched her face. "Don't worry, Kira. You won't be alone long. He's coming for you. By the way, I approve of him."

Elise picked up the object she'd set aside and placed it against Kira's chest.

"Jin will wake up soon," Elise promised.

If Kira hadn't recognized that round shape as Jin, she never would have known it was him. His spot in her mind was unnervingly quiet.

Elise dropped a kiss on Kira's forehead. "My daughter is so beautiful. Thank you for protecting her."

Kira sobbed as Elise rose. "Don't. Please."

The prospect of being abandoned by her again was more than she could bear.

Kira had never begged before—but for Elise, for Elena, there wasn't a lot she wouldn't do.

Elise paused; her expression pained.

Finally catching sight of Elise's companion, Kira's breath caught. The man towered over Elise, dwarfing her with his massive frame. His skin was as dark as the void and there were symbols etched in red on his face and arms. Horns curled up proudly from his head.

He'd be considered handsome if one was willing to overlook the fact that he was a Tsavitee general.

Vivid yellow eyes watched Kira dispassionately. To him, she was of no more significance than a bug trying to survive.

"I have to, Kira. I made a promise," Elise said as the man took her hand to draw her away. "You can't save me but you can help me. Just keep your promise to the changeling."

Summoning the strength from somewhere, Kira flipped onto her stomach to crawl after Elise. The motion caused Jin to roll off her.

Reflexively, Kira caught him before he could fall over the edge of the walkway.

When she looked up again, Elise and the general were already gone.

She was alone. Again.

Despair crashed over Kira. She didn't try to stop the tears or the grief as she sank onto the deck, her strength deserting her.

She was alone again.

* * *

A long time later, Odin's repeated hails brought her back to herself.

"Kira, answer me. Damn it, Kira, the kid is going crazy."

"I'm here."

Kira's throat felt raw and dry as if the outpouring of emotion had sucked the energy out of her.

"Finally," Odin said in relief. "Did you get Jin?"

The walkway under her body vibrated.

Kira turned her head, watching as a Tsavitee war party stamped toward her. Infantry drones, not so affectionately nicknamed demons, made up the ranks.

They spotted her.

The big one in the center barked several guttural commands in Tsavitee.

Would you look at that? The lambs had delivered themselves to the slaughter.

"Kira?" Odin asked.

Kira didn't answer, pulling herself to her feet. Runes wrote themselves on her skin as she raised her face to the ceiling.

She relaxed the stranglehold she'd somehow managed to retain over her inner monster. Her primus surged up from the deep.

* * *

The aftermath of a carnage confronted Graydon and his oshota when they arrived at the location Finn had indicated.

Streaks of blood smeared the hulls of nearby ships. Headless torsos rested precariously on the edge of the walkway, and a dismembered limb waved at Graydon from the nose of a ship.

"This is—" Solal started before trailing off.

"I finally see why you're so taken with this woman." Torvald studied the massacre with a dispassionate gaze. "This level of blood thirst is terrifying in one so young."

Graydon didn't hear, his gaze already locked on the woman perched on the beams high above. Crouched up there, her enemies' blood coating her arms and streaked across her face, she resembled a nightmare.

Her skin was charcoal gray, violet runes scrolled all over it. Her eyes flashed in the same way an animal's would, catching the light and refracting it.

Abruptly, her gaze shifted from the slaughter to them, the weight of her regard oppressive.

Feeling as if he was in a dream, Graydon started toward her. He didn't care how this had happened. He was simply grateful she'd survived.

"Careful," Torvald warned. "I'm not sure what happened, but if she ever had control, it's gone now."

The primus was a double-edged sword. It was an ultimate weapon, but it was also a weakness.

They were nearly indestructible, graced with an insane amount of speed, power, and strength. The flip side lay in how easy it was to lose yourself in the form.

It was a creature that operated on instinct. Tuann history was littered with tragic tales of Tuann who couldn't control their primus and wound up killing those they loved as a result.

They were never more vulnerable than in the years after their first transformation. It took decades of rigorous training to exert their mind over their primus. It was one of the reasons a child with Kira's bloodlines wasn't released into the galaxy unrestricted.

The Tuann knew an uncontrolled primus would cut a wide and bloody swath through the universe before someone finally put it down.

Kira was still and calm at Graydon's approach. Not reacting even when he stopped beneath her and looked up.

"*Cheva nier*, you should come down from there," Graydon said in Tuann.

Kira's primus regarded him silently.

Graydon didn't look away as he lifted a hand toward her.

Between one second and the next, Kira disappeared.

Graydon grabbed the claws aimed at his throat, smiling at the expressionless primus. "I'm sorry I'm late."

The primus's eyes searched his. After a moment, a purr rumbled from her throat.

"Beautiful," the primus whispered in halting Tuann.

With a slow blink, it withdrew into Kira's mind, the runes on her body fading.

Kira sagged in his arms. "Did I kill any of ours?"

Graydon shook his head. "No."

Even if she had, he wouldn't tell her. There was some guilt she didn't need to live with.

"Jin?"

Graydon didn't answer for long seconds. "I haven't seen him."

Kira tensed as Torvald neared, his expression curious as he studied the woman in Graydon's arms. "Was this all your work?"

Kira looked around the docking bay with a blank expression. "Probably."

Torvald quirked an eyebrow at her. "You don't sound sure."

Kira rolled her head to look up at Graydon. "Should I be flattered or scared that the man you serve sees me as important enough to leave the battle to come to my rescue?"

Torvald's head tilted as he examined Kira with interest. "You're quite smart."

Her smile was humorless. "Or you're quite bad at hiding your identity."

Torvald let out a *hm*.

Before either of them could say anything else, the smell of burning flesh filled the air.

Torvald's frown was perplexed. "What is that?"

The oshota crouched defensively as the headless body of a Tsavitee jerked and danced. The center of his chest glowed red.

With a scream, a round shape burst through it.

Jin hovered several feet above the deck, panting. Covered in blood and other internal matter, he regarded them for several seconds.

"Is it over?"

Kira leaned her head on Graydon's shoulder. "Yeah, you missed it."

Jin spun, taking in the scene. Kira's primus hadn't just killed the Tsavitee. From the looks of things, she had toyed with them like a cat did a mouse, reveling in their pain and terror.

"Lost your temper, did you?"

Kira listed to the side, her eyes closing. "A little."

Graydon had had enough of restraining himself. Finally, he acted on the impulse that had been beating at him since the second he caught sight of Kira.

He swept her into his arms before carrying her toward his oshota.

The fact she didn't fight him told him how exhausted she was. A transition to primus always took a toll on the body. He couldn't imagine how much worse it would be after months of wearing an inhibitor.

A chill swept through Graydon at the realization of how close she'd come to burning herself out. An inhibitor was supposed to be removed in stages, allowing the body to readjust to the weight of its soul's breath. Her *ki* could have easily rebounded, especially after such a large output immediately after.

"Finn and Raider?"

Graydon pressed his lips against her forehead. "They're fine, but we lost Noor."

Kira tilted her head, her face saying she heard the bone-deep grief in that one statement.

"Oh, Graydon, I'm so sorry." She reached up, touching his cheek with a gentle caress.

Understanding reflected in her eyes. She'd lost more than her fair share of treasured companions. It never got any easier.

Graydon's voice was rough. "Me too."

Kira's silence acted as a balm, allowing him to process some of his grief.

"His ancestors would be proud he died in the same way he lived," Graydon finally said.

"Maybe so, but that doesn't make the pain of loss any less." Her thumb flitted along his jaw. "Or fix the guilt we feel over having survived."

Graydon pressed his forehead against hers, his arms squeezing her a little tighter. She got it without him having to say a word.

They stayed like that for several minutes, until Graydon finally drew back.

His eyes were reddened as he cleared his throat and changed the subject.

Kira was exhausted. Now wasn't the time for this.

As if her head was too heavy for her to hold up, she set it against his shoulders.

"I left some of ours to help Finn and Raider take care of the strays," Graydon said. "They should be here soon."

* * *

"I can walk," Kira said after resting against Graydon. She didn't bother opening her eyes, judging the act more trouble than it was worth.

"I'd almost like to see that." Graydon responded in a neutral voice. "Something tells me it would be highly amusing."

Kira cracked one eye and sent him a glare. He didn't think she could do it?

The way he kept his eyes focused on the others and the slight tilt to one side of his mouth said he found her adorable.

Hm. It seemed her glare needed work. It hadn't intimidated him at all.

She had to admit, it was good to see some of the strain in his features lighten.

She knew Noor's death wouldn't be so easily forgotten.

Grief was a many-tentacled monster. Just when you thought you'd reached the end, when you'd finally dealt with all its many faces, another tentacle would reach out to wrap you in a suffocating embrace from which escape seemed impossible.

For now, though, their banter told her Graydon would be okay. It didn't lessen what had happened, but it made it so he could get through it—at least for now.

From the direction of the shipping yard, Finn and Raider made their way slowly towards them.

Neither man had escaped the battle unscathed.

A burn mark on Raider's shoulder still oozed blood, and he had a giant bruise on one side of his face. Half of his pant leg had been ripped away.

Kira found it wrapped around Finn's thigh, staunching the blood from his wound.

Her oshota had a noticeable limp as he walked toward her, his face a mask of relief.

"What happened to you two?" Jin asked.

Finn stopped and glared at Jin unhappily. "Someone got themselves kidnapped and the rest of us had to go rescue them."

"Who?" Jin asked.

"You," he growled.

While the two were arguing, Raider's gaze landed on Elise's body. Shock and grief rendered him immobile.

In the next moment, he collapsed by the fake Elise's side.

Kira tapped Graydon's shoulder. "Down."

He gave her a sidelong look. "If you fall, I won't be happy."

"I'll keep that in mind," she told him.

And then she'd promptly forget it, she added silently.

Grudgingly, Graydon set her on her feet.

Kira wobbled but caught herself.

She moved to Raider's side where he knelt by Elise, touching his shoulder gently. They jerked as he tried to swallow down his sobs.

Kira crouched beside him. "Raider, it's not her. It's not Elise."

He met her eyes, his face ravaged by loss and grief. As far as Kira knew, Elise had been the only one Raider had ever loved. Dashed hope was almost worse than having no hope at all.

"What are you saying?" he asked.

Conscious of the number of people around them—the emperor in particular—Kira knew she had to phrase this carefully. For now.

"Think about it—why wouldn't she care that Elena was on that planet?" Kira asked.

She saw the struggle in Raider as his desire for this not to be Elise warred with the body before him.

"She might not have known," he said.

"She used House Remie to ambush us. She had to have some dealings with them. Wouldn't they have told her about the preteen with me? They saw Elena with me on multiple occasions. How could she not have known?" Seeing he was starting to think again, Kira inched closer. "Elena is the answer to years of research. Why would they risk destroying that?"

The answer was they wouldn't.

If the Tsavitee and their masters had any inkling of who Elena was related to, they would have sacrificed even Kira and Jin to obtain her.

Kira leaned closer, dropping her voice so only he could hear. "She didn't know the third code."

Raw emotion stared at Kira through Raider's eyes.

She nodded again. Now he saw it.

Shouts came from Amila and the rest of the oshota as they closed protectively around Kira and Graydon.

A ship burst through the membrane of the dock seconds later. It scraped along the tops of the landed ships as it swung wide, its cannons pointing toward them.

"Auntie, your reinforcements have arrived," Elena yelled through the ship's speakers.

Kira blinked dumbly at the *Wanderer,* where it hovered menacingly over them. "What is she doing here?"

Moving quickly, Raider snagged a nearby Tsavitee body, dumping it onto the fake Elise to hide her face.

Finished, he regarded the ship with a bit of humor. "I'm beginning to be grateful she's been your responsibility all these years."

Kira didn't have time for a sharp retort as Auralyn and Wren dropped from the belly of the ship. They landed in a crouch; their en-blades drawn.

Torvald lifted a hand and waved. "Welcome to the party."

Seeing him and Graydon, the two momentarily froze before relaxing. They straightened from their crouch at the same time.

Kira stood and glared at the bridge of the ship. "I thought I told you to stay put."

"Um—I thought you could use the help," Elena said guiltily.

Kira raised her eyebrows and then swept her gaze over the many dead bodies surrounding her with a pointed look.

"My bad. I'll be over here."

The *Wanderer* retreated, landing on the end of the walkway several feet away.

Kira glared at her *seon'yer* and Auralyn. "How did she get you two to agree to this?"

Wren straightened, not deigning to answer before he moved toward Torvald.

Auralyn's murderous expression thawed. "She's quite persuasive when she wants to be."

Kira scrubbed at her forehead. "She gets that from her mother."

Reaching Torvald and Graydon, Wren didn't salute, but judging from the stiff way he carried himself, Kira could tell he wanted to.

"The forces we had waiting outside the system have arrived along with ships from the Haldeel and the Consortium," he reported.

"They're late," Torvald grumbled.

Wren remained composed as he finished relaying his information. "They've targeted the Tsavitee warships. The royal's guards have begun sweeping Almaluk to dispose of the last of their forces."

"Tierni's okay then?" Kira asked.

Wren's attention shifted to her. "As far as I know. Several of her guard, including the one you know, took injuries. A few are dead. The humans will face repercussions for this attack."

"The Tuann were part of it," Kira said.

Graydon shook his head. "House Remie and its allies only attacked you as far as we know."

"A case could be made that it was an internal matter among the Tuann," Torvald said idly.

From his expression, Kira could tell that was exactly the argument they'd make to the Haldeel, leaving the Consortium out on the ledge by themselves.

Raider's hands clenched, his disquiet mirroring Kira's.

They didn't know all that happened, but judging by the androids involvement, Zepher and the faction supporting them likely had a lot to do with the attack.

As distant as her relationship had become with the Consortium and humans, Kira had no interest in watching them fall.

Even if there weren't still some among their ranks she cared about, she felt they were essential for the coming war.

A war the Tsavitee had just demonstrated they were already preparing for.

Kira stiffened as Lorcan wandered into the shipping dock.

"Graydon," she warned quietly as his oshota let the man pass. "He was with Remie when they attacked us."

Hearing her words, Lorcan's smile widened. "Such a stiff greeting for someone who saved your ass."

Kira's mouth snapped shut as her hands flexed. Reaching for her primus or *ki* was out, but that didn't mean she couldn't do some damage if needed.

Graydon held a hand in front of her to stop her. "It's fine. He was acting under our orders."

Lorcan made a kissy face at her before sauntering toward Torvald. He slung his arm over the bigger man's shoulders before turning to say several things into his ear.

Torvald nodded several times before Lorcan dropped his arm and sauntered off.

Kira watched it all, feeling a sense of disconnection.

"He's a Face," she said softly.

A clandestine Face from the looks of things.

She knew he reminded her of Graydon. She just hadn't been able to put her finger on why.

Graydon didn't confirm or deny, instead changing the subject.

"Your Himoto volunteered to stay behind and provide cover so we could reach you," Graydon said after a beat. "The Haldeel will take his sacrifice into account before making any decisions."

The somberness in Graydon's expression told her even if they didn't, the Tuann would.

Kira didn't have to ask how serious the situation had been. Graydon's expression and the rest already told her.

She didn't know how to handle the thought of Himoto in danger. It wasn't the first time, but a cold feeling in the pit of her stomach told her this time was different.

"Liara and your rear admiral are with Himoto," Graydon said. "Your admiral was wounded, but it's possible he survived."

But not probable, Kira knew, reading his tone.

A feeling of inevitability filled her. She'd always known one of them would go out this way.

Funny thing—she thought it would be her.

Kira stared outside the docking membrane, watching the battle rage as reinforcements rushed into the fray. The advantage the Tsavitee had was eliminated as the ships cooperated, working together to turn the tide.

A Tsavitee cruiser turned, preparing to flee.

The rest refused to let it. Several split off from the main pack to harry its sides.

It wasn't long until they'd dealt critical damage to the ship. Seconds later, unable to defend against the sustained power of the allied ships, the cruiser exploded.

The surviving allied ships turned their attention to the remaining ship.

"What now?" Raider asked, joining her and Graydon as they watched the destruction.

Kira didn't answer for several long minutes.

"When I woke up from my coma all those years ago, I could never understand why I couldn't accept it was over. Now I know." Kira's gaze moved to Graydon's. "It wasn't over. Everything was simply on hold."

The memories of all they'd lost the last time they'd fought a war shadowed his eyes as Raider looked at her with grim resignation.

"And now they're back," he said softly.

"Yes, they are," Graydon said grimly.

His fingers touched hers. She caught his hand and held it tightly.

As she looked up at him, she caught a promise in his eyes. One thing was different now. She wouldn't face what was coming on her own.

She couldn't even if she wanted to. The Tuann wouldn't let her.

TWENTY-FIVE

"WE'RE READY FOR you now," the Haldeel attendant informed Kira when she made no attempt to walk into the room.

"Thank you," Kira said, backing up the words with a gesture of gratitude.

Knowing she couldn't stand out here any longer without drawing attention, Kira steeled herself to enter.

She stopped as soon as she crossed the threshold, a shuddering breath leaving her at the sight of the still figure lying on the bed.

The backs of her eyes tingled and her nose stung as she fought the emotions that wanted to rise.

"You stupid old man," she whispered.

Himoto lay unmoving in the bed, his body barely forming a bump in the sheets. Like this, the strength of his charisma and the personality that defined him was gone, leaving behind the shell of who he'd been.

The fight for Almaluk had been hard fought—both over the planet of Jettie and within the station.

Thousands had died.

The planet was the hardest hit, but the station suffered losses too. Among them, her mentor. The father figure who had kept Kira anchored when the rigors of this universe threatened to wash her away.

Gingerly, Kira approached the bed, stopping next to it. She bent her head, her hands trembling before she clenched them into fists.

Himoto would have chastised her for her lack of control if he'd still been alive.

She could almost hear his voice as he said, "Kira-chan, such emotion is unnecessary."

The tears she'd thought she'd forced down made a reappearance. She sniffed before slipping her hand into Himoto's.

She flinched at the cold feel of his skin.

"I'm so mad at you. I'm not ready to say goodbye. There was still so much left to say."

Kira's expression crumpled before she steeled herself again.

"I always hated it when you cited the greater good, but I guess this time I can't argue." Kira scrubbed a hand over her cheeks, wiping away the tears that kept falling without her permission. "Your actions preserved the alliance. If you were here, I know you'd say that the tradeoff was worth it."

Kira shook her head, her voice clogged with tears. "I can't bring myself to agree with you, though."

The door opened behind Kira, and a woman stepped into the room.

The stranger came to an abrupt stop, her gaze lingering on where Kira still held Himoto's hand. "I'm sorry. I thought the room was empty."

To Kira's surprise, instead of excusing herself, the woman stepped forward, moving to the other side of Himoto's bed.

Her appearance was tidy, with her hair pulled into a sleek bun. She wore the formal dress uniform of the Consortium.

Her face was small and delicate and carried the stamp of an Asian heritage.

Kira's gaze dropped to the name and rank emblazoned on the woman's chest. Lieutenant Himoto.

"You're his daughter," Kira said finally.

The woman hummed in agreement. "And you're the woman my father raised instead of me."

A flash of discomfort crossed Kira's face.

The woman waved a hand in dismissal. "Don't take that to heart. I made my peace with who he is a long time ago."

Despite the seemingly harsh words, the lieutenant's hands were gentle as she tucked the blanket more firmly around him.

"Mom always said heroes made for shitty parents. She was right." The woman's expression was introspective as she gazed at her father.

Kira remained quiet, not knowing how to respond to that.

She'd always known Himoto cared for her but that he cared for the common good more. It was a hard truth to accept when she was younger.

The lieutenant's eyes met Kira's as she gave her a crooked smile. "He left me something to give to you. A last message, if you will."

Kira stayed silent, reluctantly taking the coin the woman handed her.

She rubbed her thumb against the raised ridges, realizing it was a data storage unit.

The lieutenant aimed a brief nod Kira's way and moved toward the door. "I'll leave you alone."

Feeling off-balance, Kira stared at Himoto's still form.

Gathering her courage, she put her thumb on the top of the coin and pressed, allowing it to read her thumbprint.

Himoto's voice filled the air. "Kira-chan, if you've received this, it means I'm either dead or incapacitated and can no longer protect you from the shadows. There are many things you don't know from all those years ago. My appearance the day you escaped the camp was no accident. The Consortium always knew of its presence. I was the liaison appointed so they wouldn't get their hands dirty."

Kira stumbled from the bed, collapsing into a chair.

"The Tsavitee told us they could help humans evolve. At the time, we didn't know how they planned to do that. I'd like to think I would never have allowed it if I knew they would use children, but part of me knows the temptation of a super-soldier would have corrupted my honor. Putting a face on suffering always changes things. I'm not sure I would have been strong enough to do the right thing if I hadn't met you. My greatest regret in this life is what happened to you and the rest. I've spent the years since trying to rectify my mistakes."

Kira pressed a hand to her chest, trying to stem the emotions boiling inside. She'd be lying to herself if she said she hadn't ever thought of this possibility.

His appearance that day had been too fortuitous and coincidental.

She'd overlooked it because of how sincere he'd been helping her move forward afterward.

"I killed everyone I could find who had a link to that place. I also know you've located several other camps in the years since. I hid your movements from those in the Consortium who would have tried to stop you. Make no mistake, Kira—they would have killed you if they found out."

Himoto's voice underlined his sincerity.

"On this disk is everything I've compiled over the last decade. I've never been able to find the mastermind no matter how hard I look. Perhaps you will do better. Good luck, daughter. I'm proud of the person you've become."

Kira sat for hours beside Himoto's bedside trying to reconcile everything he'd told her.

Finally, she stood, putting the coin in her pocket and stepping outside.

She paused when she found Jace sitting on the floor, his back against the wall. He looked like he hadn't slept since the battle, his face gaunt as ghosts haunted his thoughts.

Kira crossed the hallway, sliding down into a sitting position next to him.

"They made me his successor," Jace confided after several minutes of silence.

Kira grunted. She'd figured as much.

"I don't know how to do this job like him." The look in Jace's eyes was raw and full of pain.

Kira set one hand on his knee and shook it. "You don't. You do it like you."

His snicker was soft.

"How are things?" Kira asked.

"Do you mean me or the alliance?" he returned.

Kira lifted a shoulder. "Whichever one you prefer to focus on."

"I'm surviving. Came out without a scratch, thanks to the admiral. He took the charge of a demon that was meant for me." Jace's grin was halfhearted. "Killed it too."

Kira leaned her head against the wall. "The old man was always a bit of a badass."

This time Kira caught a note of genuine amusement in Jace's laugh.

"You could say that again." Jace shook his head. "As for the alliance—it's holding by a thread. The Haldeel is giving the Consortium the chance to root out the dissenters, but one stumble and we're done."

Jace flipped his hand as if dumping something on the ground. "What a situation to inherit."

Kira punched him on the shoulder and stood. "You can handle it. Just ask yourself what I would do and do the opposite."

"Don't be a stranger," Jace said as she prepared to leave.

She held up a hand. "I don't think I could even if I wanted to."

Realization crossed his face. "That's right. You're still part of the Consortium."

This time, real laughter shook his shoulders as Kira stalked away.

"Don't push me or you'll regret it," she said over her shoulder.

"I'm not worried; I'll make sure to end the call before you finish gloating," he called after her.

Kira shook her head as she walked out of the medbay and headed toward the part of the station set aside for the Tuann contingent.

She felt worn and threadbare, the emotions leaving her raw inside. For the first time, the thought of another war didn't leave her feeling paralyzed.

Whatever came, she'd meet it head on. She couldn't let fear of loss keep her isolated anymore. It was time to gather her allies—not that she thought they'd give her much choice.

She'd almost reached the section given to the Tuann as temporary quarters when a disturbance pulled her from her distraction. Jin darted toward her in the commotion.

"What's going on?" Kira asked.

Before he could answer, she caught sight of Selene being led through the halls, a phalanx of oshota surrounding her, Baran at their lead.

Kira blocked their path. "What are you doing with her?"

Selene's expression was serene as she shook her head slightly, telling

Kira not to do anything foolish.

Baran's eyes held sympathy as he met her gaze. "She is Tuann. We are bringing her home."

"You can't take her," Kira said through gritted teeth.

"Kira," Graydon said from behind her.

Kira's shoulders rose as she took a deep breath before facing him. "You promised me."

At that, Graydon moved in close, lowering his voice. "Remember what I said before. Only if they don't expose themselves in a way we can't hide. Her orphanage came under attack by a Tsavitee war party. The way she used *ki* to defend it during the bombardment sent up a beacon to every Tuann on the planet. I can't hide this even if I wanted to."

Kira looked at the floor, feeling the same impotent rage that had characterized so much of her youth. "What will happen to her?"

"She'll be taken to Ta Sa'Riel where her fate will be decided," Graydon said.

Kira's head rose. "Her fate?"

By Tuann logic, Selene should have been on the fast track to being turned over to her birth House.

Graydon nodded. "I've made the argument her actions prove her ability to survive independent of her House. The emperor and his council will review the matter."

"You want me to let this happen," Kira said through numb lips.

He pressed his hand against the back of her head, pulling her into his chest. She felt him drop a kiss onto her head. "I want you to play this smart. Don't burn bridges unless you have to."

Graydon released her, following Baran as he escorted Selene away.

"What do we do?" Jin asked in a soft voice.

Kira didn't answer, accessing a channel she'd never thought she'd use again. "The only thing we can."

* * *

In a darkened room on the other side of Almaluk, a man reached for the communicator on the bedstand next to him.

"What is it?"

Kira's voice came over the line. "The Tuann have Selene. I thought you should know."

Kira didn't wait for his response, a click signaling the end of the transmission seconds later.

Alexander sat up before pacing to a blank wall and touching its side. A window appeared, allowing him to stare at the space outside.

Their years of exile and freedom were coming to an end.

The feelings that knowledge brought were complicated. It had been so long since the forty-three walked in the light. He didn't know if they could survive in the new paradigm.

Their psyche had been scarred by their beginnings. In many ways, their development was stunted, never allowing them to evolve, much less heal. They were so desperate to cling to the safety of the known, they would sacrifice anyone who threatened that.

Alexander had always known their peace couldn't last. Soon, the events set in motion nearly a century ago would come to a head. Would the Tuann be the thing they feared or their salvation?

The forty-three were about to find out.

TERMS

Adal – Loosely translated it means the reckoning – challenging to dangerous undertakings

Adva Ka – A rite of passage Tuann must pass

Aksa – Fist sized animal who is stubborn and blood thirsty

Alja – Haldeel word for spy. Often used in reference to the ilsa

Almaluk – the crown jewel of the Haldeel empire. It doesn't have a fixed location but rather wanders space.

Azala – Child

Azira aliri – Cat ear shaped flower

Aza – Polite form of address, ex: Sir or Ma'am

Balial – the material with anti-ballistic properties often used in the clothes Kira is given by House Roake

Buka – a carnivorous fish raised by the Haldeel

Cheva nier – My love

Choko trees – A tree on Ta Sa'Riel

Coli – Affectionate term of endearment similar to sweet heart

Colina – A formal form of coli

Etheiri – Place of remembrance

Etair – Horse-like creature

Feilli – Symbiotic creatures in the ocean

Fendrik – An enemy on Roake's border

Iffli – Insult. Roughly translated – mutt, half-breed, waste

Ilsa – alien arachnid that is sometimes used as a spy or pet

Kattas – Warrior forms

Keeva – Alcoholic drink

Ki – Soul's breath

Kithiw – derogatory term by the tsavitee used in reference to humans. Loosely defined it means fodder or food

Kueper – A snack wrapped in a pastry

Loaw – Hoverbike

Lu-ong – Dragon like creature who is able to manipulate ki.

Mea'Ave – The soul of the planet

Ooros – Beast of burden, pulls carriages, looks like a cross between a bison and woolly mammoth

Ooril – Night animal

Oshota – Elite Tuann warriors – their name means shield

Seiki Stone – Drains ki

Seon'yer – Teacher or guide

Sirav Rytil – Second chances

Sye – direct translation means all and none. It is the third neutral gender of Odin's people, being neither female or male

Tala dog – Cross between boar and wolf and armored tank

Tilu – A Tuann invention that looks like butterfly wings and allows the user to fly

Tijit – A small angry rodent

Uhva na – Trial of the Broken. A rite of passage those of House Roake must pass before receiving a teacher who will prepare them for the adva ka

Ural – Similar to synth armor but not as advanced

Vertier Order – an order of the Haldeel that is considered sacred

Yer'se – Student or apprentice

Zala – Infant

Za/Za na/Za na ri/Za na ri na – various forms of formal address by the Haldeel

Zinyai – precious small one

Zuipi – Tuann energy/projectile weapon that looks kind of like a bow and arrow

TUANN HOUSES

Luatha – Major House - Kira's mother, Liliana, is descended from this House. Its Overlord is Liara.

- **Maxiim** – Minor house who has pledged allegiance to Luatha. Its Overlord is deceased. Joule is attempting to resurrect the House.

Roake – Major House – Kira's father, Harding, is descended from this House. Its Overlord is Harlow.

Danai – Major House – Overlord is still unknown

- **Dethos** – Minor House who has pledged allegiance to Danai. Overlord is still unknown.

Asanth – Major House

Kashori – Major House

Remie – Minor house – allegiances still unknown

DISCOVER MORE BY T.A. WHITE

The Firebird Chronicles
Rules of Redemption
Age of Deception
Threshold of Annihilation

The Broken Lands Series
Pathfinder's Way
Mist's Edge
Wayfarer's Keep
The Wind's Call

The Dragon-Ridden Chronicles
Dragon-Ridden
Of Bone and Ruin
Destruction's Ascent
Secrets Bound By Sand
Shifting Seas – Novella

The Aileen Travers Series
Shadow's Messenger
Midnight's Emissary
Moonlight's Ambassador
Dawn's Envoy
Twilight's Herald

CONNECT WITH ME

Twitter: @tawhiteauthor

Facebook: https://www.facebook.com/tawhiteauthor/

Website: http://www.tawhiteauthor.com/

Blog: http://dragon-ridden.blogspot.com/

Click here to join the hoard and sign up for updates regarding new releases.

ABOUT THE AUTHOR

Writing is my first love. Even before I could read or put coherent sentences down on paper, I would beg the older kids to team up with me for the purpose of crafting ghost stories to share with our friends. This first writing partnership came to a tragic end when my coauthor decided to quit a day later and I threw my cookies at her head. This led to my conclusion that I worked better alone. Today, I stick with solo writing, telling the stories that would otherwise keep me up at night.

Most days (and nights) are spent feeding my tea addiction while defending the computer keyboard from my feline companions, Loki and Odin.

Made in the USA
Monee, IL
21 December 2024